THE
QUEEN
OF
IZMOROZ

"She doesn't care about you, or the Rangers, or Izmoroz."

"All the Lady cares about is death and change. It is her nature. She is beyond right and wrong, good and evil. That is what it truly means to be a god."

Sonya wanted to object, but couldn't think of any way to refute what Anatoly said. Certainly not the Lady's own behavior or words. When she considered it, even Mikhail's teachings had been vague on the Lady Marzanna's morality.

"So how do Andre and Tatiana know something bad is coming?" she asked instead.

"How do you know when a storm is coming?"

"I can smell it."

He nodded. "As you get older, even before you can smell it, you'll learn to *feel* it coming. In your very bones."

"And this is like a storm?"

"One that may cover the world," he said.

BY JON SKOVRON

The Goddess War

The Ranger of Marzanna

The Queen of Izmoroz

The Empire of Storms

Hope and Red

Bane and Shadow

Blood and Tempest

THE
QUEEN
OF
IZMOROZ

JON SKOVRON

THE GODDESS WAR: BOOK TWO

orbitbooks.net

ORBIT

First published in Great Britain in 2021 by Orbit

1 3 5 7 9 10 8 6 4 2

Copyright © 2021 by Jon Skovron

Map by Tim Paul

Excerpt from *Legacy of Ash* by Matthew Ward
Copyright © 2019 by Matthew Ward

A CIP catalogue record for this book
is available from the British Library.

ISBN 978-0-356-51486-4

Printed and bound in Great Britain by Clays Ltd, Elcograf S.p.A

Papers used by Orbit are from well-managed forests
and other responsible sources.

MIX
Paper from
responsible sources
FSC® C104740

Orbit
An imprint of
Little, Brown Book Group
Carmelite House
50 Victoria Embankment
London EC4Y 0DZ

An Hachette UK Company
www.hachette.co.uk

www.orbitbooks.net

For Nerea, most generous of hearts

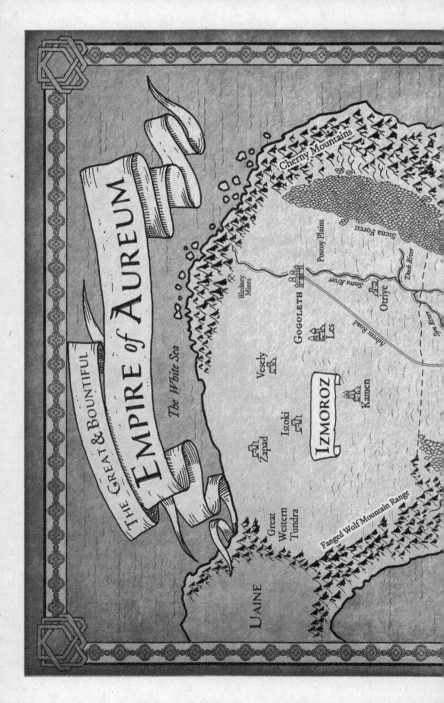

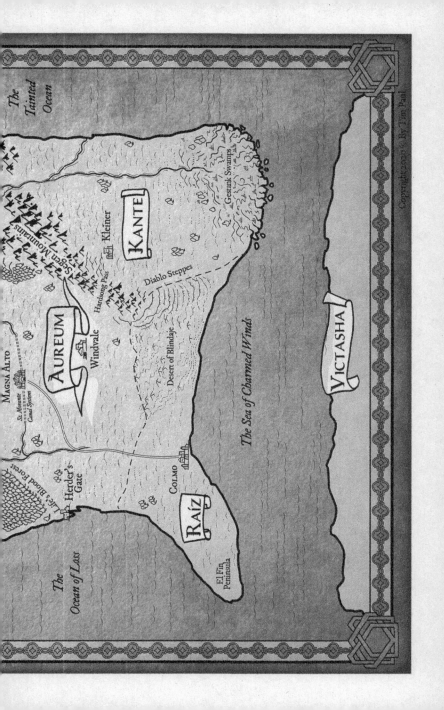

PART ☉ ONE

CHILDREN OF THE WOLF

"It does not seem fair that we be punished for the sins of our fathers. Yet we cannot ignore the unearned bounties we have reaped as their progeny. What, then, is justice?"

—Fyodor Botkin,
The Izmorozian Dream

PART ONE

CHILDREN OF THE WOLF

I

Many people thought of winter as cruel, and spring as gentle. But Sonya Turgenev Portinari, Ranger of Marzanna, knew that wasn't true.

She gazed at the thawing Great Western Tundra that stretched out around her in all its sodden glory. She knew the quiet ferocity it took for those hardy green shoots to reach up toward the sunlight from beneath the slush that now covered much of Izmoroz. And then, once the plants had at last broken through, they risked being eaten by the starving animals that had just woken from hibernation. *That* was spring. It was not gentle. It was a desperate and voracious thing that defiantly clawed its way up from the darkest depths of winter to thrive once again, no matter the cost or suffering.

Still, Sonya could not deny spring's ragged beauty. The sun shone down brightly, and purple flowers brazenly poked through the patchy brown snow. Small rivulets of water trickled here and there like tiny impromptu streams, and the air was alive with insects and birdsong.

She wished Jorge could have witnessed the tundra's transformation from the smooth, barren snows of winter he'd seen before. But he had remained at the Imperial College of Apothecary in Gogoleth so that he could impress his teachers with the knowledge of plants and herbs he had brought back from the distant and mysterious country of Uaine.

She and Jorge had not traveled across the brutal winter tundra for

3

plants, of course. They had traveled to Uaine to enlist the aid of its people, fearsome warriors who commanded an even more frightening army of walking dead. The Uaine had helped her drive out the Aureumian Empire so that Izmoroz could once again be a free and independent nation.

During the occupation, the empire had banned worship of the Lady Marzanna, Goddess of Winter. They had also sought to exterminate her servants, the Rangers of Marzanna, and they nearly succeeded. When Sonya's mentor had been killed, she had thought herself the last one. But during her journey across the tundra with Jorge, they had encountered three older Rangers who had survived the imperial purge by hiding in this vast wilderness for the last two decades.

Those older Rangers—Andre, Tatiana, and Anatoly—were the reason Sonya now returned to the tundra. She wanted to tell them that she had succeeded in driving out the empire, and they no longer had to hide. They could return to Izmoroz and its people.

Sonya was not making the journey alone, however. This time she had brought her Uaine friend and lover, Blaine Ruairc. The two of them had been trekking northwest across the thawing mud-slick meadows in the direction of the Rangers' cave for several days now. She estimated they should reach the cave later that day or early the next.

"These other Rangers be Bhuidseach as well?" asked Blaine in his guttural, rolling Uaine accent.

"Like me, you mean?" Sonya asked. "They have similar markings, although each of us looks different, depending on what animal the Lady Marzanna has chosen for us."

Beneath Sonya's long black hair, her ears tapered into delicate tips. Her teeth were as sharp as any carnivore's, and she gazed out at the land with the golden eyes of a fox. Such beast marks were called favors of the Lady, and were an indication that they had been blessed with a boon of some kind. Each piece of humanity the Ranger sacrificed made them more powerful.

But the more they resembled a beast, the more likely they were to act as one. Sonya had not truly understood what that meant until

4

a month ago, during the final clash with the empire. In the heat of battle, she had succumbed so deeply to animal instinct that she had momentarily blacked out. When she had recovered her senses shortly after, she found that she had torn a man's throat out with her teeth. And possibly swallowed his flesh. Her memory was hazy on that last point. Or maybe she didn't want to remember.

Regardless, the memory of that temporary loss of control haunted her, and she was glad. It served as a constant reminder that she must avoid asking any more boons of the Lady unless it was absolutely necessary. There were stories of Rangers who had lost so much of their humanity, they forgot who they were. She worried she might already be nearing that point.

Not that Sonya didn't appreciate the favors that the Lady had bestowed on her. Her speed, strength, reflexes, and stamina were now much greater than a human's. Her senses were also enhanced, and on the tundra that could mean the difference between life and death.

"Did you notice we're being tracked by a pack of wolves?" she asked Blaine as they tromped across the meadow.

He jerked to a halt, his expression unexpectedly alarmed.

"Since when?"

"Since this morning," she said.

He scanned the rolling hills that surrounded them, his hand on the massive broadsword at his waist. "I don't see anything."

"They're keeping their distance for now," said Sonya. "But I can definitely smell them."

"What should we do?" He looked far more worried than she would have expected for such a seasoned warrior.

She shrugged. "Nothing. If they were desperate, they'd have already attacked by now. Soon we'll be in the Rangers' hunting territory, and I doubt they'll follow us there."

"If you say so."

They began walking again, but Sonya could tell Blaine remained uneasy. He kept running his hands through his long blond hair and glancing over his shoulder. He rarely showed fear in battle, so she wondered what was bothering him.

"Do you not like wolves?" she asked.

"Does anyone?"

"Oh, wolves are okay," she said. "They can be ferocious when they need to be, but they also take care of each other, and I like that."

Blaine grunted but said nothing more.

"My father's nickname during the Winter War was Giovanni the Wolf," said Sonya. "I suppose because he had a reputation for being a vicious and crafty commander. But the man I knew was fiercely protective of his family—his pack—above all else. So I guess I also like wolves because they remind me of him."

Blaine eyed her curiously. "You don't talk about yer father much."

"Yeah. We didn't really get along, especially as I got older. We argued a lot. My mom said it's because we're so much alike, but I don't see it."

Then a long, chilling howl rose up behind them. It was followed shortly by another howl a short distance in front of them.

"Huh," said Sonya.

Blaine's hand went immediately back to his sword. "I thought you said they'd keep their distance."

"Yeah..." She frowned. "It sounds like they're surrounding us, but that doesn't make sense."

"*Surrounding* us?" Blaine drew his two-handed sword. His eyes darted in different directions.

"But we must be in Andre and Tatiana's hunting territory by now. I suppose this pack could have migrated here with the thaw and the Rangers haven't gotten around to clearing them out yet..."

That didn't seem likely, however. Andre in particular was extremely territorial. But Sonya couldn't think of any other reason that a pack of wolves would infringe on Ranger hunting grounds.

When the wolves came into view, Sonya saw that it was a surprisingly large pack for spring. Twenty wolves with mud-spattered white fur, who were spread out so that they completely encircled Sonya and Blaine. They slowly tightened the circle, their movements cautious, as if unsure of the strength of their prey. Their lips were curled back to reveal sharp teeth, and the sound of their low, rumbling growls filled the air.

Blaine nervously adjusted his grip on his sword, muttering to himself in the Uaine language. His face had gone ashen, and sweat ran from his forehead into his scruffy beard. The wolves had already smelled his fear, and now they could see it.

"Calm down and listen to me a moment." She kept her eyes on the wolves as she slowly unslung her bow and nocked an arrow. "Wolves aren't stupid. They won't go after difficult prey unless they're desperate, and these wolves do not look like they're starving. So all we have to do is show them we're too much trouble, and they'll give up. Probably."

"Probably?"

Blaine did not look like he was calming down. He wiped the sweat from his face with his sleeve as he watched them tighten their circle.

"Can't you just shoot them before they get close?" he asked.

"All twenty? When they have us completely surrounded? Not even I'm that fast. But when they go for you—"

"Why would they go for *me*?"

"Because wolves are attracted to weaker animals, and your fear is a sign of weakness to them."

"I'm not afraid!" he said sharply.

Sonya gave him a dubious look.

The wolves had gotten as close as they deemed safe, and were now beginning to rotate their circle, paws squelching, yellow eyes all fixed on Blaine. He began muttering in Uaine again.

"What is it with you and wolves, anyway?" she asked.

He was quiet for a moment, and when he finally spoke, it seemed to take a great deal of effort. "When I was a wee boy, I watched me mother get torn apart by a pack of wolves."

"Oh," she said. "That would explain it."

"Aye," he said grimly.

One of the larger wolves lunged toward Blaine. Fear must have stiffened his muscles because he took a surprisingly clumsy swing with his sword. The wolf had only feinted its attack anyway, and easily avoided it. That opened Blaine up to another wolf, who went for his haunches.

It was a classic wolf pack tactic and Sonya had expected it. She buried an arrow in its eye and the wolf fell into the mud with a splash still several feet from Blaine's rear.

The wolves went back to circling, no doubt a little more cautious now that one was dead. They continued to growl, and it felt as if they were debating among themselves whether the risk was worth it. Sonya suspected if she immediately shot a few more, they might scatter. But she was reluctant to do so. They were such beautiful animals, and she didn't want to kill any more of them than necessary. As long as she and Blaine stood their ground, the wolves would eventually go in search of easier prey. They just had to be patient.

Unfortunately, patience had never been one of Blaine's strong points, and in that moment he was too on edge to even try. He shouted something defiantly in Uaine, raised his sword, and charged the wolf directly in front of him.

"Damn it, Blaine . . . ," she muttered.

The wolf hopped backward, while the two on either side converged on Blaine's flanks. Sonya shot one, but the other reached him.

Clearly still muddled by fear, Blaine couldn't bring his sword around fast enough. The wolf latched on to his forearm and gave a hard pull. His waterlogged boots slipped out from under him and he fell. He hit the ground hard and his sword went flying. The remaining sixteen wolves ignored Sonya completely and went in for the kill.

Blaine kicked desperately at the approaching wolves as he tried to free himself from the one who held his forearm in its jaws. Sonya didn't want to risk shooting him in the chaos, so she shouldered her bow and leapt into the fray, cursing under her breath at the impatience of Uaine.

Sonya's knife flashed brightly, throwing splashes of blood into the golden spring sunshine as she carved her way to Blaine. She grabbed his collar, intent on pulling him up. But he was a large man, and the ground was so slick that she nearly fell. With so many wolves surrounding them, that might have meant their deaths. She let go of his collar, and instead fended off the darting wolves as she shouted at him.

"Get up, Blaine! Get the hell up!"

He was now covered in mud, and half-blinded by it. He groped around for his sword for several moments before he finally found it and hauled himself up.

Once they were both back on their feet, the wolves withdrew and began circling again. They had lost several more of their pack, but the smell of blood was now so strong it was like a tether around which they rotated.

"Can you still use your arm?" she asked.

"A little."

"Enough to swing that big sword of yours?"

"A few times. Maybe."

"That doesn't sound encouraging."

This was not how she'd hoped this would go. If only Blaine had listened to her. Now things had gotten out of hand and the only thing that would fix it was more death. Death that could have been avoided.

She grimly drew her bow again and shot a wolf. Its sharp whimper wrenched at her heart, but she turned and shot another. Then another. One by one they fell. They were still so incensed with bloodlust that she had to slay several before the survivors finally scattered, yelping pitifully to each other as they ran away.

They watched the wolves flee for a moment. Then Blaine, still muttering in Uaine, stalked over to one of the dead wolves and kicked it.

"Blaine!" Sonya's voice cracked like a whip.

His head jerked back to look at her, his expression bewildered.

Sonya pushed him aside, then knelt down beside the dead wolf. Its white fur was stained with both brown earth and red blood. She had killed ten of these magnificent animals today. Far too many to make use of out here on the tundra. A waste of meat and hides. And a waste of life. She didn't use to be so bothered by such things. A year ago it might not even have occurred to her. But now . . . well, she wasn't sure what had changed, but it bothered her a great deal.

She took a moment to calm herself. Then she gently laid her hand on the wolf's head and spoke the Ranger's prayer.

"One day I will return as you now return. Until then, I will travel light."

She stayed there for a time, feeling the warmth leave the wolf's body.

Finally, she looked up at Blaine. Anger must have still been in her eyes, because he took an unconscious step back. He looked confused, as if he couldn't understand why she was frustrated with him. She supposed she couldn't blame him for acting so irrationally. But she couldn't shrug off so much unnecessary waste, either.

"Let's get you patched up, then carve as much meat as we can carry. If nothing else, we can have a feast when I tell the other Rangers that they no longer need to hide out here on the tundra."

"Is wolf meat good eating?" he asked.

"No," she admitted. "But we'll eat it all the same."

2

Sebastian Turgenev Portinari had been told countless times about the beauty of Aureum, but that hadn't prepared him for the real thing.

As he traveled on the Advent Road with his mother Lady Irina Turgenev Portinari, Commander Franko Vittorio, General Savitri Zaniolo, and Private Sasha Rykov, his eyes swept almost reverently across the rolling emerald-green meadows that stretched out to the horizon on either side. The trees were covered in fragrant white or pink blossoms, and newly sprouted green wheat fields rippled with the gentle gusts of wind. A bold sun shone overhead, while fluffy white clouds floated placidly through the azure sky. After the relentless monochrome of Izmorozian winter, Aureum's spring grandeur was almost overwhelming.

He sighed. "So this is my father's homeland."

"It's stunning," agreed his mother. She looked serene, almost saintly, with the sunlight playing off her long white hair as she rode beside him.

"Is this your first time in Aureum as well, my lady?" asked Zaniolo. "I hadn't realized."

She nodded. "Giovanni spoke of it often but said he had no desire to return."

"I can't imagine why not," said Sebastian.

Zaniolo gave him one of those unreadable smiles of his. The sort that always made Sebastian feel as though the general was hiding

11

something. Of course he knew it could just as easily be a habit acquired from many years as an intelligence officer.

"Sometimes the past is best left undisturbed." Zaniolo glanced toward Commander Vittorio, who rode a little ways ahead of the rest.

Vittorio had gone through drastic changes in temperament since Sebastian had first met him. Initially, the commander had possessed an almost regal bearing, and while he could be a little stiff, he had projected a firm sense of leadership that instilled confidence in everyone under his command. But that decorum had faltered in the face of the unexpected conflict brought about by Sonya and her Uaine allies. Sebastian had been stunned, and at times even horrified, by the shocking displays of violent temper Vittorio had exhibited toward his subordinates on numerous occasions during the conflict.

In the month since they had been routed from Gogoleth and forced to flee Izmoroz, Vittorio had changed yet again. Gone were both the regal bearing and furious outbursts, to be replaced by a deep and pensive brooding. He had spoken little, slept little, and eaten little since crossing the border into Aureum. And yet for all his silence, there was a sense that the wrath he had displayed previously was still there, seething beneath the surface.

Sebastian was concerned for the commander, and had wondered if there was anything he could do to improve his mentor's mood. But Zaniolo and his mother had both advised him to give Vittorio space so that he could grieve for his losses in Izmoroz, and prepare for whatever punishment might await him in Magna Alto.

"Something big coming up the road," said Rykov.

Although Rykov was Izmorozian, he had decided to remain Sebastian's aide-de-camp and follow him to Aureum. Sebastian was grateful for the large man's stoic, unwavering presence. Rykov had been there, in his quiet, unobtrusive way, to guide and support Sebastian from his very first day as an officer of the imperial army. The aide-de-camp's loyalty was especially precious to Sebastian after the betrayal he'd suffered at the hands of his former betrothed, Galina Odoyevtseva Prozorova. Time and distance had dulled his heartbreak to some degree, but he still tried to think about her as little as possible.

Sebastian squinted in the sunlight to where Rykov pointed. He could see a large cloud of dust along the road, which suggested a group of riders ahead.

"A merchant caravan?" he asked.

"Perhaps," said Zaniolo, although his tone suggested he thought it was something else.

Commander Vittorio made no comment, and merely continued to plod ahead, so they followed him.

Once the riders finally came into view, Sebastian saw that it was an imperial cavalry unit of twenty strong heading toward them. They moved in perfect formation at a steady canter, their bright steel breastplates and helmets shining in the warm Aureumian sun.

"Well," Zaniolo said dryly. "Here is our welcome party, although I don't expect it will be a particularly warm reception, given our recent failure."

They all looked to Vittorio for what they should do, but again he made no comment. He did, however, rein in his horse, so the rest followed suit. There they sat and waited as the soldiers approached.

"A word of advice, Captain Portinari," Zaniolo said quietly.

"Yes, General?"

"Our arrival in Magna Alto will undoubtably be complicated and fraught with tension. I will do my best to shield you and your mother from any major repercussions, but for me to succeed, I will need you to only speak when addressed, and even then as reservedly as possible without giving offense. Do you understand?"

Sebastian still didn't have a sense of how much trouble Vittorio was in, or how that might impact him and his mother. But he had few allies and even fewer options at this point.

"I understand, General. And thank you."

He gave Sebastian a faint smile. Then they waited in silence until the soldiers reached them.

The captain of the cavalry unit, a clean-shaven man of middle age with close-cropped black hair beneath his round officer's cap, called for his unit to stop.

"I am Captain Leoni of the Forty-Sixth Imperial Cavalry," he

13

boomed in a hard, formal tone. "By the authority of Her Imperial Majesty, Empress Caterina Morante the First, I command you to identify yourselves."

There was an awkward moment while they waited for Vittorio to speak, but the former commander only glared down at the pommel of his saddle and said nothing.

Finally Zaniolo prodded his horse forward and smiled broadly.

"Now, now, Captain Leoni. There's no need for all this ceremony. Surely it has not been so long that you have forgotten Commander Vittorio or me?"

"I am sorry, General," Leoni said earnestly. "But I have been given explicit orders to stand upon the strictest formalities."

Zaniolo looked a little disappointed, but not surprised. "I see, Captain. Then I might as well begin." He gave the captain a smooth salute. "General Savitri Zaniolo, formerly of the imperial garrison in Gogoleth."

Leoni returned Zaniolo's salute, then looked expectantly at Vittorio, but the commander kept his eyes downcast, his jaw flexed with tension.

When it was clear Vittorio still refused to speak, Zaniolo glanced back at Sebastian and nodded.

Sebastian saluted the captain and said, "Captain Sebastian Turgenev Portinari, formerly of the Four Hundred and Fourth Imperial Cavalry."

Again Leoni returned the salute.

After yet another awkward moment, Sebastian's mother spoke up. "I am Lady Irina Turgenev Portinari of Izmoroz, mother of Captain Portinari and widow of the late retired commander Giovanni Portinari of Aureum."

Leoni bowed respectfully in his saddle. "Your Ladyship."

Rykov saluted. "Private Sasha Rykov from Izmoroz."

Since Rykov ranked below the captain, Leoni was not required to return the salute, and only nodded. Then he gave the silent Vittorio a hard look.

"Are you Commander Franko Vittorio, formerly of the imperial garrison in Gogoleth, exiled from Aureum until such time as Her Imperial Majesty ordered your return?"

Vittorio's lips curled up into a grimace, but he still did not look up. "I suppose I must be."

Exiled? Sebastian was stunned. Zaniolo had told him that Vittorio had been sent to Izmoroz as punishment for an indiscretion of some kind, and he'd later mentioned that the empress might not be pleased that Vittorio was returning to Aureum after such a defeat. But Sebastian hadn't realized that Vittorio had been *banished* from Aureum. Simply crossing the border had been in direct violation of the empress's orders and therefore a crime against the empire. What had the man been thinking?

"Franko Vittorio," Leoni continued sternly. "You are commanded by the empress to accompany me to Magna Alto, where you will face judgment. Any attempt to disobey this order or flee my custody will be considered treason. Is that understood?"

"Yes, Captain." Vittorio's lips writhed as he spoke, as if the words tasted foul.

"Very well."

Leoni ordered his unit to form up around Sebastian and his companions, then, as one mass, they continued south toward Magna Alto.

But now the beautiful landscape seemed somehow less inviting to Sebastian. Were they to be criminals, then? He tried to catch Zaniolo's eye, but the general's expression was neutral as he rode. Somehow, Sebastian found that even more unnerving than his usual unreadable smile.

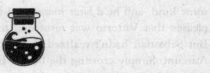

3

In all the time Jorge Elhuyar had studied under his mentor, Anton Velikhov, master apothecary, he had never argued with the man. Until today.

He looked up from his work at the lab table and said, "I'm sorry, Master, but I must refuse."

Velikhov tugged at his beard while he roamed aimlessly around their apartments. "I don't mean a *lot* of blood, of course. Just a small amount to study. Jorge, you understand how significant this would be for the college. Blood that can raise the dead? Who knows what we could learn from such a thing. And if we could somehow duplicate it, the number of applications would be staggering."

"I do understand, Master, but I'm asking you to also understand that Bhuidseach Rowena and her fellow Urram Le Bàs are considered sacred to their people. Merely to ask for a sample of her blood would be offensive."

He stopped his wandering to look exasperatedly at Jorge. "You won't even *ask*?"

"No, Master."

Velikhov threw up his hands and stalked back to his bedroom, muttering to himself.

Jorge took no pleasure in refusing his master, but Rowena had taken him into her confidence, and he had sworn to respect the secrecy of the Uaine knowledge of necromancy. Even mentioning offhandedly to Velikhov that it was done by blood transference had been a mistake. That tiny bit of knowledge had sparked a hunger in the old master that Jorge had never seen before.

He sighed and returned to his work on the cold resistance potion he had been forced to put off yet again this past month. Not that he was complaining. It had been a supreme honor to stand in the college's main lecture hall and present his findings on the Uaine herbs, plants, and fungi he had discovered during his time there.

But he'd been so busy that he'd had to decline Sonya's invitation to return to the tundra to search for her fellow Rangers. Instead she'd taken Blaine. That was to be expected, of course, but Jorge still hadn't sorted out his feelings about either of them. Even thinking about them being out there without him set his stomach into knots. Was it jealousy? If so, of whom was he jealous, exactly? Both of them? And why, when he knew that he could not marry either of them, did he continue to entertain notions of it? He should be happy for his friends that they had found each other. And yet...

There was a light knock on the door, which reminded Jorge that there was someone else he'd been neglecting while he'd been preparing for his lecture.

"Rowena, the door should be unlocked. Please come in."

Bhuidseach Rowena Viridomarus drifted into the room like a tall, thin wraith. Her milk-white hair and skin was the mark of being a necromancer, or Death Touched. Traditionally, necromancers wore long brown robes, but lately Rowena had been experimenting with Izmorozian gowns generously provided by Galina Odoyevtseva Prozorova. The gown she wore today was lavender, and while Jorge wouldn't exactly say that it made her eerie appearance any more attractive, he could not deny that her ghostly paleness, combined with the elegant gown, made her very striking.

"Do I interrupt ye?" she asked in her rolling brogue. She hadn't picked up the language quite as well as Blaine, probably because she mostly kept to her own people, who occupied the abandoned garrison outside Gogoleth. The townspeople were still not comfortable with the Uaine undead warriors, called sluagh gorta, so it was probably for the best they remained separate.

"It's no interruption," he assured her. "I promised to help you. I'm only sorry it's taken me this long to invite you over."

She pulled a stool from the corner and sat down across from him. "I am in no rush."

"Yes..."

He kept his tone neutral, but that was actually something that worried him a little. The Uaine had been brought over to liberate Izmoroz, and were then supposed to march on Magna Alto, capital and heart of the great Aureumian Empire, where they would no doubt be able to claim untold riches. Except they didn't seem in any hurry to do so.

It was true the Uaine had suffered enormous casualties among their living warriors during the battle for Gogoleth. But the true power of the Uaine army was that any who were killed could be immediately resurrected as sluagh gorta, so their numbers had not actually diminished. In fact, since the sluagh gorta were nearly indestructible, the Uaine army was arguably even more formidable now. Jorge told himself that they were merely taking the time to recover from the fierce battle and devise the strategy for their invasion of Aureum. But each week that passed without any visible signs of preparation or progress made it harder to believe that.

"Does something trouble ye?" asked Rowena.

With both Sonya and Blaine gone, she was probably the closest friend he had in Gogoleth and he was tempted to unburden his worries to her. But it would certainly put her in an awkward position, so he shook his head and smiled.

"Nothing you could do anything about, I'm afraid," he told her.

"Maybe ye miss Sonya en Blaine?" she suggested.

"That's part of it, I'm sure. Perhaps I'm so used to having them around that I'm at a bit of a loss without them."

"Do ye think they bring back more Bhuidseach like her?" she asked.

"The old Rangers?" He shrugged. "I'm honestly not sure. Our previous interaction with them was...not positive. And frankly, they didn't seem all that interested in the affairs of regular humans in Izmoroz. They might prefer to stay where they are."

She frowned. "But they es Bhuidseach. They have responsibility to their people."

"Perhaps that's how it's seen among the Uaine. And that's certainly how Sonya personally feels about it here in Izmoroz. But not all cultures insist that their...*gifted* members contribute so altruistically. Within my own culture, for example, the Viajero can perform extraordinary feats of magic. Some of them live in the cities and help people, but others join troupes that wander throughout the empire seeking fame and fortune. And still others enter one of the monasteries along El Fin Peninsula where they hope to strengthen their bridge to God in Heaven. Some even retreat in solitude to the Blindaje Desert, though I'm honestly not sure what they do out there."

"I know little about Raíz," said Rowena. "I would like to see it someday."

"It's a beautiful land, quite different from anywhere else on the continent." Jorge smiled sadly, relishing the small pang of homesickness. Then he briskly rubbed his hands together. "Now, I promised to teach you how to make the salve that will prevent your sluagh gorta from freezing during your return trip across the tundra."

"Aye." She nodded.

"Before we begin, I must warn you, it is a complicated process that will require a great deal of time and patience to master."

She gave him an odd, closed-mouth smile and leaned toward him so that a lock of white hair fell across her colorless eyes. "My friend Jorge, surely ye know by now there es nothing I won't do to ensure the success of my people."

"Wonderful. Then let's get started."

THE QUEEN OF IZMOROZ

4

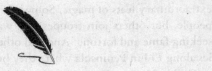

Galina Odoyevtseva Prozorova placed the book on her lap and wearily rubbed her eyes. Mere months ago, she had considered the collection of writings by Iosif Kantemir, *The Purpose of Man, Nature, and Governance*, to be dull reading. She had occasionally waded through one of his essays, but only because she felt some knowledge of political systems was necessary for a well-rounded scholar. Oh how she missed those halcyon days.

Following the liberation of Izmoroz from the empire, the Council of Lords had reformed to take over governance of the country. It had been a glorious and historic day filled with inspiring speeches and great feasting. It was a day that would forever be fixed in her memory.

But since that day, nothing else had happened. Cities that had been damaged during the conflict continued to languish. Even stately Gogoleth still showed the disfiguring scars of battle. Yet the people who had the power to do something about it argued endlessly about minor details on how aid should be provided, squabbling among each other like petulant children.

As always, when Galina saw a problem, she turned to books for advice on how to remedy it. The previous Council of Lords had been disbanded at the end of the Winter War, years before she had been born, so she knew little about how it had functioned. The obvious first step, then, was to read books written by or about the most famous statesmen from Izmoroz's past. How had they broken such deadlocks?

And going forward, how could a country without a single ruler still provide strong leadership? If she could find answers to those questions, she could pass them along to her father, one of the most prominent members of the council, and they could finally begin to heal their poor, beleaguered country.

So she read every book on the subject she could find: *The Izmorozian Dream* by Fyodor Botkin, *The Noble Council* by Nikolay Pirogov, and now *A Land Without Kings* by Timofey Korotkov. Unfortunately, they were all such laborious, overwrought tomes that even a scholar of her caliber had difficulty parsing them at times. Worse still, the results of her research thus far were . . . not promising.

Yet there had to be a way to inject strength into her country's flailing new government, and she would find it. With that resolution firmly in mind, she returned to Korotkov's belabored prose.

Soon after, she was interrupted by a knock on the study door.

"Yes?"

Masha peeked her head inside.

"Angelo Lorecchio is here to see you, miss."

Galina closed her book once again. "Thank you, Masha. Please send him in."

Lorecchio was undoubtedly a sly character, but Galina found she rather enjoyed the imperial deserter's visits. She didn't know how much she trusted his professed motives, but she found in him an intellectual equal, and that was a novel experience for her. He was also not a bad-looking fellow. There seemed to be a subset of Aureumian men whose looks actually improved with age. Apparently, Giovanni Portinari had also been such a man. Perhaps that meant that Sebastian would—

She cut off that line of thinking immediately. It would only bring her pain and sadness, neither of which she could afford during this critical time for Izmoroz. She fixed a smile to her face as Lorecchio entered the room.

"Dear Angelo, you really should have a title of some sort, don't you think?" she asked as he settled into his customary chair across from her.

"Goodness no, Galina Odoyevtseva," he said. "I have no title because I have no authority. I am merely an adviser, and all those I advise are free to take or ignore my words as they see fit."

"Well, then, if you are so very informal, perhaps you should speak less formally and simply call me Galina."

"I beg you not to deny me the pleasure of speaking your melodious name," he replied.

She smiled ruefully. His slippery demeanor belied a deeply stubborn nature underneath. As always, she was fond of such contradictions.

"Well, then, to what do I owe the pleasure of your visit?" she asked.

"Sadly, I bring news that could be somewhat...troubling to you," he said.

"Oh?"

"Apparently, our illustrious Ranger of Marzanna and Captain Blaine left Gogoleth some weeks ago with the intent of returning to the tundra."

"That hardly seems troubling to me," said Galina. "The less I see of that...*creature*, the better. Is Elgin Mordha concerned for the safety of his countryman?"

"The Tighearna has expressed no such worries to me," said Lorecchio. "But while speaking with Bhuidseach Rowena, I learned Sonya Turgenev's purpose in returning to the tundra. Apparently there are three other Rangers who have been hiding there since the end of the last war."

Galina's eyes widened. "For twenty years?"

Lorecchio nodded.

"Well, they must be quite old by now. Assuming they wish to return to society, I question how much use they would be to us should the empire return."

He gazed at her a moment, his eyes hooded in the shadow of his iron-gray brows. "It isn't their military prowess, or lack thereof, that should concern you, Galina Odoyevtseva."

"Oh? And pray advise me, what should my concern be?"

"Do you recall, on the night of our victory over Aureum, that I shared my concerns regarding Sonya Turgenev's negative view of the Izmorozian nobility?"

Galina's eyes narrowed. "Of course I do."

"You have seen firsthand the influence a single Ranger can exert over the peasants of Izmoroz. Can you imagine how much power *four* of them would wield? What if they, as a group, decided to supplant your new Council of Lords to rule this country themselves?"

"I have a difficult time imagining Sonya ruling anything," said Galina.

Lorecchio nodded. "But what of these older, more experienced Rangers? Hardened by years of war, estranged from society for so long, I wonder if they would have much sympathy for your struggling council of nobles."

"The council is not struggling, it's merely——"

"Please let us be candid, Galina Odoyevtseva. Currently, it is a mess. And why wouldn't it be? Men with little experience in governance are suddenly thrust into the role of leadership, and the only precedent they know, so you have informed me, is one of weakness and inefficiency. It is only natural that they should struggle with how to proceed."

He was painfully correct, of course. According to Galina's research, the previous councils had been just as beset by internal disagreement as the current one. Some arguments had gone on for months without resolution, and in one notable case, *years*. In fact, that years-long deadlock, which had concerned placing some modest limits on annual tithes, had only been resolved when its most prominent opponent died.

Furthermore, the books she'd read described no method to achieving strong leadership without a single ruler because the council had been purposefully designed to *prevent* strong leadership from existing in Izmoroz. Lord Korotkov had perhaps put it most succinctly, and to Galina's mind most naively, when he wrote:

What purpose would Izmoroz have for kings or emperors? Such men could never understand or appreciate the individual needs of each lord or their people. I tell you, good citizens, there is more potential harm in the system of monarchy than there could ever be gain. What's more, the will of one man could never match that of a nation united in brotherhood. I need but look to the failure of our neighbor in the south to know that ours is the superior system of governance.

That "neighbor in the south" had of course been Aureum during the early years of an empire that had gone on to conquer over half the continent, so it was clear Korotkov's evidence had not borne out for him.

Galina gave Lorecchio a pained smile, striving not to appear defensive.

"The council simply needs time to find their footing. To figure out a new system. A *better* system."

"But do you think these Rangers will give them that time? You can plead for patience to me, and perhaps even to the peasants." He leaned forward, his tan, weathered face etched with concern. "But when have you ever known Sonya Turgenev to be patient with others?"

He was right about that, too, of course. This might be just the opportunity Sonya needed to incite peasants to rise up against the nobility.

She inclined her head. "Very well, Angelo. You have convinced me this is indeed troubling news. So what do you propose I do about it?"

"It's a tricky situation, to be sure," he said. "But I believe that between the two of us, we can devise the proper remedy without any bloodshed."

She put her book to one side and placed her hands in her lap. "Then let us begin immediately."

5

Weary and caked in dry mud, Sonya and Blaine found the entrance to the Rangers' cave shortly before nightfall. The narrow opening in the ground was easier to spot in the thinner snow cover than it had been on her first visit. A small channel had been cut down the length of the narrow tunnel to guide the snowmelt like a tiny river.

Blaine peered down into the hole.

"Will I fit?"

Sonya gazed speculatively at his broad shoulders. "Andre fit, so I think you'll be fine. But maybe toss the meat in first."

They tossed the bundles of wolf meat down into the tunnel. Sonya smiled, thinking how surprised the Rangers might be by the sudden bounty that appeared. She knew she'd been rude to them on her first visit, but perhaps this would earn their forgiveness.

She got down on all fours and straddled the channel of snowmelt, then worked her way down the tunnel.

"Andre? Tatiana? Anatoly?" she called. "I'm back and I have great news!"

She didn't hear any response, which was odd. She didn't think Anatoly was able to leave the cave anymore, so even if the other two were still out hunting this late in the day, the grouchy old wolverine should still be there.

Finally the tunnel opened out into the massive rock cavern where the Rangers had made their home for the last twenty years. As before,

25

the floors and walls were covered in grimy fur rugs, with a few wood and bone structures here and there where meat and hides might be hung for curing. Except they were all bare now. On her last visit, there had also been a number of stubby tallow candles flickering merrily throughout the cave, but now there were only a few set in a small cluster beside a pile of furs.

"Where are the Rangers?" asked Blaine as he squeezed out of the narrow tunnel behind her.

Then the pile of furs shifted and a gravelly, barely intelligible voice said, "Long, long gone."

That was followed by an intense coughing spell.

"Anatoly?" Sonya hurried over to the old Ranger.

He lay on the pile of furs, covered by the same ragged, patched wool blanket as before. He looked even smaller than last time, and more frail, as if he had not been eating well. His beady dark eyes were unreadable as he looked up at her. The lips of his long black snout curled up to show pronounced canines. It could have been a smile or a snarl. He had so many favors of the Lady, he hardly looked human at all anymore.

"So it's you, little fox? My nose is as bad as my eyes these days, so I couldn't tell who had come. But I might have guessed you'd be back."

"Have Andre and Tatiana abandoned you?" she asked the old wolverine.

"They needed to go, so I told them to go."

"Why? What are they doing?"

"Dark times are coming. Terrible times. They went to prepare themselves."

"What do you mean 'dark times'? I've freed Izmoroz from the empire. We should be celebrating."

Even as she said that, she wondered if *celebrating* was the right word. It hadn't been a total victory, after all. Many innocent people had died during the conflict. The empire had been driven off for now, but was sure to return eventually. And Sonya had failed to free her brother from the grip of that viperous commander, Vittorio.

But Anatoly didn't seem to hear her anyway. Instead, he stared at the slow trickle of water that ran down the tunnel and into the pebble-strewn stream nearby. Then his eyes fell upon the sacks of meat, and he grunted.

"You brought presents this time, at least."

"When was the last time you ate, Anatoly?" asked Sonya.

"I don't remember," he said.

"Let me cook something for you. Then we'll cure the rest. That should last you a little while at least."

He nodded. "Thank you, *Lisitsa*. I know it is inevitable, but I'm not eager for the Lady's final embrace." He squinted at her. "And by the look of things, you better understand why now."

The last time Sonya had spoken to the Lady, she had begged for a way to defeat her brother without killing him. The Lady had granted her request, and as payment had slowly, mercilessly, wrenched out her teeth one by one.

Now she ran her tongue across the sharp fox teeth that had grown in place of her human ones as she nodded.

"Yes, Anatoly. I understand."

There was plenty of salt and saltpeter stored in the cave, so once they'd cooked and eaten a meal, Sonya and Blaine got to work curing the rest of the meat.

As they hung the treated meat up on the bone and wood frames, Sonya said, "Before, I was worried some of this would go to waste. Now I wish we'd brought more."

"We could *get* more," said Blaine.

She narrowed her golden eyes thoughtfully. "I suppose that wolf pack won't be back anytime soon. And the reindeer migration is just starting, so it might be good timing." She glanced over at the now snoozing Anatoly. "But I feel bad leaving him alone right now."

"I can go," offered Blaine.

"You? Hunt reindeer?"

He looked offended. "A' course! I been hunting deer since I was a boy!"

She shrugged. "If you say so."

While Blaine was off somehow hunting deer with a giant sword,

Sonya turned her attention to cleaning the cave. The smell had become quite unpleasant since the other two Rangers had left.

Anatoly watched her wash his ratty old blanket, wringing his claw-like hands anxiously.

"I said it's fine," he muttered.

"It was disgusting," she told him. "And if you don't stop fussing, I'm going to wash you, too."

He shrank back into his pile of furs and glared at her.

Finally she finished with the blanket and handed it to him. He grabbed it eagerly, as if it had caused him physical pain to be separated from it.

"Anatoly?" she asked.

"Hmm?" He pressed his face to the blanket and inhaled deeply, although there was no way it smelled the same after she had washed it.

"Why did Andre and Tatiana leave?"

"I told you. Dark times are coming. They went to ready themselves."

"But I liberated Izmoroz just as the Lady commanded me. Things should be getting better now, not worse."

He gazed at her a moment. Rather than his usual peevish retorts, he seemed to be genuinely considering what she said.

Finally, he replied, "Rangers don't often get direct commands from the Lady, but when we do, we must obey. That is the 'right' thing for us to do. Always. So you did no wrong, little fox. But you are a fool if you think that following the Lady Marzanna's orders will ever make things *better*."

"But she said—"

"She doesn't care about you, or the Rangers, or Izmoroz," he cut in. "All the Lady cares about is death and change. It is her nature. She is beyond right and wrong, good and evil. That is what it truly means to be a god."

Sonya wanted to object, but couldn't think of any way to refute what he said. Certainly not the Lady's own behavior or words. When she considered it, even Mikhail's teachings had been vague on the Lady Marzanna's morality.

"So how do Andre and Tatiana know something bad is coming?" she asked instead.

"How do you know when a storm is coming?"

"I can smell it."

He nodded. "As you get older, even before you can smell it, you'll learn to *feel* it coming. In your very bones."

"And this is like a storm?"

"One that may cover the world," he said.

"Then where did they go to prepare for it?" she asked. "What do they plan to do?"

"They didn't tell me. Because I'm old and grumpy and told them they were fools to even try." He heaved a gurgling sigh that threatened to turn into another coughing fit, but didn't. "Damn foxes. You always get people riled up."

"Me?" She'd never considered that her actions would have an impact on the other Rangers. They certainly hadn't seemed to take her very seriously the last time she'd been there.

Anatoly's shoulders bounced a few times, as if he was still holding off the cough. He lay back down in his blankets and closed his eyes until it passed.

"Yes, yes," he muttered. "Some might call it inspiration. But I know better."

"But..." A chill crept up Sonya's spine as she considered. "If the Lady Marzanna is not trying to make things better, then..." She almost didn't want to ask. "What have I inspired?"

He lifted his head and looked at her again with his beady black eyes.

"That is an excellent question. Maybe you're growing up, little fox."

Then he laid his head back down and went to sleep.

Sonya sat there and watched his slow, even breathing. She could hear the muted gurgle of fluid in his lungs that never quite went away. And there was a faint smell of decay about him. It seemed likely that his days were numbered regardless of how much food he had. Perhaps that was the real reason Andre and Tatiana had left him behind. They could already tell he wouldn't last the journey.

29

She was tempted to stroke his shaggy gray head, but knew it would infuriate him, so she held herself in check. What sort of life had he lived down here in this cave, dependent on other Rangers, unable to even hunt? Why did he cling so stubbornly to it? Was he really that terrified of the Lady's final embrace?

But perhaps it wasn't so difficult to understand. Sonya had always told people that Rangers didn't fear death. That the Lady would take care of her, even in those final moments. But Sonya still recalled the brutal frozen pain of her touch, and the almost sadistic leisure with which she'd torn off Sonya's ears, gouged out her eyes, and yanked out her teeth. Did Sonya really still think she could count on mercy from the Lady in the end?

She heard Blaine's heavy tread near the cave entrance. A moment later, a nice-sized reindeer carcass slid down the tunnel and splashed into the stream. Then he emerged grinning widely.

"See?"

She stared at the reindeer a moment. "How did you kill this with a sword?"

"A sword and a *rock*," he clarified. "You stun it first, see? Then you run in quick t' finish."

She smiled as she dragged it over to the curing rack and began to skin it. "I admit. I'm impressed."

"So what now?" he asked.

"We'll cure this, maybe start making some candles with the fat that he can finish on his own. And then..."

Her smile faded. She looked back at the dying old Ranger sleeping in his pile of furs.

"And then?" Blaine asked gently.

She sighed. "I guess we'll head back to Gogoleth. Anatoly is certain there are bad things coming. Worse than what we had before, maybe."

"Aye?" Blaine looked as uneasy as she felt.

"It's strange," she said. "When Anatoly told me dark times were coming, I didn't actually feel that surprised. It was like I..." She considered for a moment. "Have you ever had that feeling like you've

30

been somewhere before, or done something before, even though you know you haven't?"

He nodded.

She looked down at the dead reindeer, which had a large gash in its throat from Blaine's sword. She could smell the iron tang of its blood.

"It was almost like I remembered it from a dream."

Sebastian had dreamed of seeing Magna Alto, but not like this.

The city did not disappoint, of course. It was the grandest thing he'd ever witnessed. It was easily five times as big as Gogoleth and had been built onto a mountain. The city walls at the base of the mountain were a gleaming white marble. The major thoroughfare of the city, Ascendant Way, gradually spiraled up the mountain so that the entire thing bristled with brightly colored buildings and culminated in the sparkling gold of the imperial palace at the very top.

But Sebastian had a hard time savoring the city's majesty. He imagined anyone who arrived against their will under armed escort would have felt similarly conflicted. Not that they had been mistreated in any way. Captain Leoni had been the soul of courtesy, particularly where Sebastian's mother was concerned. But he had also made it very clear that they were all his prisoners and he would tolerate no dissent or delay.

During the first few days of captivity, Zaniolo had tried to thaw the captain's demeanor with idle soldier's talk but met little success. He never seemed frustrated by his failures, however, and even when he gave up the effort, he did so with a show of high spirits and a knowing smile, as if to say that was how he'd expected it to go, but he'd had to try anyway.

Vittorio continued to say little, do little, and eat little during the trip. But his brooding wrath seemed much closer to the surface now.

32

Perhaps it was Sebastian's imagination, but it seemed like whenever Leoni was occupied with something else, the ex-commander would glare openly at the captain with dark, furious eyes. Leoni had been kind enough not to restrain them. But if Vittorio did something so foolhardy as to attack the captain while surrounded by imperial soldiers, that nominal freedom might be taken away. Sebastian wondered if he should warn Leoni about the possibility, but remembered Zaniolo's request to only speak when necessary. It also felt like that would be a terrible betrayal to Vittorio. Betraying his former commander and mentor at perhaps the worst moment in his life would be the actions of a disloyal coward. Imagine if Rykov had betrayed Sebastian during *his* darkest hour during the battle in Gogoleth? Such a thing would have been devastating. No, Sebastian must remember the good man he met all those months ago and stand by him now.

Despite his resolve, it was an anxious and exhausting ride to Magna Alto. But at last their horses crested the top of a hill and the magnificent city came into view for the first time.

"My word . . . ," his mother sighed.

"Is this your first time to Magna Alto, my lady?" asked Leoni.

"It is, Captain. And such a sight to behold."

He seemed pleased by her awe. "It's said that it took twenty-three years and more than a hundred thousand laborers to build."

"Astonishing," she agreed.

The captain pointed to a line of white marble that stretched east and west from the outer city wall, ending somewhere beyond their view. "Do you see those edifices, my lady? What do you suppose they are?"

"Additional defenses?"

He chuckled heartily. "Far more than mere walls, my lady. That is the Saint Morante Canal system, a miraculous feat of Aureumian engineering that took over a decade and tens of thousands of workers to build. It stretches west all the way to the Poca River, and east to the Estraneo River, which I believe originates at your Sestra River. This allows Magna Alto, formerly a landlocked city, to be the hub of both land and water trade. Not only that, it provides fresh water for drinking and irrigation to support Aureum's renowned agricultural region."

"Truly wondrous," she said.

Sebastian stared at the miles of proud, uncompromising white that had been carved in a straight, unwavering line through the uneven landscape. It seemed like a declaration that not even the whims of Nature could hamper Aureum's ambitions. And this canal was clearly why Vittorio had been so concerned about bandits on the Sestra. Their river piracy had directly impacted Magna Alto.

Except they hadn't been bandits or river pirates, he reminded himself. They'd been rebels. Not selfish opportunists but regular townspeople unhappy with the empire's rule. Perhaps not so different from the poor people of Les...

"Apologies, my lady." Captain Leoni's voice broke into Sebastian's thoughts. "We should continue on to the palace without further delay. I was ordered to present my charges directly to the empress with all due haste."

Sebastian's mother nodded. "By all means, Captain. We cannot keep the empress waiting."

He smiled gratefully, then signaled to his men and they began their descent.

The road sloped gradually downward until it leveled out about a half mile from the outer wall of the castle. Sebastian could see the glint of steel at the top of the wall, most likely a sentry. The gate was easily twenty feet tall and made of stout oak beams bound in iron. Even the ancient entrance into Gogoleth looked flimsy by comparison.

"Unfurl the flag," Captain Leoni told one of his men.

"Yes, sir!" The soldier unfurled a flag with a white falcon on a golden background and fixed it to the back of his saddle.

"The imperial crest," Zaniolo told Sebastian as they rode. "It's a signal to the gate guard and all within the city that the good captain is acting on direct orders from the empress and should not be impeded in any way."

Sure enough, the gate opened immediately and they entered the city without hindrance.

"You know, Sebastian." Zaniolo leaned over and spoke just loudly enough to be heard over the sound of the horse hooves pounding on the cobblestones. "You could have easily wiped out Leoni's entire company with your magic when we first encountered them."

"Sir?" Sebastian's eyes went wide.

"I'm not saying you should have," Zaniolo said quickly. "And it's far too late now. But it's important not to forget one's advantages. You've seemed a tad discouraged since our . . . well, let's be frank and call it an arrest. But don't ever think of yourself as truly helpless, my boy."

"Y-yes, sir."

As they rode through the city streets, people looked out of windows and doorways with mild curiosity. A pack of children came scampering out of an alley and tried to keep pace with them for a little while, shouting and waving at the soldiers. Captain Leoni smiled good-naturedly and instructed one of his men to throw a few coins. The children shouted with glee as they stopped to wrestle over the coins that bounced across the cobblestones.

Peasants that actually appreciated their imperial protectors? Sebastian thought it a welcome change after dealing with the ungrateful bumpkins back in Gogoleth.

Ungrateful bumpkins? The thought jarred Sebastian with its harshness. That wasn't how he really saw the simple farmers and laborers he'd grown up around. It was more like something Vittorio would have said.

He glanced back at the commander, who stared ominously at the back of Leoni's head as though he did not even see the bustling city around him. Sebastian still vividly recalled the night of the Ascendance, when Vittorio had looked into the night sky with glistening eyes as he'd spoken of his longing to once again see his beloved Magna Alto. Yet now his own wrath seemed to have blinded him to the very thing he'd so desired to see. If he was to be punished for his crimes, Sebastian thought the least the man could do was enjoy its meager rewards. But no. Vittorio seemed to have succumbed to his own seething, impotent rage. For the first time, Sebastian felt a stirring of pity for the man.

They followed the spiraling main road up the mountain toward the palace. Sebastian noted that the closer they got, the brighter and more luxurious the homes were. Toward the bottom, the buildings had been mostly stone and mortar with slate shingle roofs. They had been small and packed in tightly. Neat and well kept, but not ostentatious in any way. As they progressed along Ascendant Way, the structures became larger, more spread out, and made of brick, sometimes with plaster facades painted in bright colors. Then, as they neared the palace, the buildings became more like estates, each as large as Roskosh Manor, with copper roofs turned green from age, and surrounded by sweeping lush gardens dotted with colorful flowers.

"The Silver Ring is always a feast for the eyes in spring," said Zaniolo.

"The Silver Ring?" asked Sebastian.

"This neighborhood," said Zaniolo. "Only the most prestigious citizens of the empire live here."

"The nobles?"

Zaniolo shrugged. "Nobility means something different in Aureum."

Sebastian's mother gave him a curious look. "Oh?"

"Aureum was once a republic," said Zaniolo. "The idea of a noble class is a relatively recent concept installed by the first emperor, Alessandro Morante, near the end of his life. Titles were generally given as rewards to those who had served him in some exceptional way. And they could be taken away just as easily if that person failed him. It's a tradition that has continued to this day." He looked at Sebastian and frowned thoughtfully. "You know, it's possible that your father was given a title by the empress after winning the Winter War. Perhaps a count, or a duke."

"Really?" asked Sebastian.

"He never mentioned it," said his mother. "But he'd never been particularly impressed by titles. Least of all, his own."

"Since he married you, was he given the title of Lord Portinari of Izmoroz?" asked Zaniolo.

Sebastian's mother shook her head. "Nobility in Izmoroz is only by blood. When he is of age, Sebastian will be the first lord of our family estates since his grandfather perished after the war."

"I thought my grandfather perished *during* the war," said Sebastian.

"No, it was shortly after."

"What—"

"But that is a topic for another time," she told him firmly.

Sebastian gave a reluctant nod. He still didn't know what had become of his grandparents or his aunt, all of whom had died before he was born. And he knew nothing of his father's parents or siblings. It was entirely possible he had relatives in this very city. The only family he'd ever known was his parents and sister.

He frowned. "Will Sonya be Lady Portinari someday?"

"Assuming she outlives me," replied his mother.

"Hardly a foregone conclusion, given the powerful enemies she's managed to collect," said Zaniolo.

"Will the empress retake Izmoroz soon?" asked Sebastian.

"It depends on how well the war is going in Kante. My last information on that matter is months old at this point." He looked at Leoni. "Perhaps the captain has more current news."

Leoni returned his look but did not respond.

Zaniolo winced, as if the silence itself was a reply. "I see."

"Is it not going well?" asked Sebastian.

"It's a rare soldier who can resist bragging about a recent victory. But none care to speak of defeats. Unfortunately for some..." Zaniolo turned around in his saddle to look back at Vittorio. "That might put the empress in a less benevolent frame of mind when meting out punishment."

At last they reached the golden walls of the palace. Now that he was able to look more closely, they were not solid gold as they'd seemed from a distance, but made of marble with a great deal of gold inlay. As with the outer gate, the palace gate opened immediately for them and they clattered into the courtyard beyond.

Captain Leoni commanded his men to form up around Sebastian and his companions, and they all dismounted. Except Vittorio. The ex-commander still sat on his horse, his eyes wide and unblinking as he stared at the palace before them as if only now realizing where he was. His jaw muscles twitched spastically and he seemed unaware that everyone else had come down from their horses.

"Sir." One of the soldiers reached up and tapped his arm with what Sebastian thought was a great deal of respect, considering the circumstances.

But Vittorio's eyes narrowed to slits and he glared balefully down at the soldier.

"Unhand me!" he snarled.

Surprised by the sudden outburst, the soldier went immediately for his saber.

"At ease." Leoni's voice was like cold steel as he walked over to them.

Vittorio shifted his scowl to the captain, and Sebastian couldn't help feeling a twinge of embarrassment for his old mentor. His ire was almost childish, like a toddler about to throw a tantrum. But Leoni regarded him with cool disdain.

"If you prefer, Franko, I can have you brought before the empress in chains."

The two men stood there for a moment, then Vittorio sucked at his teeth and began to dismount. "There is no need for threats. I merely object to being manhandled. I will obey all that you command."

"Wonderful," Leoni said dryly.

He selected a few men to accompany them, perhaps on account of Vittorio's belligerence, then dismissed the rest to care for their mounts.

"Please follow me," he said, then led them across the courtyard and into the palace proper.

7

Sebastian recalled that first time he entered Roskosh Manor. He had felt awed, perhaps even daunted by its opulence. The lush rugs, the sensuous oil paintings, the gilded frame mirrors, and the profusion of oil lamps had made it immediately clear that he was somewhere special.

But to compare Roskosh Manor to the imperial palace of Magna Alto would be like comparing a child's scribble to a great work of art. Lady Prozorova had no doubt made a valiant effort, but any attempts to achieve the sort of splendor Sebastian saw now would have been doomed from the start. Her heavy rugs and coarse oil paintings would have seemed as odious in these glorious halls as piles of dung.

The polished marble floors of the palace gleamed with inlaid gold. Some walls, and even parts of the ceiling, were covered in intricate stained glass that allowed the generous Aureumian sunlight to cascade into the space like the gentle fingers of God Himself. The sections not taken by windows were painted with vast delicate frescoes. There was so much color and life everywhere Sebastian looked that his heart began to ease. He found it difficult to imagine that anything truly terrible could take place amid such magnificence.

But when he glanced back at Vittorio, his worry returned. The ex-commander walked at the same even pace as everyone else, but there was now something wild in his eyes. It reminded Sebastian disconcertingly of his sister's expression when she'd been in the heat of battle in Gogoleth. There was an almost feral desperation about him. Fight or flight. There was little hope of flight now, of course. But what about fight? Vittorio had professed his love for the empress many times, but Sebastian knew from experience that love could transform into hate when one felt betrayed. It was difficult to imagine, but might he attempt to attack the empress once they stood before her? Could the stress of their current circumstances make him that unstable?

Sebastian glanced over at Zaniolo, but the general did not seem the least bit worried. In fact, there was an eagerness in his expression, as though he greatly looked forward to what would come next. Did he think that Vittorio deserved whatever harsh fate lay in store for him? Once again, it felt disloyal to contemplate such things. And yet, when Sebastian thought about it, he realized that a soldier's loyalty should ultimately be to the empress, not a commander, regardless of past circumstances.

Captain Leoni led them through winding passages until they reached a set of closed double doors guarded by two soldiers, who immediately opened the way.

"We are *eagerly* expected," murmured Zaniolo.

A long rectangular room lay beyond lined on either side with marble columns. The wall at the far end contained a massive stained glass window that appeared to depict the story of the Ascendance, when Emperor Alessandro was rescued from the treacherous senators by God. Within the image, the emperor, dressed in a white robe, looked serene while a giant hand lifted him up into the heavens. Far below, dressed in black robes, the senators shook their fists and seemed to shout in silent fury while flames curled around their feet.

The sunlight through this glass tableau shone down on the throne and illuminated Caterina Morante the First, Empress of Aureum. She looked to be about Commander Vittorio's age, with hair as dark as Sonya's, but streaked in gray and pulled back into a tight braid that allowed a few tresses to lay artfully across her shoulders. Her gown was white and gold brocade, with ruffled sleeves that stopped midway down her arms. Her olive complexion was similar to his own, and her eyes were a warm brown. Her posture was erect, almost stiff, but there was a startlingly amused expression on her full red lips, and one of her sculpted black brows was raised in a playful arch.

Behind the empress was a line of soldiers in burnished gold-plated chest armor and helmets, with long red capes draped over one shoulder. They wore jewel-encrusted sabers at their hip, and fixed to one arm was a small golden shield with the falcon crest of the empress. Sebastian thought it likely that these were the imperial honor guard. Merely looking at them set Sebastian's mind more at ease. Even if Vittorio went into an uncontrollable rage, there was little he could do against such a formidable group of soldiers.

Captain Leoni led them slowly and with great solemnity toward the empress and her honor guard. But his gravity seemed at odds with the empress's obvious amusement. Perhaps Sebastian's first impression had been correct after all, and nothing truly terrible could happen in such a beautiful setting.

Once they stood before the empress, Leoni dropped to one knee. The rest followed suit, except Sebastian's mother, who gave a deep curtsy.

"Your Majesty," said Leoni. "I have returned with Franko Vittorio, former commander of the imperial garrison in Izmoroz, and his company, as requested."

"Please rise." The empress's voice had a rich, velvety quality to it.

They all stood immediately.

"Captain Leoni," she continued. "As always, I am grateful for the stalwart and thorough service rendered to me by the Forty-Sixth Imperial Cavalry. It is a comfort to know I can always count on you and your men to fulfill my wishes exactly."

Leoni gave a sharp salute. "It is my privilege to serve, Your Majesty!"

The empress's eyes locked on Sebastian in a way that made him slightly uncomfortable, though he could not say why. While her words sounded formal, her expression remained playful and amused.

"I have no doubt that you are Sebastian Turgenev Portinari, son of Giovanni Portinari. Dressed as you are in imperial uniform, you seem the very image of your father as a young man."

"You honor me, Your Majesty." Sebastian wasn't sure if he was even still a captain of the imperial army. But he decided it was better safe than sorry and saluted.

The empress turned to Sebastian's mother. "And this handsome woman must be Giovanni's widow, Lady Irina Turgenev. I see he was able to find the true beauty of the northern lands."

Sebastian's mother curtsied deeply again. "You are most gracious, Your Majesty."

"You have my condolences for the loss of your husband. Know that I too grieved, as did the whole empire with me. Though retired, the premature death of one of the greatest military minds of our age was truly a tragedy."

Premature? wondered Sebastian. Hadn't the empress ordered his father's death?

As if in answer to his question, the empress's gaze shifted to Vittorio, and all her amusement and playfulness vanished. Her voice took on a hard edge as she spoke to him.

"I believe that was the first of your *many* transgressions since assuming command in Izmoroz, Franko."

Sebastian had been so transfixed by the empress that he hadn't paid any attention to Vittorio. So he was startled when his former commander groaned like a wounded beast and fell to his hands and knees. His expression still held a desperate energy, but the wrath had been replaced with agony, as if the reprimand from the empress caused him physical pain.

"I beg your forgiveness, Your Majesty! I know I have no right, but I throw myself upon your mercy. Please, give me one more chance! Please!"

Sebastian stared at Vittorio as he groveled on the cold marble floor. In all the time he'd known him, he'd never seen such self-demeaning behavior. The man he had once considered the very pinnacle of manly grace was now behaving like a spoiled child who'd been caught with his hand in the cookie jar.

And what did the empress mean by the first of his many transgressions?

Empress Caterina watched him grovel for several moments in silence, her face unreadable.

At last she spoke. "These theatrical acts of contrition may have worked on me in the past, Franko, but no longer."

Then her expression curled into distaste.

"Antonio, make the dog stand on his hind legs, please."

"At once, Your Majesty!" One of the honor guard came forward and roughly yanked Vittorio to his feet.

The ex-commander stared at the empress with wide, pleading eyes. He truly did look like a contrite puppy.

"Franko, enough." The empress seemed barely able to look at him. "The more allowances I make, the worse you become. I simply cannot give you any more chances. First, you killed Commander Portinari without my authorization."

"What?"

Sebastian knew he had promised Zaniolo that he'd only speak when spoken to, but the exclamation slipped out before he could stop himself.

The empress turned to him and her expression softened. "Did you think I would order the death of one of the greatest living heroes of the empire? Is that what *he* told you?"

"Y-yes, Your Majesty."

Her expression darkened. "I see. And I suppose he also neglected to mention that after I learned of the tragedy, I commanded that you and your family be brought immediately to Magna Alto. Is that so?"

Sebastian once more felt the stirring of guilt at betraying his former mentor—but no. What loyalty should he feel to the man who lied about his own culpability in his father's death? What else had his supposed mentor lied about?

So with new resolve, Sebastian said, "That is correct, Your Majesty. He told me I had been ordered to stay in Izmoroz and fight off the Uaine invaders."

The empress's baleful expression turned back to Vittorio, who was still held in Antonio's grip.

"So you not only ignored my orders, but *contradicted* them. You were just going to throw Giovanni's sixteen-year-old son at the Uaine?"

Vittorio cringed. "Please, Your Majesty, I am a fool, a weak, pathetic——"

"Silence. I have not finished listing the new crimes we may now add to your already long list of transgressions. You will hear them all."

"Yes, Your Majesty." There was a hollow misery now etched into Vittorio's expression.

"I have also been informed that you beat several subordinate officers nearly to death without provocation. And of course, you not only failed your mandate to maintain peaceful rule in Izmoroz, but lost it to the Uaine Empire. Now, thanks to your incompetence, a horde of leering undead are practically at our doorstep. What's more, word of the success of the Izmorozian insurgency is spreading to other territories, which might well incite further unrest elsewhere. All of this you have done *after* I so generously gave you the chance to make amends for your atrociously poor judgment as captain of my honor guard when you killed a *valued subject of mine* in one of your *childish fits of rage!*"

She paused for a moment to collect herself, during which time Vittorio remained silent, his eyes staring unseeingly at the floor.

The empress's expression softened slightly. "Even after all your misdeeds and failures, Franko, if you had simply fled to Victasha or braved the Ocean of Loss, I would not have pursued you. Instead you knowingly broke your banishment and returned to Aureum because you had the arrogance to believe you could still wheedle your way back into my heart."

"My empress . . . ," he moaned.

She shook her head sadly. "I was fond of you once, Franko. But you have squandered that affection so profoundly that there is nothing left of it."

"Please, Your Majesty!" He tried to step forward, but Antonio gripped his arm, preventing him getting any closer. "Everything I do is out of love for *you*."

"The only thing you love is yourself," she told him.

He continued to strain against Antonio's grip as he spoke. "No, Caterina! I swear I love you more than life itself! I would do anything for you! I worship you! God knows that I speak the truth!"

The empress came suddenly to her feet, her expression furious. "How dare you blaspheme!"

"It is no blasphemy, Your Majesty!" cried Vittorio. "I swear to God that my whole life has been dedicated to you!"

"Is that so?" Her expression cooled as she continued to look at him. "I had other punishments in mind, but since you insist that God be your witness, we will let God be your judge. Tomorrow at dawn, you will be flung from the highest tower in Magna Alto. Perhaps God will save you, just as he did my great-grandfather."

Vittorio stared at her, his mouth working but no sound coming out. Clearly he had not expected a death sentence.

She turned her back on him. "Take him away."

Antonio pulled him toward the doors, and he stumbled along, looking numb.

The empress looked at Zaniolo, as if seeing him for the first time. Her expression and tone became brisk and businesslike. "General, I expect a thorough debriefing on the debacle in Izmoroz within the hour."

Zaniolo bowed smoothly. "Of course, Your Majesty."

"You!" Vittorio was nearly to the exit, but stopped short, his face twisted into the purple fury Sebastian had seen at the battle at Sestra River. He struggled against Antonio's grasp as he shouted at Zaniolo. "Traitor! Rat! You were spying on me the whole time?"

Zaniolo gave one of those inscrutable smiles. "Now, now, Franko. Surely you didn't think Her Majesty would give you command of even such a minor territory as Izmoroz without some supervision. Not after your *history*. If so, you were an even bigger fool than I thought."

Vittorio bellowed with incoherent rage and became so frantic, a second honor guard had to assist Antonio in dragging him out of the room.

8

Sonya did what she could to help Anatoly, but even after weeks of regular meals, his health did not improve. She wished Jorge was there. Perhaps his potions could cure the old wolverine's ailments, or at least make his final days more comfortable. She debated staying with him until the Lady finally came for the final embrace, but he would have none of it.

"Why are you still here?" he snarled on more than one occasion. "Don't you have fox things to do? Starting revolutions, eating babies, and the like?"

He acted as though her presence was an inconvenience of some kind, but she wondered if it was the looks of pity she couldn't completely conceal that made him so cross.

One night, as she and Blaine settled in on the far side of the cave, Blaine gently suggested it might be better if they left.

"And let him die alone?" she asked.

"Maybe that's what he wants," said Blaine. "I think maybe I would."

"Really?" Sonya was surprised. Blaine was such a friendly, outgoing person that she assumed he would want to seek the comfort of loved ones in his final moments.

He stared up at the cave ceiling.

After a moment, he said, "When I finally meet Bàs, that reckoning is for me alone."

"What do the Uaine believe happens after death?" asked Sonya. "Is the soul of the dead person in the sluagh gorta? And does it stay there the whole time before they're brought back? Or does it go somewhere else while it's waiting?"

He was silent for such a long time that she wondered if he'd fallen asleep.

But then he said, "Sorry, Sonya. Only the Urram Le Bàs are allowed to talk about such things, and I don't think they'd tell anyone who wasn't Uaine."

"Oh. Uh, sure. I understand."

Blaine had never been reluctant to talk about his religion before, and he'd never seemed all that devout. In fact, he seemed far less deferential toward Rowena and the other Urram Le Bàs than many other Uaine. But perhaps even he had his limits.

"I guess it's sort of the core of your whole religion, isn't it?"

"Aye. What about Rangers?"

"We return to the Lady Marzanna for our final embrace in the Eventide, then we pass to what lies beyond."

"And what lies beyond?"

"We don't know."

"So your religion doesn't claim that anyone knows what happens after death?" He seemed impressed for some reason.

"Well, the Lady knows of course," said Sonya. "But she's not telling."

Now he just looked confused. "Why not?"

"It's not for us to question the Lady." She said it automatically, but then wondered if she still believed that, given her conversation with Anatoly.

"I see..." He didn't sound like he much cared for the blind obedience, either, but clearly didn't want to cast judgment on her religion.

After a moment, Sonya sighed. "I suppose if Anatoly wants to die alone, we should honor that wish."

"Aye," said Blaine.

"Once the meat is all cured, we'll head back to Gogoleth."

"I think that's for the best."

47

"You miss Jorge, don't you?"

"Don't *you*?"

"Of course."

They stayed another week, then said goodbye to Anatoly. He responded with a "Good riddance!" before flopping down on his pile of furs and gnawing intently on a piece of salted meat as if they were already gone.

Sonya had spent far too much time in the cave during the last month, so it was a great relief to feel the mild spring breeze on her cheek as she emerged from the Ranger's den. The snow was nearly gone now, and the mud had mostly dried. In their place were gold and green fields, interrupted by the occasional meandering brook.

She searched the area around the cave to see if perhaps Andre and Tatiana had left some sign of which way they'd gone. But either they'd covered their tracks, or the clues had all melted away. Regardless, she had no way of knowing whether she would ever even see them again. She would have loved to get another opinion on some of the things Anatoly had said about Lady Marzanna. The idea that the goddess didn't have Izmoroz's best interests at heart, the idea that her efforts might not have actually been for the good of her people...

"Was this whole trip a waste of time, then?" asked Blaine as they began the long trek back to Zapad.

"I don't know," she said. "We made Anatoly's last days more comfortable, at least. And he...taught me some things, I guess. About Rangers."

"Oh?"

She merely shrugged, and he did not press her. Perhaps he understood that just as there were things about Bàs that he couldn't speak about, there were some things about the Lady Màrzanna that a Ranger shouldn't speak about. Besides, she wasn't sure she really understood it yet anyway.

It wasn't as though Anatoly had completely altered her view of Lady Marzanna, of course. She'd always known the Lady could be cruel. But perhaps she'd still clung to the idea that the goddess cared at least to some degree about the welfare of Rangers and the people of

Izmoroz. The suggestion that they were nothing but tools was deeply troubling. If true, it called into question a lot of Sonya's assumptions of what it meant to be a Ranger. And to be Izmorozian.

A chill ran through her as she recalled something Andre had said during her first visit. *Our responsibility is to facilitate death and change, to make way for something new. Not just the death of people, but the death of countries and cultures. The Lady Marzanna has made it clear that it is time for Izmoroz to die.*

She'd argued against that idea ferociously at the time. Even now it didn't seem possible that was the Lady's intention. It simply couldn't be true.

Could it?

9

Sebastian and his mother were given adjoining suites to stay the night in the palace. Each room was spacious, with a four-poster bed, a wardrobe, and a fine birchwood writing desk.

"It will certainly be nice not to have to sleep on one of those dreadful, straw-filled mattresses at the roadside inns, won't it?" his mother said once the soldier who had escorted them left. She stood with hands clasped and gazed at the room with satisfaction.

"I suppose." Sebastian tried to get a sense of how she felt about their larger situation but, as usual, was unable to discern anything. "Mother, what should we do?"

She turned to him, a look of bemusement on her face. "Do?"

"Are we under arrest? Should we expect some sort of trial and punishment? Am I still a captain? Was I ever truly one?"

She nodded thoughtfully as she brushed his blond hair behind his ears. "I see. You're uneasy about having so many unknowns regarding our current situation."

"Well *yes*."

"I understand, my darling. And I wish I could assure you that everything will be all right, but in truth I have no idea. Nor do I have an answer to any of your questions."

"Then how can you be so calm about all this?"

"I only appear that way, darling, because I am not in the habit of showing vulnerability in the company of strangers. And really, there is no point in fretting about any of it, because there is nothing we can *do* about any of it. In many ways, we are back to the same predicament as the night your father was killed. It is clear the empress has designs for you. Simply be your sweet and earnest self, do as she says, and I suspect we will both live." She gave the room another appreciative glance. "And live well, by the look of it. I was sad to leave Izmoroz, of course, but I think I could be quite content with palace life. Now, if you will excuse me, I believe the guard mentioned something about a lady's bath."

"Yes, Mother. I suppose good night, then."

"Good night, my dearest." She walked as confidently and regally as ever as she made her way down the unfamiliar hallway in the direction the guard had indicated.

Sebastian went to his own room, where he found a small wash basin filled with water. Just as he finished freshening up, a servant in a beige tunic brought a platter of roast lamb and apples, and so he ate, chewing silently as his eyes roamed the room.

Once he'd eaten, Sebastian couldn't make up his mind whether to try exploring the palace or napping. He was concerned about getting lost in the massive palace, yet found his nerves too taut for sleep.

He found a book on the desk written by the famous Aureumian explorer, Lucio Gregori. It was about his adventures sailing on the Ocean of Loss, which lay off the western coast of Aureum. The account was well told and took Sebastian's mind off his current predicament for a little while. At least until he came to one passage:

As we sailed south along the coast, I asked the captain how well he knew these waters. He chuckled and said, "As well as any man can know such a thing. Which is to say, hardly at all."

At first I was perplexed, and even alarmed by his response. Had I entrusted our voyage to someone who was ignorant of our route? But the more I pondered it, the better I understood. We think we know this land, our bounteous Aureum. But like the great ocean, now and then we witness an effect, a ripple of some kind, that reminds us that much goes unseen beneath the surface of what we know. There is so much life and death, joy and suffering, that we do not—perhaps cannot—truly

*comprehend. And I am forced to ask myself: Am I truly exploring, or am
I merely drifting, unaware of the real world that lies beneath?*

The vague, unnamable dread of that passage struck at Sebastian's
heart with such intensity that he was forced to put the book down and
stare up at the canopy above his bed for some time. It was exactly as he
felt in that moment. Adrift on the surface of a world he could scarcely
comprehend, except to know how little he understood.

Everything Vittorio had told him was now suspect. Therefore
every action Sebastian had taken because of those words was also suspect. He was forced to review these last months and ask himself, again
and again, had he done the right thing? When they'd first arrived at
Magna Alto, he had been worried about receiving punishment. Now
he wondered if perhaps he deserved it.

There was a light tap at his door. Sebastian splashed some water on
his face, hoping it might snap him out of his gloomy reverie. But it
only managed to make him more alert, and therefore, more anxious.

He opened the door. "Yes?"

A young woman in a neat gray gown stood on the other side. "Captain Portinari?"

"Hopefully," he said.

She gave him an odd look.

"Sorry. Yes, that's me."

"Her Majesty requests an immediate audience with you in her
chambers. Please follow me."

Without waiting for a response, the woman turned and walked
down the hall.

Sebastian quickly snatched up his jacket, then hurried after her,
buttoning it as he went.

"Do you know what she wishes to speak to me about?"

"She did not confide that information to me, Captain."

Her tone was polite, but disinterested. Sebastian got the distinct
impression that further questions would yield similar results, so he
remained silent for the rest of the walk through the labyrinthine hallways of the palace.

At last they arrived before a thick oak door with the figure of a falcon carved in bas-relief. Two of the gold-armored honor guard were stationed before it, their eyes steely and grim. But the woman did not seem the least bit daunted.

"Captain Portinari to see Her Majesty, as requested," she told them.

One of the guards nodded, then knocked on the door.

"Come in." The empress's smoky voice filtered in from the room.

The guard opened the door and gestured for the woman and Sebastian to enter.

The empress's chambers were naturally much larger than his, composed of multiple rooms. The center of the main room was taken up with a narrow table surrounded by a sofa and several plush chairs, all upholstered in silk.

The empress was off to one side at a sprawling desk, quill in hand, and a pile of parchment before her. She looked up from her work and gave Sebastian the same playful smile he'd seen in the throne room.

"There you are, Captain Portinari. Thank you for coming so late in the day."

Sebastian dropped to one knee and bowed his head just as he'd done in the throne room. "It is an honor, Your Majesty."

"Yes, yes, there's no need to go into all that when it's just the two of us in my own chambers." The empress put away her quill and gathered the pile of parchment into a neat stack. "Abriana, you may go."

"Yes, Your Majesty."

The woman turned and left, the guard closed the door, and Sebastian was indeed alone with the empress in her chambers. He recalled what his mother had said earlier. Do everything the empress said, and they would get to live. Probably.

She eyed him still kneeling on her rug. "Dear heavens, Sebastian, do get up off the floor."

"Y-yes, Your Majesty." Sebastian stood up, feeling light-headed for a moment. He reached one hand to the arm of the sofa to steady himself.

The empress stood up from her desk. She wore only a long silk dressing gown belted at the waist with a sash.

"You must excuse my informality, Sebastian." She made her way over to one of the large upholstered chairs. "There's only so much pomp I can stand in a day."

"Of course, Your Majesty."

"And please don't hover."

"Apologies, Your Majesty!" He sat down on the sofa across from her.

She leaned back in her chair and gazed thoughtfully at him a moment. He sat up straight, knees together. He had no idea what else to do with his hands, so he placed them awkwardly on his thighs.

"Hmm."

She leaned forward, took a decanter of red wine from the table, and poured herself a glass. Then she leaned back again, crossed her legs, and continued to gaze at him as she took a sip.

Finally she said, "Savitri told me you were the nervous type."

"Sorry, Your Majesty?"

She smiled slightly, as if enjoying his discomfiture. "General Zaniolo. He's given me his full report on what transpired in Izmoroz."

"I . . . see, Your Majesty."

Would Sebastian and his mother's fate come down to whether Zaniolo had given him a favorable report? And while he thought Zaniolo liked him, could he really say that for certain? In fact, he had never truly felt like he could tell what the sly general was thinking. And if the general were to lie, or even merely highlight what might very well have been legitimate mistakes, could Sebastian hope to defend himself? Was there, in the end, even a defense for his actions?

"I'm sorry to hear about your betrothal," the empress said. "Sounds like a nasty bit of business."

That was not one of the topics he had expected Zaniolo to cover. "Th-thank you, Your Majesty. Yes, it was."

She sighed and swirled the wine around in her goblet. "I'm afraid you'll find that the more power one possesses, the less one can trust the true motives of one's companions, particularly when it is of a romantic nature."

Sebastian wanted to ask her if she'd had her heart similarly broken, but feared the question might be too personal.

"Speaking of power," she continued, "show me that outrageously expensive diamond that Franko purchased on behalf of the empire without my permission."

"Y-Your Majesty, I had no idea—"

She only needed to raise a finger for him to immediately stop talking and take out the diamond, which he habitually kept on a leather thong around his neck. He untied it from his neck and handed it to her.

She dangled it by the strap so that it twisted lazily, glittering in the lamplight, while she took another sip of wine and admired it.

"Well, I can see now why it was so expensive. I don't think I've ever known its like," she said. "And I trust it was effective in application?"

"Very much so, Your Majesty."

At times, too much so, he thought. Even though it had been an accident, the fate of Les still haunted him. In fact, the darkness of those memories only seemed to grow more intense and suffocating with the passage of time. It had gotten so uncomfortable that he avoided thinking about it as much as possible.

"Hmm," the empress said again.

She continued to watch the gem twist as she drank more wine. Sebastian could not even pretend to guess at what her thoughts might be. She didn't seem angry with him. But he had learned with painful slowness that, unlike him, some people were capable of hiding their true feelings quite well.

Finally, she said, "Tell me, Sebastian, were you happy under Franko's command?"

"I'm . . . not sure what you mean, Your Majesty."

"Come now. He's no longer your superior officer, so you don't need to worry about that. And he hasn't been executed yet, so you don't have to worry about speaking ill of the dead, either. Be candid with me. Were you satisfied with what he had you doing?"

Sebastian had no idea what the correct response was. His only clue was what his mother had told him. Do what the empress said. And the empress had told him to be candid.

"I confess I felt . . . troubled with the direction in which he pushed me to use my magic."

"Oh?" She leaned forward, looking interested.

"It's not that I...well, I *understand* that the military application of magic is important. But when I first received this gem, I had envisioned..." He wanted to talk about his beautiful ice bridge, but he recalled how the commander had shamed him for having such naive goals.

"Go on." It was a command, gentle but firm.

He took a deep breath and continued. "I'd hoped to do profound good in this world, like Stephano Defilippo. I wanted to create, rather than destroy. Given some time and the right materials, I know I could learn how to rebuild whole towns in a day. Not..." He swallowed. "Not level them."

"Ah." She leaned back, looking strangely satisfied. "Zaniolo told me you accidentally demolished a town in Izmoroz and he suspected you might harbor some guilt about that. You acted in a moment of pique, no doubt agitated by your sister, who I hear is shockingly belligerent. Losing one's temper at your age, particularly toward a sibling, is hardly unusual. But for someone with your abilities, the consequences are far more dire."

He stared at the empress, unable to fathom how she could assess and understand so much so quickly, and with such empathy.

She smiled. "Do you think I have never lost my temper? And believe me, the power I wield can destroy far more than a single town."

"I had not considered—"

"Of course not, Sebastian." She leaned forward and pressed her hand to his cheek in an unexpected display of affection. "And thank you for being so honest with me. I know it couldn't have been easy."

He felt his cheeks beginning to flush. "I—I—I...thank you."

She continued to hold her palm to his cheek for a moment, rubbing her thumb up and down on his temple. Then she leaned back in her chair and smirked. "You forgot to say *Your Majesty*."

"Apologies, Your Majesty! I—"

She cut him off again with the wave of her hand. "What you've told me will be very helpful in deciding what your next assignment should be."

"My next assignment, Your Majesty?"

"Naturally, such a bright young talent like yours cannot be squandered. But I want to find something more suitable for you. Clearly hunting rebel insurgents doesn't play to your strengths."

"I'm afraid you're right, Your Majesty."

"We all have our weaknesses." She smirked at him again. "Except me, of course."

"Of course, Your Majesty," he said quickly, and possibly meant it as well.

Her smile faded and she sat up in her chair. "Now I know this will be difficult for you, Sebastian, since he is your former mentor. But I would ask that you attend the execution of Franko Vittorio tomorrow at sunrise. I think it will help you put this whole sordid affair to rest so that you can look toward the future. *Our* future. The empire is in great need, and I believe you can do much good."

"Yes, Your Majesty. That's all I've ever wanted. To do some good."

She nodded. "That is what I like to hear. Now, why don't you go get some sleep."

10

Sonya couldn't decide if it was her or the world that had changed.

It was subtle at first. When she and Blaine finally reached Zapad, the villagers seemed to look at her differently. Maybe her new-found doubts about Lady Marzanna's motives were coloring how she looked at others. Or maybe the doubts merely allowed her to see what had always been there. Either way, when people spoke to her, or even looked at her, there was an unease she hadn't noticed before.

They still treated her with respect, of course. But it now seemed motivated more by trepidation than reverence. Had it always been like that? Had they all known the Lady did not truly care for them? Had they acted deferentially toward Sonya merely to avoid punishment? Had Sonya been a fool to think their behavior had, at least in part, been motivated by affection?

The closer they got to Gogoleth, the more pronounced people's sense of unease grew. When they reached Vesely, she thought perhaps it would be different. She had always considered it an especially welcoming place. But when they arrived, people would not even look her in the eye. The children did not come out to entreat her to stay at their homes. Even Yuri, the village elder, invited them into his home in a way that suggested he was doing so because he felt he had to, not because he wanted to.

When they sat down at Yuri's hearth fire, Yelena did not stay behind to keep them company while he collected food for the meal from the other villagers. Instead she silently handed them the jar of vodka, bowed respectfully, and left.

Sonya and Blaine sat and silently drank for a few minutes before she finally said, "I don't understand what happened."

"What do ye mean?" asked Blaine.

"Are people treating me differently now?" She gave him a hard look. "And don't just say what you think I want to hear. Tell me the truth."

He seemed to struggle with his answer for a moment, probably tempted to do exactly what she'd just told him not to. Finally he sighed and nodded.

"People do seem to be a wee bit...scared of you."

"Okay, so I'm not just imagining it. Something has definitely changed."

Again he hesitated. Blaine was not great at hiding his feelings, and there was clearly some kind of conflict going on inside him. Finally he nodded. "Aye."

"What are you not telling me?"

He stiffened at her question. "I don't know anything."

"But you have a guess. Or a suspicion at least?"

He shook his head, but couldn't look her in the eye. What could be so terrible that he didn't have the heart to tell her? She thought about pushing him harder on the subject but decided to hold off for now. Maybe he'd pluck up the courage on his own. He knew her, after all. She wasn't scary. Not really.

Yelena and Yuri returned carrying a steaming pot of stew between them. Sonya was disappointed that it wasn't Dima barging in and calling her *Strannitchka*. Yelena had once said that there would come a time when he wouldn't feel comfortable being so familiar with her. Had it already reached that point? If so, what had caused it?

The two old people set the pot down beside the hearth, then Yelena retrieved two bowls and spoons from her cupboard while Yuri waited silently by the door.

"We hope you enjoy the meal." She handed the bowls and spoons to Sonya and Blaine, then quickly headed for the door.

"Yelena, wait," said Sonya.

Yelena froze, but did not turn around.

"What's with everyone?" asked Sonya.

"I'm ... not sure what you mean, *Strannik* Sonya." She still wouldn't look at her.

"Everyone's being so distant. It's like they're scared, or maybe angry? I don't understand what happened."

"It's not for me to say."

"Tell me anyway," she said firmly.

There was a long pause. Then Yelena spoke with a surprising tremor in her voice.

"Is it true? Are you the daughter of Giovanni the Wolf?"

Sonya had not been expecting that.

"Well ... yeah. I've never hidden the fact that my last name is Portinari."

"We did not know the devil's full name. We only knew him as Giovanni the Wolf."

"The *devil*?"

"What else do you call someone who wages war with unarmed peasants by razing their fields and slaughtering their livestock?"

"He ... did that?" She'd known her father had been haunted by his actions in the war, but she hadn't realized he'd been to blame for the terrible famine that had followed.

"Is it also true that the wizard who destroyed Les was your *brother*?"

Regret lanced through Sonya. She still vividly recalled watching her brother flee with that viper Vittorio. Maybe there was nothing she could have done or said would have gotten through to him. But it still felt like she had failed him somehow.

"Yes, he is my brother."

"Whom you refused to kill." Yelena's eyes bored into hers with surprising intensity.

Sonya stared back at her. "I mean ... he's my *brother*."

"But *your* brother did not afford the same mercy to *mine* when he cornered him and his fellow rebels in a cave outside Otriye!"

"But that's ..." Sonya's voice was quiet. "That's not me, though."

60

"Isn't it?" flared Yelena.

"I'm a *Ranger of Marzanna*. I protect the people." Even as she said it, she thought of what Anatoly had said and heard the doubt in her own voice.

Yelena shook her head. "You still think *Strannik* bring us comfort?"

Yuri pulled at her sleeve. "Please, my dear..."

She yanked her arm free, her eyes still locked on Sonya.

"Do you think we find some assurance in your presence? You, the servant of Winter and Death?" She chuckled mirthlessly. "Are you still such a child?"

"I saved Izmoroz from Aureum!" Sonya's voice grew firm. She knew this for certain. "I drove out the empire!"

"And replaced it with a horde of necromancer barbarians! Do you think that's an improvement?"

"No, I just..."

Anger began to rise in Sonya's gut, but she tamped it back down. She would not lash out defensively at this old woman who had treated her so kindly in the past. A woman who had legitimate grievances.

"Look." She tried to keep her voice calm. Reasonable. Compassionate. "The Uaine are just guests. They won't be here much longer."

"Is that so?" Yelena looked scornful. "And just when are they leaving?"

"I don't..." She glanced over at Blaine, who had remained silent throughout this exchange. Even now he would not look at her. "Blaine, do you know?"

He said nothing.

Sonya turned back to Yelena. "You can trust me. I swear. I will make sure the Uaine leave. No matter what my father and brother have done, I still love this land. I'm still Izmorozian."

Yelena looked like she was about to retort, but Yuri squeezed her arm, his face pleading. "I'm begging you, Yeletchka. No more. For *all* our sakes."

Yelena took a deep breath, then gave Sonya a curt bow. "I have answered your questions as you commanded. I hope you are satisfied with my service, *Strannik* Sonya. Please excuse me. I am feeling unwell."

Yuri guided her gently out of the house, glancing fearfully back at Sonya, as though expecting a reprisal.

But Sonya's eyes were fixed on Blaine, who looked miserable as he stared down at his untouched bowl of stew. She struggled to keep her voice even.

"What are you not telling me?"

"I have heard no plans of leaving Izmoroz," he said quietly. "In fact, even though I am a captain, I have not been invited to any council meetings in some time."

"Since how long?" Sonya's voice was bleak. She already knew the answer.

"Since I met you."

"Because they know you're a terrible liar and you wouldn't be able to keep it a secret that they have no plans of leaving Izmoroz anytime soon."

He looked up at her, his eyes red and glistening with unshed tears. "We don't know that, Sonya. Maybe—"

"Maybe when we get back to Gogoleth," she cut him off, "I'm going to have a long talk with Tighearna Elgin Mordha."

II

Sebastian had seen death before, but it had always been sudden and in the heat of battle or conflict. So when he awoke the next morning, the weight of a formal execution hung heavily on his heart. He had also slept poorly. Nightmares haunted him, though he couldn't remember the details. It was not the first time he'd had them since leaving Gogoleth, but they felt worse somehow. More urgent, though toward what he didn't know.

His uniform had been cleaned and neatly pressed, so he put it on. As he did so, he wondered where Rykov was. He had not seen his aide-de-camp since they had arrived at the palace the day before. He missed his friend's quiet, reassuring presence and hoped they were not treating him poorly just because he was Izmorozian.

The execution was held at the highest tower of the palace. It wasn't the same tower as the one Alessandro Morante had been thrown from by his fellow senators. That building had been torn down as soon as Morante had seized power. But this tower had been added to the palace specifically to commemorate that event. Sebastian wondered if anyone else had been thrown from it, or whether Vittorio would be the first.

The tower was open to the air, but narrow, so only a limited number of people could attend. The empress was there with two of her honor guard. Aside from Vittorio, the only other people present were Sebastian, Zaniolo, and a tall, thin older gentleman with the uniform and decorations of a general. He had a white beard that was carefully waxed into a point, and a thick mane of white hair that stuck out in all directions when he removed his cap.

The sky was ruddy with pink predawn light, and the ceaseless gusts of chill wind were so shrill that the guard holding Vittorio had to shout to be heard.

"Franko Vittorio, you have been found guilty of multiple crimes against the empire, and have been sentenced to death by falling. Do you have any last words before you are flung from the parapet?"

Vittorio wore only a simple white tunic and tan trousers. His eyes still seethed with the dark rage he had displayed the day before, but he seemed much more in control of himself now. In fact, he seemed determined to meet his end with the decorum for which he had been known throughout much of his time commanding the imperial army in Izmoroz.

Sebastian found a sudden sadness well up in his chest. He might never understand why Vittorio had squandered his own greatness, but he pitied him nonetheless. And perhaps there was still some guilt, despite the empress's assurance the night before, that Sebastian was not being punished for his own failures as well.

"Your Majesty," Vittorio said solemnly. "If God decides to spare me from death, will you abide by His judgment?"

"If you survive a fall from over a hundred feet, I would be disinclined to try killing you again," she said.

He bowed his head. "Thank you, Your Majesty. Then I will let God decide my fate, for only He knows the innocence that dwells within my bosom."

"How long did he take to compose that one?" murmured Zaniolo.

Sebastian didn't appreciate the levity in this unhappy moment, but the other general smiled tiredly at the quip.

Vittorio turned toward the reddening horizon, the wind whipping his hair and shirt. His hands were bound behind him and the honor guard reached out to take his arm, but Vittorio shook him off. Then he moved bravely up onto the parapet without any assistance. He stood for a moment, watching the sun slowly emerge. He whispered something quietly to himself, perhaps a prayer. Then, his eyes still gazing forward, he stepped off the edge and disappeared from view.

There was the sound of several short impacts, as though he had perhaps bounced off a few ledges or a buttress on the way down. Then at last there was the faint sickening thwack of flesh hitting cobblestones far below.

"Well." The empress looked solemn, her eyes gazing up into the sky as the pink gave way to the bright blue of morning.

Sebastian knew that Vittorio had loved the empress, and wondered if in some way, she had once loved him in return. Sebastian wondered how a man might change so much that someone falls out of love with him.

He felt an unpleasant squirm in his stomach at that thought. After all, Galina had claimed to fall out of love with him because he had changed. Or had she merely pretended to love him from the start? He could drive himself mad thinking about that, and anyway, it was over, so he supposed there wasn't any point in wondering the answer.

He turned to Zaniolo.

"What happens now, General?"

Zaniolo nodded. "I believe Her Majesty has already decided on your next assignment."

"Indeed I have," said the empress. "Which was one of the reasons why I invited General Paolo Barone to join us this morning."

The white-haired general smiled affably at Sebastian. "I knew your father quite well in our youth, Captain. And I've heard great things about you from Savitri. I look forward to working with you."

"Yes, sir." Sebastian was a little startled that the empress had already reassigned him but saluted sharply.

"Captain Portinari, you are to join General Barone's battalion," said the empress. "They will soon be deployed to Kante."

Sebastian's heart, still heavy with sadness from Vittorio's death, now tightened up with dread. "To the war, then, Your Majesty?"

"Not exactly, Captain."

"This is more of a...rescue and rebuilding mission," said Barone. "Our main force in Kante has achieved their first major victory by taking the town of Kleiner. But they received heavy casualties. If we do not arrive with reinforcements and medical supplies before the Kantesians can regroup and mount a counter assault, all their sacrifice will have been for naught."

"That sounds dire, sir." While he was not eager to return to battle, his concern for his fellow soldiers outweighed his reluctance.

"It is," agreed the general. "But our work will not end there. Once the situation in Kleiner is stable, we will need to rebuild the town as quickly as possible so that it can serve as a base of operations for further military action in Kante. And that is where you come in."

"Me, sir?"

The empress gave Sebastian that playful smile of hers. "After our discussion last night, I decided I'd like to test your bold claim that you could rebuild a town in a single day. What do you say to that, Captain?"

Understanding dawned on Sebastian that he was not being sent to Kante to destroy, but to restore. He knew he might look foolish, but he couldn't stop the relieved smile that broke out on his face. He had seen enough death and suffering to last him a lifetime. Perhaps now he could reach for the true greatness he'd always dreamed of.

"I am profoundly grateful, Your Majesty, and I swear to serve you with all my heart and mind!"

"That is what I like to hear."

Then a voice came from the stairwell. "Your Majesty!"

One of the honor guards appeared with a clank of gilded armor. He was breathing hard but gave the empress a sharp salute.

"What is it, Gino?"

"It's Vittorio, Your Majesty. He's . . . still alive."

She stared at him for a moment, her mouth slightly open. "Will he die soon?"

"It's hard to say for certain, Your Majesty. Both arms and both legs are badly broken, and the apothecary in attendance said there was a moment when it seemed like he'd died. But then his heart started beating again and he began to breathe. So there is a chance he may continue to live for some time."

The empress closed her eyes. "This is absurd." She shook her head and looked back at the guard. "Well, I did promise to let him live if he survived the fall. Instruct the apothecary to care for him as he would any patient."

Gino saluted again. "At once, Your Majesty."

The empress sighed as she watched the guard hurry away. "Will I be punished for my past kindness to that man for the rest of my life?"

She looked more put out than anything, but Sebastian felt oddly relieved. Even if Vittorio was a deeply troubled man, and even if he could no longer live the soldierly life he'd so cherished, perhaps he would find some small measure of happiness in this new chapter of his life.

And perhaps Sebastian would as well.

12

The people only grew more distant and hostile as Sonya and Blaine neared Gogoleth. By the time they reached the ancient city itself, townsfolk would sometimes go so far as to cross the street to avoid her.

Sonya still struggled with how to react. She was hurt by their fickleness, and at times furious with them. But then she would grow angry with herself for feeling that way. Yelena had made some valid points. Her anger toward Sonya's father and brother was justified. Her fear regarding the Uaine might be as well. And of course, Sonya's own doubts had made it difficult to convince her that the Rangers were a benevolent force for the people of Izmoroz.

But one thing Sonya *could* do was show Yelena and everyone else that they could at least count on her. The people wanted the Uaine to keep their promise to leave Izmoroz, so Sonya would ensure Mordha began his preparations to leave immediately. By force, if necessary.

"Sonya, why don't we stop at the college first?" suggested Blaine as they rode down the cobblestone streets at a brisk trot toward the garrison. "Maybe Jorge can help us think of the best way to handle this."

"Why would I need Jorge? I already know the best way. Tell Mordha it's time to leave. If he doesn't like that, he can fight me. Isn't that how Uaine settle their differences?"

"It is . . . ," he said reluctantly.

Blaine had been extremely anxious since she'd decided to confront Mordha directly. It was like he didn't think she could win. Well, he'd underestimated her before. Everyone did. Once again, she'd have to show them all.

"So you won't go to Jorge first?" he asked plaintively.

"Nope."

Blaine suddenly reined in his horse. "I'm going to get him anyway."

She was hurt that he had so little faith in her, but she wasn't about to show it. "Fine, do what you want."

She continued toward the garrison. Blaine stayed where he was for a moment, the distance slowly growing between them. Then he nodded and turned his horse north toward the college.

Maybe it was for the best that he wasn't there. She didn't know what would happen once she beat up Mordha in front of the other Uaine warriors. Would they challenge Mordha's authority? Or would they try to retaliate to reclaim his honor? Either way, things could get ugly. And even if Mordha was agreeable to her demands, would Blaine leave with them? Or would he want to stay in Izmoroz? She tried not to get her hopes up, and promised herself that if he decided to leave with his people, she wouldn't be angry. Well, she would try not to be, anyway.

She hadn't been to the garrison since she had attempted to "rescue" her brother in early winter. Looking back on that misadventure, she had to admit that she could have handled it better. Maybe if she'd tried to see things a little more from Sebastian's point of view, rather than dismissing what he said and immediately jumping to anger, he wouldn't have been so vulnerable to that mustachioed commander. So many tragedies could have been avoided if she'd only managed to bring Sebastian over to her side. So much death could have been avoided. Unless of course the Lady Marzanna had *wanted* all that death...but no. Sonya refused to believe that. Her faith might be a little wobbly right now, but not even she believed her goddess could ever wish so much catastrophe upon her people.

The garrison structure hadn't changed a great deal since her last visit, but the ravages from battle and the occupation of people accustomed to tents and nomadic living were evident. Some buildings were charred from fire, others looked like they'd been used as target practice or canvas to draw crude murals. None of them appeared to house the Uaine. Instead, most of the open area around the buildings was covered with their traditional tents. The Uaine themselves sat around their campfires, cooking food or polishing armor and weapons. And of course the mass of sluagh gorta, ever silent and still, stood off to one side like ghastly toy soldiers waiting to be used.

The tents were packed in too tightly to get Peppercorn through so she tied him up next to the Uaine ponies. She headed through the cluster of tents toward Mordha's, which was easy to pick out because of its size.

"Bhuidseach Sonya."

Sonya saw Jorge's necromancer friend, Rowena, sitting at one of the campfires. She looked oddly out of place in a peach gown that might have been worn by one of the Izmorozian nobility.

"Hey," Sonya said tersely, not slowing her pace.

Rowena got up and followed, her long legs allowing her to catch up easily.

"I didna' realize you returned," Rowena said in that quiet, toneless way of hers.

"Just got back," said Sonya.

"Jorge will be happy," said Rowena. "He missed you and Blaine."

Sonya nodded and kept walking.

Rowena glanced around. "Is Blaine not with you?"

"He went to see Jorge."

Rowena smiled. "He couldna' wait, either."

Sonya decided not to respond to that. It probably shouldn't have bothered her that Rowena was so close to both her best friends, but it did. It wasn't that she didn't like Rowena, but there was a quiet smugness about her that got on Sonya's nerves, and right now her nerves were frayed very thin.

"Ye need to speak to the Tighearna?" Rowena asked as they neared his tent.

"Yes."

"I will let you do so. Be well, Sonya." Then she turned and headed back to the bonfire she'd been sitting at before.

"Sure, you too, Rowena." She wondered if the necromancer would be so pleasant after she kicked them all out of Izmoroz.

Sonya knew that among Uaine it was polite to announce oneself before entering a tent, but she just pushed open the flap and stepped inside. As usual, Mordha and Lorecchio were sitting together on the fur rug talking quietly in the Uaine language. They looked up and did not seem surprised by her angry expression.

"Bhuidseach Sonah," said Mordha.

"Mordha, it's time we talked about when you're leaving Izmoroz," she said.

He grasped the small cask of whiskey at his knee with one large hand, and patted the rug beside him with the other. "Okay. You come and drink. We talk."

She shook her head and remained standing. "Have you started preparations for your invasion?"

He gazed at her a moment, his scarred, bearded face impassive. "No."

"When do you plan to start?"

He shrugged. "When I decide it is time."

"Not good enough, Mordha."

"You are displeased," he observed.

"Yeah."

He began pouring himself a drink from the cask. "I do not care."

She glared at him a moment. It wasn't like she'd expected him to immediately start falling all over himself to apologize. But this rudeness felt purposeful. Like he was trying to intimidate her. After they'd fought their way across Izmoroz together, did he really think that would work?

"Mordha, you seem confused so let me be clear. Leaving Izmoroz isn't optional. I don't care if it's to Aureum, or back to Uaine, but I want you to begin making plans to leave immediately."

"No," he said.

"No?" She couldn't hide her surprise. At this point, she'd actually expected Lorecchio to step in and smooth things over, maybe offer a few weak excuses and some vague promises. But again this felt purposeful. Provocative, even. More intimidation tactics? Was he forgetting that the whole reason they had originally formed their alliance was because she had beaten Blaine in one-on-one combat? The anger seethed in her. This disrespect, after they'd fought side by side, was unsupportable.

"No." He turned his back on her.

"I guess I'm going to have to *make* you leave."

He looked back at her. "How?"

"A duel."

He looked amused. "You want to fight me?"

"Obviously." She was right. He *did* underestimate her, just like everyone else.

He nodded as he knocked back his drink in one swallow. "Okay. Fine. We fight."

He slowly stood up and looked around the tent. "In here? Or outside?"

"There's not enough room in here."

He nodded again. "Outside."

She stepped aside, watching him carefully as he walked past her toward the open tent flap. She didn't think he'd do something like stab her in the back, but he'd clearly lied before, so she knew she couldn't trust him. He, on the other hand, didn't give her a backward glance as he stepped out into the open.

Once he was outside, he shouted something in Uaine, and everyone perked up, looking eager. Since even Blaine was frightened of Mordha, he must be a fearsome warrior. Obviously, the Uaine realized this would be a fight worth watching. They quickly cleared an open space and gathered around.

"Sonya!" Jorge's voice rang out.

Her eyes didn't leave Mordha, but she could hear the tension in her friend's voice, and as he drew near, she could smell the fear on his skin.

"It's okay, Jorge," she called over her shoulder. "This won't take long."

"What in God's name are you doing?"

"What can I say? You were right, We should never have trusted them."

"Please, Sonya!" She could see him out of her peripheral vision now, pushing his way through the crowd toward her with Blaine close behind. "For once in your life, don't be rash. Let's talk this out. I'm sure we can all come to—"

"Mordha!" called Sonya. "Are there any words I could use that would make you leave?"

He calmly shook his head.

"There, you see how it is," she told Jorge.

"Surely there must be some mistake..." Jorge looked around desperately until he spotted Rowena in her peach gown at the back of the crowd. "Bhuidseach Rowena! Can you help clear up this misunderstanding?"

"There is no misunderstanding, Jorge," she said. "If we leave this land, it will be when we choose, not when the beast witch commands us."

"*If?*" He looked stunned, and more than a little hurt. "But..."

"I like you, Jorge, but I told you before. There es nothing I won't do to ensure the success of my people."

He could only stare at Rowena. Sonya hated to see him hurt, but it was best he understood the situation.

She turned her attention back to Mordha, who had waited impassively. Patiently, almost.

"You ready, Mordha?" She drew her knife.

"Aye." Mordha stood there, his hands empty.

"Do you...want to get a weapon?" she asked.

He shook his head. "No need."

Her lip curled up into a snarl. "You are really asking for it, aren't you."

The crowds formed a loose oval shape around them, with Sonya and Mordha at either end. There was roughly twenty feet of dirt between them. She was tempted to just throw her knife at him, but the point wasn't to kill him, even though she was angry enough to consider it. The point was to force him to respect her.

So she charged him. He was much bigger than Blaine, but not as fast. She could see his shoulder shift as he prepared to strike. She ducked under his fist, expecting to reach his midsection in the next moment. But before she did, his knee shot up with unexpected speed. She rolled to the side, barely avoiding getting her nose broken.

She continued through the roll until she was back on her feet. His leg had somehow caught her by surprise, but now he seemed slow to turn. She darted back in to slash at his flank in that moment of vulnerability.

Except he'd feigned the slow pivot and, without even looking at her, swept his fist in a backhand. It would have connected with the side of her head, but she dropped her knife and kicked her legs out in front of her, catching herself in a bridge. It was an awkward position, but before he could take advantage of it, she saw her opening. His near arm was still moving backward and his legs were still facing forward, which left that side of his midsection completely open. She shifted her full weight to her hands, brought her knees to her chin, then struck out with her heels. The force of her thrust would knock the wind of him and possibly break a few of his ribs.

But again his sudden speed surprised her. He twisted his torso, reached around with his far hand, and grasped her ankle. Then he yanked so hard that he threw her several yards. She somersaulted in the air and managed to land on her feet, skidding to a halt in the loose dirt.

"Okay, okay, I get it...," she muttered to herself.

Three times she'd fallen for his feint. *She* was the one who had been underestimating *him*. He was both faster and smarter than he looked. He used his appearance to his advantage, pretending slowness so that he could take his opponent by surprise. He kept baiting her with something that looked like an opening, but wasn't. She had to wise up and stop falling for that trick.

Although first she had to get her knife back.

Unfortunately, he stood between her and where her knife lay on the ground. It was only a few feet away from him, yet he didn't seem interested in taking it. In theory she could just circle around him and snatch it up. But she was done underestimating her opponent. If she tried that, she'd leave herself open as she crossed in front or behind him. Considering both his reach and his speed, he might be able to close the distance.

Instead she charged right at him. His eyebrows lifted in surprise at her boldness. Probably once most people figured out how fast he was, they became more cautious. As she drew near, she feigned like she was going to roll between his legs. When he lowered his hands to intercept, she instead leapt into the air and used his big hard head to vault over him. She landed behind him in a crouch, grabbed her knife, spun, and slashed at his leg.

Her blade sank into his calf, but the resistance felt strange. Like she was stabbing wood instead of flesh.

And it didn't slow him down for even a moment.

That same "wounded" leg shot out, the toes of his boot slamming into her stomach so hard it sent her into the air. Then while she was still in midair, he caught her by the neck.

He held her dangling there and gazed impassively at her. The kick had made her bite her lip and she tasted blood. She snarled through her sticky red lips. This time he really had underestimated her. He was wide open, she was close, and she still held her knife. Without hesitation, she thrust it into his chest.

Except her target once again felt strange. Not like regular flesh at all. And no blood seeped from the wound. There was also no change in the expression on his face.

It dawned on her that perhaps Tighearna Elgin Mordha was not entirely human.

A hot desperation rose in her as his grip tightened around her throat. She stabbed him again, then again. Still he did not react. She went for his face and he caught her wrist with his free hand, squeezing hard enough to force her to drop her knife. Then he slammed his massive, scarred forehead into her nose.

Stars and blood splashed across her vision as her head snapped back from the impact. She was stunned for a moment, and her body drooped like a rag doll. Then he casually slammed her to the ground.

She struggled to get up, but he knelt next to her and shoved her head back against the ground with one meaty hand so her cheek was pressed into the dirt. Then he punched her in the stomach with the other hand so that all the air whooshed out of her.

"Now do you see the difference between us?"

He was not gloating when he asked the question. If anything, he seemed a little sad.

"Wha...wha..." She now fought as much for breath as she did against her opponent. But still she lashed out with fists and feet as she tried to free her head from the press of his palm. "What are you?"

"I am one who is tired of being used as a tool, just as you have been. Will you serve me?"

"Nnnnnnever!"

"Hm," he said, seemingly unbothered. "We shall see."

He gripped her head and slammed it against the ground once more, then stood up.

"Out of respect for our past alliance and the heart of Blaine Ruairc, I will let you live this time. But now it is *you* who must leave Izmoroz. At once."

"No..." She fought against the pain and the darkness that tunneled her vision as she forced herself to stand. "I would rather die..."

He nodded. "If that is your wish—"

"No! Wait!"

Jorge pushed his way through the Uaine and over to Sonya's side. "Please, Sonya. I'm begging you. Don't do this."

"Jorge?" Her vision was so blurry she could hardly make out his expression.

"You know what will happen if you die. *She'll* bring you back, but with even less of yourself."

He was right, of course. And how much more of herself could she lose before she was...something else?

"Sonya, let's retreat for now, okay?"

"R'treat?" she slurred. The concussion was coming on strong.

He nodded emphatically, squeezing her hands. "We'll go...*to Raíz*. I can show you my homeland. It's so beautiful, and you can rest there and decide what to do next. Figure out how to beat him."

"Beat 'm..."

"Exactly! Well? Doesn't that sound like a good plan?"

She stood for a moment, trying to think about it, or about anything really, as her body weaved back and forth like a drunk. If Jorge hadn't been holding her so tightly, she might have tipped over.

"'Kay...," she muttered. "We do that..."

He smiled gratefully, tears in his eyes. "Thank you, Sonya. Thank you."

Then he looked at Mordha, who had watched it all impassively.

"It will take us several days to reach the Aureumian border, maybe longer with her injuries."

"You have one week to be gone from Izmoroz."

"Thank you, Tighearna."

Jorge turned to where Blaine stood within the crowd of his fellow Uaine.

"Blaine?" He looked at once hopeful and anxious. "Will you... come with us?"

Blaine's face was tense, and his eyes were raw from tears. But he shook his head and turned away from them.

That was when Sonya's legs gave out from under her.

In a haze of confusion and despair, she was vaguely aware that Jorge laboriously hauled her across the garrison fields. The Uaine parted before them, allowing them to pass without comment, their expressions solemn. Perhaps even respectful. Sonya did not understand them, and she realized now that she probably never had.

They finally reached the horses. Jorge managed to shove Sonya up onto Peppercorn, where she could cling to the pommel of the saddle and lay her pounding, befuddled head on his coarse mane. The last thing she saw before she lost consciousness was Jorge climbing up onto his own horse, taking her reins, and leading them out of the garrison.

13

Watching Jorge drag a concussed Sonya out of the garrison was among the saddest things Rowena had ever seen. She'd always liked Jorge, of course, but his steadfast loyalty in the face of what was surely a terrifying situation brought a warm flood of respect to her chest. It was the first time she had ever felt such fellowship with someone outside her own people, and it grieved her that they could no longer be allies.

But there was still a great deal of work to be done, and many trials ahead. They must be strong, or they would perish.

She glanced over at Blaine, saw the pain etched into his face, and decided she was not the only one who needed that reminder.

She walked over to him, the crowds of Uaine parting for her as they slowly drifted back to their tents.

"Blaine," she said quietly.

He did not look at her, but only stared at a bare patch of ground.

"Hail, Bhuidseach," he said without enthusiasm.

She was not offended, though. She knew, perhaps better than any other, the conflict in his heart.

"Did you convince yourself it would last forever?" she asked.

"I suppose I did."

"I hope you at least enjoyed yourself while you could."

He shrugged. Rowena guessed that he had probably enjoyed himself where Sonya was concerned, but perhaps not Jorge. It was unfortunate, but relationships with people outside the Uaine came with any number of impediments. Perhaps Blaine would protect his heart a little more carefully next time, and not hope for so much.

"For what it's worth, I wasn't enthusiastic about this particular plan. I felt turning her own people against her and provoking her into a duel was in poor taste. I'm surprised Galina Odoyevtseva even thought of it."

Blaine only nodded.

"What happened to those other Rangers you went searching for?" Rowena asked. "That was the one variable we thought might ruin the plan. I don't know if even the Tighearna could face four beast witches at once."

Blaine still would not look at her as he spoke. "We only found one of them, and he was dying. The other two are still out there somewhere."

"Could they become a problem?"

"Maybe, maybe not. They're quite old."

They stood in silence for a moment, the chilly spring wind pulling at their hair.

Finally, she said, "You had better pull yourself together before you speak to Mordha. He won't show the same patience as me."

Blaine said nothing.

She sighed. "Life is long, Blaine, and one never knows the twists that fate might have in store. Perhaps someday we will be allies again."

"Even if that happened, would they forgive me?" he asked plaintively.

"You do not require forgiveness. You did what you must for the good of our people, and for the world. Remember your—"

He finally looked at her, and his eyes flashed with fury. "Don't you dare say my brother. Not a day goes by that I don't think of him."

She inclined her head. "Well, then. I need hardly say more. Do I?"

He glared at her a moment longer, then looked away and shook his head. "No. I understand. And...thank you for giving me a nudge. I'm sure the Tighearna would have been...less gentle."

"We are still the same clan, Blaine. And I loved your brother, too."

14

Jorge found it surprisingly easy to leave Gogoleth. He took Sonya back to his rooms at the college and gave her a tonic and poultice that would mitigate her concussion to some extent. While she lay on the sofa in a daze, he packed up a few things. Velikhov wasn't at home, but after some thought, he decided it would be okay for him to take the travel lab as well.

By the time he was ready to go, Sonya was feeling well enough to at least totter along on her own. They made their slow way back down to the stables, packed up the saddlebags, and headed out. Occasionally he caught a glimpse of one of the Uaine observing from a distance, no doubt making sure they were truly leaving. He suspected they would follow all the way to the border. Neither Mordha nor Lorecchio were the sort of men who took chances.

As Jorge and Sonya rode through the ancient cobblestone streets, he thought it unlikely he would ever return, and he found that idea didn't bother him. Perhaps he had once dreamed of continuing on as a professor at the college and living the expatriate life. Or else coming back to Raíz to open the first proper apothecary shop in Colmo. In either case, he had assumed he would graduate from the college first. After all, he had worked hard to get there. He had also worked hard to *stay* there. Being the lone Raízian in Gogoleth, and possibly all of Izmoroz, had not been easy. He could have been resentful, or at least disappointed, that he was leaving it all behind without receiving the intended fruits of his labors.

But mostly, he was relieved.

He had tried so hard to love Izmoroz. But after a year and a half of effort, he found that the only thing he truly loved about Izmoroz was the concussed and dispirited woman riding beside him.

"Fuck them all," he muttered.

He was generally not one for cursing, but this seemed an apt moment to indulge. And Sonya certainly didn't object. He couldn't imagine what she might be going through, and he still wasn't quite sure what had happened. The people treated her differently, that was true. While there had always been a nervousness in their eyes whenever speaking to her, they now expressed open fear. And seeing her in such a helpless state, there was a great deal of disgust as well.

He didn't know what had caused this dramatic shift. Clearly the Uaine were involved. But why? What could they possibly gain by driving Sonya out of the country? Did they truly think she was the only obstacle to taking Izmoroz for themselves? And why did they want it? As Sonya herself had once put it, why would anyone want such a poor, war-torn country?

They took the Advent Road south, and stayed at an imperial hostel that night. They'd probably have to stay off the main road once they crossed over into Aureum, but for now, it was the quickest and safest way to reach the border before Mordha's ultimatum.

That first night, as they lay side by side in the utilitarian beds that could be found at every imperial hostel from Gogoleth to Colmo, Sonya spoke for the first time since they'd left Gogoleth.

"Jorge?" Her voice was scratchy and faint.

"Yes?"

"Are we really going to your home?"

"Well, it's a long way, obviously, but I don't know where else we could go. I suppose we could go to the tundra, but..."

He could see her shake her head in the near darkness. "I know you don't want to go back there."

She was silent for several moments. When she spoke again there

81

was tension in her voice. "What if all this..." She seemed to struggle for a moment, then blurted out quickly, "What if this was the Lady's will?"

"You think she wanted Mordha to beat you senseless?" asked Jorge.

"Not just that. *All* of it. What if she intended for the Uaine to take Izmoroz from the beginning. They worship her, too, you know."

"I thought they worshipped Bàs."

"It's the same entity. I asked once."

"I see. Still, don't the Rangers serve her faithfully? It hardly seems right to just get rid of you like that."

"'None can truly know the will of the Lady Marzanna.' That's what Tatiana told us the night we met those old Rangers." She was silent for a moment. "I think I'm starting to understand them better. But I don't know if I can really *accept* it like they do."

"So you found them?"

"Just Anatoly. He was dying, Jorge. He was a Ranger dying and about to meet the Lady for his final embrace..." She looked over at him, her golden fox eyes gleaming in the dark. "And he was *terrified*."

Jorge didn't know what to make of that. Sonya had declared many times that Rangers welcomed the embrace of their death goddess.

"Had he...lost faith?" he asked tentatively.

"Maybe. Or else he gained clarity."

Jorge had no idea how he might comfort his friend. Exiled from her country by foreigners who had gained power because of her own actions. Rejected by her lover. And now a crisis of faith? He'd often thought that she'd been overconfident because she'd put too much stock in her status as a Ranger of Marzanna. But now that her goddess ego had been deflated, he found that he dearly wished to see that cocky grin grace her fanged lips once more. He had no idea how he could bring it back, however.

Finally Sonya asked, "You think the people will be okay with the Uaine still there?"

"I think so," said Jorge. "There really aren't that many of them, after all. And say what you will about her, that Galina Odoyevtseva is as smart as they come. She'll see Izmoroz through these rough times."

Sonya snorted. "The *doll*? That'll be the day." Then she sighed. "Well, there isn't anything we can do about it right now. I'm going to have to get a lot stronger before I challenge Mordha again."

"That's the spirit," said Jorge. "And really, how much worse could it get in the meantime?"

15

Little Vadim hadn't played near the edge of the village in a while. Not since that Ranger had slaughtered a bunch of imperial soldiers right before his eyes. But the soldiers had all left, and news had reached Istoki the day before that even the Ranger was gone now. So Vadim thought perhaps it was finally safe for him to venture out of view of the cramped little home he shared with his parents and siblings. Besides, he was nine years old now, and his mother had told him that he must start acting like it.

Just to be extra careful, he had gone to the *western* edge of Istoki, as far from the spot where he'd encountered the Ranger as one could go and still be in the village. He sat on top of an old, broken piece of fence and played with his rag doll. He assured his doll that there was now nothing to be scared of. No soldiers, no Rangers. Perhaps even the nightmares would stop.

He looked out at the freshly plowed fields that stretched to the west. They would begin planting tomorrow, which was always a busy but exciting time. Even Vadim would help this year, since he was nine. Plenty old enough to carry his own weight, his mother had said.

As he stared out into the field, noting with trepidation just how big it was and just how much work it would actually entail to cover it all, he noticed that the earth was moving toward him.

No, not the earth. But something brown and gray upon the earth.

A great mass of brown and gray, moving with slow but purposeful steps. Like marching.

He stared at it for a long time, trying to figure out what it might be. An animal migration of some kind? Unfortunately, Vadim had poor eyesight for long distances. His mother always talked about going to one of the bigger towns like Kamen, or even Gogoleth, to get him some spectacles, but she hadn't actually done it yet. She said maybe after his tenth birthday.

Finally, after watching the mass move toward him for a long stretch of time, Vadim realized that it was people. People with white hair, gray skin, and brown robes. He'd never seen anything like it. He wondered what kind of people they were.

Then something came rushing toward him. He felt a sharp pain in his stomach, and he was knocked off the fence.

He landed on his back in the damp soil. Pain throbbed in his gut, radiating outward. He tried to move, but all he could do was lift his head. He stared uncomprehendingly at the thick, wooden end of the spear that protruded from his stomach. Blood was everywhere. Just like when the Ranger came. Except this time, the blood was all his.

Then a shadow fell over him. He looked up to see the gray people with white hair, now quite close. So close that he could see their yellow, lifeless eyes, and grinning lipless mouths.

Dimly, he thought he knew what kind of people they were now. Dead people.

As his eyes slowly closed, he hoped they would just let him be, and not make him join their dead army.

That wish, at least, was fulfilled. A moment later, one of the undead stepped indifferently on his head, crushing his skull.

The army of sluagh gorta continued to trample his lifeless body until there was nothing but ragged bits of flesh, bone, and cloth.

Clan Seacál had at last arrived in Izmoroz with the full might of the Uaine Empire.

INTERLUDE

Dreams did not require logic, and neither did the Eventide.

On the highest peak of a boiling ocean, two beings met once again. One of them, known as Winter, or Chaos, or Death, or sometimes even Marzanna, shimmered white ensconced in eternal darkness and spoke with a voice like the whisper of razor blades.

"My dear sibling, I confess I am disappointed in your lack of ingenuity. Using the same tactic as last time? I expected better of you."

The other being, known as Spring, or Order, or Life, or sometimes even Zivena, pulsed and surged like the innards of a great beast, and spoke with a voice thick and gurgling.

"Unlike you, dear sibling, I do not have a compulsive need to reinvent. It worked once, and I see no reason why it will not work again. You, on the other hand, seem to have outsmarted yourself."

"In what way?" asked Marzanna.

"Your wayward children are not minding you very well."

"They do not need to. Even in their defiance, they serve me."

Zivena paused, as if considering the sincerity of those words. Then she asked, "What of your precious *Lisitsa*? The poor thing seems quite lost."

"I admit that she still has a long way to go yet, but I am confident she will ultimately serve her purpose."

"And what purpose is that, exactly?"

"Wouldn't you like to know."

Zivena paused again. "Aren't you concerned about the Armonia?"

"Aren't you?"

"I think I'm well positioned to deal with any conflict that arises."

Marzanna shivered with laughter. "Is *that* what you think?"

PART TWO⊙

EXPLORERS OF THE LOSS

"A person cannot truly understand home until they have left it behind."

—Lucio Gregori, *A Voyage on the Ocean of Loss*

ion Snyden

16

Sebastian was glad that Vittorio had regained consciousness before he departed for Kante. But he was not quite prepared for the shock of seeing his former mentor so transformed.

In Sebastian's mind, Vittorio was the perfect picture of masculine poise. Large, imposing, and dignified. And even in the darkest depths of despair when he'd lost much of his decorum, the man had still seemed strong, virile, and capable in a way Sebastian didn't think he could ever match.

Yet the man he now saw before him was none of those things. Vittorio seemed to have aged in a shockingly short amount of time. His hair and proud mustache were shot through with gray. His eyes were watery and seemed weak, as though his vision had suffered damage. He had lost a great deal of weight, so that his once proud, rosy cheeks were now gaunt and sunken. His formerly strong hands looked frail and delicate as they lay upon the blanket tucked up to his armpits. Both his arms and legs were still in splints, and the apothecary had said that even when they finally healed, he would likely be unable to walk without the aid of crutches and leg braces.

Sebastian wondered if he should feel some satisfaction that the man who had been responsible for his father's death had been reduced to this. But he didn't. He had been pondering for weeks now why it was so difficult for him to completely put Vittorio behind him like the empress had suggested. Perhaps it was because so much of his own self-worth had been built on the assurances of this man. Now that the man had been brought low, and his assurances rendered questionable at best, Sebastian felt that what little firm ground he'd managed to set beneath himself had been rendered unstable. Possibly even illusory.

He had come to see if there remained any vestige of the man in whom he'd put so much faith. But the person who looked back at him now seemed almost a stranger.

"Ah, there you are, my boy. So good of you to visit."

Even his voice sounded feeble. Quavering.

"It's, uh, good to see you so alert, sir."

"Now, now, Sebastian, you mustn't call me *sir* any longer." Vittorio gently chided him. "You'll have to get used to the idea that I'm not your superior officer now."

Sebastian sighed. "Truthfully, I'm not sure what I should call you."

"How about Franko?" Vittorio suggested. "That would please me greatly."

"If that's what you prefer." The idea actually made Sebastian uncomfortable, but he didn't want to hurt the man's feelings. "Are you...okay? Is there anything you need?"

Vittorio shook his head. "Don't worry about me. Her Majesty has generously offered me a menial position in the palace staff once I have fully recovered."

"Oh. That's wonderful."

"I just hope I won't be too much of a burden."

After an awkward pause, Sebastian said, "I was sorry to hear that... you know, that you may not make a full recovery." It seemed insufficient, but he didn't know what else to say.

But Vittorio didn't seem troubled in the least. "Don't be, my boy. Nothing in this world is free. Not even miracles."

"Is that what you think it was, then? God spared your life?"

A strange gleam came into Vittorio's eyes. "Whether it was God who spared me, I cannot say. But it was most certainly a miracle."

Sebastian didn't quite know what to make of that, and wondered if perhaps there had been some damage to Vittorio's mind as well.

"And what about you, Captain?" asked Vittorio. "Have you been given your next assignment?"

"Yes, I've been assigned to General Barone's battalion. We will be reinforcing the main force in Kante and rebuilding the town they currently occupy as a new base of operations."

"Rewarding work, no doubt. I look forward to hearing about your experiences when you return."

Then he let out a long, unrestrained yawn.

"My apologies," he said when he was finished. "The potions they have me drinking make me quite sleepy. I appreciate your visit, but I fear I must get some rest."

"Please don't let me keep you," said Sebastian. "And take care of yourself... Franko."

"You, too, Sebastian." Vittorio was already beginning to sidle down in his bed as though better positioning himself for sleep.

Not knowing what else to do, and feeling his lack of salute keenly, Sebastian left.

He was on his way to bid farewell to his mother when he came across Zaniolo in the hallway.

"Ah, Captain!" the general said cheerfully. "Ready to deploy with Old Barone, are you?"

"Yes, sir," said Sebastian. "We depart tomorrow."

"Excellent. I think you'll find his leadership style a pleasant change from the rather stern approach to which you're accustomed."

"I look forward to it," said Sebastian. "By the way, sir, have you seen Rykov? I asked General Barone if he would be joining our battalion, but he hadn't even heard of him."

"Oh, that's right. I meant to tell you. A few days ago Rykov requested a leave of absence to settle some family business back in Ízmoroz."

"Really?" Sebastian couldn't hide his look of surprise.

Zaniolo grinned. "I know. It's hard to imagine that hulking brute having a family, but I suppose everyone must."

"No, I just thought... well, since he is my aide-de-camp..."

"Come now, Portinari. The very idea that a mere captain needs an aide-de-camp is absurd. He was more like an overgrown babysitter."

"Oh." Sebastian felt his cheeks redden. "I hadn't realized..."

"Mind you, it was understandable that Vittorio assigned someone to look out for you, considering how shockingly green you were when you first arrived in Gogoleth." He gave Sebastian a reproachful look. "But I think you've outgrown such things, don't you?"

"Y-yes, sir. Of course. Thank you for explaining it to me."

"No trouble, my boy. I'm glad you understand. Now, if you'll excuse me, I need to make a report to the empress on some developments in the north."

"Concerning Izmoroz?" Sebastian knew he probably wasn't entitled to the information, but couldn't help himself.

Zaniolo paused for a moment, as if deciding something, then shrugged. "Concerning your sister, actually."

"Sonya?"

"She does have a rather... *distinctive* look, as you know, and I've received several reported sightings of her at various imperial hostels on the Advent Road, heading south."

"Toward Aureum? Why on earth would she come here?"

"I was hoping you might answer that question," said Zaniolo. "The Uaine have been most diligent in rooting out my network of informants, unfortunately, so we know very little of what's going on in Izmoroz at the moment."

Sebastian shook his head. "I haven't the faintest idea. She's never had any interest in Aureum, and loves Izmoroz with an almost zealous passion. I would think the only way she'd leave is if she was forced out."

"Hmm." Zaniolo considered that for a moment. "But why come to Aureum? If she was forced to leave Izmoroz, one would think she'd rather flee to her allies, the Uaine."

"Unless it was the Uaine who kicked her out," said Sebastian.

Zaniolo seemed surprised. "Is your sister really that fickle in her allegiances?"

"No, she's just that difficult to get along with."

"I see. Well, I thank you for the insight. I'm sure the empress appreciates it as well. Good luck to you in Kante."

Sebastian saluted. "Thank you, sir."

As Sebastian continued on to his mother's room, he wondered what Sonya might do once she got to Aureum. Would she try to find him and his mother again? Would she come all the way to Magna Alto for another misguided rescue attempt? At this point, he wasn't sure if he would put anything past her. That last time he'd seen her, with gleaming animal eyes, jagged teeth, and a face streaked in blood, she'd seemed half mad.

He knocked quietly on his mother's door.

"Please come in," she said, aloof and stern.

He opened the door. "Hello, Mother."

Her expression softened, and her voice warmed. "Ah, my darling. Come to say goodbye before your next grand adventure?"

"I have."

The empress had kindly moved his mother to a larger suite, since she would be staying at the palace for the foreseeable future. She was seated on a sofa, sipping tea. A porcelain teapot sat on a table in front of her.

Sebastian sat down across from her and helped himself to one of the small cookies that always came with the tray and that his mother never ate.

She gave him a speculative look. "Are you nervous, my darling?"

"About my assignment? No, the empress has made it clear that my primary purpose is to help rebuild a war-torn town. That will be a welcome change from being ordered to kill my sister. Although speaking of her, Zaniolo just told me that Sonya might be on her way to Aureum."

She gazed at him for a moment, her expression unreadable. Then she closed her eyes and sighed.

"That's how I feel," Sebastian said wryly. "You don't think she'd come looking for us again, do you?"

"Sebastian, I gave up trying to figure out your sister's motives long ago. I advise you to do the same. Frankly, I don't even think *she* knows why she does things sometimes."

17

Sonya didn't know where she was, what she was doing, or really even who she was anymore.

She and Jorge left the Advent Road once they'd drawn close to the Aureum border. They then cut west across the rocky, mostly uninhabited land along the border until they reached the southern edge of the Fanged Wolf Mountains. From there, they kept the mountains to their right and crossed into Aureum through the dense Life's Blood Forest.

Life's Blood was a predominantly deciduous forest, and the trees were just coming into bloom with spring. Sonya found the scent of flowers so intense at first that she had to tie a cloth across her face so that she didn't feel completely overwhelmed by it. Gradually she acclimated enough to take the cloth off, but even then, the flowers masked the scent of game, making hunting more challenging.

The temperature grew gradually warmer as they traveled southwest along woodcutter tracks. Eventually it became so hot that she had to take off her jacket. Now she wore only her breeches, boots, and a belted tunic. She felt strangely vulnerable to be traveling out in the open without a coat or cloak of any kind, although now that she was entering more southern climes, she knew she would have to get used to that.

Sonya had traveled all over Izmoroz. Under Mikhail's guidance when she was young, and later on her own. Every square mile of her homeland was at least passingly familiar to her, and she had grown accustomed to always knowing where she was. Now she was in Aureum, and it was all so unfamiliar, she couldn't quite shake the uneasiness in her heart.

By contrast, Jorge's spirits seemed to rise the farther they got from Izmoroz. Since Sonya felt a keen sense of homesickness, she could easily understand why he was so eager to return to his own home. But she couldn't seem to bring herself to share in his enthusiasm. Partly because she had no idea what she would do once they got there.

Jorge had told her she could rest, recover, and figure out how to beat Mordha. But how could she do that when she didn't even know what Mordha was? Not entirely human, she was certain of that the moment she'd stabbed him. But if he wasn't human, what was he? Did he have a weakness of some kind? Or was he truly invulnerable? How strong would she have to become to beat him? And how would she achieve that strength?

Of course she knew an obvious answer to that last question. She could ask another boon of the Lady. As she and Jorge sat by the crackling campfire one night, she ran her tongue across her sharp teeth and wondered, if she were to ask for another boon, what would be the price next time? And how much of her mind would be left after? As tempting as the idea was to seek out that strength, she realized that she also found it profoundly frightening.

Besides, even if she did become strong enough to defeat Mordha, would the people of Izmoroz even want her back?

"You've been stuck in your head a lot lately," said Jorge.

"Yeah, sorry," Sonya said. "I guess I'm not very good company."

"I know you have a lot on your mind, and it's understandable that you would be struggling. Perhaps it could help to talk it out."

Sonya stared moodily into the fire as she poked at it with a stick.

"You know, I should have seen it coming."

"Which part?" asked Jorge.

She sighed. "Mordha's betrayal, the people turning on me. All of it."

"The potential for Mordha to betray us was always there. I warned you about it before we'd even left Gogoleth. Once we met them, I admit I let my own optimism, naiveté, and fondness for Blaine and Rowena cloud my judgment. But in retrospect, I can't say I'm overly surprised by what happened. Except perhaps that Blaine refused to join us."

"The Uaine are really tight-knit. I don't think he could ever leave his people. Maybe even if part of him wanted to."

Jorge thought about that for a moment, then nodded. "Perhaps. But really, Sonya, I can't see how you could ever have foreseen your own people turning against you like they did."

"Mikhail warned me years ago." She took out her knife and began to sharpen it on her small whetstone. Mostly just to give herself something to do. "He told me that in times of conflict, people turn to the Rangers out of desperation, not admiration. He said I should never mistake fear for reverence. And that's exactly what I did. Maybe I thought I was different. Special." Her expression grew sour. "But in the end, I was like all the Rangers who came before me. It only took a small push for the people to show how they truly felt."

"Yes, that 'push.'" Jorge's eyes narrowed. "Someone must have spread the word about you being related to both Giovanni the Wolf and the Wizard of Gogoleth."

"I bet it was Angelo," said Sonya. "Sounds like the underhanded sort of thing he likes to do."

"He would have needed help getting it to the locals, however. Galina Odoyevtseva, perhaps."

Sonya looked surprised. "Galina?"

"I keep telling you, she's terribly smart. And it's not as though you endeared yourself to her, the way you were always so disdainful of courtesy and the nobility."

"You think she was afraid I was going to get rid of the nobles?"

"Weren't you?"

"Well . . . not get rid of them *completely*. Maybe just take away some of their power."

"Does Galina Odoyevtseva strike you as the sort of person who lets people take away her family's power?"

"No, I guess not. But what's she going to do with all those Uaine around? I mean, does her family even have any real power now? If Mordha decides to take charge, how is she going to stop him?"

"That," said Jorge, "is an excellent question. Especially since we now know he's someone not even you can defeat."

"You saw me stick my knife in him, right?"

"Of course."

"It was like . . . stabbing wood or something. It didn't feel like a real, living person."

"Could he be sluagh gorta?"

"I thought you said they couldn't speak or remember things."

Jorge shrugged. "That's merely what Angelo told me. It certainly seemed to be the case with their army. But perhaps there is more than one kind of sluagh gorta. For all we know, they could have been concealing vast amounts of strength from us."

"Yeah," Sonya said quietly. "I guess that means even Blaine and Rowena might have kept secrets from us."

They stared at the fire for a little while, the silence broken only by the occasional pop from an overheated rock.

"Well, on that depressing note, we should get some sleep," said Jorge. "If we get an early start tomorrow, I think we should be able to reach your surprise by midday."

Sonya's eyes widened. "My surprise?"

He grinned. "I thought that might perk you up a little. Trust me, you'll like it."

The next morning, Sonya did her absolute best to find out what the surprise was, but Jorge stoically withstood her barrage of questions, vague threats, and occasional pleading.

"You are not good with surprises, are you?" he asked as they steered their horses down the narrow trail.

"It's torture," she declared. "And you're enjoying it."

"A little," he admitted. "But only because I know it'll be worth it."

Sonya knew he was only doing it to help her. It gave her something to focus on, and as much as she complained, she was grateful for that. The scents, sounds, and landscape around them still left her feeling off balance, but rather than let them overwhelm her, she finally began sorting through them, identifying each in turn with a fresh determination. After all, any aspect could be a clue to her impending surprise. And perhaps in her careful scrutiny, she was able to appreciate just how lush and green it all was. How the scents of flowers and soft, rich earth mingled. How the golden sunlight filtered down through the thick branches to illuminate motes of pollen that danced upon the gentle breeze. How the air was filled with the mating songs of birds and insects so that it was an almost overwhelming cacophony of life. Spring in Izmoroz might be a desperate and clawing thing, but here in Aureum, it was a radiant diva returning triumphantly from the off season. And the way the salty air mingled with . . .

Sonya stopped. "Are we close to the sea?"

Jorge grinned. "I should have known you'd smell it first. Perhaps you don't remember this, but after your . . . adventure with the giant orca—"

"Lord Massa."

"Yes. After I dragged you back into the cave and stabilized you, you began rambling for a while. Talking about whatever seemed to come into your head."

Sonya winced. "I hope I didn't say anything too horrible."

He blushed and looked away. "You were . . . colorful on a number of topics. I promise I won't hold you to any of it. But one thing that really struck me was when you told me your old teacher Mikhail had sailed on the ocean and you wanted to do that someday."

"I . . . sort of remember that?" She vaguely remembered thinking about it, at least. She certainly didn't remember talking about it to Jorge, though.

"Well, I happen to love sailing, so it saddened me to learn that you'd never been on a ship. So I promised myself one day I'd take you on one. I'd like to get back to Raíz as soon as possible and there's a seaport on the coast of Aureum near here called Herder's Gate. So I thought this would be a good time to make that happen."

By then the forest had begun to thin, and Sonya could see a vast green meadow beyond. The meadow seemed to stop abruptly after about a hundred yards, but she could smell the tangy salt air even more strongly.

Sonya urged Peppercorn out into the meadow where the unfiltered sunlight lay like a warm blanket on her shoulders. They soon reached the far end of the meadow, which dropped off suddenly at a cliff's edge. Far below, and stretching all the way to the horizon, was the ocean, waves sparkling in the morning sun. Vast, majestic, and deadly, it was as glorious as the tundra in winter.

"It's called the Ocean of Loss," said Jorge as he reined in his horse beside her. "It's said that if you travel more than a few miles from the coast, your boat might be swept out into the endless seas, never to be seen again."

"It's beautiful," she said. "And we'll be sailing on it?"

"Herder's Gate should be a couple of days' ride south of here. We'll just follow this cliff until we get there. Then we can board a ship that will take us directly to Colmo, the capital of Raíz and my home."

As they rode along the edge of the cliff, Sonya couldn't tear her eyes away from the sea. It was nothing like the drab and inhospitable White Sea in the north. This ocean teemed with life. Fish jumped out of the water, their scales glittering in the sun. Sea birds swooped down to catch those fish. Plants and strange translucent creatures bobbed along with the current. It was a whole system of life unlike any she had ever seen before. It was a wondrous sight she would have never experienced if she'd stayed in Izmoroz.

"Huh. I guess there are good parts about going someplace new," she conceded.

"I hoped you'd say that," said Jorge. "Just wait until we get to Raíz. You're going to love it. I promise."

And for the first time, Sonya thought that maybe she would.

18

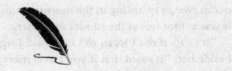

"I'm sorry, my Galechka, but what you propose is simply impossible,"
said Lord Sergey Bolotov Prozorova.

He turned his back on Galina and returned to his desk as though
that were the end of the conversation.

But Galina had no intention of leaving it at that. She had her father
cornered in his study, and she would either be satisfied or know the
reason why not.

"Papa, if you are so adamant on this, then surely you must have a
compelling explanation, and I would like to hear it. All I ask for is a
simple majority vote among council members to elect a minister to
organize the reconstruction effort. Surely with someone to lead—"

"That's just it, Galechka." Her father turned back to her, his brow
furrowing behind his spectacles. "Granting special power to a single
council member is simply not the Izmorozian way."

"I am painfully aware of that, Papa. Just as you must be aware that the
traditional system of governance in Izmoroz is woefully ineffective."

His expression hardened. "It may be slower than you would like,
my daughter, but that does not make it ineffective. I understand your
youthful impatience, but we must be cautious of what precedent this
would set. Izmoroz has avoided collapsing into tyranny in the past
because we refuse to act rashly or take the easy way out by handing all
the power to a single individual."

Galina took a deep breath. It did not calm her as she had hoped, but at least it prevented her from saying something she might regret. Specifically, that while the traditional Izmorozian government may have prevented itself from devolving into tyranny, it had failed to prevent tyrants *outside* the country from taking over. Bringing up such an obvious slight in that moment would hardly be productive.

"I'm not proposing to hand all power to a single individual, Papa." She kept her voice evenly measured. "As I explained, there would be a system in place to act as a counterbalance among various ministers who would all be elected by a simple majority vote from the council."

"And how would I propose this whole plan to the council?" he asked. "Why would any of them want to give even a *portion* of their power over to someone else?"

"So that we might heal this broken country of ours, Papa. Need I remind you that Les, a town of great importance to the economy, remains a pile of rubble, its inhabitants living in squalor or else refugees in neighboring towns that were already struggling to support their own inhabitants."

"Yes, well..." Her father gave her a pained expression. "There are members who question whether that is even a matter for the council."

"I beg your pardon?" Her voice rose in both pitch and volume. "If rebuilding a cornerstone of our national economy is not the responsibility of the council, then pray, please tell me, Papa, what *is?"*

He moved back over to her, his expression conciliatory. "Now, now, my Galechka, this is why I ask you to be patient. It is precisely that question we are trying to determine. Les is among Lord Levenchik's territories, after all, and there are some who believe that it is therefore his responsibility to rebuild it."

"Can he afford to do so?" she asked.

"Well, no, he has not been particularly wise with his money. It's all the mistresses, I suppose...," admitted her father. "Regardless, there is currently a proposal before the council that the other lords *loan* him the necessary funds. But of course now there is a great deal of disagreement on the terms, rate of interest, and so forth."

Galina stared at her father. She had never been so frustrated with him in her life. It was as though he was willfully ignoring the reality of the situation before them.

"Are you telling me that our people are starving and dying of exposure because the nobility are *haggling over interest rates*?"

"Such things are important, too, Galina."

Now Galina turned away from him, so that he would not see the look of vexation she could no longer conceal. It was even worse than she'd thought. How had Izmoroz ever accomplished anything in the past? Was her beloved nation like some massive, snow-covered jellyfish that merely bobbed along with the current, accepting whatever fate or chance bestowed?

She tensed up as she felt her father's hand on her shoulder.

"I know you are frustrated, my Galechka," he said quietly. "You did a marvelous job rallying the people and winning our independence from Aureum. But the time of thrilling battle is over. Now it is the time for sober and careful debate. You must trust me when I say that we will sort this all out before long. I promise you. We will protect the future of Izmoroz."

She glared at him over her shoulder. "And I promise *you*, if the council continues to drag its heels, there won't be a future to protect."

Then she shrugged his hand off and stormed out of his study.

As she strode down the hallway, she silently chastised herself for putting on such a dramatic display. It was exactly the sort of outburst that might cause her father to dismiss her concerns as the unreasonable passion of youth. She was not unreasonable. She was merely fed up.

"There you are, miss! It's terrible!"

Galina had never seen her maid so distraught. Masha was wringing her hands, her eyes wide, and her complexion a deathly pallor. Strangely, the sight of it allowed Galina to regain some of her own composure.

"Calm yourself, Masha. Tell me what's the matter."

"It's probably easiest if you just follow me, miss."

Masha led her into one of the less used drawing rooms, where she found Mathilde anxiously hovering over a peasant Galina had never seen before. He was slumped into the sofa and looked so exhausted he was barely conscious.

"Mathilde, who is this man?" asked Galina.

"This is my cousin Gennady Shukhov Zworykin from Zapad," said Mathilde. "The one who first told me about Ranger Sonya."

Galina felt a slight pang at the mention of Sonya's name. Was it guilt? Surely not. All Galina had done was communicate the truth to people. Reveal what they should have always known all along. That Sonya was just as dangerous as her brother, and her background terribly compromised.

"I see." Galina turned to the exhausted man. "And I assume, Gennady Shukhov, there is a good reason you are currently smearing dirt, sweat, and grime all over my family's sofa?"

"B-begging your pardon, miss." Gennady's hand shook so badly he could barely accept the tea that Masha handed him. "I come as fast as I could. The news is bad. So bad, and I didn't know where else to turn now that Ranger Sonya's gone."

"You did well to come here." Galina couldn't help feeling pleased that she had become the person they now turned to for help. "Tell me this news."

"I seen an army of the dead."

Galina strove to rein in her irritation. "Yes, we do have some Uaine with their undead warriors stationed outside Gogoleth."

He shook his head. "No, I seen those when Ranger Sonya first brought 'em. This was a different one. A *bigger* one. Ten times as big, I reckon. Maybe more. I seen 'em coming out of the tundra. So many I couldn't count. Just a river of marching corpses that trampled over everything and everyone in their path. Any person who gets near is stabbed or trampled to death."

"I . . . see."

Galina felt queasy. If Mordha was preparing for his assault on Aureum, it made sense that he would want to marshal all his forces. But why had he hidden his true numbers from his allies? Why had Angelo not mentioned it to Galina during their many conversations?

And was it a coincidence that this second army arrived shortly after Sonya had been forced to flee Izmoroz?

Suddenly, the protection of the Uaine that she had counted on to keep Aureum at bay no longer felt so benevolent.

"Masha, have the carriage brought around. We leave for the garrison at once. I will have answers."

19

"They certainly have made themselves at home here," said Galina as she and Masha wove between the tents that the Uaine had set up across just about every available space on the garrison grounds.

"Yes, miss."

"Yet the buildings themselves seem completely unoccupied. Do the Uaine have something against permanent structures? A religious belief, perhaps?"

"I don't know, miss."

Galina scanned the line of tents until she found one that was clearly larger than the others. She supposed it must belong to Mordha, and made her way in that direction. The truth was, she didn't know Mordha well. Most of her communication with the Uaine had been through Angelo. But as Angelo was so fond of pointing out, he had no real authority. Mordha was the one responsible for what was either a profoundly negligent gap in communication, or a blatant betrayal. She fervently hoped it was the former—that there was *some* reasonable explanation for this new, and according to Gennady, significantly more hostile army. Otherwise... well, she had heard what happened when Sonya tried to directly confront the man. If Mordha's true aim was total conquest of the continent, she had no idea what method or tactic she might employ that would succeed in ousting him from Izmoroz.

There were no guards posted outside the tent. Since she couldn't

107

knock on a tent flap, and she didn't want to simply barge in, she cleared her throat and called out.

"Hello? Tighearna Elgin Mordha? It's Galina Odoyevtseva Prozorova. I was hoping we might discuss something of an important and sensitive nature."

"Come," came the deep, rumbling reply.

She pushed open the tent. It was warm and stuffy inside. Mordha sat on a thick fur rug, stripped down to the waist. Galina was unnerved to see that the horrible scarring that covered his face also covered the rest of his body. A man and two women were intently rubbing a thick ointment into the scar tissue and did not look up when she entered.

"Apologies for interrupting..." Galina had no idea what she was interrupting but she felt her face redden.

Mordha didn't look embarrassed in the least. "What d'ye want?"

"I was..." She forced her eyes away from the people rubbing down his bare, scarred chest, and kept her focus only on his face, unpleasant as it was. "That is, I've heard reports of a second army of sluagh gorta that has entered Izmoroz, and I'm concerned that those leading this new deployment do not put the same value on Izmorozian life that you have exhibited in the past."

"Aye?" He looked like he didn't quite understand. She could never tell how strong his command of the imperial tongue was.

"To put it more bluntly, Tighearna, they're killing my people."

"Ah." He nodded. "No' on purpose."

"Well, that is heartening to know. But regardless of intention, the problem remains."

"Aye."

They stared at each other in silence as Galina grappled with her frustration.

"You do *understand* the problem then, Tighearna?"

"Aye."

"So how do you propose we solve it?"

He shook his head. "Some problem canna' be solved."

She waited a few moments, expecting he would explain himself further.

When he did not, she asked, "Why is it you cannot simply command them to take more care with their march? Perhaps go *around* the farms and villages that are in their way rather than trampling through them?"

He shrugged his thick, scarred shoulders. "Big army of sluagh gorta and only one Bhuidseach to command them." He stretched his mottled arm forward, the hand flat with fingers pointing toward her. "Can only aim sluagh gorta forward and hope."

"Then surely you could send your other Bhuidseach to intercept, and they could assist in more complicated maneuvers that would spare the remaining towns and villages."

"Aye," he agreed. "But no' send."

"And why not?"

He gazed at her, his expression impassive. "No' want to."

She stared at him for a moment, not quite sure she believed what she'd just heard.

She took a deep breath. "I'm sorry, did you just say——"

"Ah, Galina Odoyevtseva, sorry for not greeting you upon your arrival. I only just received word you were visiting." Angelo stepped into the tent, all smiles.

Galina turned her glare on him. "Yes, your Tighearna was just explaining to me that he will do nothing to curb the *second* army of sluagh gorta that are currently plowing across my beloved Izmoroz, leaving a trail of death and devastation in their wake."

She expected him to try evading her rather pointed remarks, but he only nodded, his expression still pleasant.

"Yes, I'm afraid it can't be helped."

"And why is that? He has just admitted to me that if he sent the other Bhuidseach, all of whom seem to merely be idling around in the garrison, they could easily maneuver the army around towns and villages, thereby sparing countless lives."

"Ah, I think there is a bit of a cultural misunderstanding," said Angelo. "You see, the Tighearna cannot send the Bhuidseach anywhere because he has no authority over them. He only commands the living Uaine. The dead belong to them, and they have final authority over what to do with them."

"I see. So I'm speaking to the wrong person, then?" She scowled at Mordha. "I thought I was speaking to the person in charge, but clearly that was not so."

Mordha seemed unfazed by her jab, which only upset her further.

She turned back to Angelo. "Very well, I will speak with the Bhuidseach then, and entreat them to spare my people."

His expression took on a pained look. Rather like her father's when he tried to explain a minor complication with potentially inhumane consequences.

"Yes, well, I am happy to ask if one of them will speak with you. I suspect Bhuidseach Rowena Viridomarus would be the one most likely to indulge your concerns."

"*Indulge* my . . ." She took another slow breath that failed to calm her. "Very well, please lead the way."

They walked among the tents in silence for a moment, Masha following at a respectful distance. But Galina could only bear the unspoken tension for so long.

"I suppose it was precisely this awkwardness you were attempting to avoid when you neglected to mention a second, less controllable army of undead during our *many* conversations."

"Now, now, Galina Odoyevtseva, don't act like such a child. Why on earth would I give away such sensitive information without reason? You and I get along well, and our interests have aligned in the past, but don't confuse that with friendship or trust. We both have our goals, and I doubt you would risk compromising yours for my sake."

"And what, pray tell, is your goal?"

He gave her a beatific smile. "Freedom. True and eternal. By any means necessary."

There was something uncomfortably zealous in his eyes, so Galina decided not to press him further. One thing at a time.

They stopped in front of a tent marked with several symbols painted in black. Or perhaps they were words in the Uaine language. Galina had never seen it written down.

"Please remain here," said Angelo. "I will ask Bhuidseach Rowena if she is willing to listen to your plea."

Galina watched Angelo slip into the tent. It was quite late in the day and she was surprised to see no light coming from within, as though Bhuidseach Rowena preferred sitting in the dark. She stood before the closed tent flap, ignoring the curious stares of passing Uaine, and listened to the quiet guttural murmur as Angelo and Rowena spoke to each other in Uaine.

It was Rowena who stepped out of the tent first. She wore her traditional brown robe and held the gowns Galina had given her draped over one thin pale arm.

"Galina Odoyevtseva, thank ye for lending these to me. 'Twas an interesting experience."

Galina wordlessly accepted the gowns, feeling this was not an encouraging start to the conversation.

"Angelo tells me ye are upset at the harm caused by our sluagh gorta as they march?"

"Very much so, Bhuidseach Rowena."

Rowena nodded. "Then ye will be pleased to know that their march is nearly ended. We are stationing them in the abandoned town of Les until we are ready to march on Aureum."

"While that is some relief, it hardly accounts for your cavalier attitude toward those we have already lost."

Rowena shrugged. "They are already dead. Do you wish me to turn them into sluagh gorta? It is unusual to bless outsiders in such a way, but it has been done in the past. With such a fearsome conflict ahead, I may be able to persuade my brethren that it would be worth making the allowance."

Galina's eyes widened. "No, I most certainly do *not* want you to turn my people into your undead servants."

Rowena gave her a puzzled look. "Then what else is there t' do?"

Galina had never been rendered speechless before, but the necromancer's undisguised indifference to the cruel fate of so many innocent people was staggering.

After a few moments of struggle, Galina's eyes fell upon Angelo, who gazed at her from within the tent, his face half hidden in its shadows.

"You can be certain I will tell the Council of Lords about this," she said.

"Yes," he said blandly. "How are they faring, by the way? Made any progress on...well, *anything* really?"

She glared at him, then spun on her heel and stalked off, Masha hurrying behind her. The Uaine might think they could act with impunity, but she would find a way to prove them wrong.

20

Sebastian wondered if it was strange, or even somehow wrong, to feel cheerful while riding to war.

General Barone's army comprised two cavalry units and five infantry units. There was also a specialized medical unit of Aureumian apothecaries and a small troupe of Viajero from Raíz who reportedly could use their expressive magic to dull the pain of even the most grievously injured.

Sebastian was thrilled to learn that there was also an engineering unit composed of carpenters, stonemasons, and other craftsmen who specialized in construction, agriculture, and irrigation. He knew that learning the engineering principles behind a structure would help him build those structures with his magic more effectively. With such a wealth of knowledge at his disposal and a great deal of practice, he felt certain he could fulfill his promise to the empress.

The battalion headed south on the Advent Road from Magna Alto for the first few days, then east following lesser roads. Unfortunately, with the bulk of the soldiers on foot, the general believed it would take a couple of weeks for them to reach the Segen Mountains that marked the border between Aureum and Kante. An army did not move quickly, Sebastian had learned. He prayed that the imperial troops in Kante could hold out long enough for them to arrive.

Sebastian had been allowed to retain his rank of captain, but he had not yet been put in command of any troops. While he would never have expressed such feelings to either the general or the empress, he was relieved. The men last under his command had all been killed, and he felt a great deal of guilt over their loss. The fewer people under his responsibility, the better.

Sebastian instead rode with Barone's entourage, comprising the general's personal guard and his aide-de-camp. Sebastian was still a little embarrassed by Zaniolo's gentle chiding about Rykov, but now he was able to appreciate how essential an aide-de-camp truly was for a man with as much responsibility as the general.

Of course Sebastian still missed Rykov. He feared he had never really appreciated, and certainly hadn't expressed, how much comfort he'd derived from the man's presence. Sebastian might not have truly needed an aide-de-camp, but he had most certainly needed a friend, and Rykov had been that for him. He'd never judged Sebastian, never discouraged him. He had only ever supported and protected him in that quiet way of his.

Thankfully, Sebastian's loneliness didn't last long because he discovered that he got along well with Barone's aide-de-camp, Marcello Oreste. Marcello was from western Aureum, and roughly the same age, with a broad handsome face, and merry eyes beneath his dark bangs.

"I don't really know much about Kante," said Sebastian as the two rode side by side at the front of the general's entourage. Like most days in Aureum, the weather was sunny and pleasantly warm, with a refreshing breeze that swept across the meadow in gentle gusts.

"Oh, Kante is a horrible, smelly place," Marcello said cheerfully.

"Smelly?" asked Sebastian.

"On account of the swamps. The southern part of the country is nothing but swampland, but even in the midlands you can smell it. And the parts that aren't swamp are mostly rocky and barren. A profoundly ugly place, all around." He frowned thoughtfully. "The women are pretty, though."

"Oh?"

"Yes, blond hair like yours, but with round freckled cheeks, and great big breasts." He held his hands out, palms up, fingers spread wide, presumably to illustrate the average size of their bosoms. "So soft and ample, you could drown in them and you wouldn't even mind."

"I–is that so?" asked Sebastian, who felt his own lack of romantic experience keenly. He'd never even attempted to touch Galina's breasts, although admittedly she hadn't been particularly well endowed.

"And Kantesian girls are very docile for the most part," said Marcello. "Unlike Aureumian girls."

"I've heard Aureumian women are unmatched in beauty." Sebastian had only seen the empress and a few servants at the palace, but he recalled General Marchisio's vivid descriptions.

"Oh, that's probably true," said Marcello. "But Aureumian girls all have sharp, unsparing tongues, and they are *very* difficult to please."

Sebastian doubted anyone had a sharper tongue than Galina Odoyevtseva, but didn't really want to bring her up to Marcello.

"Still," he said, "I would very much like to, uh, meet some."

Marcello grinned. "Well, why didn't you say so! I tell you what. The town of Windvale is close to where we'll be setting up camp tonight. It's small, but not a bad place at all. I've been a few times. Once we've taken care of our responsibilities, I'll ask the general to grant us leave to head into town for the evening. A couple of dashing young officers like us, we'll sweep those Aureumian girls off their feet!"

"Oh, I don't know if that's a good idea. After all, our mission is—"

"Are we going to get to Kante any sooner by spending the evening in our tents than we would in a tavern?"

"I suppose as long as we weren't out too late . . ." The idea of meeting some Aureumian women was appealing, but Sebastian also found it quite daunting. "But I wouldn't want to put you out."

"Nonsense," said Marcello. "You're doing me a favor. It's been ages since I really cut loose."

There was a strange eagerness in the aide–de–camp's eyes that did nothing to allay Sebastian's nerves.

21

Marcello had called Windvale a small town, but Sebastian thought it would have been considered midsized in Izmoroz. The roofs of the neat stone houses were shingled with a dark orange baked clay that was not as fine as the slate or copper roofs of Magna Alto, but still far more attractive than the thatch and wooden shingles so common in Izmoroz. The streets were all carefully laid cobblestone, with deep gutters on either side that kept the center clean.

The sun had already set, so there were not a lot of people about. But one large building had a pair of glowing lanterns out front, and the windows shone with a warm, ruddy light.

"That's our destination." Marcello pointed to the brightly lit building. "The Grapeseed Tavern is where all the young people gather after work around here. We're sure to find some of those famously beautiful Aureumian girls you're so curious about."

"Oh, well, I...don't really..."

Marcello laughed. "I'm only teasing, Portinari. You make it too easy. Besides, young men like us shouldn't feel bad about taking an interest in beautiful women. It's only natural, after all."

"I suppose..." Sebastian nervously adjusted his officer's cap, feeling even more self-conscious than usual.

"Will you relax?" Marcello patted his shoulder. "Follow my lead and you'll be fine."

Sebastian gave a mute nod.

Marcello narrowed his eyes. "Do you even know *how* to relax, Portinari?"

"Not according to my sister," muttered Sebastian.

Marcello stopped, suddenly looking very interested. "You have a sister? Why didn't you say so before? How old is she? Does she have hair like yours?"

"Er, she's a few years older than me and she has dark hair."

"Ah, what a shame," said Marcello.

Sebastian was fairly certain that even if she did have blond hair, her fox eyes and pointy teeth would have been enough of a deterrent. Or the fact that she was a seditionist wanted by the empire.

"Okay, enough stalling, Portinari," said Marcello, even though he'd been the one to halt their progress. "If I accomplish nothing else tonight, I will teach you how to relax."

Then he yanked open the tavern door with one hand and shoved Sebastian in with the other.

The inside of the tavern was hot, stuffy, and quite crowded. All the tables were filled with boisterous, talkative people. Some were evidently couples, their hands clasped together, or heads leaning forward so that their faces were mere inches apart. Others were rowdy-looking groups of young men or women talking gaily over each other, arguing and gesticulating broadly, yet laughing and clapping each other merrily on the back. The contrast to the grim and serious-faced young people of Izmoroz was striking. Sebastian felt terribly out of place and even more nervous than before. They all seemed to be having such a good time, and he genuinely didn't know if he was capable of giving in to such whole-hearted exuberance.

"Not a bad night," remarked Marcello as he surveyed the crowd. "A little slow, but that's probably better to ease you in, huh, Portinari?"

"Slow? The tables are all taken, so where should we—"

"Follow me, I think I found a place."

Sebastian followed Marcello over to a table where two young women sat drinking wine and talking in the animated way that seemed to come so easily to civilian Aureumians.

"Good evening, ladies." Marcello bowed with a flourish. "Might we join you for a drink?"

The women gazed up at them speculatively. One had hair as black as Sonya's, except it was twisted up in a complex braid, and her eyes were a tender brown. The other one had brown hair and sharp green eyes, and her hair was pulled back in a simple ponytail. The black-haired one narrowed her eyes at Sebastian, and he felt his whole body stiffen, as if he were a frightened rabbit ready to bolt. Then her burgundy lips curved into a smile and he relaxed, at least a little.

She nodded at Sebastian. "This one, yes." Then she turned to Marcello. "You, I'm not so sure about."

He pressed his hand to his chest and affected a look of hurt. "I beg you not to judge me so harshly, madam. My motives are purely altruistic. You see, my friend Portinari here grew up in the grim lands of Izmoroz and therefore has never learned how to have fun. I swore to myself I would teach him this most essential Aureumian skill and when I saw the two of you, I thought, 'Marcello, old chum, if there are any two people in this fine establishment who might assist you in your noble goal, it's those lovely women over there.'" He pressed his hands together as if in supplication. "So won't you help me, dear, dear ladies?"

The black-haired one rolled her eyes and looked at her friend. The friend shrugged and lightly tapped the side of her cup with one finger.

"I could use some wine, soldier boy."

"I'll see to it at once." Marcello turned sharply and strode purposefully over to the bar.

Sebastian stood there awkwardly until the black-haired one looked up at him.

"Well, blondie? Are you waiting for a written invitation?" She patted the seat beside her.

"Th-thank you." Sebastian sat down. "Miss . . ."

"You can just call me Mia." She inclined her head to her friend across the table. "And that's Camilla."

"Hi." Camilla waved her hand.

"A pleasure to meet you both. My name is Sebastian Turgenev Portinari."

"That's a mouthful," observed Mia. "Mind if I just call you Sebastian?"

Sebastian knew such informalities were far more common in Aureum, but it still caused him to blush. "I—I would be honored, um, Mia."

She seemed to find that amusing for some reason. "You're Izmorozian, then?"

"Half," he said. "My mother is Izmorozian, and my father was Aureumian."

"But you grew up in Izmoroz?"

"I did."

"I've never been up there. What's it like?"

He gave her a pained smile. "Cold and gloomy for the most part. Not like here…" His eyes swept the room, once again taking in all the lively conversation. They all seemed so carefree. So innocent. As though death and war had never touched them.

He turned back to them. "It's a welcome change."

"You know," said Camilla, "someone told me the other day that Izmoroz left the empire."

"Can they do that?" asked Mia.

Camilla shrugged.

"I'm afraid they have," said Sebastian. "For now, anyway. I'm certain that once the campaign in Kante is successful—"

"Have you taught Portinari how to have fun yet?" Marcello placed a large jug of wine and cups for Sebastian and himself on the table, then sat down beside Camilla.

"He's talking about campaigns," Camilla told him.

Marcello sighed. "So that would be a *no*."

He poured a cup of wine and handed it to Sebastian. "Drink this."

"I don't generally—"

"Now," he commanded. "Don't make me pull rank."

"Marcello, I'm not sure—"

"One drink wouldn't be too bad." Mia took the cup from Sebastian. She maintained eye contact with him as she sipped from it, then held it out so it was only an inch from his lips. One black eyebrow raised. "Would it, Sebastian?"

Sebastian's ears were burning and his mouth was suddenly dry. He had no idea if she was about to attempt pouring the drink down his throat herself, and decided he really didn't want to find out. He smiled as he accepted the cup from her and took a small sip.

"N–not at all, Mia. Thank you."

"I knew you two were the right choice." Marcello beamed as he poured his own drink. "We'll bring out his Aureumian side in no time!"

He held up his cup and they all toasted. Sebastian watched with unease as the other three drained their cups. Then, when Mia gave him a questioning look, he quickly swallowed his down. He'd had wine before, of course, and this wasn't even as strong as the mulled wine he had at the Ascendance. Surely he would be fine.

As Marcello refilled their cups, Sebastian tried to change the focus from their "noble" but rather embarrassing goal of teaching him how to have fun.

"So, er, what is it you two do?"

"Oh, we're just shop girls," said Mia.

"Shop girls?"

"My dad owns the general store here." Mia took a swallow of her wine. "Camilla and I work behind the counter."

"I see," said Sebastian as he sipped his own wine. If there was only one store, then all the goods traded with other towns must come through there. "It sounds like an important responsibility. Is it very taxing?"

"Better than working out in the fields," said Camilla.

"That's why I joined the army," said Marcello. "Much easier than picking grapes."

"More dangerous, though," said Mia.

Marcello leaned back in his chair, looking smug. "Ah, what's a little danger, right, Portinari?"

"I don't expect there will be a great deal of danger," said Sebastian. "After all, we're just there to—"

Marcello gave him a hard look. "Portinari, let's not bore the ladies with army talk."

"Oh, right." Sebastian took a gulp of wine. He had to admit, it did help calm his nerves.

"Yes, it's true we're on our way into enemy territory," said Marcello, ignoring his own suggestion. "But true glory is its own reward, and what's life without a little risk, eh?"

As Marcello gave the ladies an expectant look, it dawned on Sebastian that it wasn't so much "army talk" his friend wished to avoid as anything that didn't support the image of the dashing military hero he was attempting to cultivate. Marcello was posturing to impress the ladies.

Although Sebastian really did like the aide-de-camp, he found this ploy not only dishonest, but offensive.

"Have you ever been in a battle, Marcello?" he asked.

Marcello glanced at Sebastian, and his easy smile grew a little tense. "My whole life has been a battle, Portinari." He turned back to the ladies. "You know what I mean?"

"A battle in which people were trying to kill you?" clarified Sebastian.

Marcello struggled to maintain his usual cheery demeanor. "Well, not directly, no . . ."

Sebastian knew he was ruining this moment. That everyone else at the table was merely engaging in harmless flirtation and he was screwing it up. But he couldn't help himself. Battle, war, death, suffering. These were not things that should ever be taken lightly. And they were certainly not fodder for banal coquetry. The very idea made his blood seethe.

"Have you ever watched those you care about die in front of you?" asked Sebastian, his voice quiet and tremulous as he thought of the men who had been slain while under his command. Men he had promised to protect with his supposed power. "Have you *killed* another in conflict? Someone your commanding officer assures you deserved their fate but when you look deeply into your heart you cannot help but wonder: *Did* they deserve it?"

Sebastian's head was now filled with the sights and sounds of Les as it broke apart. The deaths he had turned away from, and the screams

121

he had tried to purge from his memory. It wasn't just Les that haunted him, though. There were the unsuspecting people he had burned alive in Otriye as well. And the miners at Bledney he had boiled with their own blood. He had done *all of that*. Some of it might have been at Vittorio's behest, but all of it he had done willingly.

He found he was now standing. He looked down at his shaking fist. It was still healing from the wound his sister had given him. It ached a little but he no longer resented her for inflicting it on him. Perhaps he was even grateful that her actions had prevented him from causing further bloodshed. If not for her, he might have torn Gogoleth asunder in his childish wrath.

Yes, childish. And unforgivable.

He realized this remorse had always been there, lurking low in his bosom. How had he managed to tamp it down for so long? How had he avoided acknowledging his crimes even to himself? No matter what Vittorio or the empress said, those deaths would always be on his conscience.

"As a soldier, part of our job is to kill the enemy. But does *anyone* deserve to be killed?" He opened his fist and stared down at the blotchy scar on his palm where the arrow had pierced through. "You ask yourself that question yet you cannot find an answer, regardless of how hard you try. Meanwhile night after sleepless night, the horrors you have witnessed and *perpetrated* weigh on your chest like an anchor. Did it have to be this way? Could I have done something different? Will I ever find peace?"

He looked up, fighting the tears that now threatened to break free. "Do I even *deserve* peace?"

Then he noticed that the other three were staring at him, eyes wide, mouths open. Even Marcello.

Sebastian had said too much. Shown too much. He really had ruined this evening.

He bowed to them. "I apologize for my outburst. I truly appreciate all your efforts to help me acclimate, but I think it's best for all of us if I bid you a good evening."

He turned and headed for the door.

But then he felt a hand take hold of his arm. He turned and found Mia beside him. He could not fathom her expression, which seemed a welter of concern, pity, and perhaps fear.

She stood on her tiptoes and pressed her soft lips to his cheek for a moment.

"I hope that someday you find the peace you're looking for," she whispered. Then she gave him a sad smile, and returned to the table.

Sebastian held his hand to his cheek, his expression baffled as he turned and walked out of the tavern. He did not know how to respond to such a gentle gift given so freely. Perhaps because he had never known anyone who possessed such impulsive kindness.

Well, except Yasha. She might have done something like that.

Sebastian came to a sudden stop in the street outside the Grapeseed Tavern.

It was impossible, but in that moment he wanted desperately to talk to his sister. It didn't matter what either of them had become or what they had done. He just wanted to sit with her late into the night on one of their beds like they did as children. She would grin at him and ruffle his sandy hair, which he both hated and loved. They would whisper so as not to wake their parents, talking sometimes till dawn. He could not remember anything they had spoken about, but he remembered the feeling of their shared life. Their shared understanding. More than anything, he wanted that feeling again. In those moments, at least, he thought he had known some peace.

But could such a thing ever happen again? Could he ever be that close to his sister again? To anyone, for that matter?

That was the part which seemed the most impossible.

22

Sonya did not tire of the ocean, no matter how long she stared at it. It looked as immense as the tundra, yet it was ever-moving, ever-changing. So much life teemed beneath the surface, just out of view. Some of it, like schools of fish, were easy to understand. But other things that Jorge described, like octopuses and man-o-wars, were more difficult to grasp. And the idea that some of these wonders could never be seen, or even truly known, because they reached depths beyond humanity's ability to reach...that she found staggering. She still wrestled with this new feeling of unfamiliar surroundings, but she knew she needed to get past that. After all, a ranger must range. Even if the Lady Marzanna didn't care about her and Izmoroz had rejected her, she could still be a ranger of some sort. Couldn't she?

As Jorge had predicted, they arrived at the town of Herder's Gate a few days after reaching the coast. The homes were stout stone constructions sealed tightly with mortar. Apparently the coast was often lashed by fierce storms during the summer and fall, so it made sense to have such squat, sturdy buildings.

As they led their horses down the narrow cobblestone streets, the air was permeated with the overpowering smell of saltwater and fish.

Jorge heaved a sigh. "It's starting to smell a bit like home."

"Colmo is on the ocean, isn't it?" asked Sonya.

"Technically the Sea of Charmed Winds, which is on the other side of the El Fin Peninsula," he said. "As the name implies, the water

124

and wind are a lot calmer there. But yes, it still smells like the ocean." He took in another deep breath and smiled. "I hadn't realized just how much I missed that smell until now."

They hitched their horses up, then bought roasted fish on sticks from a street vendor and ate them as they walked through the immense docking system that seemed nearly as big as the town itself. It looked like a forest of ship masts, each thick wooden pole tangled up in a bewilderingly intricate system of ropes and pulleys with functions Sonya could only vaguely guess at. The vessels ranged in size from small fishing boats that clearly couldn't accommodate more than two or three people at the most, to towering three-masted ships that looked like floating wooden castles.

Sonya wasn't sure what Jorge's criteria was in selecting boats, but after walking the docks for a short while, he found a midsized ship with two masts that seemed to please him.

"Ahoy!" He waved to the men who were busy loading cargo on the ship. They all had the brown skin and black hair of Raízians.

One of the sailors stopped and gave him a curious look. He was tall, with braids similar to Jorge's, except tied up in a red scarf. He wore baggy yellow pants made of a thin, silky material, and a leather vest that showed off his bare, veiny muscles. He also had a number of blue drawings on his arms. Sonya remembered Jorge telling her about those. A Raízian tradition called tattooing.

The man asked, "What can I do for you, friend?"

"Where are you headed?"

"South."

"As far as Colmo?" asked Jorge. "And would you be willing to take on passengers?"

The man's eyes narrowed. "How many?"

"Only two." Then Jorge's expression grew pained. "And...two horses."

The man's expression went from wary to sour. "Sailing with horses is messy. It'll cost you."

Jorge's expression grew more uncomfortable. "We don't actually have a great deal of money on hand—"

"Never mind then." The man turned his back on them and continued helping the others with cargo.

"But," Jorge pressed on, speaking to the man's back, "I'm certain my family would reward you *generously* when we reach Colmo."

The man glanced over his shoulder, his eyes narrow. "What family?"

Jorge closed his eyes and sighed, as if what he was about to say took tremendous effort. "My name is Jorge Elhuyar."

"Bullshit," the man said.

Jorge nodded, as if that's what he had expected. He took a large gold ring out of his pocket. In place of a gem, the ring had a flat gold circle with a symbol imprinted on it. He put the ring on his first finger and held it out for the man to see. The man stared at it for a moment, then his eyes slowly widened, and a broad grin stretched across his face.

"Why, Señor Elhuyar, what an honor!" He clapped Jorge enthusiastically on the back with his calloused hand. "I'm Captain Cajal! Welcome aboard the *Endless Summer*!"

When the other men heard him, they stopped loading cargo and turned to stare. Several whispered among each other, and Sonya's sharp ears picked up: "An Elhuyar? Here?" She'd already suspected that Jorge came from a powerful family in Raíz, given how both Angelo and Galina had fallen all over themselves to be polite once they learned his last name. But the way his countrymen were reacting, she wondered if he was something akin to royalty there.

"It's nice to make your acquaintance, Captain," said Jorge, looking embarrassed.

"And is this your lovely..." Cajal seemed to take Sonya in for the first time and paused, his smile frozen. He took a beat, then continued as if he hadn't hesitated. "Your lovely wife?"

Sonya realized that this man, and possibly everyone she would encounter from now on, had never seen beast marks before. They would not understand what they were, or what she was. Probably no one outside of Izmoroz would. In that awkward moment of silence, she felt self-conscious in a way she'd never known before. It was a horrible, squirming sort of sensation that lingered long after.

"Oh, uh, no, she's just a friend," said Jorge. "This is Sonya Turgenev Portinari."

Cajal's smile remained firm, although it now seemed to be tinged with a bit of relief. "That's wonderful, Señor Elhuyar. Just wonderful. Welcome aboard, miss."

"Uh, thanks." Still feeling this unpleasant new self-awareness, Sonya smiled with a closed mouth so he wouldn't see her sharp teeth.

"Well, we should have all this cargo loaded up within the hour," said Cajal. "Some of it is time sensitive, so we'll want to set sail right after. Should I send someone to retrieve your horses, Señor Elhuyar?"

"Oh, uh, no thank you, Captain. Sonya and I will go get our horses and be back here before you depart."

"As you wish, Señor." Then he turned to his men, who were still staring at Jorge and Sonya. He clapped his hands and said in a much less friendly voice, "All right, you lot of rum-soaked sponges! Back to work or so help me, you'll be making the trip home on the keel!"

As the sailors hurried back to their labor, Sonya and Jorge made their way up the dock to where they had tied their horses.

"So... how important *is* your family?" asked Sonya. "Really?"

"Honestly? Anything I say would sound like the most horrendous boasting, so I'd rather you just see for yourself when we get there."

"Why does it embarrass you so much?"

"It's... hard to describe," he said. "When I was a child, I wasn't embarrassed at all. People told me to be proud of my family and I was. But when I was older, I was able to see how different everyone else lived, and I began to see how... separate I was from most people. It made friendships and relationships difficult, because I was never really on equal terms with people."

"Is that why you came all the way to Gogoleth to study?"

"No, the college in Gogoleth is the best place to study apothecary in the entire empire." He winced. "Or it *was*, I suppose, since Izmoroz is no longer a part of the empire. Anyway, while it wasn't my primary reason for going there, I did enjoy the relative anonymity I found. And now, after knowing what that feels like..." He shook his head.

"As much as I'm looking forward to seeing my family, I dread feeling the full weight of that name again."

"Yeah." Sonya wondered if perhaps they both felt isolated by qualities they had once seen as good. "Say, Jorge. Be honest with me. Are people going to think I'm weird looking? Or ugly?"

He gave her a sharp look. "Why do you ask that?"

"You saw the way that captain looked at me. He didn't know what I was or how to react to it."

"Ah, your, uh, gifts of the Lady."

"Let's just call them beast marks," said Sonya. "Because they don't really feel like gifts right now."

"Well, I hardly even notice them anymore," said Jorge. "And I certainly don't think you're ugly."

"Yeah, but you're my friend."

"People might be a little unnerved at first. But I'm confident you'll quickly win them over with that famous Sonya charm."

She grimaced. "I'm not feeling very charming these days."

He put his arm around her and pulled her in close as they walked. "Your confidence took a blow in Izmoroz, so it's only natural you feel a little...unsure right now. You'll just have to trust me when I say that it will be fine."

She looked at him, and he seemed so *certain*. They were going to his land. His people. So surely he knew what he was talking about.

"Of course I trust you," she said.

23

Jorge had been born on a ship. He'd heard his mother tell the story many times.

He had apparently been reluctant to enter the world and was well past due. She had grown tired of heaving his bulk around, so when a friend suggested that the natural movements of the ocean were known to induce labor, his parents had immediately chartered a ship large enough to accommodate the entire Elhuyar family, a crew of sailors, plus a midwife, an apothecary, and a Viajero songstress gifted in pain-stifling and invigoration melodies. They had set sail with the intent of cruising along the coast to the tip of the El Fin Peninsula, where they might enjoy some of the many cenotes that dotted the area. But a terrible storm had come up suddenly, which was unusual for the famously calm waters of the Sea of Charmed Winds. The crew had been caught by surprise, and the ship was halfway to Victasha before they regained control of the vessel. "And *of course*," Jorge's mother would say every time she told this story, "that was when you decided to come out and say hello, my treasure."

Nothing terrible happened. As usual, Jorge's father had planned for every contingency, so the staff was well equipped to handle his birth on the open sea. They did, however, cancel their trip to the cenotes, much to the ire of Hugo, Jorge's older brother, who was then seven years old. As far as Jorge knew, Hugo to this day had still never seen the renowned El Fin cenotes, although now it was because he said he had far more important matters to attend to and could not waste time on such frivolity. Hugo took his responsibilities as the eldest child of the Elhuyar family very seriously.

Because of those circumstances of his birth, Jorge always felt he had a special kinship with the sea. During his time in Izmoroz, he had missed many things. The weather, the food, his family, and the constant inundation of art, music, and culture. But for some reason, he had not thought of the sea. It was as though he had forgotten how well it soothed his nerves. However, the moment he and Sonya had reached the coast, he had felt his chest loosen, and his worries ease. It felt as though he had been holding all that tension during his stay in Izmoroz without realizing it.

Now Jorge stood at the bow of the *Endless Summer* and stared out at the dark waters that glittered under a full moon, savoring the moment. Perhaps it was his imagination, but the stars seemed brighter and more plentiful than they were up north. A cool sea breeze tugged at his braids and shirt, but rather than chill him, it felt like a balm on his weary soul.

He wished Sonya could have enjoyed the moment with him, but she was still struggling to find her sea legs, and was now below in their cabin, miserable and unable to keep anything in her stomach. He supposed he shouldn't be surprised that she had succumbed to seasickness so easily. It was her first time out, after all.

As they had traveled south from Izmoroz these past few weeks, he had watched her lurch from anxious to despairing, occasionally to something that looked a little like hope, then back to an uneasy restlessness. In Izmoroz, he had thought his friend unassailable in her confidence and cheer. But it seemed much of her resilience had come from her identity as a Ranger of Marzanna. Now that she had lost faith in both herself and the supposed protection of her goddess, her struggle was readily apparent.

He felt bad that he had lied to her earlier, but he hadn't been able to bring himself to heap any more unease on her. The truth was, he didn't know how people would react to her unusual appearance. It might be a difficult hurdle to overcome, even for his own family.

But he'd smiled and told her everything would be fine. He hoped it would be.

After a time, Captain Cajal joined him at the bow.

"Evening, Señor," he said respectfully.

"Good evening, Captain."

"If this weather holds, we should make good time to El Fin, and from there it'll be an easy stretch to Colmo."

"Glad to hear it."

"How are you liking the *Endless Summer*?"

"She's a comfortable and reassuring vessel," said Jorge.

The captain nodded, looking pleased. "That she is."

"I'm sad Sonya can't enjoy the voyage quite yet, but this is her first time at sea, so it may take her another day or two to acclimate."

The captain's expression became uneasy. "Yes...Uh, the men have been after me to ask you about her."

"What about her?" asked Jorge, although he was fairly certain he knew.

"Well, uh, with all due respect, Señor, her looks make the crew mighty nervous. What *is* she?"

Jorge was actually glad this was coming out into the open. Sailors could be intensely superstitious, and to have that fear festering for many days at sea would likely affect the crew's morale, and possibly lead to a hostile or even dangerous atmosphere.

"Sonya Turgenev has been many things," he told the captain. "Hunter, warrior, rebel, perhaps even hero. Maybe she will be some or even all of those things again one day. But for now, she is merely a refugee fleeing from a war-torn land that did not understand or appreciate her."

He was silent for a moment, his eyes fixed firmly on Cajal's.

"She seeks sanctuary, and the Elhuyar family will give it to her. Is that understood, Captain?"

"Perfectly, Señor."

The captain might understand, but judging by his expression, he did not think this alone would ease the worries of his crew. Cajal ran a tight ship, so there was little fear of mutiny. But it was still a long ways to Colmo, and a distrustful crew could make for a very unpleasant voyage.

The captain took his leave and Jorge continued to gaze out at the black waters that sparkled with starlight. He was filled with such a strange mixture of eagerness and nervousness. He desperately wanted to see his home and his family again. Not only did he miss them terribly, but he wanted to show them how much he had matured. He almost felt like a different person than the one who had left Colmo over fifteen months ago. And yet, as the youngest—as the *baby* of the family—he was afraid that they would not see it. That they would still treat him like they always did. As someone who needed to be coddled...

He was taken out of his reverie by an ominous rumble. Even in the dark sky it was easy to spot the mass of roiling purple clouds that flickered with lightning off the starboard quarter. A moment later, he heard the bell ring.

"Batten the hatches! Haul in the sail! Stow the rigging!" Cajal's voice roared over the strengthening winds as the rain began to fall. "Señor! Get below!"

Jorge had sailed through many storms and had no intention of going below deck, where he would get all the unpleasant turbulence and none of the fresh air. But he made his way to the forecastle, where he would at least be somewhat sheltered from the wind and the rain.

"Jorge, what's going on?"

Sonya had just come up from below. She looked wan and haggard from seasickness, but her golden eyes were wide with curiosity as she watched the sailors clamber about in the rigging, furling the sails and lashing them in place.

"There's a storm coming in. They happen fairly often along this coast, and they can be quite intense. If the crew doesn't take in the sail quickly enough, we could lose control of the vessel and be swept out to the open sea. With the strong westerly current, it would be nearly impossible for us to return. That's why it's called the Ocean of Loss."

"Amazing..."

She seemed far more thrilled by the idea than he thought she should. But he supposed she might still not grasp the full vastness of the ocean.

Meanwhile, the winds were blowing harder, and water heaved in great frothy waves that crashed into the side of the ship, slopping spray onto the decks. Those sailors on deck still securing cargo had to cling to whatever they could hold every time the ship pitched to the lee or else they risked being carried overboard. Those in the rigging had an even worse time. The cold winds raked across the shrouds, threatening to dislodge the sailors as they unfastened the sails and loosely furled them. Despite the urgency, they needed to take care or they might damage the canvas, which would cause more problems later.

"Is there anything we can do?" Sonya shouted over the now howling gale.

Jorge shook his head. "We'd only get in the way," he yelled back.

He saw her rain-slick frown and realized that dangerous action was probably a welcome diversion for her.

"You could make sure no one falls overboard."

"Got it!"

He wasn't sure she could actually do anything if someone went over the rail, but she accepted with such eagerness that he let her think she was being useful as her golden eyes scanned the ship expectantly.

The *Endless Summer* had a seasoned crew, and the sails were well stowed before the storm's full strength reached them. The moon and stars disappeared altogether and the only light came from the spastic flicker of lightning in the seething clouds. The rain shifted to hail. Ice as large as peas stung their faces, and the wind shrieked like a swarm of ghosts. It was a truly spectacular storm.

"Wow, this is great!" Sonya gave him the first open-mouthed smile he'd seen since their departure from Herder's Gate.

He was about to point that out to her when an angry voice cut through the gale.

"Damn it, Señor, I told you to get below!"

Captain Cajal looked furious as he made his way toward them across the rolling, icy deck. "I don't care what family you belong to, on my ship you'll do as I say, or I'll have you—"

There was a sharp snap and the line securing a stack of barrels broke. The ship pitched hard to port and the barrels rolled downhill toward Cajal. A cry went up from several sailors, but none could get to him in time.

Except Sonya.

She launched herself at the captain without hesitation, catching him around the middle with both arms. Her momentum took him off his feet and out of the path of the barrels. Even over the cacophony of the crashing waves, hissing hail, booming thunder, and howling wind, Jorge heard the barrels shatter as they crashed into the rail. Half the contents pitched into the choppy waters, and it was clear to all who witnessed the event that if it hadn't been for Sonya, the captain would likely have gone overboard as well.

Instead Cajal lay sprawled out on the slush-covered deck with a fanged and grinning young woman straddling him, her wet black hair dripping down on his face.

Jorge saw a multitude of emotions cross the captain's leathery face, but it was clear that chiefest among them was gratitude. He decided then that whatever reservations the crew of the *Endless Summer* had about Sonya had just been cast overboard with the barrels.

24

Irina Turgenev found that palace life suited her rather well. Her quarters were spacious and comfortable. The meals were lavish and attended by intelligent people who contributed to lively and engaging conversation. Daily baths were not only permitted, but presumed. And the weather was so unstintingly pleasant that not a day went by she didn't enjoy a stroll through the imperial gardens.

If there was one flaw amid all the splendor, its name was Franko Vittorio. The empress, for reasons Irina could not fathom, had not only allowed the monster to live, but to stay on at the palace as a menial servant. Perhaps the fact that he had been brought so low should have elicited some feeling of pity in Irina—or on her less generous days, a smug sense of satisfaction. Instead, his hovering, ostensibly dutiful presence at the palace left her feeling ill at ease. She could not say why. Perhaps it was merely because, without the mustache she was accustomed to seeing, she found his bare, quavering, and sweat-dotted upper lip unnerving. Or perhaps it was because she could not bring herself to believe that even a near-death experience could so wholly change such a nasty and arrogant beast.

"Really, I don't know why you allow him to linger in such a ghastly state," she told Zaniolo when he came to visit her apartments one afternoon. "If he's already died once, I should think a second time would be far less traumatic."

Zaniolo smirked at her in that oily way of his. "Ah, my dear Lady

Portinari. Your unique combination of ready charm and casual cruelty never ceases to amuse me."

She ignored his backhanded compliment, as she usually did. "Surely you must have some concerns about allowing a convicted traitor to skulk about the palace."

He shrugged. "You've seen the man. Squeaking and clanking about on those leg braces of his, he certainly won't be sneaking up on anyone, and he can hardly hold a cup anymore, much less a sword. I can't imagine what trouble he could cause, and honestly, I think it gives Her Majesty some pleasure to see him reduced to such a groveling insect. After everything he's put her through, I'd say she's earned that."

He sat down beside her on the sofa and took one of the sickly sweet cookies that Aureumians always insisted on including with their tea sets.

"Besides," he said around a mouthful of cookie, "he's not without supporters."

"Who in their right mind would support such a spiteful, treacherous person?"

"Before his indiscretion of murdering the empress's lover in a fit of jealousy, Vittorio was tremendously popular throughout the empire. People often compared him to your husband, actually."

Irina sniffed. "In his dreams."

"To those of us who know him well, yes. But most people are spared a deeper look. Regardless, I suspect he always felt some sort of competitive resentment toward your husband and that was one reason he disobeyed the empress and had him killed."

"But surely even the dullest of officers now realize that the man is an unstable menace."

"The officers, perhaps. But the regular soldiers who make up the backbone of the imperial army are still quite fond of him."

"Well, it's not as though such people have any real influence."

"Individually, no. But collectively, the empire would collapse without them."

"Would they really turn against their own leadership like that?"

"I'd like to think not, but I haven't gotten to this point in my career as an intelligence officer by believing in the best of people. To make matters worse, I fear the empress's choice of execution methods was a grave mistake. People have begun drawing parallels to the fate of the empire's illustrious founder, Alessandro, a man they worship almost as a god himself. Ironically, their devotion to the empress's great-grandfather is due in large part to her own efforts."

Irina sighed. "What a mess. Still I suppose none of us could have predicted he would actually survive."

"Indeed," said Zaniolo. "Of course Captain Antonio and I have both gently suggested to Her Majesty that perhaps it would be best to make Vittorio disappear in some way that didn't draw attention. But she made it clear that she isn't interested in revisiting the topic. So for now, as long as he doesn't cause a fuss, we must allow the harmless lunatic to wander the halls."

"I wish I could believe he's truly harmless, General," said Irina. "But if nothing else, he'll likely spit some poison or other into Sebastian's ear once he's returned from Kante."

"I shouldn't worry about that too much," said Zaniolo. "Sebastian won't be returning from Kante for some time, and hopefully by then the empress will have given us permission to find a way to dispose of him without riling his supporters."

"Speaking of which, have you heard any news?"

"Regarding the campaign in Kante?" he asked.

"Regarding my son, General. You know I care little for politics, and wars are nothing but political tantrums."

Zaniolo smiled. "Yes of course, my apologies. To my knowledge, General Barone is making excellent time across Aureum and should reach Hardsong Pass within the next couple of days. I'm afraid news will become far more sporadic once they cross into the mountains, however."

"I see." Irina wasn't pleased that the closer Sebastian got to danger, the less she'd know, but she was not surprised. "And what of my daughter? Before he left, Sebastian mentioned that she was heading into Aureum?"

"That's what we thought at the time. But it appears she only cut across the northwest corner before boarding a southbound ship in Herder's Gate. Since she was accompanied by her Raízian companion, I think it's safe to assume they're heading for Raíz, and most likely Colmo."

"Curious," said Irina. "Still, now that she's back in imperial territory, perhaps you could order the local soldiers to bring her to Magna Alto? If the empress allows Vittorio to roam freely about the palace, surely she would allow me to at least *try* to reform my daughter. I would consider imprisonment or confinement of some sort during that period entirely reasonable. I would even be willing to give up my fine quarters to live with her in such a place."

"I'm afraid it's not as simple as that, my lady. First of all, your daughter has shown herself capable of dealing with an entire cavalry unit on her own, so I suspect it would take more than a few soldiers to apprehend her. Second, if these most recent reports are accurate, her Raízian companion has turned out to be none other than a member of the Elhuyar family."

"The Elhuyars?" asked Irina, not bothering to conceal her shock. The Elhuyars were not nobility, because Raíz didn't have a noble class. But with the financial power they'd held, they might as well be kings. While it was true the empress reigned supreme, surely even she would not be so foolhardy as to antagonize a family that might cripple the entire economy merely by ceasing operations. "How on earth did my daughter get mixed up with them?"

"Apparently the Elhuyars were indulging their youngest son's passion for apothecary in Gogoleth. Presumably that's where he befriended Sonya."

"I don't know whether to be thrilled or horrified," she told Zaniolo.

"It wouldn't be a bad match," said Zaniolo. "Especially since he seems to have a high tolerance for your daughter's antics."

"For now, at least. In my experience, frivolous men tend to weary of spirited women once they reach a certain age."

"The men or the women?" asked Zaniolo.

"Either," she said darkly.

"Well, as with the topic of Vittorio, I'm afraid there isn't a lot either of us can do about it at present. Now, if you'll permit a suggestion, I think you need something to take your mind off all of this. I'd like to introduce you to a small group of fellow expatriates who also reside in the palace. I think their company would do you a world of good."

Irina winced. "I loathe the word *expatriate*. It sounds so *eccentric*."

"But accurate in your current situation."

"I suppose." Her eyes narrowed as she watched him innocently nibble on his cookie. "I do wonder at your sudden solicitude for my well-being, however."

"As it happens, I have something of a . . . *task* for you."

Irina laughed. "For a moment, I thought you were expressing genuine concern for me."

He grinned. "What a curious notion."

"It was quite disconcerting," she agreed. "So what is this *task* you have in mind, and why would I be inclined to perform it?"

"During my absence, a great number of things have changed here at the palace. Most of them I can either adapt to or handle on my own. But there is one thing that requires a more indirect hand."

"These expatriates, I presume."

"One in particular. Ambassador Ceren Boz of Victasha."

"Victasha? Oh my. I hadn't realized the empire was even on speaking terms with our neighbor to the south."

His smile grew pained. "So you understand the delicacy of the matter. It is a somewhat recent development. Her Majesty is quite taken with the ambassador, but I find her presence here at the palace to be worrisome."

"And so you would like me to insert myself into their group and report her activities to you."

"Just so. You see, she is always . . . *alarmingly* well informed on imperial matters that she should not be privy to, and I would like to know how she manages it."

"Interesting," said Irina. "But you still have not told me why I would be inclined to accept this task."

His gaze swept the lavish apartment where Irina resided. "The empress has been quite generous with you, hasn't she?"

Irina raised an eyebrow. "I had assumed it was a gesture to curry favor with my son."

Zaniolo gave her a sidelong glance. "My dear lady, as I understand it, the empress had your son wrapped around her finger after a single ten-minute conversation."

She sighed. "That boy really does need to work on his resilience to charisma."

"Quite true," Zaniolo agreed. "To be fair, she pulled out all the stops: inviting him to her private quarters, wearing only a silk robe. She is still a very handsome woman, after all. And she offered him more or less exactly the sort of duty he longed for. Clearly she sees great promise in him."

Irina gave him a level stare. "I shan't inquire too deeply at present on what exactly that promise entails."

"I wouldn't," he agreed.

"So returning to our original topic, in essence you expect me to earn my keep by becoming an imperial spy?"

"I generally don't use the word *spy*. People make far too many assumptions," said Zaniolo. "But if that's how you prefer to view it, I have no objections."

Irina was not certain she was cut out for espionage, but she was also not inclined toward owing favors, even to an empress. If this squared her debt, so much the better.

"Well," she said after a moment, "I admit, I could use the stimulation."

"Wonderful." Zaniolo snatched one more cookie as he stood. "Why don't I take you to them now, then? I believe they're gathered in the garden around this time of day."

25

The one thing Irina missed when she moved from the farm back to Nadezhda Square was her garden. She was the first to admit that she had not been particularly well suited for raising young children. She had of course done her best, but during Sonya and Sebastian's early years, the garden had been her sanctuary, and at times her primary means of maintaining sanity. And while she'd had a few potted plants in the townhouse, they hadn't given her the same feeling of peace that came with being completely surrounded by the beauty of nature mindfully cultivated by human hand.

The imperial garden offered all the peace, and required none of the labor. It also provided a wide variety of fragrant flowers that could never have survived even the warmest months in Izmoroz. Combined with the reliable Aureumian sun that shone overhead, Irina could think of no more pleasant place in the world.

She usually took her stroll through the garden in the morning, which was likely why she had never seen the small gathering of expatriates. The gardens were quite large, but if she'd ever been there at the same time as the three of them, she was certain she would have noticed, because they stuck out quite a bit.

The youngest of the trio, perhaps in his late thirties, had long, greasy brown hair and pale, pockmarked skin. He wore a very unflattering set of loose gray garments that looked as though they were made of sack cloth, belted at the waist with a ragged bit of hemp rope.

His shoulders were slumped, and his dark eyes had a haggard, almost haunted expression.

The second was a woman with brown skin similar to a Raízian, but with delicately slanted eyes that had a merry twinkle, as if she was amused by everything she observed around her. Irina could not discern the rest of her expression because she wore an elegant silk veil embroidered with gold thread. Her hair, mostly black but gray at the temples, was pulled back with more silk fabric. In fact, she seemed to be dressed entirely in silk of some type or another. While the fabric itself was shapeless, it was just transparent enough to suggest the outline of her body, which Irina thought was an intriguing effect that she might like to employ, now that her own figure was not quite as pleasing as it had been when she was younger.

Irina guessed that this woman was the ambassador she must suss out, but her attention was most arrested by the third person in the trio, a man perhaps Giovanni's age. Also like Giovanni, he had a brawny confidence that immediately negated any sense of feebleness concerning his age. His skin was darker than any man she had ever seen, and his thick ropes of gray hair were pulled back into a tight ponytail. Unlike the others, he wore an Aureumian-style belted tunic and trousers. It flattered his physique well enough, although Irina thought she would like to have seen him in a uniform instead.

The three expatriates were deep in quiet conversation when Irina and Zaniolo arrived, but broke off as they drew near.

"My friends," Zaniolo said with his usual smile. "I bring another member to join your illustrious ranks. May I present Lady Irina Turgenev Portinari of Izmoroz."

Irina curtsied. "Happy to make your acquaintances."

Zaniolo gestured to the young man with haunted eyes. "This is Hexenmeister Friedrich Cloos, a master enchanter and metallurgist from Kante who realized that Aureum's victory is inevitable and defected at the earliest opportunity."

The man stared at Irina with unblinking eyes for a moment, then bowed his head. "An honor to meet you, my lady." He had a thick, glottal accent.

Zaniolo gestured to the veiled woman. "And this is Ambassador Ceren Boz of Victasha, who is here to make certain we never entertain notions of southern conquest."

The ambassador's eyes continued to twinkle merrily as she inclined her head. "Delighted to meet you, my lady."

Then Zaniolo turned to the dark-skinned man who reminded Irina so much of her late husband. "And this remarkable fellow is Captain Mosi Aguta, an explorer from the distant country of Aukbontar. He was rescued from a shipwreck off the coast of the Tainted Ocean. Sadly for him, but fortunately for us, we have not yet been able to devise a means for him to return to his homeland, so he appears to be stuck here for the time being."

Aguta was the only one with the courtesy to get to his feet, so Irina rewarded him by offering her hand, which he accepted immediately with a sure, yet gentle touch.

"My lady, it is a pleasure," he said in a round, melodious accent.

"Likewise, Captain," she said.

"Won't you have a seat?"

"Thank you." She sat on the cold stone bench beside Aguta, with Ambassador Boz and Hexenmeister Cloos across from them.

"Well, I had best be going so you can return to muttering disparaging remarks about Aureumians," Zaniolo said cheerfully.

Ambassador Boz let out a light, tinkling laugh behind her veil. "Always so droll, General. A good day to you."

He bowed. "And to you, Ambassador."

Irina and her three new companions watched in silence as Zaniolo made his way out of the garden. Once he was completely out of sight, Boz turned to Irina.

"Do you trust him?"

The question was asked lightly, as if it was of little import. But Irina understood it was anything but. The ambassador certainly went right to the point, didn't she. If Irina said she *did* trust Zaniolo, it might soothe any suspicions Boz harbored about the general. But that seemed unlikely. If she was as savvy as Zaniolo suggested, her suspicions would likely be founded on reliable information, perhaps even hard evidence. No, it was better to play it safe and divest herself of not just this particular Aureumian, but perhaps even *all* Aureumians. She could easily play the role of impartial foreign observer here by happenstance, as it was somewhat true in her case.

"Of course I don't trust him," she told the ambassador matter-of-factly. "In Izmoroz, our interests aligned, so I felt confident I could predict his actions. But now that we are in Magna Alto..." She shrugged. "I'm not sure what his motivations are. So I feel I must watch him far more carefully. But he has his uses, so the risk is worthwhile."

Aguta grinned broadly at her. "I believe you will appreciate our little group quite a lot."

"I hope so, Captain," said Irina. "Although I'm ashamed to say that I had never heard of a country called Aukbontar before today."

"That is because you have only recently been discovered."

"Have we?"

"By us, anyway. Our people had no idea you existed. In fact, I am only here by chance. My crew and I were attempting to locate an archipelago south of Aukbontar said to contain secret magic, but the region is notorious for its intense and frequent storms. We were caught in one such storm and swept out into the Tranquil Sea—what you call the Tainted Ocean. Our masts were all destroyed and we were left to drift for weeks. By the time our vessel reached your continent, I was the only survivor."

His eyes trailed off, and his expression became solemn. Irina could only imagine the suffering he must have experienced during such a harrowing journey.

"I'm sorry to have stirred up such painful memories," she said.

He shook his head and smiled.

There was an awkward pause, then Ambassador Boz asked, "Is it true that Izmoroz has broken off from the empire? I've heard a great many rumors, but no one in imperial intelligence, including Zaniolo, will confirm it."

Irina wondered if Boz was really looking for confirmation about that, or if she was still feeling out how candid Irina would be. Irina saw no reason to conceal this particular information, and if it allowed her to gain some measure of trust with the ambassador, so much the better.

"It's true for the time being. Although I suspect that once the empire's main forces are no longer occupied with Kante, they will retake it."

"You do not think Izmorozian forces will be able to hold them off?" asked Aguta.

"What Izmorozian forces?" said Irina. "They haven't had a standing army in decades. They only drove out the empire this time because they allied themselves with the Uaine."

"The Uaine aided the Izmorozians?" Ambassador Boz asked. "I've heard dreadful rumors about them."

Boz acted as though she hadn't realized the Uaine helped Izmoroz, but Irina wondered if that too might be subterfuge. Either way, it was a bit late to reverse course, and she didn't see any particular harm in divulging what little she knew about the Uaine. In fact, the best way to get information from the ambassador might be to start by giving some. But she would have to take care she did not present it in a way that made her complicit with the empire.

"As with most things, some rumors about the Uaine are probably true, others false. They do command an army of the dead, if that's what you were wondering."

Ambassador Boz's eyes lost some of their cheerfulness. "The thought had crossed my mind."

Irina had just given her something valuable. She could tell. This could be the start of an interesting arrangement. While it was true she was working for Zaniolo, she saw no reason she couldn't develop her own advantageous relationship with the ambassador. Perhaps with time and a little patience, she could even convince Boz to offer sanctuary in Victasha to Sonya when the empire finally grew tired of her rebellious escapades and tried to hunt her down. It would be a tricky balancing act, playing Zaniolo and Boz off each other without alienating either of them, but Irina felt she was more qualified than most to attempt it.

"I confess I don't know a great deal about the Uaine," she told the ambassador. "My wayward daughter knows them far better. After all, she was the one who enlisted their aid to liberate Izmoroz in the first place."

"Your *daughter*?" asked Cloos.

"I'm afraid so." Irina affected a weary resignation not far from the truth. "She has tremendous talent, but she's quite feisty, and never one to mind her parents."

Aguta's eyes narrowed. "Lady Portinari, are you a hostage of the empire, then?"

"It's difficult to say . . ." Irina affected a dramatic moment of hesitation. Goddess, it came so naturally, it was like she'd been born to this. "You see, my son is a captain in the imperial army. So it is complicated, to say the least."

"I'd say so." The ambassador's cheerful gaze had returned, but there was now a keen interest that accompanied it. "Portinari . . . that name rings a bell. Are you at all related to the Commander Portinari who first conquered Izmoroz for the empire?"

Irina had her now. Somehow she just knew it.

"My late husband, actually."

Ambassador Boz laughed her tinkling little laugh again and something like greed glittered in her eyes. "It seems you are a very useful woman to know."

That was exactly how Irina had intended the ambassador to view her. And here she'd been thinking that she wasn't cut out for espionage. Well, she supposed that even she could be wrong now and then.

26

The previous evening, Sebastian had been certain of so many things. The following morning, however, he was only certain of one: that he had acted like a complete fool.

As the bugle sounded to wake the army, and the first rays of morning filtered through the canvas of the officers' tent, he lay on his sleeping roll and felt the hot sting of shame in his gut. He was tempted to blame the drink, but two cups of wine was hardly an excuse. Perhaps it had weakened his resolve to some degree, but he had still been in full control of his faculties when he gave in to his base emotions in front of near strangers and ruined his friend's plan for a lighthearted, romantic evening.

But the true mistake had been in thinking he could even partake of such an experience in the first place. At least he understood that now. After what he had done in Izmoroz, what right did he have to enjoy himself? He could not even say how many lives he had taken. It didn't matter that the empress had calmly brushed his guilt aside. *He* knew that he had done terrible wrong, and he would no longer hide from that fact.

"No time to dawdle, Captain," Barone said cheerfully as he walked down the narrow aisle between bedrolls.

"Yes, sir."

Sebastian forced himself to rise, though his limbs felt heavy, and his mouth tasted of ash.

Barone gave him a gently teasing smile. "I hope Oreste didn't wear you out too much. We've got a long march ahead of us if we're to reach Hardsong Pass before sunset."

The general probably assumed Sebastian had stayed out as late as Marcello, who had stumbled into the tent reeking of sour wine only hours ago.

There didn't seem much point in correcting the misapprehension, so Sebastian merely said, "Understood, sir," and began rolling up his bedding.

Sebastian packed his saddlebags, then trudged out of the tent and over to where his horse was picketed. The whole army was up and about by then, humming with murmured conversation peppered with the occasional clank of weapons and armor. The morning air was still cool and damp, but the sun had already begun to warm things up. It was another beautiful day in Aureum, although Sebastian's present mood would have found the dismal gray of Izmoroz more complementary.

As he hitched his bags to his horse, he spotted Marcello, looking very worn out as he fastened his own saddlebags to his mount.

Sebastian heaved a sigh and headed over to him. The least he could do was apologize for spoiling the mood last night. Hopefully the aide-de-camp's late return at least meant they had rallied after Sebastian's departure.

"Marcello," he said as he drew near.

"Oh, hi, Portinari." Marcello glanced at him, looking uncomfortable. Then he went back to fussing with his saddlebags. It seemed he was still mad, which was completely understandable.

"I'm . . . sorry about last night," said Sebastian.

Marcello turned back to him, looking surprised. "*You're* sorry?"

"Well, yes. I should have been honest enough with myself to know I wasn't up for an evening out. And I most certainly shouldn't have spoken as harshly as I did. I do hope I didn't spoil the entire evening for you and the ladies."

Marcello pressed his lips together, his face tense. Then he squeezed Sebastian's shoulder.

"Portinari, you ninny. *I'm* the one who should be apologizing. Here I'd been, swaggering about like I was some big important hero. And for what? To impress some girls I'll likely never see again?" He let go of Sebastian's shoulder and turned away. "I've been living the comfortable life as aide-de-camp to the kindest and least demanding general in the Aureumian Army, without even a glimpse of actual combat. Meanwhile, you were up in that northern hellscape fighting desperately against vicious insurgents and man-eating undead, forced to make impossible choices merely to survive." He shook his head. "I'm ashamed of myself, Sebastian. I'm sorry I spoke so insensitively."

Now it was Sebastian's turn to stare in surprise. His friend made it all sound a lot more noble than it had actually been, but he appreciated the consideration regardless.

"Well," he said at last, "I suppose we're still getting to know each other. So things like this are bound to happen now and then."

Marcello smiled gratefully. "I suppose that's how we get to know each other better."

Sebastian allowed himself a return smile, but though he was glad he had patched things up with Marcello, it didn't ease the dark sorrow that had nestled itself in his chest. Even having such a kind and thoughtful friend as Marcello gave him a vague sense of guilt, as if it was a luxury he did not deserve. After all, he was responsible for a multitude of sins. Now that he fully recognized that fact, he wondered with increasing dread whether he had any hope of redemption.

The bugle sounded again, signaling it was time to form up and prepare for another long march. Sebastian and Marcello dutifully mounted their horses along with the other officers, then ensured that the infantry had formed up properly. General Barone rode slowly down the line for inspection. Once he had finished, he nodded approvingly and the bugle sounded a third time to begin the march.

They rode for hours across the lush green fields of Aureum. Far ahead there was a dark, snowcapped line on the horizon that slowly grew over time, rising up like a curtain. From a distance, the Segen Mountains seemed an impenetrable wall of rock topped with a blanket of snow and ice. But as they drew closer, Sebastian could see the

Jon Skovron

outline of the man-made valley called Hardsong Pass. The bulk of
the infantry stretched before him, so he was still some ways from the
pass, but he could see the top, its clean edges a stark contrast to the
surrounding jagged and irregular peaks. It looked as though a mighty
blade wielded by a giant had simply sliced out a section of mountain.

"How did they make Hardsong Pass?" Sebastian asked Marcello.

"I think it was a combination of Raízian magic, Aureumian engineering, and some apothecary art that can create explosive black
powder."

"Really?" Sebastian thought back to the fiery signal the Uaine had
launched into the sky when they attacked Gogoleth. Vittorio had said
they were a Raízian invention. "Like fireworks?"

"Oh, you have them up in Izmoroz, too?" asked Marcello.

"Not really. I've only seen it once, and it was used to signal the start
of an assault, not to carve a mountain."

The closer they got to Hardsong, the more unnatural it looked.
Unnatural and, Sebastian thought, not particularly safe. The passage
was too narrow for the infantry to march in their usual formation, so
they had to funnel down to only five across, stretching the entire battalion out to twice its usual length. Even then, there was precious
little room for maneuvering, with only a few feet on either side. And
according to Marcello, the pass was several miles long.

Since it was already growing dark, Barone decided they should
make camp and begin the crossing the follow morning. Once he'd
finished his duties, Sebastian took his plate of rations out into the cool
evening air to contemplate the strange edifice while he ate.

In a way, it gave him an odd sort of comfort. This achievement was
on par with something that his elemental magic could accomplish.
It was unexpectedly reassuring to see proof that he was not the only
one with such uncanny power at his disposal. But there was another
feeling as well. When he looked upon the cleaved mountain, he was
reminded of what he had done to Pustoy Plains and felt a quiet unease.
It was clumsy, brutish, and arrogant. Above all, it was against nature.

The next morning did little to quiet his unease. There was an anxious wait as the front of the line slowly filed into the man-made gap.

150

His apprehension did not lessen when it was his turn to enter. The sheer rock rose up on either side so high that it blocked out the sun entirely. The sky became nothing but a strip of blue far above, and it was so dark, they had to light torches at regular intervals along the line so that the soldiers could keep watch for uneven footing.

Sebastian's gaze followed the unnaturally flat cliff face up to the sharp, right-angled edge at the top.

"Perfect place for an ambush," he muttered, more to himself than anything.

"But who could get up that high?" pointed out Marcello.

"True," admitted Sebastian. Scaling these sheer walls would have been impossible. To properly set an ambush, a group of hardy mountaineers would have to have climbed up the outside of the mountain well before the range had come into view of the imperial army. They would then have had to survive the brutal winds, freezing temperatures, and thin air at the peak of the mountains, staying completely out of sight for well over a day. He wasn't sure anyone could survive such harsh conditions.

The hours seemed to drag even more slowly in the pass, partly because there was nothing to look at, and partly because Sebastian couldn't shake the vague feeling of unease. It was difficult to say how long they'd been at it. Since the only visible sky was directly overhead, all he could say for certain was that it was still before noon because he hadn't yet seen the sun.

Then the line came to an abrupt halt. They'd been plodding along in the dim lighting with nothing to see for so long that several soldiers were caught unawares and bumped into the man in front of them. A chorus of grumbled curses went up for a moment before the captains silenced them.

"What's going on?" asked Marcello, standing up in his saddle as he tried in vain to see the front of the line.

Then a soldier came running up the narrow gap along the side. His face was flushed with exertion as he sprinted past.

"He's probably heading for the general," said Marcello. "I better go see if I'm needed."

He awkwardly wheeled his horse around in the confined space, and followed.

Sebastian waited with the rest of the soldiers. He noticed that many of them were also glancing nervously up at the cliff edges far above, probably assuring themselves with the same reasoning he'd used. Somehow it didn't quite put the worry to rest for any of them.

A short while later, General Barone, followed by his personal bodyguards and Marcello, rode along the line. He stopped when he reached Sebastian.

"Captain Portinari." His expression was grave.

"Sir!" Sebastian saluted sharply.

"Follow, please. I may have need of you."

"Yes, sir!"

Sebastian fell in behind Marcello, hoping his friend would give him some clue what lay ahead. But Marcello did not turn back to look at him and remained silent.

They rode past the engineers, the Viajero, and hundreds of infantry, all standing at attention, to the very front of the army. There Sebastian was finally able to see what had caused the army to stop.

The pass was blocked.

They had almost reached the end. Sprawling, dark green meadows were maddeningly within sight. But to reach them, the entire army would have to climb ten feet of rock debris that had somehow been piled up before them. Perhaps the men themselves could do it, but only if they abandoned the horses and wagons that contained the vital medicine and supplies so desperately needed by the main force.

"How could this have happened?" murmured Marcello. "Magic of some kind, sir?"

"It's possible," replied Barone. "Our intelligence on Kantesian magic is sketchy at best."

It looked to Sebastian like a contained avalanche. His eyes followed the cliff up. Near the top he thought he could just make out what appeared to be three parallel grooves cut into the rock.

"General, do you see that?" He pointed.

Barone took out his telescoping spyglass and looked at it for a

152

moment. "Dear God, it looks like *claw marks*." He aimed his glass on the opposing cliff. "And on both sides."

"A *beast* did this?" Marcello's eyes widened. "From *up there*?"

Then they heard an ominous rumble at the rear of the line. It sounded like thunder, but too close and far too drawn out. It was accompanied by shouts of surprise that quickly turned to fear and pain. Sebastian watched with horror as the line rippled toward them, as if soldiers in the back were pushing forward despite the fact that there was no room to do so.

"We've just been hemmed in," Barone said grimly. Then he shouted. "Shields up! Watch for falling rock!"

"Are we under attack?" Marcello's voice sounded strained.

The soldiers shifted around so the shield bearers could cover the others with their massive iron-bound shields. Sebastian grasped the gem that hung from his neck and scanned the edges of the cliffs.

He heard a strange groan and hiss coming from the southern cliff. When he looked in that direction, all he could see was an ominous cloud of vapor hovering along the edge. Within that cloud he could just make out two immense eyes that glowed an eerie and unnatural magenta.

"A monster!" shouted one of the soldiers and the line began to shift.

"Steady, damn you!" roared Barone. "Archers at the ready! Fire on my mark!"

"Sebastian, can it really be a monster?" whispered Marcello.

Before he could reply, Barone snapped, "Portinari! Can you do anything?"

"I'll try, sir!"

Sebastian wasn't sure what he could do, mainly because he couldn't really see it. He tried to feel the fluids inside it, as he'd done with the miners. Yet perhaps his limited sight prevented him from doing that, because what he felt didn't make sense. He perceived boiling water, which certainly accounted for the steam, a great deal of metal, and some sort of...*presence*. It didn't feel like a living thing exactly. Nor was it like one of the Uaine undead. It was something he had never encountered before.

"Archers, fire!" Barone commanded.

The archers let loose with a volley into the cloud, but the glowing eyes didn't react in any way.

"Portinari!" yelled Barone. "Anything?"

Sebastian considered a moment. He couldn't do anything to the creature directly, but he could control the air around it. Perhaps if he cleared the cloud, he could see it better and find a way to attack it.

"I think there's something I could try . . . ," he said.

The monster hissed again as a massive, shining claw emerged from the cloud and began to carve out another chunk of rock directly above them. Small bits of rubble rained down on the soldiers.

"Do it now, Portinari!" said Barone. "Before we're all buried alive!"

"Yes, sir!"

Sebastian desperately gathered up the air around them and flung it straight up the narrow chasm. Not only did it clear the steam, but it also sent the creature hurtling through the air. Sebastian hadn't expected something so large to be so light. It was out of view before anyone had even gotten a good look at it, which was a mixed blessing. They were safe for now, but still had no clear idea what had just tried to ambush them.

"Wh-what just happened?" asked Marcello.

But the general ignored him, his eyes fixed on Sebastian. "Good work, Captain. But we've got another problem. If the Kantesians command monsters, they might be mounting an attack on our main forces as we speak. This could all be a delaying tactic to prevent us from reinforcing them."

"Yes, sir," said Sebastian.

Barone eyed the wall of rocks blocking their path. "It would take the rest of the day for our engineer corps to clear this out. And for all we know, a single day might make the difference between life or death for our men in Kleiner."

"Understood, sir," said Sebastian. "I'll clear it at once."

"Sebastian, what are you talking about?" Marcello asked plaintively.

"Patience, Oreste," said Barone. "Just watch."

Sebastian gripped his gem and looked carefully at the pile of rock in front of them. Even gale-force winds wouldn't make it budge. He could simply melt it all down, he supposed, but that would be a lot of lava to move, and they were packed in so tight that if he lost control of it, he would endanger himself and everyone else. But perhaps he didn't need to move it so much as *reshape* it . . .

"Apologies in advance, sir," he said to Barone. "The weather is about to get rather unpleasant."

"I appreciate the warning, Captain," said Barone.

Sebastian gripped the diamond and began to construct the sequence of events in his mind. He had never tried to use three elements at once before, so he would need to do this with great care.

First he gathered clouds above them. Dense, black clouds that turned the dim light in the pass to absolute night. Next he heated the rocks until they began to glow orange and soften. As the pile continued to sag, threatening to spill toward them, he brought the wind, funneling it through the pass so that it pressed on melting rock. It gave way slowly, grudgingly until it was almost like a ramp leading toward the pass's exit. Then Sebastian shifted the temperature so that the storm clouds above began to spit first rain, then hail. The glowing orange sludge hissed spitefully as the ice pellets struck, cooling the top layer so that it lay more heavily on the lava beneath, pushing it further into the shape of a ramp.

He continued to alternately heat and cool the rocks in this way until he had formed a fully functional ramp over the debris. Only then did he finally let the winds stop.

He stood for a moment to appreciate his handiwork. Then the world seemed to spin and he lost his balance. He hit the ground hard, pain barking up his elbow. A moment later, hands lifted him into a sitting position.

"Portinari, what in God's name was that?" Marcello asked excitedly. "That was all you?"

Sebastian was too tired to speak, but he grinned at his friend, basking in their shared pride.

"Didn't you know, Oreste?" Barone asked cheerfully. "We have the world's most powerful wizard in our ranks."

Even the title *wizard*, which Sebastian had boasted of himself not so long ago, was now enough to rein in his euphoria. His smile faded and he forced himself to stand without aid.

"It's nothing, sir."

"On the contrary, Captain. It's possible you have just saved the lives of every soldier currently stationed in Kleiner. I would not call that nothing."

Sebastian looked at him for a moment. "True, sir."

Barone nodded. "Consider this, Captain. No matter our past mistakes, as long as we persist, there will always be opportunities for atonement. But it is up to you to seize them."

The empress had likely relayed Sebastian's own past mistakes to the general. So Barone knew the terrible things he had done, yet unlike the empress and Vittorio, he was not excusing those actions. He was instead offering a way forward. A road that would likely be long and hard, but might one day lead to redemption. And perhaps for now, that was all Sebastian needed.

"I understand, sir. And...thank you."

27

"Lord Levenchik, I don't think you fully comprehend the gravity of the situation."

Galina strove to keep her tone pleasant, but it was becoming increasingly difficult. She had never spoken with Lord Konstantin Belousov Levenchik before, and knew him primarily by his infamous reputation as a philanderer. It took only a few minutes of interaction for her to suspect that *philanderer* was too kind a word.

Upon arriving at his manor, she had been brought to a parlor decorated primarily in reds and deep purples with what she considered an unseemly amount of satin. She had seated herself on the one chair in the room that could not possibly hold another person and waited, politely declining as attractive young maids in scanty uniforms attempted to ply her with wine or vodka. When at last his lordship appeared, she wondered what she had been waiting for all that time. Certainly not for him to dress, because he was clad simply in a red satin robe. Perhaps it was his hair, which had been immaculately curled into elegant blond ringlets.

Levenchik then tried to ensnare her in banal pleasantries, but she had quickly cut to the chase, hoping to reach through his artifice and have a candid conversation with the man beneath the womanizing facade.

She now suspected there was absolutely nothing beneath the facade.

"Yes, yes. It's all *very* grave, isn't it." He stretched out on a purple sofa, his robe barely covering his nakedness. He sipped his wine, then held out the glass for her to admire. "Won't you have some, my dear? It's an absolute perfect vintage."

"Again I must decline, my lord. Now, as I was saying, we are under siege, and it is your poor town of Les that suffers most. First demolished by an imperial wizard, and now occupied by an unsanctioned army of the undead. If you were to bring these concerns to the council and demand an emergency resolution to deal with the matter, I have no doubt it would improve the situation dramatically."

She actually doubted it quite a bit. But she had grown desperate, as evidenced by her current effort to seek aid from the person who represented perhaps the most grotesque expression of nobility in all Izmoroz. She understood why none were eager to confront the Uaine, but surely *someone* among the nobility besides Galina had the courage to stand up to them.

"Hm, yes, my dear Galina—may I call you Galina?—I greatly appreciate your concern for my poor beleaguered town of Les."

"As I have said to my father and several other council members, Les is an essential part of our national economy. The fate of Les is the fate of us all."

"My heart brims with your kindness, Galina, which is matched only by your unique beauty. Perhaps you and I can speak more about it over dinner? It is nearly suppertime after all, and you see..." He gave her what she suspected was intended to be a smoldering look. "I am a man with *voracious* appetites."

She took a deep, calming breath, though at this point she didn't know why, as it never succeeded in calming her these days.

"Will you speak to the council about this matter?" Her voice strained with irritation.

He leered. "Perhaps I could be...*persuaded*."

"I will not sleep with you," she said bluntly.

"But—"

"Under any circumstances."

He sighed. "A pity. I'm quite a skilled lover, I'll have you know."

"With all the practice you've had, I should hope so." She stood. "Since it seems our business is concluded, I will take my leave."

He gave her a wide-eyed look. "Not even a farewell kiss?"

She glared at him for a moment, wishing that she had even a shred of the power that the Portinari siblings possessed so she could wipe that look off his face, and perhaps him off the face of the earth. But that was not to be her lot apparently. So she decided the best course of action was not even to give him a response. She turned on her heel and, brushing aside the offers of several maids, showed herself out.

As she climbed into her carriage, she considered what options she had remaining.

None presented themselves.

She stared out the window, not really observing the buildings that slid past. In these moments when her resolve faltered, she thought of Angelo's smug look as he taunted her impotence. The monster. And to think she had fancied him. Why was she always drawn to such secretly horrible men? Could there be some defect in her? Perhaps too many romantic novels at an impressionable age? Regardless, she would be damned if she let him get away with his treachery. She would find a solution, no matter the cost.

But if she truly meant that, perhaps she should have consented to Levenchik's carnal bribery after all...

No, even if she had done so, there would have been no way to ensure that he would actually speak to the council afterward. Perhaps there was some other pressure she could apply? But what? All of Gogoleth knew of his infidelity. The man was without shame. In all likelihood, Levenchik was a dead end. But who else did she have left to turn to?

No one came to mind.

There was one rather uncomfortable idea that had been lurking in her consciousness for several days now. She did not like to think it, but *perhaps* she had been too hasty in getting rid of Sonya. In retrospect, it was clear that Angelo had pushed her toward the idea for his own reasons. If Sonya were still here, she might have once more rallied the people of Izmoroz, this time to fight back against the Uaine. Instead, she had been banished in part because Galina had been afraid she would undermine the authority of the nobility. The real irony of course was

159

that now Galina wondered why she had wanted to protect the nobility when not one of them would help her alleviate the suffering of the people of Izmoroz. Though she was loath to admit it, in this regard Sonya had been correct. The current system was flawed, if not completely broken.

Galina returned to Roskosh Manor in a gloomy mood, longing for a hot bath that might improve her spirits. But waiting in her apartments was a very apologetic-looking Masha and an elderly peasant who looked vaguely familiar.

Galina regarded the man for a moment. He stared nervously down at his toes, twisting his shapeless fur hat like he was still trying to kill the animal it had come from.

"I have not had a very good day thus far, Masha. I hope this fellow will improve my temper."

"Apologies for the unexpected intrusion, miss," said Masha. "Do you remember Olin?"

"Olin, is it?" asked Galina. "Do lift your head so that I can get a good look at you."

"S-sorry, my lady." Olin looked up at her, his temples beaded with sweat. Was she really so intimidating?

"I'm not Lady Prozorova yet, but regardless, I do recognize you. One of the original group from the Sturdy Sturgeon, correct? In fact, as I recall, you were the first person in Gogoleth to make contact with Sonya Turgenev."

He smiled, looking a little relieved. "Yes, miss. That's me. I'm so pleased you remember."

"There is very little I forget. Now what brings you to my home?"

His expression grew anxious. "There's . . . ah, people that wants to meet you. Masha done told me everything you been trying to do to get rid of them Uaine. I think these people could really help you out with that."

"Oh? And pray tell me, who are these helpful people?"

His expression grew more uncomfortable. "I'm so sorry, miss. I promised not to say. They, uh, they want me to bring you to them. Secretly, like."

"And where is it they hope you will bring me?"

"The, uh, Stena Forest."

"I see." Galina turned back to Masha. "Anonymous aid that I must seek out in the least inhabited region in eastern Izmoroz. I don't need to tell you how troubling this request is."

"No, miss."

"And you still think I should comply?"

Masha hesitated for a moment. "I do, miss."

"Why?"

"I've known Olin my whole life. His daughter was like a sister to me. I trust him more than anyone else in the world, excepting yourself of course, miss. If he says these people will help you, I believe him."

"Is that so?"

"Yes, miss."

"Then you are asking me to trust you, as you trust him?"

"Yes, miss."

Galina closed her eyes and sighed. Hadn't she just admitted to herself that she had run out of options? She had vowed to do whatever it took to free Izmoroz. If potentially putting herself in physical danger was the only recourse left to her, then so be it.

She opened her eyes and looked first at Masha, then at Olin.

"Very well. We will go to Stena Forest and hope these people are truly allies. Masha, have the carriage brought back around while I freshen up."

"Uh, begging your pardon, miss," said Olin. "A carriage won't do where we're going."

"Wonderful," Galina said without enthusiasm. "I suppose I had better change into my riding clothes, then."

28

Galina had not thought much about Sebastian these past months. In fact, she had made a point of thinking about him as little as possible. But as she rode across the Pustoy Plains toward the Stena Forest with Masha and Olin, it was difficult to put him out of mind.

This was the place he had first unleashed his full power, and the blighted land would likely bear the ugly marks of that event for generations. There was not a single blade of grass or tree for miles. The ground upon which their horses galloped was blackened and hard. Sebastian had once explained to her that it was cooled magma he had drawn from beneath the surface of the earth to show Commander Vittorio that he could wield "magic with military application." At the time, he had been deeply troubled by his own actions. And yet only a few months later, he had perpetrated far worse.

How could a man change so dramatically? Galina still wondered if it had been some inner weakness within Sebastian that had allowed him to take such a dark path, or if it had been a testament to the pressures of military culture in general, and Commander Vittorio in particular, that was to blame. The most likely answer was a combination of all those things. Not that it exonerated her former betrothed of his crimes in any way. After all, not even Vittorio had been so brutal and reckless as to massacre an entire town. That had been all Sebastian's doing. And she would never forgive him for it.

They rode all that day, then camped for a night on the hard, rocky ground. Galina had never camped before, and found that she disliked it intensely. It was cold and lacking even the most basic comforts. Without any trees or cover, she had to ask Masha to hold up a blanket like a curtain so she could have a semblance of privacy as she relieved herself.

The next morning, she awoke sore and irritable.

"I don't know that I've ever seen you in riding clothes before, miss," said Masha as she stirred the embers from the previous night's fire in hopes of heating water for tea.

"Naturally not." Galina looked distastefully down at her beige trousers. "I am aware that some women, such as my mother, will find any excuse to wear riding clothes, as it shows off their shapely legs to great advantage. In my case, however, all it reveals is that I walk about each day on a pair of matchsticks."

"Oh no, miss. They don't look at all like—"

"You know I dislike being patronized, Masha."

"Yes, miss. Sorry. But I'm certain there must be some nice young man out there who is quite fond of matchsticks."

Galina glared at her with one eyebrow raised. "I do hope that wasn't a feeble attempt at humor, Masha."

A smile momentarily ghosted across her maidservant's lips. "Perish the thought, miss."

After a barely serviceable cup of tea, they continued east to the Stena Forest. It was by far the largest forest in Izmoroz, stretching all the way down into Aureum. It was also said to be so dense in places that the light of the sun never touched the ground, and that it was inhabited by strange beasts and insects found nowhere else in the world. Galina had read several books about it, and while she'd enjoyed those books, she had never once felt compelled to visit. She supposed that someone like Sonya would have been eager to explore such a place, but as they slowed their horses and crossed the tree line, all Galina felt was a quiet, fluttering dread.

It was a stark contrast to go from the lifeless Pustoy Plains to a lush forest teeming with all manner of plants and animals. Insects buzzed, birds sang, and small rodents scampered about. There was no proper road to speak of, and the tiny path that Olin led their horses down could hardly even be called a trail.

"Olin, are you certain you know where we're going?" Galina strove to keep the worry out of her voice, but was not entirely successful.

"Oh yes, miss. I been through here several times already."

He moved with confidence, but care, his eyes constantly darting around.

"Are we ... safe?"

Olin gave her a pained smile. "As safe as one can be in the Stena."

"That is not particularly reassuring," she told him. "How deep must we go into this forest?"

"Not too deep," said Olin. "Begging your pardon, but I did tell them you were not the hardiest of souls."

"By all means," said Galina. "If it keeps me from having to trudge any farther than necessary into this bug-infested, sunless underworld, I gladly accept that description."

"Oh, it's not as bad as all that, miss." Olin turned back to look at her. "Why, if you look at it the right way, this forest is one of the most beautiful—"

There was a blur of movement and Galina found herself abruptly staring at an empty saddle.

Masha's scream echoed through the trees as Galina looked wildly about. She heard a low growl, followed by rustling. She turned and saw Olin's feet flailing wildly from a nearby thicket. After a moment, he grew still.

There was another deep growl, and then the largest cat Galina had ever seen rose up from the brush. A leopard of some kind, judging by the spots. It was indeed a beautiful animal, but its white-furred mouth dripped with blood.

"Wh-what should we do, miss?" Masha's voice shook with panic.

Galina, however, had become icily calm. She did not know how or why, but it was as though the dread she'd felt upon entering the forest had evaporated in the face of actual danger, and her mind now worked with clockwork precision as she pondered their options. Should they run? Or would such prey-like behavior only attract the leopard? Perhaps if they backed away slowly, it would allow them to leave. It already had Olin, after all. How many people could one leopard eat?

"Don't make any sudden movements," Galina told Masha.

Though in the back of her mind her instincts shrieked at her to run, Galina remained still and watched the leopard begin to tear into Olin's flesh.

Once it seemed fully occupied, she whispered, "Follow me."

"Y-yes, miss."

Masha didn't point out that Galina had no experience in dealing with man-killing leopards and seemed grateful merely to have some direction. Galina's horse was also on the edge of panic. She stroked his neck gently and made quiet soothing sounds as she coaxed him along, one trembling hoof at a time.

"Keep your horse calm, Masha. If it bolts, the leopard may give chase."

"Understood, miss."

Galina reached out and took the reins of Olin's horse. The animal was understandably even more rattled than the others and gave a sharp whinny.

They all froze as the leopard lifted its bloody muzzle. But after a tense moment, it returned to its grisly feast.

Once the sound of flesh being rent from bone began again, Galina whispered soothing words to Olin's horse, then guided it and her own horse carefully away from danger, with Masha following close behind.

After an uncomfortable and painfully slow period of time, they were out of earshot from the leopard and Galina judged they were probably safe, at least for the moment. From there she chose to head west, back toward Gogoleth. Olin was gone and she had no idea where she was supposed to meet the mysterious potential allies. There was no point staying, and she'd had quite enough of the Stena Forest to last a lifetime.

Except after several hours, they still had not reached the edge of the forest. The sun was still out, but the dense foliage prevented her from checking its position and she was forced to consider the idea that they had not been heading west after all. They might, in fact, be lost in the largest, most untamed forest in Izmoroz.

"You have done well to come all this way without a guide, Galina Odoyevtseva Prozorova," a deep, rumbling voice said.

Galina looked around, but saw no one.

"Who's there?" Her voice sounded unpleasantly shrill in her own ears.

"Will we eat her, *Medved*?" asked a different voice. It sounded feminine, but also eerily hollow.

"No, no, *Sova*," the rumbling voice she called *Medved* said impatiently. "This is the one we have been seeking. Have you forgotten already?"

"Hmm," said *Sova*. "What about the horse? Can we eat that? It appears they have an extra."

Medved sighed. "Perhaps. Once our business is finished."

"Who are you?" Galina's attempt at a stern tone was not as convincing as she would have liked. "Show yourselves."

"My apologies for remaining concealed, Galina Odoyevtseva," said *Medved*. "But before we show ourselves, I must warn you that some humans find our forms to be…unsettling. I want you to know that we mean you no harm."

"I will bear that in mind," promised Galina, because there was really nothing else she could say. These two strange people had her at a terrible disadvantage. And yet, it seemed likely these were the supposed allies to whom Olin had been leading them.

A woman suddenly appeared perched on the empty saddle of Olin's horse. She had large yellow eyes, which gleamed oddly in the dim light that filtered in through the trees. Her hair was short and white, clumped together so that it looked like feathers. Or no, as Galina's vision strained, she saw that they *were* feathers. Galina recalled that *sova* was the Old Izmorozian word for owl.

There was a rustle in the bushes, then the largest man Galina had ever seen emerged. Except, like the woman, he was not entirely a man. He had shaggy white fur on his head instead of hair, small dark eyes, and large rounded ears. *Medved* was Old Izmorozian for bear.

"You're Rangers," Galina said quietly.

"I am Andre," said the man. "And this is Tatiana."

The woman did not say anything, but only stared at Galina and slowly blinked.

"You are the ones Olin was taking me to?" asked Galina. "You wish to form an alliance?"

Andre looked thoughtful for a moment. "Dark times are upon us, Galina Odoyevtseva. So that we could once again aid our people and serve our goddess, Tatiana and I asked the Lady Marzanna for the boon of restored youth. But the cost was...high. We have difficulty...*remembering* things. Thinking strategically has also become difficult. We still wish to serve, but we require guidance. The wisdom of humanity."

"Ah!" Tatiana leaned forward, looking at Galina with more interest. "So, Andrushka, this is the rebel *Kukla*?"

"It is," said Andre.

Galina still did not like being called a *doll*, and saying it in Old Izmorozian did not make it any more palatable. But she understood that she was on very dangerous ground, so she chose not to voice her objection.

Instead she asked, "You have heard of me?"

Andre nodded. "The Lady bade us seek you out."

"The Goddess of Winter knows who I am?" Galina asked sharply. She was both astonished and horrified by the idea.

"Not only the Lady, but the people as well," said Andre. "Most do not know your name, but speak of you as Mistress Kukla who joined with our troubled little sister to drive out the empire."

"Ah, yes, Sonya..." Did they know she was gone now? More importantly, did they know Galina had a hand in getting rid of her?

"The Lady told us that *Lisitsa* has her own path to walk, and that in her absence we must take up her cause here in Izmoroz. And so we have chosen you."

"Chosen me for what?"

Tatiana hopped in a distinctly birdlike way from the riderless horse to a tree branch just beside Galina's head. Galina noticed the Ranger wore no shoes, and instead of feet had the sharp talons of a great bird of prey. She leaned sideways, anchored by her claws, and stared at Galina with her large owl eyes.

"We have lost so much, *Kuklushka*," she said. "Our humanity. Our minds. Our very souls. We have decided that you will be those things for us. You will guide us as the strong hands you lack. Together, we will take Izmoroz as the Lady commands."

Galina noticed that she had not been asked for consent to this arrangement. Apparently, arrogance was not merely a flaw in Sonya's personality, but a general trait among Rangers. And this alliance was not without risk. By their own admission, these two were no longer in full control of their faculties. They might turn on her in a moment of beastly passion.

And yet, Galina understood that Olin, bless him, had been correct in bringing her here. It had become increasingly clear during the last few weeks that if she wished to drive out the Uaine, she needed a miracle. And she'd just been given one. Perhaps literally.

"You will obey me in all things?" she asked.

"So long as it does not contradict the will of the Lady," said Andre, "there is nothing we will not do for you. We put ourselves entirely in your hands."

Galina turned to Masha, who had remained pale, trembling, and silent this entire time. Masha had always seemed overawed by Rangers. But now Galina understood that the awe the peasants held for the Rangers was not one based on respect, but on fear. An undoubtedly well-founded fear.

"What do you think, Masha?" she asked her maidservant. "Shall we once again ally ourselves with Rangers in Izmoroz's time of need?"

"I wouldn't like to think about the alternative, miss," Masha said bluntly.

"Well said," agreed Galina. These two Rangers had just admitted they were so lost in their strange animalistic magic that they no longer trusted themselves. It did not bear thinking about what might happen to Izmoroz if *someone* did not guide them.

And why not her?

She drew herself up. "Very well, Andre *Medved* and Tatiana *Sova*. I will take you into my care."

Andre knelt before her. Tatiana hopped down beside him and knelt as well.

"We deliver ourselves to you, Galina *Kukla*," they said.

Galina winced. Apparently this was not a nickname she would be escaping. She supposed it was marginally better than the name of a beast.

"Together we shall not only free Izmoroz of its current difficulties," she told them, "but usher in a bright new future so that our glorious land will never need to fear foreign aggression again."

29

"You should not treat your condition so lightly, Tighearna," admonished Rowena as she sat beside Mordha in his tent and carefully examined the gashes Sonya had left on his torso. As expected, the wounds had not closed or changed in any way since they had been inflicted.

"I cannot treat my condition lightly," Mordha said quietly. "For the pain is endless. These small marks left by the beast witch, however..." He shrugged. "They are nothing."

Rowena sighed. For such a brilliant man, he could be infuriatingly dense at times. "In and of themselves, yes. But if you are always so reckless, you will soon be riddled with holes. How well do you think you'll be able to fight then? To move about, even?"

"I do not plan to indulge others as I did that beast witch. She is a special circumstance."

"How so?"

"When we fought, I saw it in her eyes. Doubt."

"Of course. She was afraid of you, mighty Tighearna. For all her bold talk, she feared she could not win."

He shook his head. "It was not that. It was something...deeper. Something fundamental within that beast witch has shifted from when we first met her. I don't know the cause, but I can tell she questions now. And in time she might seek real answers."

There was no one else in the tent, but one never knew who might be lurking outside, so Rowena leaned in and asked quietly, "You think she might abandon the gods and join our cause?"

"I believe there is a chance, at least. And that was reason enough to spare her."

Rowena had a hard time imagining Sonya betraying her "Lady," but then, she'd never really understood Sonya.

"Regardless, it would have broken Jorge's heart to lose her completely, so I suppose I should thank you for that small mercy."

Mordha turned to her, his scarred expression as unreadable as always. "I pressed that friendship upon you, but it seems to have taken on a life of its own."

She nodded. She would not have betrayed Mordha for Jorge, of course. But she had been pleased to discover she was capable of genuine respect and affection for someone outside of her own people.

Lorecchio poked his head in through the tent flap. He looked uncharacteristically flustered. "Do you have a moment, Tighearna?"

"For you, Lorecchio? Of course."

"Not for me, actually," said Lorecchio. "For this man."

Lorecchio stepped back to reveal an Izmorozian man nearly as large as Mordha with bright red hair. He was dressed in typical Izmorozian peasant garb, and his expression had an oddly placid, almost indifferent expression. But despite those qualities, he held himself with the easy confidence of a soldier seasoned by combat.

"Greetings, Tighearna Mordha," the man said in the imperial tongue. He spoke in a monotone that suggested it was a message he had memorized. "My name is Sasha Rykov, and I bring an offer of alliance from my master."

"And who is your master?" asked Mordha.

"One who is well positioned within the high palace of Magna Alto," said Rykov. "One who would see the empire fall."

Mordha's scarred face crinkled into a smile. "Sit and drink with me. We will discuss this potential alliance."

INTERLUDE

Marzanna and Zivena lay curled up together in a dark pit of a deep part of the Eventide, a jumble of hard wintry limbs and verdant fleshy abundance. For these two beings, rivalry had never prevented intimacy. After all, who else could ever hope to be their equal?

"Are you surprised that I am taking your wayward children from you?" asked Zivena as she stroked her sibling's frozen countenance.

"I am very proud of you for taking such bold new action, my dear sibling," said Marzanna.

Zivena scowled. "Do not pretend you are not surprised."

"I make no such claim."

Zivena smiled, looking pleased, and returned to caressing her sibling.

After a few moments, she said, "I confess I had forgotten about your other two servants. The bear and the owl joining with that doll? What a curious alliance that will be."

"Most entertaining," agreed Marzanna. "I look forward to seeing what happens."

"You sent them to her yet you do not know how it will unfold?"

"Unlike you, dear sibling, I do not dictate every action of my people. I prefer to let them choose their fates for themselves."

"Yes, well, you see where that got you with the necromancers that I have just stolen from you. Nothing but disrespect and betrayal."

Marzanna nestled more deeply into the pulsing flesh of her sibling. "So you say."

172

Zivena paused to consider. "I know your tricks. Do not pretend that even this was part of your grand design."

"I pretend no such thing."

Zivena should have been gratified with that response, but for some reason was not.

PART THREE

FORGERS OF HOPE

"Let us take, for example, the verb *to forge*. It can be the honest craft of a simple blacksmith. But it can also be the nefarious deed of a criminal who falsifies documents, money, and more. How remarkable that the same word can have two such divergent meanings! It speaks, I think, not only to the fluidity of language but of the human soul as well."

—Olivia Zambrano, esteemed linguist, from a lecture given at the Colmo College of Arts and Magic

30

Sonya once considered the Great Western Tundra to be unequaled in its immense and terrible beauty. But after a week sailing on the *Endless Summer*, she understood that the tundra was nothing compared to the sea.

The ship cruised along the Raízian coast at a speed not even Peppercorn could hope to match, and it never stopped. Traveling at such a pace, they could have crossed the tundra in only a few days. And yet, even when they rounded the El Fin Peninsula, the ocean stretched out in all directions, seemingly endless. It was amazing, of course. Yet it made her feel even more anxious than before. How could one ever master such a thing? Perhaps it was simply impossible.

She sat up in the ship's crow's nest, her knees tucked under her chin, and gazed pensively out at the boundless blue of the Sea of Charmed Winds. Supposedly an entirely different continent called Victasha lay to the south, but not even her fox eyes could catch sight of it. Jorge said it was a single country nearly as large as Izmoroz, Aureum, Raíz, Uaine, and Kante put together. He had traveled there once as a child and said it was like nothing else he'd ever seen.

The world was so much bigger than she'd previously understood. Back in Izmoroz, Sonya had been like a child, thinking herself the strongest in the land, not realizing that she hadn't even stepped outside her own house yet. If she was ever able to return to Izmoroz, would it seem smaller and less impressive, like the first time she had returned home after becoming a Ranger?

The wind was strong up in the crow's nest, pulling at her long black hair and playing across her bare arms and shins. It had gotten so hot that she'd even taken off her tunic and boots, and now wore only a sleeveless undershirt and trousers rolled up to her knees. She knew her mother would have been horrified to see her so brazenly unclothed in public. That pleased her even now.

"Mornin', miss!" said a short, wiry man with close-cropped salt-and-pepper hair as he climbed into the crow's nest.

"Good morning, Alberto," she replied, her golden eyes not leaving the distant horizon.

"Are all beastfolk this serious, miss?"

"Actually, I'm the lighthearted one."

"I shudder to think, miss." He settled in beside her, taking a sip of grog from a small jug despite the early hour.

A few days before, Alberto had tentatively asked her what she *was* exactly. She hadn't really known what to tell him and had eventually settled on "just beastfolk." She wondered now if he thought she had been born this way. Like there was a whole race of people who were part human, part animal. In a way, she wished there was. Perhaps it would have eased the feeling of isolation that had crept in among these people who did not know Rangers of Marzanna.

"Sure you're not chilly, miss?" he asked, buttoning up his wool vest. "It gets mighty cold up here in the catbird seat this early."

"It's still warmer than an Izmorozian summer," she told him.

His eyes widened. "Then what's it like up there in the winter?"

"So cold the snot freezes in your nose."

He pinched his nose, as if to banish the imagined feeling. "I reckon I'll never know the like."

"Probably not. It doesn't really have any seaports."

"Aye, that's most likely why I never met any sailors from those parts."

"You say *aye*?" she asked. "Do you speak Uaine?"

He gave her a curious look. "What's yu-aim?"

"*Uaine.* It's the country north of Aureum and west of Izmoroz."

He shook his head. "Never heard of it, miss. But we never go north of Herder's Gate, so that could be why."

"But you say *aye* like they do."

"'Tis a sailor word, miss. We got all kinds of funny things we say."

Sonya wondered if perhaps the Uaine had once sailed this far south and made contact with other sailors, but that it had been so long ago only a word or two survived to mark their passage. Or perhaps some enterprising sailors from the south went up there and brought some words back with them. Language was a funny thing. As flexible and changeable as the people who spoke it, it was almost a living entity all its own.

"What is the word *señor*?" she asked Alberto.

"That's not a sailor word, miss," he said.

"Yeah, I know. But what is it? Not imperial common tongue."

"No, it's only used by Raízians as a title of respect."

"Did Raíz once have its own language then?"

"Oh, a long time ago. I hear the Viajero still know some of it, on account of it being the language they sing in their magic songs. But ordinary folks don't know much besides titles like señor and señora."

"I guess it's sort of like that in Izmoroz," Sonya said. "Most people don't speak Old Izmorozian anymore, but elders and maybe people out in the more remote villages still know some of it. Honestly I don't know much of it myself, but I try to remember the little bit my *uchitel* taught me. That means *teacher*."

They sat in silence for a while as Alberto scanned the horizon. The day before, he'd told her that he mostly kept an eye out for storm clouds and other ships. He'd then gone into a lengthy description on how a ship could be identified by the combination of flags it was flying, but she had stopped feigning interest after the first ten minutes or so.

"So, miss...how'd you become friends with Señor Elhuyar anyway?"

He asked it in a casual tone, but she had the feeling he'd been working up to this question ever since she first started spending time in the crow's nest.

"I rescued him from some bandits," she told him.

"You?" He gave her a dubious look. "Pardon me saying so, but you're hardly bigger than a dewdrop, miss."

"I can be quite deadly." She grimaced, showing him her sharp teeth. It clearly made him uneasy, though, so she stopped. "Anyway, he was grateful and insisted on cooking dinner for me, so—"

"Wait," interrupted Alberto. "The youngest son of the Elhuyar family...*cooks*? With his own hands?"

She nodded. "He's very good, although sometimes he makes things too spicy for me."

"Amazing," he said. "I never heard of such a thing."

"Is the Elhuyar family so revered that you can't imagine them doing normal boring stuff?"

"That's one way to put it, I suppose." His eyes narrowed. "You have no idea what you're in for when we get to Colmo, do you, miss?"

"Nope," she agreed, feigning nonchalance. "Not a clue."

She had been telling herself that her best friend wouldn't be all that different once he was reunited with his fancy important family again. But there had been a subtle shift in his demeanor ever since they boarded the *Endless Summer*. And every time she talked about him or his family with Alberto or one of the other crew members, it became a little harder for her to convince herself that their friendship would remain the same. So many other things had already altered in her life. Must that change as well?

31

Sebastian hadn't been sure what he'd expected Kante to look like. Based on Marcello's vague descriptions, something like a bog or a dreary, sodden moor, perhaps. But what he discovered was quite different. While it wasn't as warm or sunny as Aureum, it had its own uniquely mournful beauty.

They rode across vast, rolling green hills dotted with stone and splashes of blue and white flowers that shivered when gusts of cool, damp breeze blew past. Dense gray clouds scuttled overhead, but they were often broken by hard patches of sun that made for a striking contrast. To the north, Sebastian could make out the distant snowcapped Segen Mountains, and far to the east, out of view, he knew lay the Tainted Ocean. To the south, also well out of view, was the Gestank Swamps.

Sebastian took in a deep breath, but the air seemed remarkably fresh. He turned to Marcello, who rode beside him.

"I thought you said Kante was smelly."

"Oh, well, that's just what I heard," Marcello said sheepishly.

Sebastian gave his friend a hard look. "You've never actually been to Kante before, have you?"

"I've never even left Aureum before," admitted Marcello.

"So all that talk about the beauty of Kantesian women?"

Marcello lifted his chin haughtily. "I have it on very good authority that they are quite beautiful."

181

"Or at least you hope so."

Marcello grinned. "I know you said your sister doesn't have your blond hair, but how is she otherwise? You're a handsome fellow, so surely she must be a catch."

Sebastian sighed. "I suppose it depends on how you feel about wanted fugitives."

"She's a troublemaker, is she?" Marcello looked thrilled. "I don't mind that. Not at all."

"What about foxes?"

"Ah, she's a vixen, then?" Marcello waggled his eyebrows.

"No, I mean literally," said Sebastian.

Marcello gave him a baffled look. "I don't follow."

"Do you know what a Ranger of Marzanna is?"

"Those fiends from the Winter War?"

Sebastian nodded. "She's one of them. In fact, she's responsible for the recent uprising in Izmoroz."

Marcello stared at him. "So your father was a famous commander, you're a powerful wizard, and your sister's a bloodthirsty monster? What is it with your family?"

"I wish I knew," said Sebastian. "But I don't think it would be fair to call my sister a *bloodthirsty monster*. If anything..." He thought back to those moments when she had begged him not to harm innocent bystanders in Les, and later on the streets of Gogoleth. He recalled his own intoxicating wrath, which had enabled him to selfishly ignore the danger he posed to others...

Who was the real monster?

"Family isn't always easy," Marcello said quietly after a few moments. "But they'll always be there for you, no matter what."

Sebastian nodded, still not trusting himself to speak. On numerous occasions Sonya had come to him and tried, however clumsily and presumptuously, to protect him. He had been unwilling to see the good intentions behind her efforts, and had instead acted like a spoiled child.

"Speaking of monsters," Marcello said after a few moments. "What do you think that *thing* was in the pass?"

"I wish I knew," said Sebastian. "I've researched magic as much as

I can, in part so that I could better understand my own. I did come across a few mentions of Kantesian magic, but it was all very vague, and there was certainly nothing about them creating giant beasts. Although I honestly couldn't say for certain it even *was* a beast. It felt almost more mechanical in nature. But even then, I couldn't sense anyone operating it. So honestly, I'm at a loss to explain it."

Marcello's brow furrowed. "Do you think there will be . . . a lot of them?"

"Surely we would have heard about it," said Sebastian. "It's not as though we haven't been receiving regular communications from the front. Something as catastrophic as an army of giant creatures would not have been omitted from reports."

"That's true." Marcello looked a little relieved.

"For all we know, it might not have even been Kantesian," Sebastian pointed out.

"I suppose," said Marcello. "But the Kantesians do have some sort of magic?"

"I believe it's called residual magic."

"Residual? That doesn't sound terribly impressive."

"Something to do with energy transferal I believe? Or soul transferal perhaps?" Sebastian shook his head. "As I said, not much is known about their magic, in part because of the language gap."

"I've always found magic to be unfair, you know?" asked Marcello. "Unfair?"

"Well the Raízians have their Viajero, and the Izmorozians have their Rangers. The Uaine have their necromancers, and I guess even the Kantesians have *some* form of magic. But what do we Aureumians have?"

"I hadn't thought about it like that," admitted Sebastian.

"Well sure. You're a wizard after all, so it wouldn't occur to you. But even then, it's not like wizards are unique to Aureum."

"True," said Sebastian. "If the legends are to be believed, a wizard can be born to any culture or nationality."

"We've got no magic to call our own. And yet, we're the ones in charge."

"Perhaps *because* Aureum has no magic," said Sebastian. "They've had to work harder than anyone else to compete."

"You mean *we*," said Marcello.

"Right, of course. We."

Sebastian still didn't really think of himself as Aureumian. He wondered if he would always feel a little removed from his countrymen in that way. He supposed he was isolated in a lot of ways. His upbringing, his abilities, even his guilt separated him from his happy-go-lucky friend. He wondered if he would ever find someone that he could share his whole self with. Maybe no such person existed. Or maybe that person had been Galina and he'd completely ruined his one chance to find someone with whom he could share his life.

32

It was all very well to imagine oneself the savior of Izmoroz, but even with the aid of a superior intellect and supernaturally enhanced servants, Galina understood that her work had only just begun. During their journey back to Gogoleth, Galina questioned her new Rangers so that she might better understand the true shape of her poor, beleaguered country.

Unfortunately, they were not as helpful as she might have hoped.

"What sort of food stores do the towns and villages outside of Gogoleth have at present?" she asked as they rode across the barren Pustoy Plains.

Andre had taken poor Olin's horse, while Tatiana sat perched on the back of Masha's horse. Both the horse and Masha were handling the unusual seating arrangement with as much aplomb as they could muster, although Galina could see her maidservant tense up whenever the eerie, birdlike Ranger behind her made a sudden movement.

"Food stores...," mused Andre quietly, as though trying to recall what the phrase meant. Were they really so far gone?

"Yes," she pressed. "With the end of winter, I'd imagine their supplies must be quite low by now, and as the Aureumian General Matteo Fontanelli once famously wrote, 'The priority of any infantry commander should be boots and stomachs.'"

Andre shook his head. "We did not check those things during our travels, Mistress."

"I see." Galina was not entirely comfortable with the title of *mistress*, but after several attempts at correcting them, they still used it. "And what about weapons?"

"Weapons, Mistress?" Tatiana perked up, causing both Masha and her horse to flinch. "Where?"

"Did you see any in your travels?" Galina asked patiently. "And even more importantly, people who knew how to wield them?"

"The little fox could," Tatiana said.

"We're not talking about her," snapped Andre. "And she's left Izmoroz anyway."

"Oh." Tatiana leaned back. "Right."

"I wouldn't expect regular folks to be able to afford a sword or anything like that, miss," said Masha. "Certainly not since the empire came."

"I suppose not," sighed Galina.

As they continued on, Galina pondered what to do next. She didn't have a lot of information to go on, so perhaps that was the first challenge to meet.

"You said the people didn't know me by name?" she asked.

Andre nodded his furry head. "The delicate noblewoman who stood by *Strannik* Sonya in the battle against the empire. That's how they know you, Mistress."

"Or they just call you Mistress Kukla," Tatiana supplied unhelpfully.

"So it would be safe to say that while most people know *of* me, my identity is not well known?"

"I think so, Mistress," said Andre.

"Perhaps we should keep it that way," said Galina.

"Miss?" asked Masha.

"Once we reach Gogoleth, we will leave the Rangers at the Sturgeon, for I fear they would attract far too much notice if we brought them to Roskosh Manor."

"Yes, miss."

"Then we will pack for a very long journey."

"And where will we go, miss?" asked Masha.

"Every town, village, and farmstead in Izmoroz," said Galina. "We cannot build a resistance against the Uaine until we know what we have. Naturally, my father would not approve of any aspect of this venture without the expressed permission of the council, which they will never grant. So we will tell him that as a scholar, I am embarking on our first post-imperial national census. And to ensure that this ruse is maintained, once we begin our journey, we will no longer use my name. As we go from place to place, I intend to begin rallying people to our cause, and I do not want word to get back to my father that his own beloved Galechka is fomenting dissent within his newly established plutocracy."

Masha's eyes were wide. "That is quite an ambitious plan, miss."

Galina smiled. "You think so? It's the best I could come up with at present. I was thinking to further protect my identity, I might return to using that porcelain mask you gave me. Or would that be too much? I wouldn't want to appear melodramatic."

Masha laughed, then looked pointedly first at the towering, shaggy Andre, then at the wide-eyed, feathery Tatiana.

"I think you will find it difficult to seem any more dramatic than you already do with two such Rangers in tow, miss."

33

The city of Colmo rose up along the southern coast of Raíz like a multicolored tidal wave. None of the buildings were particularly tall, nor were there any imposing walls or other structures created for obvious military defensive purposes. Instead, the entire city seemed given over to a bright, festive decor, as if every day in Colmo was a celebration.

Sonya had thought the Aureumian architecture constructed in Gogoleth after the war was too garish. Now she understood the reason it had felt so unappealing was because it had merely been a poor attempt at Raízian architecture. Somehow, though the sea-foam greens, salmon pinks, cornflower blues, and lemon yellows were twice as bright, Colmo seemed so at ease with its own exuberance that it felt effortless. From her view at the bow of the *Endless Summer*, the entire city seemed to shrug and say, *Of course we are like this. How else would we be?*

Jorge stood beside her at the bow, his eyes wide and glistening with unshed tears as he watched his home draw close. She gave his hand a quick squeeze, and he squeezed her fiercely back. Despite all the unknowns about this new life in Raíz, she was glad to see her friend so happy to be home.

The docking system of Colmo was even more extensive than Herder's Gate. It stretched nearly the entire length of the city so that it seemed like its own floating settlement. Not only was it large, it twisted and turned with almost mazelike complexity. But Captain Cajal navigated the narrow waterway confidently until they at last tied up to the dock with ropes as thick around as Sonya's arms.

The moment the ship drew close to the docks, Cajal shouted to one of his men.

"Luis! Run to the dockmaster and tell him to prepare an escort for Señor Elhuyar and his friend!"

"Aye, aye!" The boy leapt with impressive grace across the gap to the dock, and sprinted toward a large wooden structure closer to shore.

Jorge turned toward Cajal, looking pained. "Captain, that's really not necessary."

"With all due respect, Señor, I beg to differ. Back in Aureum, I didn't see much harm in letting you wander. But here you could be recognized. Imagine what your father would do to me if I let you walk through streets filled with your family's rivals and no one to protect you." He shook his head. "I'm afraid you will just have to bear it, Señor."

"Hey, *I* can protect him just fine," protested Sonya.

"No, Sonya, Captain Cajal is right," said Jorge. "The escort is primarily to *deter* people from attacking in the first place. If someone did attack, I know you would protect me. But I think you'd probably end up killing any assailants we'd encounter, and unless things have changed greatly since I left, there is a...balance between the Great Families that needs to be maintained in Colmo. Blood in the streets would definitely upset that balance."

"Oh. Okay..."

Sonya tried not to show the hurt she felt. This wasn't her land, after all, and she didn't know its ways. He was probably right that she would end up doing more harm than good.

Perhaps he sensed that her pride was a little wounded because he patted her back and grinned. "Besides, you've got a much more formidable confrontation to prepare for."

"Really?"

"Indeed." He gave her a mock serious look. "I fear a great deal of cheek-kissing is in store for you, Sonya Turgenev."

"Cheek-kissing?" she asked.

"Nobody bows or shakes hands in Colmo," he told her. "Especially with my family, it's all about the cheeks!"

"Huh..." Sonya liked to think of herself as a physically affectionate person. It was one of the things, along with a general plainspokenness, that set her apart from the rest of her family. And she'd certainly envied the closeness she'd seen between Blaine and his father. But kissing a bunch of people she'd just met?

"Unless you're not comfortable with it," Jorge said quickly. "I'm sure I could explain to them—"

"No." She was definitely uncomfortable with it, but the last thing she wanted was to distance herself from Jorge's family. So she mustered a brave smile. "I'm looking forward to it!"

"Great." He didn't look like he completely believed her, but he didn't press the issue.

It took several sailors and a lot of cursing, but finally the ship was secured to the dock and Captain Cajal deemed it was safe for Sonya and Jorge to disembark. By the time they'd coaxed their horses onto the dock, their escort had arrived. Three men and one woman, all in long braids. They wore leather vests that had been dyed a deep black, with feathery wings stitched into the material just below the collarbone. They stood at attention, their faces expressionless.

"Does Raíz have its own army?" Sonya asked as she and Jorge led their horses down the dock toward the escort.

"That would be illegal," said Jorge. "There are, however, mercenary guilds. The Anxeles Escuros here are probably the most well respected."

Sonya gazed speculatively at the mercenaries. Their bare arms were taut with muscle and covered in tattoos. Their hands rested on the pommel of short curved swords belted at their waists with an attitude of easy confidence. Either they were very good or very cocky. She couldn't decide which.

"So anyone can hire them?"

"Theoretically," said Jorge. "Although they're quite expensive, so not everyone can afford to hire them."

"So it's really like a private army for the rich?"

He winced. "I suppose."

The tallest of the four mercenaries, a man with tattoos swirling down his arms like waves, stepped forward. "Señor Elhuyar?"

"Yes, hello. I suppose my friend and I require an escort to my family's home."

"Very good, Señor!" He glanced back at the other three. "Form up!"

The mercenaries quickly formed a box around them, then clacked their bootheels together sharply.

"Ready to depart when you are, Señor!" the lead mercenary said.

Sonya thought it strange that they didn't introduce themselves and give their names. How could one really trust someone if they didn't know who they were? But Jorge didn't seem bothered by it. Perhaps the guild name alone was enough for him.

They led their horses down the docks and the mercenaries managed to keep their tight formation without bumping into them or each other, which was impressive. Especially since the ones in front were only watching their movements out of their peripheral vision. Sonya still didn't know what kind of fighters they were, but they certainly acted like professionals.

As they continued along the docks, the mercenary footsteps fell in a sharp staccato even louder than the horse hooves, garnering the attention of everyone they passed by. There was, Sonya decided, a bit of a show to the whole thing. She almost pointed that out to Jorge, but when she looked over at him, she saw his face flushed with embarrassment and his eyes fixed with determination directly in front, as if refusing to acknowledge the onlookers. Clearly he already knew.

The looks didn't stop even when they left the docks and entered the city proper. They mounted their horses and rode slowly through a large market that sold all manner of goods. It was just as lively as the market in Gogoleth, but instead of shouting out their wares or trying to accost people, the merchants sang and danced, like they were wooing their customers. Some stalls had sizzling meats or fresh raw fish, others had pungent cheeses or bundles of herbs. The constantly overlapping buffet of music, scents, and hypnotic movement was so dense, Sonya felt as though she was swimming through it all.

She felt Jorge's hand on her arm. "Are you okay?"

She smiled, keeping her mouth closed so as not to frighten the people around them. "Sure. It's just a lot to take in."

He seemed surprised by the comment. "I suppose it is, if you're not used to it."

"You don't find it overwhelming? Everything going on all at once like this?"

"Actually, I find *Gogoleth's* markets overwhelming. This..." He took a deep breath of the spiced, fragrant air, then shook his head and smiled. "This just feels like home."

34

Once they left the market, things quieted down. But even so, many of the building exteriors were decorated with brightly colored murals, and strains of music came wafting gently from open windows. As far as Sonya could tell, they were not taverns or other public places, but merely the homes of regular people.

"Does everyone play an instrument in Raíz?" she asked Jorge.

"No, but everyone is encouraged to take up some sort of artistic endeavor from an early age."

"What was yours?" she asked.

He rolled his eyes. "Painting. Although honestly I spent more time mixing the paints than using them."

"An apothecary in the making, huh?" she asked.

"I suppose so."

"You're a pretty good dancer, though."

He gave her a confused look.

"I saw you dancing with Blaine on our first night with the Uaine," she said.

His posture stiffened. "Let's, uh, not bring up things like that around my family, okay?"

"They don't like the Uaine?" she asked.

"They've never met them, but I'm sure they wouldn't approve of them or their . . . liberal lifestyle."

"It was just dancing," said Sonya. "It's not like the two of you were

193

tearing each other's clothes off. I don't even think you kissed, did you? And they're all about the kissing here, right?"

His face was tense and his posture was now almost painfully erect. "Still, let's just leave it out of conversation."

"Sure." She still didn't understand a lot of her friend's hang-ups around sex and romance. But she didn't want to upset him just before his big family reunion, so she didn't press any further.

The brick street slowly rose on an incline, and the homes became larger, each taking up additional space with small gardens and court-yards. Finally, at the summit of the slope was a brightly colored building easily three times the size of Roskosh Manor, surrounded by a thick high stucco–covered wall. The roofs had the same red tile as the other buildings, but it was several stories taller than any others she'd seen, and small balconies jutted out gracefully from many of the upper windows that were veiled in wafting silk curtains. The wall blocked her view of the courtyard that surrounded the building, but she could see the tops of several trees, including an orange and a lemon tree, both just beginning to bear fruit.

"That's your home, huh?" she asked.

"Cassa Estío," he said with quiet pride. "Home to the Elhuyar family for half a millennium."

"It's...nice." Sonya actually thought it was excessive, especially just for one family, but she again reminded herself that this was not her land or her culture, so she had no right to judge it.

He gave her a wry smile. "It's grotesquely opulent. But it also contains all my fondest childhood memories, so I can't help but love it."

The front gate was guarded by two men dressed in sleeveless golden robes, armed with curved swords similar to the ones carried by the Anxeles Escuros. One guard appeared to be in his thirties, but the other was a bit older, with long gray braids. He still looked quite formidable, though, his bare arms showing ropey muscle tattooed with images of the sun.

The two guards watched their approach warily until the older one's eyes suddenly widened.

"Little Señor? Is that you?"

Jorge smiled and waved. "Hello, Ignacio. My father hasn't let you retire yet?"

Ignacio gave a short rough bark of a laugh. "*Let?* My life is dedicated to the safety of the Elhuyar family. Your father would have to *order* me to retire."

The leader of the mercenaries stepped forward with a sharp clap of heels on brick. He addressed Ignacio rather than Jorge, which Sonya thought was strange.

"We are contracted to deliver Jorge Elhuyar, youngest son of Arturo Elhuyar, to his family estates. Do you consider this contract fulfilled?"

"I do," said Ignacio.

"We will add this service to the monthly bill, then."

"Thanks, Miguel," said Ignacio.

Miguel nodded. "Always happy to serve, Ignacio. Give my regards to the señor."

Ignacio grinned. "I'll make certain that your name is attached to this happy news."

"Thank you."

With that, Miguel clicked his heels again and rejoined the formation around Jorge and Sonya.

He looked at Jorge. "It has been an honor!"

Then he and his fellow Anxeles Escuros turned in unison and began marching back toward the market.

As the younger guard unlocked the gate, Ignacio beckoned enthusiastically to Jorge.

"Come, Little Señor. Let's go make your mother cry with joy."

Jorge's face was still flushed, but he looked eager rather than embarrassed now. Sonya thought perhaps she could even see something of the "little señor" in him that Ignacio remembered so affectionately. It was, she decided, very adorable.

The younger guard stayed at his post, while Ignacio led them through the gate into a small alcove beyond. He gave a sharp whistle and two little boys hurried out and took their horses into an adjoining stable. Then Ignacio led them through another gate and into the expansive courtyard.

Sonya was, on the whole, not particularly fond of nature that had been so tamed and manicured that it looked man-made. But when she saw the gardens that stretched before her, she decided that, at least in this case, she was not looking merely at tamed nature, but nature used as a medium for artistic expression. The regular geometric pattern of shapes and colors had something almost hypnotizing about it, and as she gazed upon it, she felt a knot of tension ease in her chest.

"What *is* this?" she whispered.

"A Viajero garden," said Jorge. "It soothes a troubled mind."

She looked at him with surprise. "It's magic?"

"Expressive magic is, on the whole, more subtle and elegant than what your brother does."

"I don't think I've ever experienced it before," she said.

He smiled proudly. "Well, get ready to experience a *lot* of it. The Elhuyar family commissions a *lot* of Viajero work."

"Great."

She actually found magic that influenced her emotions to be a little invasive, but she supposed it would just be one more thing, along with kissing strangers, that she'd have to accept if she wanted to live in Colmo.

As they followed Ignacio through the peaceful, lush garden, she felt it continue to work its soothing charm into her chest. It wasn't that it felt bad, exactly. She was fairly anxious about meeting Jorge's family after all, so it probably did her some good. It was just...strange to know that the feeling came from outside herself.

Finally they reached a massive fountain where a short, plump, older woman sat painting a portrait of the marmalade cat that slept nearby on a sun-drenched stone bench. The woman had long, intricately plaited iron-gray hair and wore a pale pink dress that left her round, brown arms bare. She was so absorbed in her work that she didn't notice their arrival.

Jorge cleared his throat and said, "Hello, Mama."

Sonya had assumed Ignacio exaggerated when he said they would make Jorge's mother cry with joy. He had not.

The round-faced woman turned, her expression first confused, then shocked, then shining with happiness. She leapt up from her chair, knocking the painting off its easel and startling the cat.

"Jorge! My baby! My God, you have returned my baby to me! Thank you, God!"

Then she dropped to her knees, her hands clasped together in prayer.

"Oh, Mama...," Jorge said fondly in a tone that suggested this level of intensity was fairly routine for her. He knelt down next to her. "I'm happy to see you, too."

Her hands shot out and gripped the sides of his head so suddenly that Sonya tensed up. Then she yanked his face to her and loudly and fervently kissed his cheeks, one after the other. Jorge bore this patiently, a beatific smile on his lips.

Jorge's mother gazed at her son fondly for a moment before releasing him, then sighed and abruptly stood back up, now looking calm and very much in charge.

"Well, my treasure, I am overjoyed to see you but why are you back so early, and who have you brought with you?" She eyed Sonya speculatively and her gaze narrowed. "Not a new wife, I hope."

"A good friend," he said firmly. "Sonya Turgenev Portinari, meet my mother, Señora Magdalena Elhuyar."

"It's good to meet you, Señora." Sonya could hear the nervousness in her voice.

"Hmm," said Magdalena as she continued to scrutinize her. Then she leaned over to Jorge and in a very loud whisper said, "My son, there is something... *unusual* about your friend's eyes."

"Yes." Jorge glanced at Sonya. "It's considered a... *blessing* in the Izmorozian religion."

Technically that was true, even if Sonya no longer felt like it was. Since Magdalena was clearly a religious woman, the idea seemed to please her greatly.

"Ah, good! Not enough young women value faith in God these days."

Sonya considered correcting her to say that it was actually a *goddess* who had done this to her, but decided against it. Especially since the

197

woman was rapidly approaching with outstretched arms. Her insides squirmed as she received the same wet, loud kisses on her cheeks, but she bore it bravely. Or at least she liked to think she did.

"Sonya, you are welcome here!" Magdalena proclaimed.

"Thank you, Señora."

Magdalena patted her cheek. "And such manners, too. Jorge, you always did have good taste in friends."

Sonya smiled, again careful to keep her mouth closed. If only her own mother had been here to witness this casual acceptance from one of the most powerful people in Raíz. Although admittedly, the perennially reserved Irina Turgenev might have died from the shock if she'd been here to see it.

198

35

After another day's march across the cool, damp meadows, the imperial battalion reached the Kantesian town of Kleiner. From a distance, Sebastian thought the cluster of squat structures looked similar to one of the larger peasant towns of Izmoroz, like Kamen. But there was one key difference. The homes and buildings of this town used a surprising amount of stone, iron, and tin in their construction.

"Ore must be plentiful in Kante, if even peasants use it," he said to Marcello as they neared the town.

"Well, we didn't come here for the swamps," said his friend.

It was an offhanded remark, but it stuck with Sebastian because it was something to which he hadn't given much thought. Why *was* the empire invading Kante? He'd heard it described before as a "border dispute," but Sebastian wondered if a conflict more than a day's ride into sovereign enemy territory could still be considered that. Was the empress's interest in Kante primarily for its natural resources? It was true that while Aureum had rich and fertile farmland, they had very few mines or direct access to metals. That was why keeping the peace at Bledney Mines back in Izmoroz had been so important. And perhaps now that such a supply had been cut off, at least temporarily, the push to claim other sources was even more urgent.

General Barone called for the army to halt. Then he led a small group into the town that included Sebastian, Marcello, and the captains of the engineer corps, apothecary company, and Viajero troupe.

The engineer, Captain Branca, was a squat, grim-faced man with sharp, calculating eyes. By contrast, the apothecary, Captain Dandolo, was a jolly-looking bearded fellow who never seemed entirely sober. The Viajero, Captain Reyes, was a tall, slim man. Sebastian hadn't had a lot of contact with Raízians, so he couldn't say if Reyes was typical of his people, but there was something striking about him that inevitably drew the eye. He was not particularly handsome, so perhaps it was his movements. Even the slightest twist of his hand on the reins of his horse, or the nod of his head, seemed to capture a grace and care that reminded Sebastian of the astonishing performances given by the traveling Viajero troupe he'd seen as a boy. It was as if the man danced through life.

As they rode into the town, Sebastian noticed many of the buildings were damaged. Wooden roofs had collapsed or were half-burned. Even some of the brick walls had been smashed through. Imperial soldiers stood at attention before the entrance to each of the intact buildings. Their posture remained as erect as any he had seen in Aureum, but their faces were haggard and weary. It was the dull look of those who had recently seen battle that Sebastian remembered all too well from Gogoleth.

Finally a man came hurrying out of one of the intact buildings. He was a solidly built Aureumian dressed in an officer's uniform. His arm was tied up in a sling, and he had a bandage wrapped across his head, covering one eye. Despite these injuries, he moved crisply to stand at attention before Barone.

"Colonel Totti reporting, sir!" said the officer as he gave a sharp salute.

Barone nodded calmly. "At ease, Colonel. Where is General Benniti?"

"Died of his wounds a week ago, sir," said Totti.

"I'm sorry to hear that," Barone said gravely. "He was a good man."

"Thank you, sir."

"I take it you've been in command, then?"

"Yes, sir," said Totti.

"What is our current status?"

"Roughly two thousand capable infantry, and a little over three hundred gravely wounded, sir."

Barone's bushy white eyebrows rose. "Only three hundred?"

Totti nodded. "We've had little in the way of medical supplies, so the recovery rate has been low."

"I see," said Barone. "What about the local population?"

"A hundred or so noncombatants. A large portion of them are wounded as well."

"Structural damage to the town?"

"About forty percent of the structures have some damage, with roughly fifteen percent deemed dangerous and uninhabitable."

"Supplies?" asked Barone.

"Food and water are sufficient, but as I said, medical supplies are severely depleted."

"Any activity from the enemy?"

"No sign of them, sir. We took heavy losses, but we gave them a good thrashing."

"Let us hope they remain licking their wounds until we are prepared to give them a proper reception, then."

"Yes, sir!"

Sebastian looked around, wondering where the Kantesians were. If they were noncombatants, why were so many of them injured? And only a hundred people for such a large town? He examined the nearby building tops more carefully. Scorch marks suggested the town had been assaulted with flaming pitch launched from catapults. Such a sweeping attack would have made it difficult to reduce civilian casualties. He supposed the ferocity of the conflict must have made it necessary for them to take such extreme measures. Otherwise their actions would have been little better than what he had done to Les...

Well, there was nothing he could do about it now. What he *could* do was repair and rebuild. And it was important to remember that once the empire succeeded in taking Kante, these people would become new citizens of the empire. Therefore, he would need to build trust with them even as he built their homes. It would not be easy, he knew.

But he had not come all this way for an easy mission. He had come to finally use his talents to do some good in this world. He would help these people, even if they never expressed gratitude, even if they spat in his face. He would help them even if they hated him.

Because perhaps then he might hate himself a little less.

36

Galina had thought she'd known what the word *poverty* meant, but she had been mistaken. Terribly, woefully, *shamefully* mistaken.

Oh, she'd understood the concept well enough. But the moment-to-moment reality was something else entirely. Crushing, unrelenting, and infuriating, it weighed upon the people of Otriye like the yoke of an ox. Yet it was not the shoulders of beasts that bore the load, but feeble men, timid women, and malnourished children. Nothing in all the books she'd read had prepared her for such a wretched experience.

She'd spoken to a few peasants at some of the farmsteads along the way, but this was the first village they had visited. As she rode down the single dirt lane with Masha, Andre, and Tatiana, she was horrified not only by the filth, but the stench that permeated the place.

"What...is that smell?" It reached her even through the white porcelain mask that covered the upper half of her face.

Tatiana cocked her head and clacked her teeth together. "It is the scent of death, Mistress Kukla. The invisible touch of Lady Marzanna."

"Mistress." Masha pointed toward what appeared to be the largest home in the town. It was connected to a mill along the bank of the Sestra, but the paddles of the waterwheel appeared to have broken off and it no longer moved. A boy sat on the stoop of the house, slowly twisting fibers into a thin rope. He was grimy and unkempt, and there was a dull, listless look in his eyes.

Galina reined in her horse and the others followed suit.

"Masha, go ask that boy what's happened here," she said.

"Yes, Mistress."

Masha nudged her horse over to the house and spoke to the boy. The boy looked back at her with his dull expression and shrugged, then went back to his work. Masha looked over at Galina with large, sorrowful eyes now brimming with tears. It seemed she was so heartbroken by the boy's wretched state she could not force herself to press him further.

Galina sighed. She'd never particularly cared for children of any sort, much less dirty uneducated ones, but she knew that if she planned to unite the people of Izmoroz, she would have to acclimate to them eventually. It might as well be now.

She rode over to Masha and the boy, and the Rangers followed her.

"What are you doing there, boy?" she asked.

He didn't look up at her as he spoke. "Making a line."

"For what purpose?"

He looked up at her then, shrugged, and went back to his work.

Galina turned to Masha and the two exchanged a helpless look.

"Ah, *mal'chik*!" Andre climbed from his horse and hunkered down beside the boy. "You're making a line for fishing."

The boy stared at him for a moment. "*Strannik*," he whispered.

Andre nodded, his beady black eyes blinking calmly.

The boy looked down at the line in his hands. "I don't know why I'm making it. There are no fish."

"No fish?" asked Andre.

"The river's been poisoned."

Andre looked up at Galina. "Do you know of this?"

Galina shook her head. "Perhaps it's a result of the Uaine and their undead living beside the river for the last few months. Or I suppose it could even be some consequence from Sebastian's magic during the battle."

The boy suddenly stared at Galina, and his eyes were no longer dull but filled with so many conflicting emotions, she could not hope to sort them out.

"You know Captain Sebastian?"

"I knew him once," she said.

"Is he your friend?"

"No," she told him.

"Good," said the boy. "He's a bad man."

"He has done bad things," said Galina. "But how do you know him?"

The boy looked away again. "He took my father away. And he...
killed so many people here. Burned them alive. And..." He looked
back at Galina but now his eyes welled up with tears. "And it was all
my fault."

Then the boy suddenly broke into sobs. Ugly, loud, heaving sobs
that were so violent it appeared he might throw up.

When Galina and her father had argued, she had been frustrated
with him for dismissing the suffering of Izmoroz in favor of some
flawed and impractical political ideal. It had been disappointing to see
the man she'd looked up to for so long speak so callously. Yet even
then, the suffering of peasants had been more of a concept for her than
a visceral reality. Her arguments to revive Les had been more eco-
nomic and strategic in nature.

Now, as she looked down at the blubbering, weeping child, she
saw him not as a concept or commodity, but as a person. Peasants
were not hopeless, degenerate cretins in need of domination. They
were innocent, helpless victims of the arrogance and incompetence
of the rich and powerful. They were not to be feared and loathed,
but embraced as inspiration for this frustration—no, this *fury* that she
found now dwelled within her bosom. They were stark evidence of a
broken society.

Galina slid down from her horse and laid her slim hand upon his
dirt-crusted cheek. He calmed somewhat at her touch.

"What is your name, child?"

"L-Luka," he said.

"And why do you blame yourself for the wizard's crimes, Luka?"

"Because I told him where everybody was hiding. I—I didn't
know. I thought it was bandits, but it was just regular people. But I
didn't know that then!"

Galina nodded. Many of the rebels that Sebastian had burned alive in that cave had probably been townspeople. Between the poisoned river and the decimated population, no wonder Otriye was in such a terrible state.

"I could assure you that it wasn't truly your fault, but I doubt that would lessen your suffering," she told him. "Instead I ask, would you like to help me make things right?"

He gave her a dubious look, like he wanted to believe her but couldn't quite let himself. "Can you do that?"

Rather than answer him directly, she turned to Andre and Tatiana. "It's time to go hunting," she told them.

Their eyes widened with eagerness. "Yes, Mistress."

"Bring back as much food as you can by sunset."

Without another word, they wheeled their horses around and took off at a gallop. Galina watched them ride away, then turned back to Luka.

"Gather the surviving townspeople here by sundown, and I will show you the bare minimum of what I can do."

Boots and stomachs, she thought.

37

A life of leisure, it turned out, did not suit Sonya well. Perhaps she had enjoyed it the first few days. In fact, it might have even been somewhat restorative. She'd slept in late, enjoyed long breakfasts with Jorge and his family, explored the sprawling Cassa Estío, and listened to the musicians that came nightly to play for the family in the small auditorium that seemed to have been constructed expressly for that purpose.

But after those first few days, she began to feel restless. She was supposed to be getting stronger without asking the Lady for another boon so that she could return to Izmoroz and challenge Mordha again. That meant honing her fighting ability more sharply than ever. Yet how was she supposed to do that? It wasn't like she could just go out and find some bandits to kill. Jorge had made it clear that as a guest of the Elhuyar, her behavior reflected on them, and there was that whole balance between the Great Families thing. She didn't want to complain. It would have been insulting not to show gratitude toward the family that had taken her in. So she tried her best to adapt and behave.

But without anything else to focus on, her anxiety increased. Past regrets returned over and over again. Why had she trusted the Uaine so completely? How had she convinced herself that, unlike every other Ranger who ever lived, the people of Izmoroz loved rather than feared her? And perhaps because she was now surrounded by Jorge's family, she thought constantly of her own. How could she have failed her brother so badly? Was he okay? Alive, at least? What about her mother? What was Irina Turgenev doing? Where was she? Was she safe? Happy? And why was Sonya such a terrible sister and daughter that she was only now wondering these things? These thoughts raced through her mind, making her restive and ill-humored.

To quiet her troubled mind in the late hours of the day once everyone else had retired to their rooms, Sonya began to raid the prodigious liquor cabinets of the Elhuyar household. Nearly every night she drank herself into unconsciousness as quickly as possible with an unhealthy desperation. And invariably she would suffer for it the next morning.

"Sonya." Jorge's expression was uncharacteristically firm as they sat around the table for breakfast one morning in the Elhuyars' sun-drenched dining room. "You need to do something."

"Um." She stared with bleary eyes at the large cup of coffee and milk that Raízians favored with their breakfast. She wondered if her stomach would even accept such a thing. "Like what?"

"I don't know. Go into town and do some shopping or something." She gave him a skeptical look. "Shopping? Me?"

"Leave her alone, Jorge," said his sister. Maria was always cheerful, but there was a careful watchfulness in her eyes, like a cat, that suggested she was not as easygoing as she presented herself. Unlike Raízian men, young women seemed to wear their long dark hair loose and full. "Sonya's been through so much, the poor dear. She doesn't have to do anything she doesn't want to do."

"*I* know far better than *you* what she's been through, Maria," Jorge replied testily. Sonya had noticed that his habitual patience with other people did not extend to his own siblings. "Just as I know far better what she needs."

Maria rolled her eyes, then gave Sonya a warm smile. "Men, right? They think they know so much, but what do they really know? Nothing!"

"Uh-huh," Sonya said, wishing they would all stop talking so loudly.

"See, this is exactly what I'm saying," declared Jorge with a broad sweep of his hand. Sonya had also noticed that Jorge acted far less meek now that he was home among his own family. "Sonya, you're in a rut. You need to get out there and do something!"

"I agree with that," said Hugo, Jorge's older brother, as he strode into the room carefully fixing the silk cravat around his neck. "A person without work is not a person."

Hugo looked a lot like an older version of Jorge, but was nearly the opposite in temperament. His face always had a fastidious, almost fussy set to it, as if he vaguely disapproved of most of what he saw but was too polite to bring it up. He was rarely still, and the only family member who did not enjoy either the long breakfasts or the evening concerts. Instead, he seemed utterly dedicated to the various interests of the Elhuyar family, whatever they were.

"Life isn't just about *work*, Hugo," Maria told him. "Isn't that right, Papa?"

"Hmm," said Señor Arturo Elhuyar, who sat at the head of the table. The patriarch of the family remained something of a mystery to Sonya. He was often present, at breakfast, in the courtyard, at the concerts, but rarely contributed anything. He seemed mostly content to sort through ever-present stacks of parchment, occasionally marking things with a quill or making notes in a small, leather-bound ledger. Beyond an initial "You are welcome here, Sonya," he had not spoken to her once, or even seemed to notice that she was in the room.

"You see?" Maria smiled triumphantly at Hugo. "Papa agrees."

Sonya wasn't sure how Maria had interpreted her father's grunt as agreement, but Hugo didn't contest it.

"Yes, I know life isn't *only* about work." Hugo took a small pastry from the plate without sitting down. "I'm merely saying that it is a necessary component of life, like food, water, and air. It is quite simple. If you don't have work, you don't have meaning. If you don't have meaning, you will despair."

"Oh, listen to the family philosopher here." Maria seemed to be addressing the entire table now, her arms outstretched. "What other deep wisdom do you have to impart, Señor *Fyilósso*?"

He glared at her while he slowly chewed. "What kind of word is *fyilósso*?"

"It's a *Raízian* word, which you would know if you truly cared about your people."

"Sorry if I'm not as political as *some* people." Still standing, Hugo poured coffee from a carafe into a ceramic mug, then mixed in milk from a small pitcher. "But I don't have time to waste on such frivolity. I have our family to think about. Isn't that right, Papa?"

"Hmm," said Arturo, still not looking up from his parchment.

"See?" Hugo gave Maria a smug look, once again somehow able to perceive assent where Sonya saw none.

"Children, children, no arguing at the table."

Magdalena swept grandly into the room and seated herself at the foot of the table opposite Arturo.

"We are not children, Mama," Maria said frostily. "Nor are we arguing. We are discussing weighty matters of our time. *Your* generation may have given up on our people, but ours has not."

"Ach, it's too early for such talk." Magdalena waved her hand dismissively.

"Mama," said Jorge. "Don't you think it's unhealthy for Sonya to be cooped up so long? She should *do* something. Perhaps go into town."

"Yes, that's a good idea," said Magdalena. "Maria, after breakfast you will take Sonya shopping. I'm tired of seeing her walk around in those rags."

"But, Mama!" objected Maria. "I was going to—"

"Earn money for the food and drink you consume in this house?" interrupted Magdalena.

"No, but—"

"Then you were going to help your brother manage our properties?"

"Well, no—"

"Then this is what you will do today to contribute to the family that you love and cherish so much." Magdalena smiled beatifically, as if she had just given her daughter a generous gift.

Maria looked like she was about to retort, but then sighed and bowed her head. "Yes, Mama."

38

Sonya and Maria walked to the market accompanied by two of the Elhuyars' private guard. Sonya had to admit that the fresh air and sunshine were helping her shake off some of her hangover, but she wasn't particularly looking forward to the shopping. She'd never had an interest in clothes or jewelry, much to her mother's frustration. But it seemed that once Maria accepted her fate as Sonya's shopping guide, she had decided to embrace the role fully, and it was clear she took great pleasure in such things. So Sonya did her best to participate.

"How about a dress?" Maria asked as they made their way through the bustling, musical marketplace with the two guards trailing respectfully behind. "I don't mind wearing trousers now and then, but in this weather, dresses are much more comfortable."

"I haven't worn a dress since I was six," Sonya told her.

"Are you joking?" Maria looked shocked. "Why not?"

"Because you can't hunt in a dress."

"Well, you're not hunting now, are you?"

Sonya sighed. "I guess not."

Maria seemed to perceive that it was a delicate subject and quickly changed tacks. "But trousers are wonderful, too! I know a place that makes them very light and airy. Perfect for Raízian spring weather. You'll love them."

"Okay." Was this what Sonya's new life in Colmo would be? Leisurely breakfasts, fretting about clothes, attending concerts? She didn't want to disparage other people's lifestyles, but she really didn't know how much longer she could take it.

Maria led them through the market, dodging a group of dancers modeling the latest imperial half capes, a singer praising the fine seasoning of his cured hams, and a painter who had created a canvas that expressed the experience of drinking his wines so evocatively, Sonya felt a moment of intoxication when she looked at it. All of it seemed to pull at her, worming its way into her anxious heart.

"Is there magic in all of it?" she asked Maria.

"In what?" Maria's eyes scanned the market, looking for a particular merchant.

"The dancing, the singing, the painting? All of it?"

"A little," said Maria indifferently. "They aren't Viajero, so it's not going to compel you to buy what they're selling. But we are a passionate people, and magic dwells within even the simplest artistic expression."

"I didn't know that." Sonya hadn't had a great deal of exposure to the arts beyond the simple folk songs of the Izmorozian peasantry and the wild dances of the Uaine. Her brother had been more interested in such things. Especially poetry. "Is there magic in poems as well?"

"Of course there is." Maria looked incredulous, as if it was a bizarre question. "Can you not feel it?"

Sonya shook her head.

Maria frowned sympathetically. "Maybe you just haven't been exposed to *good* poetry. I'll have Mama invite Pedro Molina to present one of his plays for us. Every line he writes is a poem that will press upon your very soul. You'll see."

Sonya nodded politely, though she doubted it would feel that way to her. Perhaps some people were predisposed toward that sort of thing, but she was not one of them.

"Now," Maria said, "let's find some clothes that will please both you and Mama."

Sonya allowed Maria to lead her over to a stall where a number of silky, semitransparent articles of clothing hung. It all looked so delicate that even a bramble bush would tear it to shreds, and the colors were so bright that one might as well be jumping up and down, shouting to be seen by everyone around them.

Still, she bore Maria's fussing ministrations, dutifully lifting her arms out so that Maria could see how a particular blouse looked, or holding a pair of silken trousers at her waist so that Maria could stand back and examine the effect.

"Well?" asked Maria. "What do you think?"

"Pick whatever you like," said Sonya. "It doesn't matter to me."

This seemed to displease Maria a great deal. "Come now, Sonya. You need to take more care with your appearance."

"Why?" asked Sonya.

"Why? Well…" Maria considered this a moment. "Your clothes should be an expression of you. Of who you are!"

"Who I am?" If only she knew. A Ranger out of Izmoroz who doubted even her own goddess. A hunter who could not hunt. A sister and daughter who didn't even know where her family was.

"Don't overthink it, Sonya. Just—"

"Shh!"

Maria looked stunned but before she could retort, Sonya closed her eyes and held up her hand.

"Do you hear that?"

"Hear what?" asked Maria.

It was the sound of a crying child.

"This way."

Sonya moved with a swiftness and surety that she had not exhibited or felt in a while. It was such an abrupt change that Maria and the family guards stared in surprise for a few moments before hurrying after her.

As Sonya wove through the crowds, she continued to hear the keening, terrified sobs of a little girl in fear for her life. The sound cut through all the music and bustle of the market like a hot blade through butter. Sonya's pulse quickened, and a terrible eagerness welled up within her. A hunger. Whoever had frightened that child so badly would regret it.

"Sonya, wait! It's not safe to leave the market!" called Maria, falling farther behind because she was hampered by her dress and impractical shoes.

Sonya only increased her pace as she broke free from the crowds and followed the child's sobs out of the market and into the twisting alleyways that lay beyond.

The alleys were so narrow that little sunlight reached them, but the dim lighting made no difference to Sonya's keen golden eyes. She had not brought her knife, so she snatched up a sliver of jagged, broken pottery that lay on the ground as she continued down the alley.

She turned a corner and at last reached the source of the sound. A small Raízian girl of perhaps four or five was being held roughly by an imperial soldier. Three more soldiers stood nearby, grinning. An older Raízian man sat on the ground, his hands clasped in supplication as he begged them to release his granddaughter.

"Sure." The soldier gripped the little girl's arm so hard it made her cry even louder. "Just as soon as you pay up."

Sonya smiled with an open mouth that revealed her sharp, predator teeth. A little saliva leaked down onto her chin.

"Such a present," she said in a throaty growl. "Is it my Name Day already?"

The four soldiers looked over at her with a start, as if they hadn't even noticed her arrival. Fat, lazy, complacent soldiers.

"Who the hell—" said the one holding the girl.

Sonya threw the sliver of pottery and it embedded in his eye. He released the girl and let out a shriek, his hands hovering near his face as if afraid to pull it out. Sonya dashed forward and kicked the protruding piece further into his eye, jamming it so far back that it reached his brain. His screech was cut short, and he dropped silently to the ground.

It took a moment for the other three to recover from the shock. They finally moved in when they saw their comrade die, but even then, Sonya could smell the fear mingled with their outrage. She scooped up the dead soldier's sword and held it loosely in one hand, still grinning. A proper swordsman like her father might have gone for the torso or the head, but Sonya was not a swordsman. Instead she went for wrists and ankles, dodging and weaving around their slow, clumsy swings.

She could already feel the beast *Lisitsa* within rising like the tide. But rather than let it engulf her like she had on the streets of Gogoleth, she rode it as the *Endless Summer* rode the sea. She allowed her feral instincts to lift her up, to sharpen her movements and enhance her strength, without letting it take over completely. It was a balancing act, to be sure, but for the first time in a long time, Sonya felt as though she actually had some equilibrium.

One soldier quickly lost the fingers of his sword hand, cut off at the top knuckle. As he howled with pain, Sonya ducked and rolled under the second soldier's overly wide stance, slicing his unarmored inner thighs as she went—not deeply, but enough to make it difficult to move. She dodged to the side, avoiding the third soldier's thrust, then stepped in past his guard and stabbed her sword through the narrow opening between his chest plate and armpit to pierce his lung.

Sonya yanked the sword out of that soldier and brought the blade around in time to deflect a clumsy overhand strike from the fingerless soldier, who had switched to his off hand and was clearly not as good with it. Sonya pivoted on one foot, flipping the short sword into a reverse grip as she came around, then thrust it into the soldier's neck.

She spun back the opposite way, switching the grip to a forward position again and slicing open the neck of the remaining soldier who had thought he'd been sneaking up on her.

Sonya watched him clutch at his gushing neck and topple over. Then she tossed the blood-drenched sword on top of his body and looked over at Maria.

Jorge's sister had arrived with the family guards just in time to witness the carnage.

"You asked who I am?" Sonya said quietly. "*This* is who I am."

She turned to the quaking little girl, who now clung to her grandfather, staring up at Sonya with wide, terrified eyes.

"You're safe now."

The girl did not look like she felt safe. Sonya realized that every child she had rescued over the years had probably also been terrified.

That knowledge hurt, but what else could she do? Perhaps it was time to accept that a servant of the Goddess of Death could protect, but never truly give comfort.

"What is the meaning of this?" boomed a familiar male voice.

Sonya looked toward the other end of the alley and saw a group of Anxeles Escuros striding toward them. They were led by Miguel, the man who had first escorted her and Jorge to Cassa Estío. His hand was at his sword as though he were about to draw it, but then he saw Maria and came to a stop, his eyes wide.

"Señorita Elhuyar?"

"Hello, Miguel," she said.

Then he looked more closely at Sonya. "You were with the young señor a few weeks ago."

Sonya nodded.

He was silent for a moment as he stared at the dead soldiers and the girl with her grandfather.

In a much less challenging tone, he asked, "What happened here?"

"Miguel, I promise you she was only protecting the girl," said Maria.

Miguel turned back to Sonya, his eyebrows raised in surprise. "*You* did this?"

Again, she nodded.

"By yourself?"

"Hardly an accomplishment," Sonya said. "They were weak, even by imperial military standards."

He gazed at her a moment longer, then turned to Maria. "Accounting for this will be . . . difficult, Señorita."

Her look of worry deepened. "Is there anything you can do?"

His brow furrowed for a moment. "I think we can manage something."

"Whatever it costs," Maria said.

"Wait, what are you talking about?" asked Sonya.

"You just killed four imperial soldiers," Miguel said. "We will have to cover this up somehow. It would be much easier if you were a guild member rather than a guest of one of the Great Families, but—"

"What if I become a guild member, then?"

That brought Miguel up short. "You? A member of Anxeles Escuros?"

She had said it offhandedly, but as the idea took hold she realized that joining the most respected mercenary guild in Colmo might be her best bet at getting stronger.

"You can see for yourself that I'm good in a fight."

"But you're not even Raízian."

"Oh, is there a rule against that?"

He considered a moment. "I suppose not. But you would have to get permission from our guild master. And even then, some might challenge you."

"That's okay, I'm used to having to prove myself. It's not easy being both tiny and deadly, you know."

"Sonya, are you sure about this?" asked Maria. "You know you can stay with my family as long as you like."

"I appreciate the sanctuary that you and your family have given me, Maria. Truly I do. But I don't think I'm suited for life at Cassa Estío. Jorge was right, as usual. I need to be *doing* something. To be a part of something. Maybe this is it, maybe it's not. But I won't know until I try."

Maria's eyebrows knitted in concern. "I don't think joining a mercenary guild is what my brother had in mind when he said you should do something."

Sonya laughed. "Oh, I know. But he won't be surprised I did."

217

39

Once Sonya had said goodbye to Maria, she followed Miguel and his fellow Anxeles Escuros through the streets of Colmo beneath the golden afternoon sun.

The area they walked through was not as clean or luxurious as where the Elhuyars lived, but it didn't seem like a slum, either. The beige stucco buildings were well cared for, and covered in the large, colorful murals so common in Colmo. The rich, multilayered sound of a Raízian guitar drifted through the air as they walked.

Sonya noticed that when they weren't escorting a client, the Anxeles Escuros walked quietly rather than marching in strict formation, confirming her suspicion that the task had been as much show as anything else. She also noticed that though they still looked quite formidable in their black leather armor and curved swords, people they passed did not seem frightened of them, or even particularly excited by their presence. Instead they often waved casually, or called out a cheerful hello, to which Miguel responded with a solemn raised hand and a slow nod.

"People don't seem very intimidated by you," she said to Miguel.

"Why would they be?" he asked. "We step in to keep the peace now and then, but for the most part, we are merely skilled men and women who work for the big families, just like them. We are the same."

"They could never fight like you," said Sonya.

"And I could never throw a pot, or smith a blade, or tan a hide like them. What is so great about fighting? Can it make a bowl to drink from, a hammer to build with, or a coat to wear? Can it feed a child, make a home, or keep someone warm?"

Sonya gazed into Miguel's large brown eyes.

"No," she said. "It can't."

"It is at times a necessary skill, which is good for those of us who earn a living from it. But it is not better than any other skill."

There was, she realized, an arrogance in how she viewed herself in relation to everyone around her. Maybe because she'd had to compete with her exceptionally powerful brother for attention throughout her childhood, she'd grown up thinking that strength and worth were the same thing. It was no wonder, then, that when she'd finally been out-matched in strength by Mordha, her sense of worth began to crumble. It had been built on a faulty foundation.

Sonya and the Anxeles Escuros continued to a large, two-story building that took up an entire block. There were few windows on the main floor, but the second-story structure had a number of decks that cut into it. The decks were covered by canvas awnings on top, and dense black netting on the sides, so it was difficult for even Sonya to see inside. She could just make out black-clad figures sitting on benches or at tables drinking beverages. The guild lounge, perhaps?

An Anxeles Escuros stood guarding the front entrance. Miguel held up his hand as they approached.

"Good afternoon, brother. Darkness knows light."

"And light knows dark," replied the guard. Then he looked at Sonya. "Who is this you bring into our home, Miguel?"

"She wishes to speak with the Xefe about becoming one of us," said Miguel.

The guard's eyes widened. "*This* one? Are you joking?"

"Here we go...," Sonya muttered. She thought she'd at least be able to get through the door before they started to object.

"I'm not joking," Miguel said calmly.

The guard turned to Sonya, his face becoming set as he spoke in a loud, formal tone. "What is your name?"

"My name is Sonya Turgenev Portinari." She tried to keep the irritation out of her voice and mostly succeeded.

"And you seek to join Anxeles Escuros?"

"I do."

"Then I, Eduardo Magallón of the Anxeles Escuros, challenge you!"

The low murmur of conversation in the covered balconies above abruptly ceased.

Miguel gave Sonya an apologetic smile. "It is his right."

"It's fine," said Sonya. "I'll try not to damage him permanently."

Miguel nodded, then he and the rest of his men stepped aside. Sonya could hear loud whispers above as people began to gather along the balcony railing behind the black netting. Apparently they had an audience.

"Are you sure you want to do this in public?" she asked Eduardo.

"It would not be an official challenge otherwise."

"I see." The old Sonya might have made some boast, telling him he was about to be embarrassed in front of his fellow guild members. But the new Sonya, full of questions and doubt, merely squared her stance and prepared to fight.

She was about to ask Miguel if she could borrow his sword, but then Eduardo unbelted his own sword and placed it on the ground. Then he stood before her, looming more than a foot taller, his fists practically double the size of hers and rough with scars and calluses. He wasn't nearly as big as Mordha, of course, but she was done making cocky assumptions about others.

So she decided to take a defensive approach at first to gauge his abilities. He came at her swiftly, his fists flickering forward and back in a blink, rarely leaving himself open for more than a moment. And unlike a lot of male fighters she'd encountered elsewhere, he did not forget that his feet could be used as weapons as well. In fact, for such a large man who could easily rely merely on brute force, his movements were impressively precise. She threw out a few experimental blows, and while he wasn't quite as nimble as her, he was able to block her probing attacks quite easily. As they shuffled back and forth before the entrance to the guild, neither landing a substantial blow, she decided that he was actually quite good. She was glad about that, since she had no interest in joining a group of unskilled mercenaries.

Yet in the end, he was still human, while she, for better and for worse, had left much of that behind.

When she struck in earnest, he didn't even see it coming. Her palm slammed into his nose and his head snapped back, sending an arc of blood into the air. Then, while his balance was off, she swept his legs and he went down. As he fell back, she lunged over him, gripped his head with both hands, and shoved it straight down toward the brick street. It would strike with enough force to knock him out, perhaps even break his skull. She felt the exultant surge of *Lisitsa* claiming her prey.

But there was still some humanity in Sonya, and she was here to make allies, not enemies. So at the last moment, she planted her feet and stopped his head an inch from the street.

They were motionless for a moment, him lying on the ground, her holding his head. He stared up at her, blood flowing from his nose. Then he let out a single laugh.

"You may proceed," he said.

As Sonya helped Eduardo to his feet, a chorus of cheers rose from the balconies. She looked up at the outline of figures clapping, laughing, and whooping behind the netting, then turned to Miguel with a questioning look.

"The old retired ones still come to drink here, but they don't get to see much action anymore," he said with a hint of embarrassment. "It's possible you may be the highlight of their week."

Not knowing what else to do, she waved up at them, which renewed their cheers.

"Shall we go inside?" asked Miguel. "I'd say you've earned your meeting with the Xefe."

The entrance led to a long hallway, with several passages breaking off to the right and left. The other three guards said their goodbyes to Miguel, wished Sonya luck, then walked down one of the side passageways. Miguel and Sonya continued down the main hallway until it terminated at a wooden door that looked like any other, except for the black wings painted on it, and the word XEFE.

"What does it mean?" asked Sonya as Miguel knocked on the door.

"It's the Raízian word for *chief* or *boss*," he replied.

"I thought Raízians mostly spoke the imperial tongue."

"We do. But there is no law directly forbidding the use of our ancestral language, and some words have lingered too long in our tradition to ever be forgotten. Besides, these days people find it comforting."

Sonya wanted to ask him what it was about these days that made people seek that comfort, but then the door opened, and a tall Raízian man with a thick, carefully braided gray beard was gazing down on her. There was a mixture of surprise and wonder in his eyes.

"Is this a fabled Ranger of Marzanna you have brought me, Miguel?" he asked in a rich baritone.

Miguel looked at her. "Are you?"

"I . . . was." Sonya felt a mixture of surprise and relief that this Xefe instantly recognized who and what she was. If nothing else, she didn't have to explain everything. "But I have fulfilled my vow to the Lady Marzanna, and I am no longer in Izmoroz, so . . . I don't know what I am now."

"An unaffiliated Ranger? Very interesting," said the man. "Come in and let us talk."

He gestured with one hairy hand, then turned and stumped back into his room, displaying a noticeable limp. The room was cramped, with far too much furniture for such a small space. Even so, it was difficult for Sonya to find a place to sit, because the majority of the furniture was covered in precarious stacks of parchment, bedraggled books, and half-rolled scrolls.

The man picked up a glass decanter filled with wine and poured a little into three glasses.

He held one out to Sonya. "In my opinion, wine is one of the few good things the empire has given us."

She laughed and accepted the glass. "I agree."

"I'm called Javier Arzak, or Xefe if you prefer. What about you?"

"My name is Sonya Turgenev Portinari. I am called *Strannik* by the people of Izmoroz, and *Lisitsa* by the Lady Marzanna and my fellow Rangers."

"Ah, a fox, is it?" he asked.

Her eyes widened. "You know Old Izmorozian?"

He chuckled. "I am old enough to remember a time when it was merely called Izmorozian."

"I see." She had thought him around the same age as her parents, but apparently he was even older.

Javier continued to look at her with great interest as he took a sip of his own drink. "So, little fox, why are you in Colmo?"

"I'm here because my friend asked me to come," she said.

Javier looked questioningly at Miguel, who sat nearby nursing his own drink.

"Jorge Elhuyar," he told Javier.

Javier nodded. "Impressive friends, little fox. So what do you plan to do now that you are here?"

"Honestly, I'm hoping you'll give me a job. Cassa Estío is nice, but I realized I can't just sit around, or I'll go crazy. I need to get stronger so I can take Izmoroz back from the people who have it."

"I thought Izmoroz was just liberated from the empire."

"Yeah, and now it's occupied by the people who helped liberate it."

"Ah." Javier nodded. "One must always be cautious about forming alliances." He held up his glass and stared at the ruby liquid for a moment. "With that in mind, the Rangers of Marzanna are of course renowned for their fighting prowess. The most powerful ones are *also* known for succumbing to a . . . savagery that cannot always distinguish friend from foe on the battlefield."

"Oh." He really knew a lot about Rangers. Sonya wondered if he might have encountered some in the past. "Yes, that can be true."

"So my question, little fox, is how far along are you in your goddess's process to transform you into a pure killing machine?"

Sonya stared at him, outrage slowly building inside. But what if he was right? According to Anatoly, that might indeed be the Lady's whole purpose for the Rangers. She was, after all, the Goddess of Death, and they were her servants—or tools. Thinking of Anatoly, who had likely died by then, grieved by none, brought a sudden pang of sadness to her heart, and her outrage deflated beneath its weight.

"There was a moment back in Gogoleth," she said quietly, "right after my most recent...*change*, where I blacked out for a moment and the beast took hold. But I have it under control now."

"And do I only have your word on that?"

"No, Xefe," said Miguel. "Eduardo challenged her at the door. She could have easily dashed his head against the street, but repaid his antagonism with only a bloodied nose."

Javier gazed carefully at him for a moment, tugging on his braided beard. "So you vouch for her, then?"

Miguel considered a moment. "I do."

"I see." Javier took a sip of his wine. "What brought her to your attention in the first place?"

"She was out shopping with Señorita Elhuyar and stopped to defend a little girl from imperial soldiers."

Javier let out a low chuckle. "That explains your fondness for her then. A fellow champion of the weak. I'm sure her proximity to the Elhuyars didn't hurt, either. What happened to the soldiers?"

"She killed them," said Miguel.

"Ah," said Javier.

"Sorry," said Sonya. "I didn't realize it would be such a big deal."

Javier gave her a stern look. "Killing imperial soldiers on what is technically imperial soil is indeed a big deal and will require a great deal of work on my part to smooth over. If I were to allow you into the guild, you would have to restrain your anti-imperial impulses. At least for the time being."

She perked up. "For the time being?"

He smiled and drained his glass. "That is a conversation for another time. Meanwhile, as long as you promise not to go around killing imperial soldiers on a whim, I believe I can offer you some work."

"Really?" She hesitated. "But I don't think I could march around in perfect formation."

"I don't think you could, either," he agreed. "But that is not all Anxeles Escuros do. Some jobs require more discretion, and more danger. Some require people who do not flinch from death."

"As you know, Xefe," she said, "Death is my mistress."

He nodded. "Then I think we have a place for you here, little fox."

40

In the past, Jorge had not always loved it when his mother bullied his friends into doing what she thought best. But in Sonya's case, he was glad. He really hoped that getting out of the house would help her adapt better to her new environment, and give the family liquor cabinet time to restock as well.

Yet now Jorge was having his own problem finding purpose. He had spent years of his life focused on the venerable art of apothecary, which most Raízians considered dull, dry, and dispassionate. He'd resented such judgment, and to some extent, that was what had led him to apply at the College of Apothecary in Gogoleth. He'd wanted to study somewhere that the art of potion-making was respected. And while he may not have loved living in Izmoroz, he had always been grateful for its reverence of such quiet, patient work.

Except he was astonished and somewhat alarmed to find he couldn't muster up that same old focus and inspiration now that he was home.

"I don't understand it, Hugo," he told his brother as he stared down at Master Velkhov's ingenious mobile lab, which he hadn't touched once since his return to Colmo. "It used to be almost like a compulsion, you know?"

"I recall," said Hugo, not looking up from a thick, leather-bound ledger. "You were obsessed. When you weren't mixing noxious concoctions, you were blabbering on about them endlessly. It was very annoying."

"So how could I go from being obsessed to completely disinterested?" Jorge slumped into a plush, leather chair near his brother's desk and sighed heavily.

Hugo stopped writing a moment and looked over at Jorge with his fastidious gaze.

"Because, little brother, an obsession is not the same thing as a passion. Obsessions tend to burn hot, then sputter out."

With that, Hugo went back to his work.

Jorge didn't know when his fussy older brother had become so wise, and he found he didn't particularly like it. Unfortunately, what Hugo said made a lot of sense. But it left a big question in its wake. If apothecary wasn't truly his passion, then what was?

"Oh, by the way," said Hugo, still scratching away with his quill on his ledger. "I overheard Mama planning several romantic dinners for you with a choice selection of the current crop of nubile young women from the most reputable families. I thought you'd like to know."

Jorge closed his eyes and wearily rubbed them. "I'd forgotten about that part of living here."

"You don't have to *marry* one right away," said Hugo. "I was engaged to Martina for two years before we married."

"How often do you see her?" asked Jorge.

Hugo shrugged as he continued to write. "My work is here. She doesn't seem to mind."

Jorge wondered if that was a good sign for a marriage but decided to let it pass. "What about Maria? Is she engaged to anyone yet?"

Hugo laughed. "She spends all her time in the Viajero Quarter, talking about politics and smoking hashish."

"Maybe I should do that, too, then," said Jorge.

"Please, little brother. You are many things, but political revolutionary is not one of them."

Jorge smiled. He'd been vague with his family on why he had returned from Izmoroz prematurely, and none of them had pressed him. He was fairly certain his mother believed he'd just been homesick. He was tempted to tell his brother the real reason now, just to see the look on his face, but decided against it. His brother was not known for keeping secrets, and his mother would be furious with him for taking such risks.

Then Maria poked her head into the room.

"Jorge. There you are."

She had an odd look, her eyes a little wider than usual.

"How was your shopping trip?" he asked. "Was Sonya completely miserable the whole time?"

"Uh..." Her eyes darted to Hugo, who was still writing in his ledger. "Can I talk to you a moment, Jorge?"

"Ooh, secrets," said Hugo in a teasing voice, though he still didn't look up.

"Shut up," she told him. Then she glanced back meaningfully at Jorge. "Well?"

"Sure." Jorge stood and followed his sister out of the room and down the hall.

She pulled him into the library, which was unoccupied and lit only by a few flickering candles near the entrance. She gripped his upper arms and frowned at him.

"Jorge, who is Sonya?"

"What do you mean?" he asked carefully.

"I *mean* that I just saw her kill four imperial soldiers in the blink of an eye and I want to know what kind of person can do that."

"Ah." His chest tightened with panic. Apparently, forcing her out of the house hadn't been a good idea after all. "Did anyone see?"

"The Anxeles Escuros. She's with them now."

Even worse. "They *arrested* her?"

Maria shook her head. "No, she's trying to see if they'll let her join."

"Really?" Jorge wasn't sure that was good news, exactly, but it was better than the alternative. "I suppose it might keep her out of trouble at least..."

Maria's eyes narrowed. "Sonya said you wouldn't be surprised and you're not."

"If anything, I probably should have anticipated something like

227

this," he admitted. "She's . . . prone to violence when it comes to imperial soldiers. I wanted her to get out of her rut. I should have realized that killing some imperials would do the trick."

"She did seem to be in a better mood afterward," said Maria. "But, Jorge, she was *merciless*. A true killer."

"Please don't tell Mama."

She gave him a searching look. "Are we safe, little brother? Is our *family* safe?"

"Perfectly," Jorge assured her. "If anything, we're more safe than we've ever been. Sonya would never let anyone hurt her friends."

"Okay, fine. I guess I believe you." Then her eyes narrowed. "You still haven't answered my question, though. Who *is* she?"

"It's . . . complicated."

"Bullshit."

Jorge sighed. "Have you heard about what's been going on in Izmoroz?"

"Of course. It's all they talk about in the Viajero Quarter right now. The northerners have broken away from Aureum. They spat in the face of the empress."

"Sonya is more or less responsible for that."

"Stop."

"I'm serious. She convinced the Uaine to join us, then led the charge against the imperials herself."

"*Us?*"

Jorge winced. "Don't tell Mama that, either."

She still looked doubtful. "If what you're saying is true, why is she here? She should be a hero in her own land, not a refugee in ours."

"Like I said, it's complicated. And honestly, I'm not sure I even know all of it. As far as I can tell, the Uaine conspired with the Izmorozian nobility to turn the people against her and drive her out once they no longer needed her."

"That's awful!" But now she was smiling.

"It *was* awful," he said. "So why do you suddenly look so happy?"

"Listen." She glanced around, as though there might somehow be spies lurking in Cassa Estío's library. "My . . . *friends* have been really inspired by what happened in Izmoroz. They've been talking about making real change, right here in Raíz. And now I find out that my *baby brother* is friends with the most famous revolutionary in the world!"

"Except you hadn't even heard of her until just now," he pointed out.

"But now that I know how important she is, she *will* be famous. She *should* be! You can't imagine how eager my friends will be to meet the person who started it all. Especially since it's a *woman*!"

His eyes narrowed as he understood what she was after. "You want Sonya to help with your revolution?"

"Obviously!"

"Forget it," he said. "Just let her be. She doesn't need to take on anyone else's problems. She's done enough of that to last a lifetime. *Several* lifetimes."

"I'm sure she has," Maria said soothingly, rubbing his back like she used to when he was a little boy. "But maybe she *wants* to help. Maybe if you talk to her—"

"No." He stepped away from her lulling back rub. "First of all, she's tired and broken, and in no shape to lead any more revolutions. Second of all, even if she did come around, you have no idea what you would be unleashing on Raíz. Her abilities...what she can *do*...it's not human, and it comes at a terrible price. I won't let you or anyone else take her further down that road."

Maria regarded him for a moment, and he saw a hardness set into her expression that he'd never seen before.

"Won't *let*?" she asked quietly. "Baby brother, I think you overestimate yourself. Or else you underestimate my dedication to the cause."

41

Her name was Isobelle Cohen, and though they never talked of anything except medicine, food, and building reconstruction, Sebastian found himself stammering and blushing whenever they spoke. Perhaps it was because she was one of the few Kantesians in Kleiner who knew the imperial tongue. Or perhaps it was her eternally buoyant mood, despite the obvious hardships that surrounded them at all times.

Marcello had a different theory.

"She's eye-meltingly *delicious*," he said as they ate supper in the officers' tent.

"Don't be coarse," said Sebastian. "Not about Fräulein Cohen."

Marcello wasn't wrong, though. There was something about Isobelle that evoked a . . . *hunger* in Sebastian unlike any he'd ever known. He'd felt a strong emotional and intellectual attraction with Galina. This was much more visceral, like parts of him were waking up for the first time.

He couldn't say there was any single trait that made Isobelle so alluring. Not her bright blue eyes, or her rosy cheeks, or her curly, chestnut-colored hair that was always halfway falling out of its binding. It was not her sweet smile, or the soft white down on her upper lip. It was not her alabaster neck, or round freckled arms, or her generously endowed bosom that heaved whenever she laughed, which was often. It was not her wide hips, which swayed hypnotically as she hurried from one task to the next, or the delicate ankles that peeked out from beneath her gray dress. It was not the light tinkling soprano of her voice, or the fact that no matter what work they were doing, no matter how much they labored and sweat, she always smelled, unaccountably, of chamomile.

None of those things alone could have produced such a storm of feelings and passions within Sebastian. But all of them combined created a veritable tempest whenever he was near her.

"Honestly, Portinari," said Marcello as he bit into a piece of crunchy Kantesian bread, "I bet you looked less frightened on the battlefield than you do requesting the inventory counts on bedding from Fräulein Cohen. When she brushed that bit of dirt out of your hair this afternoon, I thought you might faint."

"Ha," Sebastian said sourly, although he'd thought much the same thing.

"So are you going to pine over her forever, or make a move?" asked Marcello.

Sebastian gave him a sharp look. "Don't be absurd. General Barone expressly forbade overly fraternizing with the Kantesians. And even if he hadn't, the stark difference in power and authority between Fräulein Cohen and myself would make any expressions of affection on her part highly questionable."

Marcello's smile turned a little crooked. "Would it really matter if her affections were authentic so long as you got to kiss those rosy lips?"

Sebastian looked away, thinking of the empty platitudes he had received from Galina Odoyevtseva in the past. "To me, it would matter a great deal."

Marcello heaved a tragic sigh. "You're too good for this world, Portinari."

"You know that's not true," said Sebastian. "I'm guilty of a great deal of wrongdoing. I'm simply a gentleman, just as my parents raised me to be."

"Well, I think it's a damn shame, seeing as how much good you could do her."

"What do you mean?"

"She's better than this squalid place deserves. You could sweep her off her feet, take her back to Magna Alto, and set her up as the fine lady she so clearly deserves to be."

Sebastian had to admit, at least to himself, that the idea appealed greatly. But it still seemed... *presumptuous*.

"Regardless," he said aloud, "you're far too unkind to describe Kleiner as *squalid*. After all, it was our soldiers who brought it low in the first place, and it is our daily efforts now that are trying to not only restore but improve upon the original."

Marcello shrugged. "If you say so."

"Gentlemen, may I join you?"

Sebastian looked up to see General Barone smiling down at them.

"Of course, sir!"

Sebastian quickly got to his feet. Marcello did so as well, although more slowly. It had only been a few weeks, but apparently the honor of dining with the general had already begun to pall on him.

"My thanks," said Barone as he sat.

They were soon joined by Colonel Totti, Captain Branca of the engineering corps, Captain Dandolo of the apothecary guild, and Captain Reyes of the Viajero troupe. Sebastian had gotten to know these men better during the first few weeks of reconstruction, and found it fascinating how distinct their personalities were. Even as he ate, Branca showed his meticulous care, chewing each slice of sausage diligently before swallowing. By contrast, Dandolo seemed barely to chew at all as he wolfed down his food so fast that Sebastian marveled he didn't get a stomachache. And of course Reyes cut his food with such elegance, it could have been a performance all its own.

"Well, gentlemen," said Barone as he speared a clump of sauerkraut on his fork. "What is our status?"

"Better than I would have expected, sir," said Totti around a mouthful of sausage. He was the one Sebastian knew the least, and there was something aggressively blunt and judgmental about the man that he didn't care for at all. "Most of the men are back on their feet, or nearly. Some fine potions your people make."

Dandolo shook his head merrily. "The credit belongs to Reyes as well. His Viajero singers have been handling the pain management, which allows us to focus entirely on the healing potions." He lifted his cup of pale yellow Kantesian wine to Reyes, who gracefully inclined his head in response.

"Excellent." Barone turned to Branca. "And what about the rebuilding effort?"

"Right on schedule," said Branca. "At this rate, and given the extent of the Kantesian losses reported by the colonel here, I think it will be impossible for them to mount a counteroffensive to take back the town before we've sufficiently fortified our position."

"Marvelous," said Barone.

"It's all thanks to Portinari, of course," continued Branca. "When you gave us your initial projections, I was skeptical. With all due respect, sir, it just seemed unrealistic. But now that I've seen the man in action, I have no doubt we'll meet the deadline you've set."

Barone smiled wryly. "I'm pleased that your faith in me is restored, Branca."

"Hmmm," said Reyes, in his melodic tenor.

"A concern, Captain?" asked Barone.

"I merely have some...reservations about being so reliant on this mysterious elemental magic of Captain Portinari's." He inclined his head to Sebastian. "No offense."

"Oh, don't worry about Reyes, Portinari," Dandolo cut in, his red face breaking into a teasing grin. "He's just sore that his Viajero are getting upstaged for once."

"I grant that such power is impressive." Reyes gave a graceful shrug. "But at what cost?"

Sebastian held his fellow captain's gaze, his expression firm. "I promise you, Captain Reyes, that you need not concern yourself with the cost."

42

The cost for Kleiner's swift recovery was, in fact, quite high. Every morning Sebastian saw new lines and more white hair as he gazed into his small hand mirror. During his time in Aureum, he had gone so long without using magic that he had almost forgotten its effects on his body. But these past few weeks in Kante, he had been pushing himself to his limits on a daily basis, and it showed.

Or perhaps he was overly concerned. After all, he hadn't told anyone in the battalion about the cost of his magic, not even Marcello, and no one had remarked upon his changing appearance. It could be that since he was looking for it, the changes he saw seemed more pronounced than they really were.

"Relax, Portinari." Marcello slapped his back as he hurried past. "You can put down the mirror. You're still pretty."

See? Sebastian's unease was surely the product of an anxious mind. Lots of men had graying temples at seventeen, didn't they?

So he began another day of work. Currently he was assisting the bricklayers, so he walked down to the stream that lay west of the town. The rest of the men were already hard at work, digging up the dense clay from the riverbank, removing stones and other debris, then shaping it into rectangles. They laid out the rectangles on a large stone slab, and it was Sebastian's job to cook them into bricks. Since he could heat them from the inside, he was able to do it much more quickly than a traditional oven.

Baking bricks was not particularly glamorous work, but Sebastian found it satisfying. At the end of each day, he could look at the large stack of his handiwork and see progress that was easily measured and indisputable. That was a nice change to the work he had done in Izmoroz, when it had been difficult to judge on any given day if he'd really accomplished anything at all.

Granted, it was not challenging work, either. After the first hour or so of the day, he hardly even needed to think about it. But over time, the cumulative effort did take its toll on his body, and in the afternoon, he would have to take breaks now and then so that he didn't exhaust himself prematurely. Sometimes he would sit and talk to the other workers. Other times he would simply gaze out at the vast rolling fields of Kante, greener than Izmoroz, yet colder and wetter than Aureum. The clouds overhead were always heavy and gray, yet there were usually hard shafts of sunlight breaking through, creating such a stunning contrast, he sometimes wished he could capture its likeness. He wondered if any of the Viajero were painters, and if they would mind doing it for him. Perhaps he would ask Captain Reyes.

He also found, perhaps unsurprisingly, that heating clay with magic was thirsty work. Thankfully, there was a clear, refreshing stream only a few paces away, so he had no problem addressing that issue as often as necessary. It was on one of those water breaks that he was fortunate enough to run into Fräulein Cohen, who had pulled a small cart of ceramic jugs down to the bank so that she might bring back water for the injured and their apothecaries.

"Good afternoon, Fräulein Cohen." He crouched by the stream and splashed cold water on his face, hoping it might brighten up his no doubt weary expression.

"Good afternoon, Captain Portinari. So good to see you." She smiled at him in a way that made him feel quite special, although he was certain she must have that effect on everyone.

"Likewise, Fräulein." He nodded to the cart full of empty jugs. "May I help you with those?"

Her ever-present smile grew gently teasing. "Surely you have your own, more important work, Captain."

"It will keep," he assured her. "And anyway, it's nothing special. I'm only making bricks."

Her ice-blue eyes widened. "Not special? *Ach nein*, Captain. What you can do is like nothing I have ever seen. Heating bricks with your mind? I did not know such a thing was possible."

"Well, I'm not really heating the bricks with my mind." He picked up a jug, brought it over to the stream, and knelt down so he could fill it up.

"It certainly appears that way." She also took a jug and knelt beside him on the bank.

"What I do is mostly instinctual," he said. "I just have a feeling for the element and act upon that feeling. But repeating the same task over and over has allowed me the luxury of examining it more closely. I can't say for certain, but I believe that what I'm actually doing is not heating so much as removing the cold."

"This seems just as miraculous to me," she said.

"Miraculous?" He had never heard his magic described in that way.

"A gift. Surely that is what you possess."

"Perhaps so," he agreed. "Although I wonder why it was given to me in particular."

"Why *not* you?" she asked.

"I'm certain there are others more . . . worthy."

She gave him a dubious look. "Is any man truly worthy of such power?"

He laughed. "Maybe not, Fräulein Cohen. But perhaps *you* would be."

She shook her head, and her expression grew uncharacteristically serious. "Oh no, Captain. I am more flawed than most."

"I can't believe that." Sebastian stood up, intent on placing the full jug back on the cart. "Nor can I imagine any reason why you might . . ."

He took one step toward the cart, and the world suddenly spun beneath his feet. The last thing he saw before he lost consciousness was the cold, wet riverbank rising up to meet his face. His final, oddly detached thought was: *At least it's soft. More than I deserve, really.*

43

Sebastian woke on a cot covered by a thin wool blanket. He was in a storehouse that had been converted into a place for the injured to rest and recover. The lighting was dim, with only a few flickering candles, and there were no windows, but he had been here often enough visiting the wounded that he recognized it.

"Captain, you are awake."

Sebastian looked up to see Isobelle Cohen beaming down at him.

"Fräulein Cohen, I must have been pushing myself too hard. I'm sorry to have troubled you."

When he sat up, she gently but firmly pushed him back down. "Your general has told me to make sure you have rested properly before returning you to work."

"I appreciate your concern but—"

"So *I* will decide when you are properly rested. And I would also like to make certain you have eaten something. Here."

She handed him a wooden bowl of soup. He smiled in thanks and inhaled its salty smell, remembering that Rykov used to give him salty broth to help him recover back in Izmoroz. Rykov always used to take care of him, making sure that he ate and slept, and didn't overtire himself. Once again he felt a pang of regret that perhaps he hadn't truly appreciated everything his friend had done for him until they'd been separated. He wondered what family concerns had prompted Rykov to return to Izmoroz. He hoped it was nothing dire.

Isobelle broke into his thoughts. "I have observed that men with great ability often lack good sense, Captain. I suspect you are accustomed to a wife telling you when you must eat and sleep?"

"Oh, I have no wife."

"Ah. And no children?"

"I'm a bit young to have children."

When he saw her confused look, a sudden unpleasant thought took hold of him.

"Fräulein Cohen, how old do you think I am?"

Her pale cheeks blushed and she looked away. "I wouldn't know."

"Yes, but if you had to guess. Will you please tell me?"

"I . . ." She looked as though she might refuse, but then saw the sudden urgency in his gaze and hesitated.

"Please be candid with me," he said. "I promise I won't be offended, whatever you say. But it would help answer an . . . important question lingering in my mind."

She still looked uneasy, but nodded. "I would guess you to be . . . thirty, perhaps? No more than thirty-five."

"I see . . ."

In all likelihood, she was still trying to be polite and guessing lower than she actually thought. So he must look . . . forty? Older? Had the others noticed, too, and merely been too polite to say anything? After all, what would they have said? *My, Portinari, you're looking rather old today.*

She looked even more uneasy. "Did I get it wrong?"

He let out a mirthless laugh. "Yes, but it's no fault of yours."

"May I ask your real age?"

"Seventeen," he said.

She looked stunned. "But why . . ."

It was clear she didn't know how to finish that sentence without saying anything worse, so it hung in the air.

"It's the magic," he told her. "Everything has a cost."

Her expression softened. "Ah. I see."

She gazed at him for a moment. Not with pity, exactly. Perhaps Sebastian flattered himself to think it was respect.

"I must attend to the others," she said quietly. "Please eat your soup, and I will be back to check on you in a little while."

He nodded and began to eat as he watched her move on to the next person. He noticed that she took the same amount of time and care with each of them, and all seemed to adore her, of course. One after another she spoke to them kindly, making even the guttural Kantesian language sound sweet. They all gazed up at her like she was an angel of mercy sent down from the heavens. For all Sebastian knew, perhaps she was. Another miracle, or gift from God. And perhaps they were all just as undeserving.

Then he noticed something odd. Other than himself, all the injured were Kantesian. When Isobelle came back to check on him, he mentioned this to her.

"Oh. Eh, yes." Her blue eyes darted one way, then another, almost like she was looking for an escape. "That is true, I suppose."

"But why?"

"Well." She still wouldn't look him in the eye and instead busied herself straightening his blanket and taking his empty soup bowl. "There were not enough healing potions, you see."

"A shortage?"

This was the first he was hearing of it. Was Captain Dandolo keeping such an important development from Barone? Or perhaps he had taken the general aside and told him discreetly so as not to cause a panic. But that didn't really sound like Dandolo . . .

"That is quiet concerning." Sebastian sat up in his cot. "I promise you, Fräulein Cohen, I will look into it."

She smiled gratefully and again eased him back down. "After you rest a bit more, Captain. I must insist."

He sighed and nodded. He doubted he could refuse her anything, especially when she had his own best interests at heart.

She moved on to her next patient and he was content to watch her care so kindly for them as he felt himself begin to drift toward sleep.

"Well, that's one way to get out of work, Portinari."

Sebastian looked up to see Marcello.

"Oh, hello, Oreste," he said mildly. "Come to laugh at my embarrassingly unmanly fainting spell?"

His friend grinned as he hunkered down beside him. "How could I miss the opportunity? Besides, just between you and me, I *know* it was all just a ploy to get closer to Fräulein Cohen."

Sebastian laughed. "You got me."

Marcello's expression grew serious. "But really, are you okay?"

"I just overexerted myself, that's all. I'll be fine by tomorrow."

"The general wants you to take the day off tomorrow as well."

"But I'm fine. Really."

Marcello shrugged. "You tell him, then."

"Well I can't right now. Fräulein Cohen said I'm not to leave without her consent."

"Oho!" Marcello waggled his eyebrows. "And so the seduction begins!"

"Hardly." Sebastian couldn't help the bitterness that crept into his voice. Now that he knew how old he appeared to her, he probably looked more to her like a father than a romantic prospect.

"Now, now. I'm sure if you gave it a shot—"

"Do you think I look older than when we met?" Sebastian asked.

"What?" Marcello looked confused.

"Do you think I've aged abnormally in the past couple of weeks?"

He squinted at Sebastian in the dim light. "I ... suppose? I can't say I was really paying that much attention, but I don't remember you having so much gray at your temples when we met." He considered for a moment. "Now that I think about it, I guess that's a little odd for someone in their twenties, isn't it?"

"Pardon?" asked Sebastian. "How old do you think I am?"

"Huh? Oh, I don't know. When we first met I just assumed you were probably in your midtwenties."

So it had begun even before this week. He wondered if anyone outside of those who knew him in Izmoroz were aware of his real age.

"So what if you've got some premature gray, Portinari." Marcello patted his shoulder. "I hear a lot of women find older-looking men more attractive."

Sebastian gave him a sour look, then turned back to watch Isobelle continue her rounds.

"Say," he said after a moment, "have you heard anything about a healing potion shortage?"

Marcello looked confused. "No, of course not. The general and I were just inspecting the inventory. We've got plenty."

"But Fräulein Cohen said there wasn't enough to give these people."

Understanding dawned on Marcello's face. "Oh, that. Well sure, there's not enough to give the *Kantesians*. I mean, we have to prepare for another attack at some point, don't we? No point in wasting our resources on prisoners of war when we'll need them for the soldiers."

"That's horrible!" Sebastian sat up in his cot. "These people aren't the enemy. They're noncombatants who were caught in the conflict before they could flee!"

"Come off it, Portinari. I know it's not ideal, but what can we do? Orders are orders."

"Aureumian or Kantesian, it's downright inhumane to allow these people to suffer when we have the means to help them," declared Sebastian. "It's atrocious, and I can't believe the general would sanction such a thing!"

"Quiet down, will you?" Marcello's eyes darted around. "You can't go saying things against your superior officers like that."

"But—"

Marcello leaned in close. "Listen, Portinari. Since we're friends and all, the next time we're doing an inventory count, I could see a few bottles *accidentally* falling into my pocket. I bet if you gave those to your girlfriend, she'd be very *grateful*, if you know what I mean." He winked.

Sebastian eased back down. Even if his friend's motives were...questionable, it would still help. He smiled weakly. "Thanks, Marcello."

"Don't mention it." He stood back up, then looked around nervously. "No, seriously. Don't mention it to anyone. But I promise I'll try. Anyway, I'll see you later, Portinari." He nodded toward Isobelle and grinned. "In the meantime, enjoy the *view*."

Sebastian watched Marcello go. He hadn't had too many friends in his life, and so he wasn't sure how to handle the obvious differences between him and Marcello. Should he be honest and express his opinions? Or should a friend be supportive no matter what? But the way Marcello spoke about Isobelle troubled him. As did the way he justified the cruel treatment of innocent people. It sounded chillingly familiar to his own mindset back in Izmoroz when he served under Vittorio. Did that mean Sebastian didn't have the right to judge him? Or did it mean he had an obligation to show Marcello a different perspective?

"It was nice of your friend to come check on you," said Isobelle the next time she stopped by.

"Yes, it was," he agreed. "Although I'm afraid he gave me some rather distressing news."

"Oh?" Her brow puckered in concern as she sat beside him.

"I don't really know how to put this delicately. Apparently, there is no shortage of healing potions. They only told you that because they want to save it for Aureumian soldiers."

She gazed at him a moment, her face oddly unreadable.

"Yes, Captain." She carefully tucked in his blanket and smoothed back his hair, then stood. "I know."

Then she returned to her ministrations, leaving Sebastian to ponder her unsurprised reaction. Was this mentality typical of the imperial army? He had been under the impression that Vittorio had been solely to blame for the crueler aspects of military practice that he'd observed. Could some—perhaps even *most*—of it be merely common practice for the imperial army? After all, one probably did not become the most powerful force on the continent by being humane.

44

Galina had not been to Kamen since she first met Sonya Turgenev. It seemed a lifetime ago, though it had only been last winter. Perhaps because she had changed so much since then. Or at least she liked to think so.

It appeared that Kamen had changed as well, but not in a good way. She remembered it being a bustling town, with a cobblestone main street and a number of well-crafted buildings. There had been an air of hopeful energy about the place, newly liberated from the empire by Sonya and her Uaine.

Now as Galina, Masha, and the Rangers rode into town, the streets were silent except for the echoing clap of their horses' hooves. It was clear most of the buildings were inhabited, but the shutters were all closed.

"Fear," rumbled Andre. "The whole place reeks of it."

"Fear of the Uaine?" asked Galina.

Andre shook his head. "Something nearer."

They continued through town until they reached the inn where Galina had met Sonya. Raucous shouts and laughter came from within, jarringly at odds with the quiet surrounding area.

Galina turned to her companions. "Let us see what the celebration is about."

The tavern was not particularly crowded. Twenty rough-looking men in poorly cured furs lounged about at the tables, drinking vodka directly from clay jars. During her previous visit, the inhabitants of

243

the inn had been peasants, but cleanly dressed and only moderately drunk. This group gave her the distinct impression that they were interlopers. A particularly well-organized group of bandits, perhaps.

A harried bartender moved with a jittery speed, as though afraid of some punishment should he slacken his pace. He was the first one to see Galina and her companions enter, and his eyes went wide, though Galina could not decide if it was hope or dread that he was expressing.

It didn't take long for the others to notice their presence. Their gruff conversations tapered off, and soon the inn was silent. But only for a few moments.

"Well, now, what's this here?" A shaggy man with a long scar across his cheek stood up, his face flush with drink. He grinned at Galina, displaying less than a full set of teeth. "Is it a costume party and nobody told me?"

Galina decided for the time being to ignore them. Instead she walked over to the bar and spoke to the bartender.

"Is there any supper left?" she asked.

"I-I'm sorry, no, my lady."

"I see." The peasants in Otriye, as well as those at the many small farmsteads she had encountered since, all seemed to share a compulsive need to call her *my lady* and she had grown weary of constantly correcting them, so she let it pass. "How disappointing."

"It's been a...*busy* few days, my lady." The bartender glanced at the men behind her who were beginning to mutter irritably, most likely because Galina was ignoring them. "Perhaps it's safest if you just moved along."

"Hold on a minute now," said the same shaggy man. "Her ladyship weren't done telling me about her fancy costume party. And besides, if she just wants a big slab of meat, I got one right here."

He leered and grabbed at his crotch.

"Charming," murmured Galina. "But I'm afraid I must decline."

"I don't recall giving you the option," he said. "See, me and my boys run things here now. We make the rules." He grinned at the rest of the men in the inn, then turned back to her. "And I say, pretty little ladies like you should be fucked raw."

For a moment, Galina felt her fear spike. Her mouth became suddenly so dry she couldn't swallow. But just like when the leopard had attacked, she clamped down hard on her emotions and forced herself to think logically about the situation. She glanced at her Rangers, who stood impassively near the entrance, awaiting her command, and she smiled. It seemed these men hadn't yet noticed her entourage.

"If I may ask, who said you were in charge?"

"Why, *I* did," said the man. "Now the empire is gone, and so is that damned Ranger. From now on, it's the strong that make the rules."

"So by that logic, if I am stronger than you, then *I* am in charge?" she asked mildly.

"You?" He laughed, as did a number of his men.

"Well, me and my servants," she amended.

"Servants?" He frowned, turning toward the doorway. When he saw Andre's hulking form, his bravado lessened considerably. The other men began whispering among themselves.

"Careful, Kuzma, those look like Rangers," said one of the other men. "Maybe we oughta let 'em be."

Kuzma wheeled around and glared at him. "This is *our* town, ain't it, Stas? We're building a place just for us. Our own kingdom. You said so yourself. But now you want to let some uppity noble and her freakish pets take it from us?"

"Maybe they're just passing through," said Stas. "No point tangling with Rangers if we don't have to."

"I'm afraid we are not merely passing through," Galina informed the clearly more intelligent and sober man, her voice stronger now that she saw the nervousness in his eyes. "In fact, I take great issue with you ruffians claiming one of the most important towns in Izmoroz for yourselves at a time when we should all be joining together in common purpose. I cannot let this pass."

"Don't let her try to intimidate you with her fancy words," said Kuzma. "Even if it is a couple of Rangers, we got twenty of the fiercest men in all Izmoroz right here." He looked challengingly around the room. "Don't we?"

Many seemed to regain their courage at his challenge and shouted their response.

Kuzma nodded, looking satisfied. "And we ain't no beast people, either. We're good old-fashioned, salt of the earth, *real* Izmorozian men. No way we can lose."

More cheers from everyone except poor Stas, who looked like he might be the only one sober enough to predict what was about to happen.

Galina turned to Tatiana. "*Sova*, these men are impeding our goals. Do whatever you want with them."

Tatiana's yellow eyes widened even more than usual, and her mouth opened eagerly. "Thank you, Mistress Kukla."

The Ranger walked slowly toward the now distinctly nervous Kuzma with her odd, birdlike strut. In an attempt to lessen her disturbing appearance, Galina had convinced Tatiana to wear a white feathered cloak that matched the white feathers on her head, reasoning it was the dissonance between human and owl aspects that was so unnerving. Rather than trying to make her look more human, it seemed wiser to emphasize the elegance of her owl aspects. Unfortunately, while her luminous owl-like appearance had certainly been enhanced, she now looked more unnerving than ever.

Tatiana approached, her head cocked to one side in that way of hers. Her arms were loose at her sides as she stared at the now visibly sweating man.

"You are in our way, lemming." She lifted one foot, and with a quick back and forth motion, tore open his throat with her talons.

A roar of alarm and outrage suddenly went up in the inn. The men scrambled for their weapons as they realized the time of manly posturing had been cut short.

Tatiana leapt into the largest group of them, vaulting onto her hands, and slashing about with her feet. Andre shambled eagerly after her, his dark bear eyes wide.

"Show me your courage, little lemmings!" he roared as he grabbed one of the men by his face and lifted him high into the air. "Let me feel some struggle from you!"

Then he ripped out the man's innards with his clawed free hand.

Wet slippery guts were flung across the room and spatters of blood misted the air. The sounds of tearing flesh and cracking bones competed with the screams of agony and terror. Galina stood and gripped the bar as she watched the unfolding massacre with queasy fascination. She didn't think of herself as squeamish, per se. She had read a number of anatomy books, after all. But those had not truly prepared her for this experience. The best she could say was that she managed not to vomit. Numb with encroaching shock, she watched Tatiana greedily slurp down one man's eyeball and wondered if the Ranger was still human enough for it to count as cannibalism.

Finally, blessedly, it was over. The only living bandit was poor Stas, who had done his best to avoid all conflict. He attempted to flee, but slipped on a patch of gore and splashed into a sticky red puddle.

Tatiana, ever quick, descended upon him, with Andre following after. But Galina called out to them. "*Sova! Medved!* To me!"

Her voice was shaky but both Rangers stopped. They seemed to struggle internally for a moment, as though trying to recall something. Perhaps themselves and their vows. Then, thankfully, they moved quickly over to Galina's side.

"Mistress Kukla!" They knelt before her.

"You have both done very well, but I want to keep this one alive."

She turned to the shaking Stas, now drenched in the blood of his comrades.

"I am Mistress Kukla and these are my Rangers." She stroked Andre's furry, blood-spattered head to further drive home the point. "We will not tolerate any behavior that conflicts with the betterment of Izmoroz. Feel free to share that knowledge with any other... *fellows* you meet."

"Y-yes, Mistress Kukla!" he whimpered.

"You may go."

He ran for the door while Tatiana and Andre watched him. Once he was gone, Galina turned back to the bartender.

"Sorry to be a bother, but would you mind cleaning up in here? I'd like to call a town meeting, if I may, and this seems to be the most suitable gathering place."

45

W ith all due respect, Tighearna, I think it would be a terrible mistake."

Rowena's bluntness was not typical for a high council of the Uaine. The Uaine rarely bothered with decorum, so when they did, it was weighty. And now Rowena felt the intensity of the eyes that scrutinized her. Mordha had called the chiefs and Bhuidseach of all six clans together for a formal discussion on whether they should form an alliance with the Aureumian traitor.

Mordha represented his own people, of course, Clan Greim of the Biting Grip, which currently had no Bhuidseach. Albion Ruairc and Rowena represented Clan Dílis of the Loyal Ones. Chief Ragáin and Bhuidseach Hueil represented Clan Gáire of the Laughing Mood. Chief Floinn and Bhuidseach Lorcan represented Clan Fuinseog of the Ashen Forest. Chief Nualláin and Bhuidseach Ruairi represented Clan Rincemór of the Endless Dance. And of course, for better or worse, Chief Conaill and Bhuidseach Sorcha were present to represent Clan Seacál of the Jackal Lords.

They were all gathered in a circle inside Mordha's massive tent. A small, sullen fire crackled in the center, making the air above it waver, though the eyes that held Rowena remained firm. It wasn't that they necessarily disagreed with her. But it was highly unusual for anyone to object so blatantly to the Tighearna's proclamation.

"And why, exactly, do you believe this to be a mistake, Bhuidseach Rowena?" Mordha asked, his expression as unreadable as ever.

"Perhaps she doubts your prowess in battle, great Tighearna," said Chief Conaill of Clan Seacál.

"Or your wisdom," chimed in his Bhuidseach, Sorcha. "It seems Bhuidseach Rowena is always questioning you, mighty Tighearna. So much for the *Loyal* Ones."

Rowena glared at Sorcha. As the only other woman present, she wished they could have been allies. Sisters in cause and reason. But from the day of her ascension to Bhuidseach, Rowena had received nothing but animosity and scorn from the elder female. Perhaps being from Clan Seacál, there had been no chance of harmony between them, since the two groups differed in deeply fundamental ways. True to their name, Clan Dílis was fiercely loyal to their allies, and therefore gave their allegiances sparingly and after great deliberation. Clan Seacál, on the other hand, was quick to throw in with whoever appeared strongest, and just as quick to abandon that ally should their strength begin to ebb. If it had been up to Clan Dílis, the Uaine would never have allied themselves with the beast witch in the first place because they had known the alliance was temporary and fragile. But in a high council of war, while Bhuidseach were free to voice their opinions, it was the Tighearna who made the final decision.

"I remain loyal to the Tighearna," Rowena said. "Any who doubt this are welcome to challenge me directly." She held Sorcha's gaze until the elder Bhuidseach looked away. Then she continued. "None can doubt the Tighearna's might and wisdom. But he is no god. He is neither omniscient nor infallible. This is why we hold these gatherings. So that we may *counsel* him. Clan Seacál seems the most eager for this alliance, but they are also the clan that knows the Aureumians the least."

"Because while *you* were cavorting with Raízians and brewing potions, *we* were leading a grueling march across the tundra with the bulk of our forces," snapped Sorcha.

"None would dispute the enormous contributions that Clan Seacál has made to this campaign," said Bhuidseach Hueil of Clan Gáire in his deep, somber voice. Hueil was the oldest of the Bhuidseach and respected by all, even Sorcha. "But that fact does not contradict young Rowena's statement. If we are to ally ourselves with the Aureumians, we must consider their character, and your clan is the least knowledgeable on that count."

While Rowena was grateful that Hueil was sticking up for her, she really wished the old man would stop referring to her as *young Rowena*. She was nearly twenty years old, after all.

"It does give one pause," agreed Hueil's chief, Ragáin. "While I think we can all attest to the loyalty of Lorecchio, we cannot assume that he is typical of his kinsmen. Indeed, I have had several conversations with him that indicate he is unique among his people, and that disparity is one of the reasons he left them."

"But if this traitor Aureumian is abandoning his people, might we assume he is also atypical of them?" asked Chief Floinn of Clan Fuinseog.

"Though, even then, he may not be atypical in the same way," said Bhuidseach Ruairi of Clan Rincemór. "He might be *worse* than the majority of Aureumians."

"We can speculate on the qualities and unspoken intentions of this Aureumian endlessly," said Chief Conaill of Clan Seacál. He was the youngest of the chiefs, and his impatience was beginning to show. "But in the end, does it matter? The Aureumian claims he can get us past the walls of Magna Alto without a grueling and costly siege. If he can, wonderful. If he can't, then we're no worse off than we were before. It isn't as though we weren't going to attack the city otherwise. And if he tries to betray us once we have taken the city, then he will know the folly of crossing the most powerful Tighearna the world has ever seen."

Conaill smiled ingratiatingly at Mordha and was undaunted by the Tighearna's habitual lack of response.

"In the end," the chief of Clan Seacál continued, "this man may hold a strategic position, but he clearly lacks power. Otherwise he would not have sought an alliance with us. So he breaks that alliance at his own peril."

"Bhuidseach Rowena," Mordha said, "as always, I am grateful for your considered advice, and I understand your concerns. But we have sat in this dour land long enough. Our people grow restless, and our presence grows more onerous by the day for the helpless sheep of Izmoroz. It is time for us to take bold action, seize our fate by the throat, and strangle it."

Rowena bowed her head. "Yes, Tighearna."

Then Mordha's gaze swept around the circle. "There is one more thing I would like to make clear this day. Some of you have mistakenly equated doubt with disloyalty, and obsequious fawning with loyalty." His eyes stopped at Sorcha and Conaill for a moment before moving on. "Let none question the loyalty of Clan Dílis and Bhuidseach Rowena again. You would all do well to ponder why it is that I always seek and consider her counsel."

Rowena kept her head bowed, but try though she might, she could not quite stave off a pleased smirk.

251

INTERLUDE

Zivena stood at the precipice of the eternal Now and gazed with bloodred eyes at the infinitesimally intricate lattice of Then, but it did not soothe her like it usually did. Her mass contracted and expanded fitfully.

"I am uneasy about the Armonia, dear sibling," she said finally.

"One should always be uneasy about the Armonia," said Marzanna, who stood with her back to her sibling, facing in the opposite direction and staring placidly at the seething, roiling mass of If. At the moment, its colors were a most pleasing display of reds, yellows, and oranges. Like a gore-drenched autumn.

"His attitude is becoming... unstable," said Zivena.

"I find it charming," said Marzanna.

"Of course you do." Zivena glanced over her shoulder for a moment. "Are you not concerned as well, though?"

"Naturally, I am concerned," said Marzanna. "But not for the same reasons you are."

"Do you have some scheme in mind for the Armonia?" demanded Zivena.

"Don't you?"

"Well of course."

"There you have it, then."

Zivena knew she would get no more out of her, and returned to contemplating the soothing complexity of Then for a few moments.

Finally she said, "Do you think Mother is cross with us?"

"Did you think she *wasn't*?" asked Marzanna in surprise.

Zivena grimaced. "Don't be impudent."

Marzanna shrugged, ripples of sharp white slicing delicate lines in the darkness that surrounded her. "How can I be anything else if you insist on willfully ignoring the obvious?"

"I'm not a fool. I know she doesn't like our games. But must she always try to spoil them? I mean, what else are we to do?"

Marzanna continued to watch the chaotic swirl of If that stretched out endlessly. It was now a very fetching purple and pink, with a few traces of blue. Like entrails just given to decay.

"What else indeed," she said.

PART FOUR

ARTISTS OF TRUTH

"It's quite simple to become an artist. One merely has to make art. There is no requirement that the art itself be good in order to claim that title. Of course, becoming a master of one's art is an altogether different enterprise, taking years, if not decades, and requiring a great deal of failure, suffering, and shame along the way. But whether one is a master or a hack, it begins the same way."

—Alejandro Cortina, renowned sculptor and winner
of the Imperial Prize for Visual Artistry
three years in a row

46

Galina walked through the village of Vesely beside a stout, jolly, and somewhat brusque man named Dima Batriov. Andre and Tatiana trailed silently behind, as they usually did until needed.

Once she'd fed the people of Otriye, they had enthusiastically pledged their allegiance to her. While it had certainly been gratifying, she knew that such an impoverished place could contribute little. The people of Kamen had been grateful that she'd driven out the group of bandits, but after weeks of pillaging, they hadn't been in much better shape.

Because of those experiences, Galina was able to fully appreciate how remarkable it was that Vesely was not only able to meet the basic needs of its people, but also exhibited a strong sense of unity.

"Your town gives me hope for all our people, Dima Batriov," she told him as they observed the blacksmith and his apprentice hammer away at what would be the first new weapons made in this town in decades.

"I'm glad to hear it, Mistress Kukla," Dima replied.

"Is Elder Yuri feeling better today?" she asked as they continued through the village.

He shook his head gravely. "I'm afraid not. His wife, Yelena, is doing what she can, but the man is old. This is what happens to old men."

"It seems more like an illness than old age to me," said Galina.

"That was why I sent Masha to fetch an apothecary from Gogoleth. I pray they make it back in time to treat him."

"You're kind to do it, Mistress."

"No, Dima Batriov, I'm merely pragmatic. Elder Yuri is a talented leader, as evidenced by the quality of your village, and if we are to succeed in driving out the Uaine, we cannot spare any such gifted individuals."

He seemed amused by her unsentimental response, but only replied with a nod of his head.

Dima took her around the rest of the village. She saw the tannery, which would be just as important as the blacksmith in arming the village. She saw the food stores, which would of course feed the combatants. And she was able to observe the people themselves as they went about their daily tasks. Once again, compared to some of the other villages and towns, Vesely was in good shape.

But it was still not enough. There was not enough iron, not enough hide, not enough food, and not enough healthy people to face a legion of undead. This was what she had observed, place after place. Perhaps if all of them had been as well positioned as Vesely, a frontal assault on the Uaine might have been possible. But Vesely's modest accomplishments alone were not enough to make up for the others, and she'd heard that villages farther out, such as Zapad and Istoki, were even worse off.

As Dima led her out of the damp, chilly spring air and into the nominal comfort of his home, Galina struggled not to show her discouragement. There were other methods of warfare, she knew. Perhaps initially she had envisioned a glorious meeting in battle with the Uaine. Now she understood how utterly unrealistic that idea was. Instead, they would have to resort to guerrilla tactics and underhanded methods. It would be a long, drawn-out, and ugly war. But she would do whatever was required. If it came down to a choice between honor or freedom for her people, there was no question which she would pick.

"Mistress Kukla, Mistress Kukla!"

As soon as Galina entered Dima's small, low-ceilinged home,

she was surrounded by his soot-faced, snot-crusted children. A few months ago she might have recoiled from them. The way they pawed reverently at the lace on her dress would have alarmed her, and the way their grimy lips pressed against the back of her pale hand might have sent her fleeing. But now she understood the opportunity that they represented.

"Hello, boys and girls," she said gravely.

"Now, now, let the lady some air," scolded Dima as he shooed them back a few steps.

"Have you been practicing your letters?" she asked them.

"Yes, Mistress!" they said in unison.

Since her arrival in Vesely, Galina had occupied her evening hours with teaching Dima's children the alphabet with the hope of eventually getting at least some of them to read. She was as concerned about Izmoroz's future as she was about its present, and intended to address the shortcomings of both.

"Show me," she commanded.

She sat by the fire and watched attentively as the children took turns writing and reciting letters on the slate she had given them. The difference in cognitive capabilities between the relatively well-fed children of Vesely and those of an impoverished place like Otriye were stark. She'd read enough on human physiology that this didn't surprise her, but it emphasized the order of priorities that would most effectively assist the peasantry in becoming educated and thoughtful members of society.

Once she was satisfied that they had memorized the previous evening's lessons, she began with a new set of letters. But the instruction was cut short by Masha, who stumbled into Dima's home looking almost giddy.

"Mistress!"

"What is it, Masha?" Galina asked. "Did you find an apothecary willing to come examine Elder Yuri?"

"Yes, Mistress, he's with Yuri now. But while we were in Gogoleth, I learned that the Uaine who had been living out at the old imperial barracks are gone."

"Gone?" Galina stood up, nearly dropping the writing slate. "Are they mobilizing? Have they begun their attack?"

"No, Mistress. That's just it. They marched south on the Advent Road. And that's not all. On our way back here, we passed near Les, where the Uaine were keeping their main army of undead, and that's empty, too."

"You're certain?" Galina asked sharply.

Masha nodded. "Empty as a beggar's stomach. I talked to a few farmers in the area, and they saw the undead headed south."

Galina frowned thoughtfully. "As if they planned to join near the Aureumian border..."

Did she dare hope that the Uaine were actually making good on their promise to leave Izmoroz of their own accord?

"*Sova.*"

"Mistress *Kuklushka!*"

The Ranger darted forward from where she had been lurking near the entrance with Andre. Galina had told the Ranger many times that using a diminutive nickname like *kuklushka*, no matter how affectionately meant, was pushing it. But sometimes Tatiana's enthusiasm for action got the better of her. Regardless, now was not the time to address such minor concerns.

"I need you to verify that the two Uaine forces have indeed joined and are marching into Aureum. Do not engage and do not let them see you. Report back to me as soon as you know for certain whether they are leaving Izmoroz."

"Yes, Mistress."

Once Tatiana had left, there was a moment of silence as Galina pondered the potential implications of this stunning new information. But the quiet was soon broken by Dima, who slapped his large belly and let out a laugh.

"Sounds like we should celebrate! I'll start pouring the vodka!"

"I'm afraid it's much too soon to rejoice, Dima Batriov," said Galina.

"Oh?" He looked confused. "But now we don't have to drive the Uaine out. All our fretting was needless. We don't need to fight."

"That conclusion, though alluring, is also premature," she said.

He gave her a pained look and scratched his thinning auburn hair. "I don't understand, Mistress Kukla."

"Who drove the empire out of Izmoroz, Dima Batriov?"

"Well... *we* did. Didn't we?"

She shook her head. "I'm afraid that it took far more than Ranger Sonya, myself, and a few unruly townsfolk to pose a threat against even the small standing imperial army at Gogoleth. No, unfortunately, it was the Uaine who drove the empire out of Izmoroz. Likewise, it has been the Uaine's presence here that has discouraged the empire from quickly returning to retake Izmoroz."

His eyes widened. "Oh."

"Indeed. It is difficult to predict with any accuracy whether the Uaine will be successful in taking Magna Alto. They certainly have a larger army than before, but this time they will not merely be facing a modest military outpost, but potentially the full might of the imperial army. And of course the empress will have the advantage of Magna Alto's formidable defenses. Defenses which, by all accounts, put even ancient Gogoleth to shame. Should the Uaine lose, what would stop the empire from marching north to reclaim Izmoroz?"

She gazed down at the gaunt, waifish little girl beside her and stroked her greasy, unwashed hair. Then she looked back at the crestfallen Dima.

"It *is* good news that the Uaine have left, Dima. I don't mean to diminish that. But understand that if we do not prepare ourselves for whatever comes after, all our suffering and struggle will have been for naught."

47

I don't think I'm a good person, Miguel," said Sonya.

They sat on a rooftop, camouflaged by cloaks dyed in the same dusty brownish-red color as the tiles beneath them. Unlike the four-person Anxeles Escuros security squads, the sniper squads comprised only two people: one as lookout, the other to shoot.

"I think you're very nice," said Miguel as he watched the streets below with a telescoping spyglass. "Considerate, generous, and always a friendly word for those you meet."

"Oh, I'm nice," agreed Sonya as she examined the fletching on her arrows. "But being nice doesn't make me *good*."

Miguel lifted a finger, twirled it, then pointed down to a narrow alleyway beneath them. Sonya nodded, took up her bow, and nocked an arrow.

"Okay, I'll bite," Miguel said agreeably as he lowered his spyglass and looked at her. "What makes you so bad?"

Sonya drew her bowstring to her anchor point and waited until the courier came hurrying around the corner, surrounded by several mercenaries from a rival guild. Then she released.

"Well, I mean..." She watched the courier clutch futilely at the feathers now protruding from his neck. "I kill for money."

"Do you really, though?" Miguel gave her a searching look. "While it's true that you're paid to kill people, is that really the reason you do it? Surely you could find a less arduous means of employment.

Or you could even just sponge off the Elhuyar family again like you were doing when we first met." He handed her another arrow from her pile.

"I see your point." Sonya shot one of the panicking mercenaries in the eye and he immediately dropped.

"You don't kill people for the money." Miguel gave her another arrow. "You do it because you find personal fulfillment in it."

"And this is your argument for why I'm *not* a bad person?" she asked as she shot another mercenary.

The remaining two mercenaries finally wised up and took cover in nearby doorways.

"I suppose the real question is how you define 'bad.'" Miguel stood and stretched. "Anyone who kills?"

"No." Sonya got up, shouldering her bow. "Rangers of Marzanna are servants of death, so technically, killing is part of our religion. And it is the law of nature that some must die so that others may live."

She took a step back, then leapt across the alley to the next roof. Miguel needed a little more of a running start, but soon joined her.

"Well, our client will presumably live better with these people dead. And since you're earning a living and finding some meaning in life, so do you. Everybody wins. Except of course the people getting killed."

"I guess." Sonya drew her knife and jumped down to street level. "This just feels less noble somehow."

The mercenary nearest her lashed out with his curved sword. She parried it with her knife, then spun in close and jammed her elbow into his stomach.

"I think your mistake," said Miguel as he landed on top of the last mercenary, who was attempting to flee, "was in thinking that killing is *ever* noble. It's not."

"Hmm." Sonya stepped to one side as her mercenary doubled over and retched on the cobblestones. "Rangers of Marzanna are taught by the Lady that as long as they kill in her service, it's always noble."

She planted her knife in the mercenary's ear, driving it in up to the hilt. His body shuddered, then she let him drop to the ground.

"With all due respect to your religious beliefs"—Miguel watched the mercenary beneath his feet struggle for a moment, then stabbed him in the back of the neck with his dagger—"I think this Lady Marzanna is holding you back."

Sonya looked over at him in surprise as she wiped her knife on a dead mercenary's tunic. "Really? You think so?"

"Absolutely. The way you describe her, it sounds like your goddess is all rules and subservience. That's not how the Raízian God works at all. He lifts us up and inspires us with the music and art that He left behind to guide us. He doesn't *constrain* us."

"That does sound nice," admitted Sonya. "If only I could join your religion."

"Anyone can," said Miguel. "They just need to find some connection to the arts."

Sonya made a sour face. "I'm an okay dancer, but otherwise I'm not very good at that stuff."

Miguel laughed. "Are you kidding? You're a master." He gestured to the five people who now lay dead at their feet. "Killing may not be noble, but it can most certainly be an art."

48

As they made their way back to guild headquarters, Sonya pondered what Miguel had said. Could changing her religion really be that simple? Would the Lady even notice? Or care?

When they reached the guild, Sonya was greeted by a rowdy cacophony of rusty voices from the balcony above welcoming her home. She smiled her toothy grin up at the old men. She wasn't sure if it was her novelty as a foreigner or her grand introduction a few months ago, but she was popular in the guild, especially among the old retired mercs who often gathered in the evenings to drink and wax poetically about the adventures of their youth. Javier had offered to scold them if they were bothering her, but she didn't mind having a group of concerned, if somewhat meddling, elderly uncles.

"How many this time, little fox?" one called down. They had picked up this nickname from Javier, but she didn't mind that, either.

"Four," she replied.

"Miguel, did she leave any for you?" called another.

"She generously allowed me one," he told them.

They all laughed delightedly, like this was a great joke.

Sonya nodded to the guard on duty at the front door. "Hey, Eduardo. Darkness knows light."

"And light knows dark," said Eduardo as he opened the door. "Welcome home, Sonya."

She smiled. "Thanks." This little ritual never got old for her. It was like an affirmation of sorts that she belonged somewhere, like the Ranger's prayer.

"Sonya, do you mind debriefing the Xefe without me?" asked Miguel. "My wife said she's making my favorite dish tonight and that I better not be late."

"Sure, Miguel," said Sonya. "Tell Anita I said hi."

He nodded. "I will."

Sonya smiled as she watched Miguel hurry down a side passage to the changing rooms. The younger guild members, like Sonya, lived at headquarters, but the older ones typically had their own homes, and often families as well. The food at the guild wasn't great, so she'd managed to get a number of dinner invitations during her months with the Anxeles Escuros and had been able to enjoy all manner of home-cooked meals. She'd even somewhat acclimated to the spicy flavors so popular in Raíz. Again, it might have been her novelty as a foreigner that made her such a popular dinner guest, but she didn't mind that, either. It helped to lessen the sting that she hadn't been invited back to Cassa Estío since joining the guild.

While she had mostly adapted to life in Colmo, the thing she still struggled with was her changed relationship with Jorge. Or rather, the lack of relationship. She tried not to take it personally. She'd been living here long enough now to have a basic understanding of how the Great Families worked. While she had been the Elhuyars' guest, she had been granted the privilege of their presence. Now that she was a mercenary, she was viewed as a lower class and not someone they would generally spend their time with except when employing her. But that didn't explain why her best friend Jorge was ignoring her. Perhaps he was mad at her for joining the guild and putting herself in danger on a regular basis. Or perhaps her fears had been right, and he no longer thought much about her now that he had his family again.

Sonya walked down the hall toward Javier's office, and was surprised to see the chief stepping out and quickly closing the door behind him. He hardly ever left his office during the day. And even more surprisingly, he had a wild look in his eyes.

"Is everything okay, Xefe?" she asked.

He started, as if she'd snuck up on him, and looked down at her. "Sonya Turgenev! Perfect! God must still love me!"

She frowned. "What's wrong?"

"Nothing's wrong!" he said with suspicious force. "Nothing at all!"

"Uh…I'm just here to debrief you on the job that Miguel and I completed. I think the client will be satisfied with—"

"Yes, that's great!" He gripped her shoulders, the wild look still in his eyes. "How about you give me the details later. Right now, I think you're available for another job, yes?"

"Actually, I was planning on getting something to eat."

"Certainly. Later. But first you must speak with your new client. She requested you specifically."

"Really?" Few in Colmo knew her as anything other than *that foreign girl in Anxeles Escuros*.

"Yes. I'm afraid so."

"Afraid?" asked Sonya.

"Never mind," he said. "Come along."

Still gripping her shoulder as though worried she might flee, he turned and opened his office door.

"Ah, what perfect timing!" he declared to whomever was in the room. "Here she is, Señorita! Your favored angel!"

He firmly guided Sonya into his office, then quickly shut the door behind him.

Sonya was surprised to see Maria sitting behind Javier's desk.

"Sonya!" She stood and came over to her, gracefully avoiding the precarious piles of books and scrolls that littered the room.

Before Sonya could react, Maria grabbed her face with both hands and kissed her cheeks.

Sonya found herself blushing. Maybe it was because she'd been hearing her guild mates speak in hushed, reverent tones for months about the Elhuyars in general and the young señorita in particular.

"Hey, Señorita Elhuyar. It's good to see you again."

"Sonya!" Maria playfully slapped her arm. "Don't you dare 'Señorita' me! I'm still Maria to you!"

"Oh, uh, sure."

"So this is what you prefer to wear?" Maria picked at Sonya's reddish-brown camouflage cloak.

"This was just for a job." Sonya took off her dark orange cloak and draped it over her arm.

"Hmmm." Maria continued to scrutinize her. "I suppose all that tight black leather *is* flattering for your figure. Maybe I should start wearing it as well?"

"Sure..." Sonya had the distinct impression that something was going on that she didn't understand. Like this was a performance of some kind.

Maria laughed gaily and patted Sonya's cheek in a patronizing sort of way. Whatever game Maria was playing, Sonya didn't think she liked it.

Then Maria turned to Javier. "Presumably she's available for the assignment, Xefe?"

"Of course, Señorita," said Javier. "We are honored by your request."

Maria looked back at Sonya, a triumphant gleam in her eye. "Excellent. It's all settled, then. Sonya, I'll see you at noon tomorrow at Cassa Estío."

"Oh?" asked Sonya.

Maria grinned. "Indeed. I need a chaperone, and you're the perfect person to fill that role. So until tomorrow, *madios!*"

She tossed her long black hair, sending an invisible cloud of flowery perfume into the air, then left.

Sonya and Javier stood silently in the office for a moment.

"Xefe?" asked Sonya. "What just happened?"

Javier sighed, and his entire body sagged slightly as he began to relax.

"I wish I knew, little fox."

"If she only needed a guard, she has plenty at home," Sonya pointed out.

"I am as perplexed as you," said Javier. "I will tell you this, though. There are few things scarier than a young person from one of the Great Families with such a mischievous gleam in their eye."

49

There were some aspects of espionage that Irina quite enjoyed. Utilizing politely manipulative conversation to discern the opaque motives of others was not only a pleasant activity, but also came quite naturally to her. Yet there were other aspects, such as blatant eavesdropping, which she found not only unsavory but extremely unladylike. And yet, Zaniolo had made it clear that such activities fell under her purview. Frankly, she felt the general could have put someone else in charge of this more "hands-on" aspect. But he had pointed out, not unreasonably, that should she be caught, she would have a much better chance of talking her way out of an international incident than one of his men.

And so, since she had been unable to discern Ambassador Boz's sources through polite conversation, she was now forced to take . . . less elegant measures. After one of the usual expatriate gatherings, rather than returning to her own apartments, Irina lingered in the garden for a few moments with the intent of following Boz at a discreet distance.

Unfortunately, Hexenmeister Cloos interpreted Irina's action as an invitation for a more intimate conversation. It was clear the man was preoccupied with her, but it was not attention she particularly enjoyed. He had not yet made a direct overture, and seemed to forever lurk in the periphery, fixing her with his hollow-eyed stare as if watching an exotic bird. She had known him for some time now, yet still couldn't decide if he was merely awkward or genuinely creepy. In either case, she typically made a point of never being alone with him. But she had been so preoccupied with her plans to tail the ambassador that she had forgotten him completely until this moment.

"Ah...Lady Portinari, might I...have a moment of your time?"

Irina cringed inwardly but allowed no outward appearance of her disdain.

"Of course, Hexenmeister Cloos."

He kept his eyes downcast, as if unwilling to even chance meeting her gaze. "I have been...working on something. A project of sorts, related to metallurgy and enchantment."

"I'm glad you have been able to continue to practice your craft," said Irina. "No doubt the empress finds great value in what you do."

"Oh, I...haven't shown this particular project to her yet. In fact, I haven't shown anyone yet. I was...hoping you would be the first."

A pretext to lure her to his rooms? Perhaps. And if he were to force himself upon her, what recourse would she have? His word against hers? And even if they believed her, who was the more valuable guest, the mother of a captain with great military potential who now seemed reluctant to exercise that potential, or a traitor to their enemy with no doubt a great deal of valuable information? No, the situation was dicey at best. Yet if she were to flat out refuse him, it would likely delay her enough that she would lose the ambassador's trail.

"I am deeply flattered, Hexenmeister, and I look forward to it."

His face lit up. "That's wonderful! Perhaps we—"

"Now if you'll excuse me, I really must be going." She stood and curtsied, then made a swift exit. Anyone who observed her would no doubt interpret her speed as an eagerness to leave Cloos rather than urgency to follow Boz. A not altogether incorrect assumption.

"Oh, er, yes, I look forward to it as well!" he called after her.

It seemed Irina would have to begin contemplating ready excuses to avoid "viewing" his "project" from now on. But she couldn't worry about that at present. Zaniolo had given her to believe that the ambassador usually disappeared somewhere around midday, and he strongly suspected that this was when she met with her contacts. Irina was not to interrupt it in any way, but merely get a visual description of these contacts, and if possible listen in to the conversation. The sooner she got this sordid business over with, the better.

She hurried down the hallways where she'd seen Boz heading, but there was now no sign of her. Irina walked faster, shoes rapping on the stone floor. The hallway turned to the right a short way down and she spun sharply on her heel, hoping to catch sight of her quarry.

Instead, she bumped directly into her.

Some spy she turned out to be.

"Oh my!" exclaimed Ambassador Boz as they collided. "Lady Portinari? Are you okay?"

"Yes, my deepest apologies," Irina said, trying to conceal her panic.

"You appear to be in quite a rush." The ambassador sounded concerned rather than suspicious, but Irina knew this was a woman skilled at concealing her reactions. She would need an alibi. And quickly.

"Ah yes," said Irina. "The hexenmeister was attempting to lure me to his apartments and I felt it necessary to make a speedy departure."

Boz let out her light, tinkling laugh. "You seem so flustered, my lady. I would think a handsome widow such as yourself would be quite used to such overtures."

Irina gave a weary smile. "While that is true, I fear Cloos's particular method of wooing leaves me somewhat discomfited."

Boz's dark eyebrows curved down. "I do hope he hasn't acted shamefully."

"Not yet," said Irina. "But there is something about his demeanor that makes me apprehensive."

"He is a bit awkward," agreed the ambassador. "Like most geniuses."

"Is he a genius, then?" Irina asked, feeling a little more at ease.

Boz flashed a knowing look. "Indeed he is. Does that change your disposition toward him somewhat?"

"I don't find him any more appealing, if that's what you mean," said Irina. "But my son is quite gifted as well, and terribly awkward. So perhaps it allows me to interpret the hexenmeister's actions more generously."

"Ah, I see," said Boz. "Well, I am glad I could to some extent restore the harmony within our strange little group."

"It is a... curious collection, isn't it."

"Especially that Captain Aguta," said Boz.

"Why him in particular?" asked Irina. "I find him rather charming."

"Oh yes. It's not him specifically that troubles me, but what he represents. An entire continent on the other side of the ocean that we know nothing about? Islands with secret magic?" Boz sighed. "It's enough to keep a diplomat up at night."

"Are you concerned this Aukbontar might have ambitions of conquest?" asked Irina.

Boz's eyes crinkled. "All countries have ambitions of one sort or another. Now, if you will excuse me."

"Of course, I'm sorry to have kept you," said Irina as she stepped aside. She wondered if the ambassador's assertion regarding ambition included Victasha as well.

She waited until Boz was some distance down the hallway. Then, loath as she was to do so, she removed her shoes and padded silently after on stocking feet.

Extremely unladylike.

50

Irina followed the ambassador to the top floor of the palace, an area she had never been before. She knew the royal family apartments were nearby. Zaniolo had mentioned that Empress Morante was quite fond of the ambassador. Wouldn't it be amusing if Boz's source for supposedly confidential information was the empress herself? It would almost be worth it just to see the look of chagrin on the oily general's face.

But instead of heading toward the royal apartments, the ambassador opened a thick door and began to ascend a narrow set of spiral steps. The only thing that could be higher were the towers that jutted up from the top of the palace. Could Boz be meeting her contact up there?

Irina had never had occasion to go up into one of the towers, but Sebastian had described them to her. In such a small yet exposed location, she didn't know how she could possibly observe the exchange. But perhaps if she stayed in the stairwell, she could at least ... *eavesdrop*.

Irina sighed and began creeping slowly up the stairs. A chilly wind swept down from above, making the stone steps unpleasantly cold for her stocking feet. But only halfway up, she could already begin to make out the conversation.

"Have you been able to get in touch with anyone in Kante?" Boz's voice filtered down from above.

There was a lengthy pause.

Then Boz spoke as though replying to some unheard answer, "That's unfortunate. But I suppose we've never attempted it over such a distance, and with the mountains in the way..."

Another pause.

"Oh, well that makes sense. I suppose we'll just have to wait and see then. How are things on your end?"

It was as though the ambassador was carrying on a conversation with someone, but Irina could not hear the other speaker. Not even a murmur.

"I see, I see," said Boz. "Still, the Portinari girl? Do you think it's wise? I've heard she is rather unpredictable."

Something about Sonya? Irina had already been listening intently, but now her hearing sharpened even more.

"No, you're right. Some legitimacy wouldn't hurt. And as long as you think she won't cause more trouble than she's worth..."

Irina had truly hoped that her daughter could find some peace and quiet in Colmo with that wealthy Elhuyar boy, but perhaps that had been too much to wish for. Why did she have to have such difficult children?

"Well, I leave it to you then," said Boz. "Now, about the situation in Izmoroz..."

Irina of course also wanted to know what was going on in Izmoroz, but a familiar and therefore deeply unpleasant sound intruded below. The slow clank and squeak that announced the imminent arrival of Franko Vittorio. If he happened by and saw the door to the tower open, he might investigate. And if he saw Irina lurking on the stairs...

Well, best to make her escape now.

She hurried down the stairs and stepped through the door. She had just managed to slip her shoes back on when Vittorio rounded the corner.

"Ah, Lady Portinari!" he said, presenting the kind, gentle, and to her mind highly suspicious smile he'd been using since his failed execution. "What a delightful surprise to see you all the way up here."

"Vittorio," she said coldly as she walked past.

"Visiting the tower, were you?"

He asked it lightly, but she thought she detected a strange undertone. Could he be collaborating with Boz? Perhaps guarding the tower entrance for her? That would certainly explain how she had been interrupted so soon after she began listening in to the ambassador's conversation.

She paused, brushing back her white hair, which had been mussed by the wind in the stairwell.

"Yes, it's a breathtaking view. Although I hadn't realized how cold it is up there. I fear I did not dress appropriately."

He nodded, still smiling that simpering, mustache-less smile of his. "I was just on my way up there myself."

"Oh? I should think an open tower would be the last place you'd want to be," said Irina, unable to resist the petty jab.

But if it pained him, he gave no sign of it. "Yes, that may be quite surprising to people, yet to me it makes perfect sense. It was, after all, my moment of communing with the divine."

"I see . . ." Irina wondered if he was not so much devious as he was insane. Not that it made him any less of a threat. She still didn't understand why they let him wander the palace freely.

"Well, if you'll excuse me," she said.

"Of course, of course." He turned and continued clanking toward the entrance to the tower.

As Irina began walking away, it occurred to her that if Vittorio did go up the stairs, he would encounter Boz and whoever it was she was talking to. Perhaps if she were to once again *eavesdrop*, she might learn the identity of the other person based on his reaction.

She continued to walk slowly down the hallway until she heard him begin his slow, laborious, and loud ascent up the stairs. Then she turned back around, once again removed her shoes, and crept up the stairs after him.

"Oh, Ambassador," she heard Vittorio say once he'd reached the top. "I didn't realize you were here as well."

"As well?" asked Boz.

Irina tensed. If Vittorio mentioned that he'd just seen her, Boz would no doubt become suspicious, and Irina's cover would likely be blown.

But to her surprise, Vittorio only said, "As well as me. I've never seen anyone else up here. It's a good place to find some solitude amid the hustle and bustle of the palace."

"Ah," said the ambassador. "Yes, I also do enjoy the solitude here."

"I can see that," said Vittorio. "Well, I am sorry to interrupt it."

"No, no. It's quite all right. I was just heading down. It can be a bit brisk up here."

"Indeed it can," agreed Vittorio.

Irina hurried back down the stairs and through the hall, waiting until she was some distance away before putting her shoes back on. Had Vittorio known she was listening in? Had the two of them been putting on a little show to convince her that Boz was not actually talking to a contact up in the tower?

It must be that. After all, the only other possible explanation was that the ambassador had been carrying on a conversation with someone who wasn't there.

51

Sonya arrived at Cassa Estío shortly before noon. She recognized the old guard stationed at the front gate.

"Hey, Ignacio. How've you been?"

He looked unsure for a moment, then his face lit up. "Ah, you're the little señor's friend with the funny eyes."

"That's me." She was used to such descriptions.

He eyed the feathery wings stitched into her black leather vest. "Joined the Anxeles Escuros, I see? Very impressive."

She shrugged with exaggerated nonchalance. "It's a living."

He laughed. "That's one way of looking at it. I take it you're the chaperone that the señorita said would be escorting her?"

She nodded.

He opened the front gate. "She said to wait for her in the gardens. She should be along shortly."

"Thanks, Ignacio."

"I don't think I caught your name before, miss."

"Sonya Turgenev."

He nodded. "An Anxeles Escuros preferred by the Elhuyars? I'd say you're making a good life for yourself here, Sonya."

She gave him a close-mouthed smile. "Just so long as I don't screw it up."

Since it wasn't quite noon yet, Sonya decided to stop by the stables to check on Peppercorn before she went to the garden. There weren't any stables at the guild, so he'd been living here this whole time.

"By the Lady, you've gotten fat!" she told him.

He shook his mane, not looking the least bit sorry.

She sighed as she stroked his neck. "I guess after everything I've put you through, you've earned the good life."

He pushed his muzzle against her affectionately.

"I miss you, too, *Perchinka*."

She stayed a few minutes with Peppercorn, then made her way to the garden. It was strange to be back in this place. She saw it from an entirely different perspective now. Not merely a place of luxury and leisure, but of power and position.

"Sonya?"

She turned to see Jorge walking toward her, his dark brows furrowed.

"Hey, Jorge." She smiled, happy to see her friend.

"What are you doing here?" he demanded.

Her smile faded. Apparently, he was not happy to see her. Maybe her worries had been well founded after all.

"I'm on a job, *Señor*."

His eyes narrowed further. "Who hired you?"

"Maria."

"Damn her!" He wrung his hands together. "I can't believe she—" He shook his head. "No, who am I kidding. Of course I believe it. It's *exactly* the sort of thing she'd do."

"Jorge, what are you talking about?"

"My damned sister!" He grabbed her bare arm. "Listen, Sonya, don't accept the job."

"I already did."

"Then tell her you can't do it. Tell her something came up."

She yanked her arm out of his grip. "Are you joking? I can't do that to one of the Great Families. I'd get kicked out of the guild."

He groaned and went back to wringing his hands. She hadn't seen him this frustrated in a long time.

"Jorge, calm down and tell me what's going on."

"Fine." He took a deep breath. "Whatever my sister hired you for, that's not actually what she wants from you."

"Really?" Sonya considered a moment. "I mean, I've never had sex with a woman before, but she smells great, and that goes a long way for me. I'd be willing to give it a try."

"No! That's not what I..." He sighed. "Look, Maria is involved in some sort of...anti-imperial insurgency. She heard about what you did in Izmoroz, and now she wants you to help free Raíz from the empire as well."

"You're joking," said Sonya.

"I'm not."

"Xefe would be pissed if I just started killing imperials again. He made that very clear."

"Regardless, the *last* thing you need right now is to be caught up in someone else's cause. I've been trying to keep her away from you, but I didn't consider the idea that she'd just march down to the guild all on her own and flat out hire you. Stupid of me, really. I should have realized that as radicalized as she's become, she wouldn't hesitate to be so bold."

"Wait, this whole time you've been protecting me from her?" asked Sonya.

"Of course! She kept trying to get me to invite you over for dinner, but I knew what she had in mind. Then, when I wouldn't do it, she started working on Mama. Fortunately, Mama wouldn't hear of inviting an Anxeles Escuros as a guest." He winced. "No offense."

But she smiled. "So...we're still friends?"

He looked shocked. "Of course we're still friends. My God, Sonya, did you doubt that?"

"Well..." She blushed. "We haven't talked in a while. I thought maybe you were mad at me for becoming a mercenary. Or that maybe you didn't care about me now that you had your family back."

He shook his head in exasperation. "You're ridiculous, you know that? Sonya Turgenev Portinari, yes, we are still friends. And as your friend, I do *not* want you getting mixed up in whatever harebrained scheme my sister has cooked up."

"But I really can't back out on the job, Jorge," said Sonya.

"Fine, just...don't commit to anything, okay? My sister goes through phases where she's really passionate about something, then she loses interest. Right now it's revolution, but in a month it'll probably be Victashian erotic dance or something."

"There's special erotic dances in Victasha?" asked Sonya.

"Never mind that," Jorge said impatiently. "Promise me you won't let her take advantage of you."

"Don't worry about me, Jorge," Sonya said. "The Uaine taught me not to go around making alliances with people I don't know."

He nodded. "Okay, good. Just...be careful."

"I'm getting better at that, too," she told him.

"Jorge, my dear brother!" Maria was walking toward them, her dress and hair flowing in the spring breeze. "I do hope you're not trying to chase off my chaperone."

Jorge glared at her. "Remember what I told you, dear sister."

"How could I forget when you have told me so very many times?" Her smile remained fixed on her face, but her eyes were hard.

Jorge ignored her and turned back to Sonya.

"I'll see you later, okay? I'll try to come down to the guild soon."

"Sure, Jorge," said Sonya. "See you then."

Jorge turned on his heel and stalked off.

"Well then, Sonya, shall we be off?" Maria asked brightly.

"Where are we going?" asked Sonya.

She grinned. "To the Viajero Quarter! I just know you're going to love it!"

52

What did Sonya want? *Really* want?

This was what she asked herself as she followed Maria through the streets of Colmo. Maria cheerfully rambled on about historical anecdotes of the area, pointing out specific murals that had been made by some well-known artist or another. But Sonya barely paid attention. Instead, she wondered what she would say when Maria finally stopped playing games and got around to asking her to kill some imperials.

Sonya had come to Colmo to recover and hopefully become strong enough to one day challenge Mordha again. To free Izmoroz, as she'd always strived to do. She'd thought joining the guild would let her hone knew skills, and it had. But she also found that she *liked* her life with the Anxeles Escuros. She'd made some friends—true ones, who didn't care about *that Ranger stuff*, as they usually referred to it. They appreciated her because she was good at her job and supportive of her comrades. There was a place for her among their ranks and she found that assurance greatly comforting.

But there were also times, usually in the short stretches between jobs, when she still felt restless. Like what she was doing didn't really matter. As much as she enjoyed the camaraderie and excitement of being an Anxeles Escuros, was it really *accomplishing* anything? Was it changing the world? Helping the poor and downtrodden? Bringing justice to those who deserved it? Usually not. If anything, she was mostly just helping rich families stay rich. And because of that, it felt sometimes as though her life had become... small.

Maybe that was okay, though. Perhaps it was arrogance to think she deserved more. She wasn't even following the dictates of a goddess anymore. She was just... *her*.

Besides, these people, whoever they were, probably didn't understand what they were asking for. The risk of having her as an ally. She'd told the Xefe she had *Lisitsa* under control, and that was true. But her newfound equilibrium hadn't really been put to the test. If she was cornered and truly in danger, would she be able to keep the beast at bay? And if she lost control like she had in Gogoleth, would she lose this life she'd worked so diligently to build these last two months? What would happen to her then?

The sharp scent of sweat cut into Sonya's pondering. She stopped abruptly and grabbed Maria's arm.

"We're not alone."

They stood in a narrow, empty street that led to a small square with a fountain in the middle. The faint strains of a flute came from somewhere, though oddly, Sonya couldn't pinpoint it. Some of the murals in this area were so intricate and rich that they seemed to move and writhe in place. A massive blue flower opened and closed its petals. A cat slowly blinked. The portrait of a man lifted his wondering gaze to the heavens again and again. But there was no actual movement in the square. It appeared completely unoccupied.

Except it wasn't. Sonya could smell them. Not one person, but many. Too many to determine.

"It's an ambush," she said quietly to Maria as she took up her bow and nocked an arrow. "Get behind me."

Instead, Maria sighed and stepped forward.

"I told you it wouldn't work," she called out. "Come on out, everyone. *Slowly*, so she doesn't shoot you."

Then she smiled at Sonya. "Please don't shoot them."

The flute abruptly fell silent and Sonya watched as things that had once seemed like bushes or benches became people. In only a few moments, the seemingly open square was now full of people.

"Viajero magic?" she asked Maria.

Maria nodded. "I promise it's not an ambush. At least, not the way you were thinking. We just want to talk."

"We?"

"Maria!"

Sonya saw a woman step forward. She wore a simple white vest and trousers, showing lean muscles on her bare tattooed arms. Her black hair was cut short, and her face had a strong, chiseled look.

"Lucia!" Maria ran over to her and the two kissed. After a few moments, Maria broke off and looked back at Sonya. "Sonya Turgenev Portinari, this is Lucia Velazquez."

"Maria, why did you bring me here?" Sonya asked plaintively.

"I apologize for alarming you, Sonya." Lucia's expression was earnest as she and Maria walked over to her. "We are Viajero, and theatricality is in our nature. We meant only to make an impressive entrance."

Maria said, "I told them you were too good to be fooled by a simple illusion spell."

Lucia tilted her head to one side. "May I ask what gave us away?"

"The smell of that many people gathered was so overpowering, you might as well have lit a bonfire," Sonya told her.

"Ah." Lucia looked oddly relieved. "So there was no visual flaw?"

"Not that I could perceive, and I've got pretty sharp eyes."

"Excellent." She turned back to the other Viajero gathered. "Good work, everyone. Think of this not as a failure, but a learning experience. We must polish our smell-cloaking as sharply as we have sight and sound."

Many of them nodded thoughtfully, their troubled expressions easing.

Sonya looked questioningly at Maria.

"Viajero are immensely proud of their skill, and deeply bothered by failure," she said.

"Isn't everyone?" asked Sonya.

"Come, come," Lucia said sharply. "Do you know the hearts and minds of the people so poorly?"

Sonya's golden eyes narrowed. "Excuse me?"

"Ah, what Lucia means," Maria broke in, "is that while it's obvious to *you*, being such an accomplished and skilled person, most in Raíz don't seem to value such discipline."

"Hm." Sonya was not totally appeased. No one had ever questioned her understanding of the people before. "So what was the point of this attempted *spectacle*?"

Lucia clearly bristled at Sonya's word choice, but Maria laid a calming hand on her shoulder and she took a moment to calm herself before responding.

"We have heard of your success in Izmoroz, and we entreat you to lend us the same strength you used to free your own people."

"Success?" Sonya asked bitterly. "I don't know what you heard, but it wasn't exactly a perfect outcome. Our supposed allies, the Uaine, decided to break their word and now occupy Izmoroz. So we merely traded one oppressor for another."

"Word has come from the north that a mighty leader rose up among the Izmorozians, and the Uaine have fled."

"A leader?" Sonya asked sharply. "Who?"

"She is said to be an ally of yours? They call her Mistress Kukla."

"Mistress *Doll*?"

Sonya frowned. The only person she could think of was Galina Odoyevtseva, who wasn't exactly *mighty*.

"Have you heard how she accomplished it?" she asked.

Lucia shook her head. "All we know for certain is that the Uaine have left Izmoroz, and none know their current whereabouts."

"And how do you know all this?" asked Sonya.

Lucia gave her a coy smile. "The Viajero have ways. Regardless, with the bulk of the imperial army fighting in Kante, and Magna Alto focused on locating the Uaine, now is the perfect time for Raíz to assert our independence. And it does not seem possible that your presence in Colmo is a coincidence. God has brought you here to help us."

"I doubt that," said Sonya. "And regardless, why would I help you?"

Both of them looked surprised.

"Because our people suffer under the empire's rule, just like yours did," said Maria.

"People here seem a lot better off than they were in Izmoroz," said Sonya.

"Have you been to Raíz anywhere other than Colmo?" Lucia demanded. "Have you seen the true plight of the people?"

Sonya felt the burn of shame. She'd asked Jorge almost the exact same thing when he'd suggested that Izmoroz had not been suffering under the empire.

"I . . . haven't," she admitted.

"Then allow me to *show* you!" Lucia looked eager as she turned to the crowd of Viajero and clapped her hands. "It is time!"

The crowd began shifting around, forming into three groups. One group had a variety of instruments, another was dressed in colorful, flowing silks, and a third stood poised with strange, unusually large paintbrushes.

Lucia spun back around, and there was a striking new energy about her, as if the very air around her vibrated. She gave Sonya an imperious look.

"You are fortunate, Sonya Turgenev, for few get to experience the full expression of the Viajero Symphony of Visions. What you are about to witness is no mere illusion, but a window into other places and other times. What is, what was, and what may yet be! Prepare yourself!"

Sonya couldn't decide how much credence to give such a dramatic speech, so she only nodded.

Lucia smiled, looking amused. "You remain skeptical. Very well. You shall soon see. Let us begin!"

The musicians struck up a sharp, swift tune, the rich guitars striking counterpoint to the muted pulse of drums. The dancers began to move, clapping their hands sharply to add a third point in the rhythm as their silks began to swirl through the air. Lucia took a slow breath so that her rib cage expanded, then she looked straight at Sonya and began to sing.

The air shuddered around them, and the color from the silks began to blur and spread through the air like clouds. The painters, wielding

285

their brushes with the same precision with which Sonya wielded her knife, pulled those colors from the air and began painting a composite picture that grew increasingly dense until it not only looked real, but began to move, as if Sonya was truly watching events unfold elsewhere. And the words that Lucia sang, though in a language she didn't understand, intruded themselves in her brain so that she understood exactly what the woman was saying.

Sonya stared at a scene in a small Raízian village, dry and dusty, with sand and grit everywhere. She felt the heat, and breathed in the stench of impending death. Children lay weak, dying of hunger and thirst while their gaunt, hollow-eyed mothers wept over them, rubbing even their tears on the cracked lips of their babies. The Viajero could have called down the rains for these people. But they were not there...

Then another vision began to overlap the village. This one showed a battalion of Viajero soldiers in a vast, swampy field. Instead of using their art to help the people of Raíz, they had been conscripted into the imperial army to use it for violence, bloodshed, and conquest. They fought pale-faced men and women garbed in iron, while giant metal insects staggered about, crushing or piercing the Viajero in their path.

Seeing these two images superimposed, death upon death, suffering overlaying suffering, twisted Sonya's chest. She could hear their cries of agony, their wails of despair. The feelings flooded into her and she was helpless to resist. It felt as though the battle was being waged inside her mind, and the starvation was eating away at her own flesh. The line between vision and reality blurred. Was she standing in a square in Colmo? Or was she in a small village? Or was she on a marshy battleground? For someone so attuned to their own senses, the dissonance was alarming. She staggered, her hands flailing as she tried to find something tangible to grasp. Some concrete aspect of reality that could save her from the horrors of famine and war that roared inside her skull.

As if in response to this "attack," the beast within her welled up. This was an invasion and *Lisitsa* would not allow it. A sound somewhere between a shriek and a growl escaped her lips, and the world turned red as she lashed out in fury.

Abruptly the real world juddered back into existence.

Sonya was on her knees in the middle of the square, gasping for breath. She stared down at her hands, which were streaked with blood. She tasted salt and iron on her tongue and when she wiped her lips, she found more blood.

She looked up to see the Viajero now scattered and pressed back against the outskirts of the square, their eyes wide with shock. Maria's face was pale, and her shaking hands supported Lucia, who seemed barely able to stay on her feet. Blood ran down Lucia's bare arm from the sizable bite in her shoulder.

Sonya spit blood onto the flagstones and stared intently into Lucia's eyes.

"I see you now," she said. "I see your people. I see your pain and suffering. Your cause may be just. But you see me now, too. You see what I truly am. A beast you cannot control. A terror waiting to be unleashed."

"Oh, I see you all right," Lucia said quietly. "I see both your beauty and your ferocity. But you still do not understand. Art does not seek to control, but to release. It does not tame, but excite. It does not dictate who you are, it *uncovers* it. If God came to me and said, 'Lucia, I will give you the fiercest of hurricanes to aid you in your struggle, but be forewarned, it might harm you as well,' I would still say, 'Thank you for this gift, God. I will use it to its fullest, and if in doing so your creation sees me to my death, I will be honored.'"

Lucia moved away from Maria so that she stood unsupported. She took her bloody hand from her wound and held it out to Sonya.

"Sonya Turgenev Portinari, will you be my hurricane?"

Sonya stared up at Lucia for a moment. She did not know if the woman was inspired or mad, but regardless, she was damn impressive.

"I have a condition."

"Oh?" asked Lucia.

"Now that the Uaine have left Izmoroz, the empire might decide to take it back. If they do, will you and your Viajero help me protect it?"

"Viajero are not so good in the cold. It stiffens our muscles and tightens our throats. This was why we were not forced to help conquer Izmoroz during the Winter War. But I swear we will do whatever we can to aid you and your people."

Sonya appreciated Lucia's candor as well as her passion. They might have gotten off to a rocky start, but perhaps they were more alike than she'd first thought.

"Good enough."

Their sticky, blood-soaked hands came together with a wet slap and Sonya slowly rose to her feet.

Lucia smiled triumphantly.

"They will sing of this day for generations, my sister."

53

The following day, Sonya entered the guild headquarters with a heavy heart. Her best moments in Colmo had been here, among these honest, gallant souls. But she knew she couldn't continue to have the easy, relatively carefree life of an Anxeles Escuros once she joined the Viajero in their struggle for freedom.

She walked down the familiar hallways, headed for Javier's office, when she encountered Miguel, looking like he was getting ready to go patrol the market, a service paid for by a consortium of merchants who sold their wares there.

"Good morning, Sonya," he said cheerfully. "I didn't see you yesterday. Interesting job?"

"Yeah, you could say that." She couldn't quite meet his eyes. Miguel was the one who helped her join, after all. He'd partnered with her more than anyone else and invited her into his home. There were times when he almost felt like the big brother she'd never had. She felt that in quitting the guild she would be disappointing him somehow.

"Is something wrong?" he asked.

She smiled and shook her head. "Things are fine. Have a good patrol."

"Thanks..." It was clear he didn't completely believe her, but chose not to push. Sonya was grateful for that. "See you later, then."

"Yeah. See you later."

She wasn't sure when she'd see him or any of the Anxeles Escuros again. Even if she did, it wouldn't be the same, since she would no longer be one of them.

She continued on to Javier's office, and knocked on his door.

"Come in," came his deep, rusty voice.

She opened the door and took a fond look at the inspired chaos within. Somehow the office always seemed to change and shift its contents without ever looking neater or more organized. Did Javier try to tidy up now and then, only to grow bored of the task before it was finished? If not, why move a precarious pile of scrolls from one place to another? She'd asked him once, but he'd only laughed, as if she'd made a joke of some kind.

"Sonya Turgenev, ready for a new assignment?" asked Javier as he put his quill down and carefully blotted the paper before him on the desk. "People need killing, you know."

"I'm sorry, Xefe. I'm..." Now that she was looking into his cheerful, grizzled old face, she wasn't sure how to broach the topic. "I have to leave the guild."

"Leave the Anxeles Escuros?" He looked incredulous. "Are you returning to Izmoroz so soon?"

She shook her head. "No, I just... I have to do something else. Something that I wouldn't want the guild to be held responsible for."

"Ah." His eyes narrowed. "So Señorita Elhuyar has pulled you into her machinations, as I feared."

"I've been happy here, Xefe. Really. I'm grateful to all of you. But after what Lucia and the other Viajero showed me..." Sonya shook her head. "When they asked for my help, I couldn't refuse."

Javier sighed. "I understand, little fox. You have a generous heart. It will either be your salvation or your undoing. Unfortunately, you're right. For now, the Anxeles Escuros cannot be seen participating in seditious activity."

"For now?" There it was again. The same vague suggestion that months later he still refused to explain.

And once again he smiled slyly and shook his head. "*For now*, may I make a suggestion?"

She sighed. "I will always listen to your advice, Xefe."

"Once someone leaves the Anxeles Escuros, they may never return. So perhaps instead we should just say that you are taking a leave of absence to handle some personal matters?"

Sonya's eyes widened. "I can do that?"

"I am El Xefe, am I not? I decide what can be done. We have all grown quite fond of you, so I am certain none will complain."

She grinned as relief flooded through her. "Thank you, Xefe."

He nodded. "You're my best sniper. I would be a fool to lose you so soon."

"Your *best*?"

"Don't let it go to your head, little fox. Now, if I may make another suggestion, you should bid farewell to the old men in the cantina. They will be heartbroken during your absence."

Sonya said goodbye to Javier and made her way to the cantina on the second floor. The bar was set up just beyond the entrance to the balcony along the outer wall. The bartender, Gonzalo, had apparently been working there even longer than Javier, and he looked it. Nothing but leather skin, stringy muscles, and a fringe of gray hair pulled back into a ponytail. He waved to her as she passed and she nodded. There was something oddly pleasing about being known by the bartender.

"Little fox!"

"We missed you!"

"Where have you been?"

The old men gathered at tables out on the balcony, drinking their wine and telling each other the same stories they'd been telling for years. Sonya knew that a large part of her appeal was simply because she had never heard their stories before and, unlike many of the other young mercenaries, was willing to listen.

"Gentlemen! I have good news and bad news!" she told them.

"You're getting married?" asked Santiago, who was probably in his late sixties, but still looked burly enough to wrestle a bear.

There were several barks of laughter and several groans.

"I'm never getting married," Sonya told him.

This was followed by a chorus of cheers. She shook her head and smiled. She didn't understand why they fancied themselves her protectors, but it amused her.

"No, the bad news is that I'm taking a leave of absence to sort out some personal stuff."

"Absence?"

"How long?"

"What personal stuff?"

Sonya gave Benicio, the one who had asked that last question, a hard look. "It's called personal stuff because it's *personal.*"

Benicio looked suitably chastised, but the others pestered him anyway.

"Yes, Benicio, who do you think you are?"

"A young lady needs her privacy!"

"Honestly, some people!"

Once they felt that Benicio had been shamed enough, they quieted back down.

Then Santiago asked, "So what's the good news, little fox?"

Her smile returned, wider now so that it displayed her sharp, bright teeth to their fullest. Then she declared, "Tonight, drinks are on me!"

A new chorus of cheers rose up, even stronger this time.

54

Galina Odoyevtseva Prozorova was, as she had ever been, a great admirer of contradictions. Perhaps it was because she was a woman. After all, what could be more contradictory than the role of women in Izmorozian society? They were revered. Held up as precious beyond measure. Men fought wars for them. And yet, to Galina's knowledge, no woman had ever asked that a war be fought for her. Men were confused when a woman bristled under their authority because they did not understand that reverence was not the same thing as respect.

Yet as pervasive as the issue of gender inequality was, surprisingly little had been written about it. Perhaps because there were so few women writers. For a long time, Galina had dreamed of being the first writer to truly express the plight of women.

But now she had a different dream. Rather than merely express it, she would change it.

Why not her?

"Are you sure this is where you want to hold the gathering, Mistress?" Masha asked.

The two women stood in the decimated, empty remains of Les.

"I asked you not to call me *mistress* in private," said Galina.

"It becomes harder to remember each day," said Masha. "As it becomes harder to see the sullen girl I once knew within the fierce young woman before me."

Galina smiled. "A woman I would never have become without your support."

Masha nodded her head in acknowledgment. Then her brows knit together.

"But truly, miss. Why this place?" She gestured to the collapsed buildings and gaping cracks in the square. "Why gather everyone in this broken, ghost of a city?"

"Ghosts," said Galina, "are a symbol of past failures that we long to correct."

"That's very fine, miss," said Masha. "Who said it?"

"I did, Masha. Just now."

The two walked through the desolate city. The Uaine had left few signs of their brief occupation, but Galina supposed that wasn't so surprising. After all, it was an army that did not eat or drink, that did not leave waste. In some ways they were the perfect army. Or at least they seemed so. Galina hoped that the living passion of brave men and women might overcome the obvious advantages of the undead. Of course, she hoped even more fervently that she wouldn't need to test that idea. Ideally, the empire would take care of the Uaine, and it would be such a fierce struggle that even the victors would find themselves at a disadvantage against the Izmorozian militia. A militia she planned to begin gathering that day.

A short time later, Andre and Tatiana returned from scouting.

"They come from the west," Andre rumbled.

"They come from the north and the east," said Tatiana.

"Excellent," said Galina. "When will they arrive?"

"The first within an hour or two," said Tatiana.

Galina nodded. "Well done. I suspect it will be a long night. You should both see to your food now, and rest if you can."

"I shall see you and Masha fed first, Mistress," declared Andre.

"I fear I don't have much of an appetite at present, *Medved*." Galina found it gratifying that representatives from every town and village in Izmoroz had agreed to her request to gather at Les. But it also created a deep, tremulous unease in her stomach that only grew stronger now that she knew precisely when they would arrive.

"That's just nerves, Mistress," Masha assured her. "Best to have something in your stomach before you make your big speech, even if you don't feel like it."

"I suppose," said Galina. "Very well. Andre, please find something small for me and give it to Masha to clean and cook."

She had discovered if she didn't indicate her preference for cooked food, Andre would sometimes return with a raw, unskinned rabbit and look terribly disappointed when she didn't immediately tear into it with her teeth. By and large, the Rangers had been able to keep their more beastly impulses in check, but they still required gentle reminders on a regular basis. In some ways, they were almost like children, albeit giant, ferocious children capable of instantaneous wide-scale murder.

Andre returned an hour later with a pheasant, which Masha kindly plucked and roasted for her. Galina didn't find the idea of eating even remotely appealing, but forced it down. Later, as she watched people from Kamen, Otriye, Istoki, Zapad, and elsewhere filter into the square, she felt her stomach churn even more and began to suspect that food of any kind had been a mistake.

She waited inside one of the few buildings still standing, and even the murmuring sounds of the gathered crowds made her queasy.

Andre appeared in the doorway.

"All have arrived, Mistress," he rumbled. "It is time."

Galina gazed up into his small black eyes for a moment. Then she turned her head and vomited.

"Mistress!" His hand shot out to steady her. "Are you ill?"

"It's all right, *Medved*. Just a touch of nerves, I think."

He gave her a baffled look. "Nerves, Mistress?"

"I've never spoken in front of so many people. Nor has there ever been quite so much at stake for the future of our land." She took a sip of water from a skin, swished it around in her mouth, then spit it on the ground. "It would be a tremendous comfort if you stood by my side."

"Of course, Mistress."

She smiled gratefully and patted his thick arm. She wondered when it was that his coarse, hairy presence had gone from intimidating to reassuring.

"Mistress." Tatiana stood in the doorway, as unnerving as ever. Galina appreciated the female Ranger, and relied on her for many things, but for whatever reason, she didn't feel the same warm fondness that she did for Andre. "Masha is doing her best to placate the people, but they grow restless."

"Then I suppose we had better get started."

Galina tried to rinse the unpleasant taste of vomit out of her mouth one last time, with middling success. Then she adjusted her porcelain mask, squared her narrow shoulders, and stepped out of the building.

The roar of the crowd was immediate and did little to settle her stomach. But she smiled and nodded as she shakily made her way to the small platform that had been constructed from rubble. Andre helped her up onto the platform as though recalling some distant past in which he'd been a proper gentleman. Neither of the Rangers remembered much about their human lives, so perhaps he had.

She held up her hands until the people quieted down.

"My fellow Izmorozians, thank you for coming. It is gratifying to see so many of you here. We——"

She had to pause as they cheered. She hadn't really taken audience response into account when she'd written the speech. She smiled and waited patiently until they had settled down again.

"We have a profound decision to make that may well affect the very future of Izmoroz. As you all know, the Uaine and their foul undead have left Izmoroz. For th——"

Again she had to pause while they cheered.

"For the time being, we are safe. But we do not know how long it will last. If the Uaine successfully sack Magna Alto, they will likely cut across Izmoroz again when they haul their spoils back to Uaine, leaving more damage and death in their wake. On——"

She paused as many groaned or shouted angrily.

"On the other hand, if the empire wins, there is currently nothing to stop them from retaking our land for themselves. And we all still vividly recall what life was like under the thumb of the empire."

More shouts of anger, frustration, and fear.

"We cannot let that happen!"

Cheers.

"We will not be victims to any more conquerors!"

The cheers grew louder, but this time she shouted over them.

"We must grow strong so that we may never toil under unjust rule again!"

She allowed the cheers to peak, and when they began to die down, she spoke again.

"You may wonder how we will grow strong enough to fend off either Uaine or imperial invaders. It is quite simple, my countrymen. By coming together, by sharing our skills and our knowledge, by *learning and growing as a people.*"

She fondly touched Andre's shoulder. "*Strannik* are a boon from the Lady. There is no doubt about that. But do you really think the hard Goddess of Winter wishes us to weakly submit and allow her servants to solve our problems for us? Could it be, in fact, that she wishes us to work and train with them so that we too might grow strong? So that our entire nation becomes as fierce as winter and as dreaded as death itself?"

There was silence in the square as people contemplated her words. Some were no doubt troubled by them. Perhaps even shocked by the notion that anyone might attempt to emulate the Rangers without the explicit blessing of Marzanna. And yet, here were two Rangers standing beside her, neither of them objecting. Could it be that she was right? That the strength of the Lady of Winter could be theirs as well?

"But let us be frank with each other, my countrymen," she said. "Can we expect the Council of Lords to enact such a daring plan to form, supply, and rigorously train a national militia?"

There were uneasy murmurs.

"They claim to have the best interests of Izmoroz at heart, but have your lives improved since they took power?"

The murmurs grew louder and more angry.

"Perhaps they mean well. Let us give them the benefit of the doubt. But good intentions will not save us from the Uaine or the empire.

What we need is courage. Bold ideas. A willingness to take risks and do what needs to be done for the good of Izmoroz and its future. What we need is strong leadership to see us through these difficult times. So I ask you to decide: Who will guide us?"

She gazed down at them with clear eyes, at last untroubled by her stomach. She waited. It would happen or it wouldn't. This blessed moment was completely out of her hands and she felt a sense of peace in that knowledge.

"You, Mistress Kukla!" someone in the crowd shouted.

"Yes, you!" shouted another.

"You! You! You!" The chant was taken up across the square.

She let the shouts reverberate through the broken remains of Les. This was what she'd expected to happen. She could have placed a few trusted souls in the crowd to instigate it. But it had been important to her that the people choose her of their own volition. That they also thought to themselves, *Why not her?*

Now she gravely inclined her head in acceptance, then raised her hand for silence again.

"I am honored, and accept this burden for so long as I am needed. Now, let us take the first steps toward the future of Izmoroz."

55

The largest imperial garrison in Raíz was situated just north of Colmo along the Advent Road. Curiously, Sonya thought it looked a lot like one of the estates owned by the Great Families. It was a multi-building compound enclosed by a high, thick wall covered in the beige stucco so common to the area. That region of Raíz was largely flat, with only low scrub brush and the occasional palm tree. The approach to the garrison was quite exposed, making a surprise attack impossible. For anyone other than Viajero, at least.

Sonya, Lucia, and a group of Viajero gathered in the dining room of a sympathetic merchant family in the northern part of the city. The large dinner table had been cleared, then plain linen hooded cloaks were laid on top. A small group of painters swept their over-sized brushes across the cloaks while Lucia and her group of musicians played a song so quiet that Sonya doubted normal human ears could hear it clearly.

At first, the cloaks seemed unaffected by both the paint and the song. As the Viajero flung their brushes over the fabric, they didn't even change color. But as the painters continued to work, Sonya watched with fascination as the cloaks began to slowly fade from view.

"They're invisible now?" she asked Lucia once they had finished.

"Of course," Lucia said with the deliberately casual air that Sonya had come to realize was her version of bragging. "And once we put them on, we will be, too."

"That's amazing," said Sonya.

Lucia shrugged with her exaggerated nonchalance. "I suppose it is amazing. Now we must move quickly. The effects will only last a short while."

The painters remained in the house, while Sonya, Lucia, and the other musicians donned their cloaks. Sonya looked down at her own invisible body, then over at Lucia, who appeared to be a head floating in the air beside her, and laughed.

Lucia's eyebrow arched. "Obviously we'll need to keep our hoods up and our heads down to be completely invisible."

She pulled up her hood and bowed her head, and disappeared completely from Sonya's view.

As they left the house, the sun was beginning to set, leaving the sky a dark purple tinged in red. Sonya and the Viajero hurried north through the streets, keeping their heads bowed so as not to terrify the few people on the street with the sight of a group of disembodied heads.

Once they had reached the northern edge of the city, Sonya called for them to stop.

"We should probably move slowly from here. We might be invisible, but we're not inaudible, especially running."

"It's a good time to give you these as well." Lucia handed Sonya a pair of wax earplugs that would protect her from the effects of the Viajero music. "When I take down my hood, that will be the signal that it's time for you to move in."

Sonya fit the wax earplugs into her ears. They had been made specifically for her so they had a perfect seal. As soon as she put them in, the abruptly silent world was disorienting.

They walked slowly across the fifty or so yards of open space toward the garrison. Sonya was keenly aware of all the sounds she wasn't hearing. The wind that pulled at her cloak, the rocky ground beneath her feet, the breath of her comrades. All of it was hidden from her. She didn't like that feeling at all, and a nervous energy began to mix with her eagerness for action.

At last they stopped roughly ten feet from the two guards posted at the entrance of the garrison. Or Sonya assumed the others also did so with her. She couldn't see or hear her comrades, and even their smell seemed to be masked by the cloaks. She just had to hope they all remembered the agreed upon position.

Then she waited.

At first, it seemed like nothing was happening. Since she could not perceive the Viajero, she had no idea if the plan was proceeding, and her mind began to sift through any number of alarming scenarios. Perhaps they had lost their courage and fled. This was, after all, their first real conflict. And if that was the case, Sonya was the only one standing there, stupidly waiting for a signal that would never come until the invisibility wore off and then she would be stupidly standing in front of some very alarmed imperial soldiers with a great many more soldiers only a cry for help away. Could she silence them both quickly enough to prevent them from raising the alarm? Then what would she do? Flee or continue on alone? Could she handle a fortified imperial garrison single-handedly?

But even as her mind rifled through a series of worst-case scenarios, she noticed the guards gradually look sleepier. Their stiff postures sagged, their eyes drooped, and they began to stifle ever-larger yawns. Finally, they leaned back against the gate they were guarding, then slid to the ground. They didn't seem to be asleep exactly, but in an unnatural state somewhere between consciousness and unconsciousness.

Then Lucia's head appeared beside her. Still singing, she nodded.

Sonya moved forward alone, since the Viajero had to keep singing or the effects of the song would stop. She took keys from one of the guards and unlocked the gate, feeling rather than hearing the bolt shift. She pushed open the large double doors, then let the still-singing Viajero walk slowly into the courtyard as they continued their song. From there, they should be heard by every soldier in the garrison. That meant it was time for Sonya to get to work.

The layout was surprisingly similar to Cassa Estío, which meant she would be able to find her way around more easily. To the right were the stables. She peeked in and saw the horses all in the same unnatural daze. She hesitated for a moment, then moved on. Surely no one expected her to kill horses.

Then Sonya began to quickly but methodically work her way through the imperial compound. Where the Elhuyars had a theater, the imperial garrison had a training area. Where the Elhuyars had large opulent bedrooms, the garrison had dense clusters of bunk beds. She still hadn't seen any soldiers, however. Could they be out on a training exercise? If so, what could she do? Was the entire plan a failure?

But no, she should have realized: With the setting sun, it was dinnertime. She found them all in the dining hall. Some were seated at long tables, others in the kitchen. All were in that same unnerving semicomatose state. She crept closer to get a better look. To a man, their faces were all slack, almost peaceful. They looked troublingly innocent, in fact.

They weren't, of course. She knew that. And yet, to kill them when they looked like this . . .

She caught a glimpse of movement reflected in a metal tankard, and spun around just in time to dodge a clumsy swing from an imperial officer's sword. The man had taken shreds of cloth and jammed them into his ears. Judging by his befuddled look, it wasn't a perfect seal and he was suffering the same effect as the others, just to a lesser extent.

She looked down and saw that her cloak was beginning to flicker in and out of view.

He took another swing, and she dodged again. He looked a few years younger than her, about Sebastian's age. He didn't have the markings of a captain yet, but that wasn't surprising. It was probably only her brother's magic that had allowed him to rise so quickly through the imperial ranks. This poor fool was no Sebastian. Not even on a good day. And this was most certainly not a good day for him.

Yet she couldn't help admire how he fought on, forcing his slow, lethargic limbs to move again and again, trying in vain to protect the other men. The empire might be terrible, but was this man terrible? How many of them had been bullied or cajoled into service for the empire like her brother? Did they even know what their empire had done to the Raízian and Izmorozian people? They had probably been raised to believe that they truly were making the world better.

These thoughts worked their way through Sonya as she continued

302

to dodge the bumbling swings of the imperial officer. She could see his frustration with his own body, as well as his growing despair.

"Yes," she told him, though neither could hear. "It is always pointless to fight against death. And yet we must."

Then she stepped in close and pressed her hand against his back as she slipped her knife between his ribs. There was a strange sort of intimacy to it as she gazed up into his wide eyes. His lips opened and closed a few times. He died in her embrace, and she let him fall to the ground.

She turned to the others, all slack-jawed and vacant-eyed. Like surprised children. Lucia had told her this way would make the risk of losing comrades almost nothing, and that those under the song's power would feel no pain. It had seemed, intellectually, to be not only the smartest, but the kindest plan.

Yet here she was, staring down at these helpless men, and she did not feel kind. She felt as despairing as the officer she'd just killed. Today she was not the proud death that could be found in battle, but that most dreaded and inglorious death that steals the lives of those weakened by illness or age.

She walked slowly down the length of the table, tears coursing down her cheeks as she slit throat after throat.

They did not even struggle as they died, and for reasons Sonya could not articulate, that broke her heart all the more.

56

Sebastian had always been one to follow the rules. Perhaps because his sister had always been one to break them. He'd enjoyed the praise that his parents heaped on him after they'd finished scolding Sonya. He'd enjoyed being the child they could "count on."

If he was being honest, the idea of rebelling against the established order had also seemed a little frightening to him. Perhaps that fear had held him in check for much of his life. No other emotion had arisen that had been intense enough to push past the unease of breaking the rules.

Not until he came to Kleiner, where the turmoil he felt at witnessing the needless suffering of the Kantesians finally smothered his fear.

Sebastian had moved on from bricks to glass, melting sand into large sheets that would then be placed in the windows of the newly built brick homes. The process was a little trickier, requiring more thought and attention than baking clay, but it was also even more satisfying, since the end result was quite beautiful to his eye. He almost felt like an artist.

Once he'd finished his glass quota for the day, he would go visit Isobelle, who still cared for the injured Kantesians. There he would discreetly give her a new batch of healing potions.

"Are you certain you won't get in trouble?" she whispered to him. The dim candlelight glittered in her concerned blue eyes.

He smiled. "I'm not certain at all. But rest assured, if I am discovered, I will insist on taking the full blame."

She gave him a worried look, which he appreciated. "How do you even get it? Or do I not want to know?"

"The less you know, the better," he told her.

Initially, Marcello had made good on his promise, taking a few bottles from the storehouse and giving them to Sebastian as a "gift for wooing." But when Sebastian had asked for more, Marcello had said they would need to wait until the apothecaries restocked the shelves. Taking too many, too soon would draw attention.

But the Kantesians were suffering *now*, and any delay in additional deliveries would extend that suffering. Sebastian found the idea unsupportable. And so, one night, he snuck into the storehouse and stole another bottle.

And it had felt wondrous. He understood now why his sister was such an ardent rule breaker. There was a palpable thrill with the very act of transgression itself—a heady mixture of trepidation and power. There was also the relief of at least temporarily calming the anxiety he felt at knowing the Kantesians were suffering. There was the rush of pleasure he felt every time he handed the medicine over to Isobelle and saw the look of true gratitude in her eyes. And, there was an unexpected secondary pleasure when he would encounter a Kantesian who only a week ago had been moaning quietly in a bed and was now hale and hearty enough to hang the newly made window glass. The person didn't even know it had been Sebastian who saved him, and savoring that secret somehow made it all the sweeter.

On some level, he always knew that it couldn't go on forever. That eventually he would be found out. He didn't know what would happen then, and he was pleasantly surprised to discover that he didn't really care. No matter what, it had been worth it.

When the day finally came, he was on his way to see Isobelle once again, the heavy weight of a potion sloshing in his satchel. But Marcello was waiting for him outside the entrance. He grabbed Sebastian roughly by the arm and pulled him aside.

"And just what do you think you're doing?" he hissed, his expression tense.

"Uh, going to see Isobelle?" said Sebastian. "I thought you approved."

"Seeing her? Yes. Giving her stolen potions? Absolutely not."

"Ah," said Sebastian.

Marcello shook his head. "I *warned* you. Dandolo keeps his own records and the difference between what he had on record and what was actually in stock was so obvious, even drunk he noticed."

An odd, unfamiliar calm began to settle over Sebastian. It was almost a relief. "Do they know it was me?"

"Not yet, but I'm in that storehouse every day and when they come to question me—which you know they will—I have to tell them the truth."

Sebastian nodded. "Of course you do. I would never ask you to lie for me, and I'm grateful that you decided to warn me."

Marcello sighed. "Honestly, Portinari, I can't believe you'd go this far just for a turn in the sheets with a Kantesian."

Sebastian frowned at his friend. "You think I did all this just to impress Isobelle?"

"Well . . . of course."

"No, Marcello." As Sebastian spoke to his friend, he articulated something that he had not fully understood himself until that moment. "I did this because it was the right thing to do. Do you recall what General Barone told me after the encounter with that monster in Hardsong Pass?"

Marcello shook his head.

"He said, 'No matter our past mistakes, as long as we persist, there will always be opportunities for atonement. It is up to you to seize them.' I arrived in Kleiner with the hope—the first true hope I'd felt in a while—that I could do some real good. Yet how could I possibly find redemption if I willfully ignored the suffering of innocent people? So just as the general advised, I seized this chance to make something right."

"Damn it, Portinari, you're twisting his words around. Aiding our enemy at the cost of our own supplies? He never meant for you to do something like that."

"Oh, I know. But I'm done letting old men dictate what is right and wrong when I know perfectly well what I must do."

Marcello looked like he was about to retort, but Sebastian gripped his shoulders and gave his friend a serene smile.

"Thanks, Marcello. It felt liberating to say that aloud."

Marcello scowled. "You won't feel very *free* once the general figures out what you did."

Sebastian nodded, still strangely unbothered by his looming fate. The courage of the righteous, perhaps?

"I expect it will not go well for me. But still, I plan to give this last potion to Isobelle and warn her of what is to come." He looked thoughtfully into Marcello's eyes. "Will you try to stop me?"

Marcello stared at him for a moment, then began muttering curses as he stalked off.

Sebastian watched him go, feeling a swell of gratitude toward his friend. They might disagree on a number of things. Important things, even. But still, his loyalty, such as it was, meant a lot to him.

He turned and entered the dimly lit warehouse. As always, Isobelle was caring for the remaining Kantesians not yet recovered from their wounds.

"Isobelle, I'm afraid I have bad news," he said.

She looked up at him, and it seemed as though she already knew what he was going to say. She whispered something in Kantesian to the old woman she'd been sitting with. Then she stood and beckoned Sebastian over to a corner.

"This is the last I can give you, I'm afraid." He handed her the potion. "I expect they'll arrest me for treason. Likely as soon as tomorrow."

She took the bottle from him and nodded, biting her pink lower lip. "I have asked so much of you, Captain, but will you grant me one final favor?"

"If it's within my power," he said.

"Meet me by the riverbank outside of town just before midnight."

"I won't run from this, if that's what you're thinking," he told her.

She smiled sadly. "I did not think you would. But if this is to be the last day I see you, I would like to give you something."

He wasn't sure what sort of gift she could give him. For a moment, he felt a small tingle of hope. A kiss perhaps? *More*, even? But no, he admonished himself, that was hardly a gentlemanly expectation. Regardless, he knew he could not deny her now any more than he could when they first met.

"Very well. I will see you tonight at the riverbank."

Jon Skovron

57

The moon was full that night as Sebastian quietly made his way to the riverbank where he used to bake clay into bricks. He was fairly certain that Marcello had seen him slip out of the officers' tent, but his friend had made no noise or objection. Once again, Sebastian was touched by Marcello's loyalty. He promised himself he would do whatever he could to shield his friend from getting any of the blame for the stolen potions.

Kante was often cloaked in fog at night, and the bright moon made the mist glow with an eerie luminescence. Tendrils swirled around his feet as he walked out of town and down to the riverbank.

At first he saw no one by the river. Then the night winds blew, shifting the fog, and he saw Isobelle standing there, looking uncharacteristically grave. As the dense mist continued to swirl, it revealed other Kantesians standing nearby. More continued to appear out of the haze, all of them standing still and silent. He thought it might be the entire town.

It was a jarring moment that reminded him that although he'd been working with these people for months now, he really didn't know them very well. Much too late, he realized that he should have considered some form of betrayal, despite all he had done for them. His hand automatically reached for the gem around his neck.

But he stopped himself. He had already been willing to sacrifice his life for these people. Why would he consider harming them now?

"Isobelle, what's going on?" he asked once he drew near.

She gave him one of her sad smiles. "I'm so glad you came, Sebastian."

"Why is everyone else here?" he asked, feeling their eyes on him. Not unfriendly, but not exactly welcoming, either.

Her smile took on a teasing tone. "Oh, were you expecting a more *intimate* farewell?"

"Uh, n-no, I would never presume—"

"But you were hoping?"

He laughed sheepishly. "I suppose just a little."

Her smile faded. "You have done so much for us, Sebastian. For me and my people. So there are two things I wish to give you."

He waited, unsure how to respond.

"The first thing I wish to give you is an apology. I know there are some men in your battalion, like your friend Marcello, whom you care about. I hope that no harm comes to them, but I cannot promise it."

He looked at her sharply. "Harm?"

"And that leads me to the second thing I wish to give you. Your safety this night."

"Isobelle, I don't understand. What's happening?"

"Listen. You can already hear him coming."

Sebastian strained his hearing. At first he perceived nothing. But after a few moments he heard... *something* off in the distance. It was a strange rhythmic pounding, like a sharp, repetitive metallic clank. It seemed to be coming from a long way off, but it grew in volume as though rapidly drawing closer. As it did so, he also began to hear an odd groan and hiss underlying the muted clang. He felt a chill of recognition.

"What *is* it?" asked Sebastian.

"My grandfather, the former Herzog of Weide." There was both pride and sorrow in Isobelle's voice.

Then he saw it emerge from the mist. A giant metal insect, easily three or four stories tall. It had six steel legs that gouged up the earth as it ran, and a pointed, triangular head that wheezed and hissed as steam poured out of its glowing magenta eyes. Seeing its size, power, and eerie luminous eyes, he understood that it was this thing, or one like it, that had attacked them in Hardsong Pass.

"My God...," he whispered.

"Far from it, Sebastian. This is humanity's work, not God's. Here in Kante, we do not rely on supernatural aid. We take care of ourselves."

"Wait! It's heading for the town!"

He stepped forward, as though to head it off, but Isobelle took hold of his arm. He looked at her in confusion and she shook her head.

"I am so sorry, Sebastian. I know you worked hard to rebuild Kleiner. But we Kantesians are a proud people, and we would sooner our homes be laid to waste than give shelter to our enemies."

Sebastian watched in horror as the metal behemoth crashed into the town. One of its long metal forelegs swept across a two-story brick building, knocking the top off with a thunderous crack that he could hear even from afar. The creature rampaged through the town, destroying one structure after another as though they were stacks of pebbles. Screams could be heard from within the collapsed buildings that housed soldiers.

Even the storehouse, which had been reinforced with a second layer of bricks, could not withstand its hissing metal fury. But when the creature knocked down the sturdy walls, it must have struck the oil supply. A font of liquid flame burst up into the air, lighting the misty sky like fireworks. Burning oil splashed down in all directions, igniting everything it landed upon, including the monster. The creature gave another groaning hiss as the oil burned across its metal hide. It shook itself, but the air it stirred up only increased the strength of the flames. It staggered a few times, then began its clanging run once again, now a flaming monstrosity that streaked off into the night until its flickering light faded once more into the fog.

The monster had fled. But the damage was done. Most of the buildings were destroyed, and flames raged everywhere, feeding off spilled oil, imperial tents, and the timbers of shattered buildings. The fire spewed dense black smoke that mingled with the mists, obscuring the night sky.

"Goodbye, Sebastian," Isobelle said gravely. "If we ever meet again, I hope that we can truly be friends."

"Isobelle..."

He stared helplessly as she and the other Kantesians turned and disappeared into the mist-covered night. For a moment, he thought about going after them, although he didn't know if it was to punish them or join them. But then he turned back to the flaming rubble of Kleiner and realized that Marcello was in there somewhere. So he gripped his gem and ran back into the town.

Many of the soldiers had already fled their makeshift barracks and were trying futilely to put out the oil-fueled fires. As he ran past, Sebastian withdrew the air around the flames, snuffing them out, first on one side, then on the other.

He continued on to the officers' tent, which was one of the few structures still standing. But even though it hadn't collapsed, it was now a raging inferno. He could hear shouts and coughing coming from inside. It sounded like they were all trapped.

Already fatigued from his day's glass labor and lack of sleep, he gathered up the fog that lay so heavily on the night air, condensed it, then brought it down on the tent like a gushing waterfall. The fire hissed spitefully, then disappeared.

Sebastian dropped to his knees, breathing hard. He felt the cold mud beneath him seep into his trousers as he told himself to get back up. He had to go in there and make sure everyone was safe. But he could not make himself move.

"Captain Portinari? Are you injured?"

Sebastian looked up to see the Raízian captain, Reyes, looking down on him with concern.

"I'm fine." Sebastian held out his hand. "Just...putting out these fires took a lot out of me."

Reyes's eyes narrowed as he helped Sebastian to his feet. "I suppose it is not my business to say, Captain, but it has seemed to me for some time that the cost of your power is much too high."

"As long as everyone is alive, it's a cost I willingly pay."

"Let us hope your efforts were not in vain, then."

Reyes yanked open the tent.

"General Barone? Are you here?"

"Marcello?" called Sebastian.

They were greeted by a great many coughs as their fellow officers began to stagger into view. Colonel Totti and Captain Dandolo appeared to have suffered moderate burns, but everyone else was unharmed, including Marcello.

Sebastian rushed over to his friend, tears suddenly springing to his eyes. Were they tears of relief? Of remorse? He did not know.

"I'm so glad you're okay." He gripped Marcello's shoulders.

Marcello looked back at him with haunted eyes. "What happened, Sebastian?"

Sebastian hesitated for a moment, realizing he was about to compromise himself. But what else could he say?

"It was the Kantesians."

"What are you talking about?" asked Captain Branca as he wiped soot from his face.

"I saw it." Sebastian turned to Barone. "The creature that tried to bury us alive in Hardsong Pass."

Barone paused in dabbing at his watery eyes and stared incredulously at him. "Is *that* what attacked us tonight?"

"Yes," said Sebastian.

"And the Kantesians?" he asked.

"They all fled just before the creature attacked."

"And how do you know all this?" Totti demanded as he wrapped a bandage around his burned hand.

Sebastian took a deep breath. What did it matter now, anyway?

"It's because—"

"Portinari just can't keep it in his pants, General," said Marcello.

"Marcello?" asked Sebastian.

"Sorry, Sebastian, I can't keep it a secret any longer." Marcello turned back to Barone. "Despite your orders to not get overly friendly with the enemy, he's been sneaking into the Kantesian area after dark each night to diddle that nurse, Isobelle." He gave Sebastian a hard look. "Must have been a real surprise not to find her in her bed tonight, wasn't it?"

Did Marcello really think that's what happened? No, he knew Sebastian better than that. This was his way of getting him out of serious trouble by blaming him for a minor infraction.

Sebastian nodded glumly. "I'm sorry, sir."

Barone sighed. "Well, I suppose I shouldn't be too angry, since in a sense it was your libido that saved our lives. If you'd been caught in here with us, there's no telling whether you would have been able to put out the flames as quickly as you had."

"I . . . suppose so, sir. Thank you for your understanding."

"Isobelle, eh?" asked Dandolo as he gingerly dabbed salve on his burned leg. "Can't say I blame you, Portinari. She was *delicious*."

Barone looked around the charred ruins of their officers' tent. "I take it you've put out the other fires as well, Portinari?"

"Yes, sir."

"Very well, let's go and see what damage those Kantesian bastards and their metal monster have wrought. I'm afraid it's going to be a long night, gentlemen."

58

As an honored guest of Her Imperial Majesty, Irina was required to participate in certain activities. One of her least favorite among them was attending the weekly recitals performed by the empress's offspring.

The concert hall was stunning, of course. Located in the northwest wing of the palace, it had vaulted ceilings with tall stained glass windows, rows of velvet cushioned chairs on risers, and a massive crystal chandelier overhead. Whenever Irina entered, it always smelled of vanilla and strawberries, and it was clear that great pains had been taken to ensure that the acoustics were immaculate.

Sadly, perfect acoustics only emphasized what dreadful musicians the princes and princess were. The eldest, Prince Valentino, sawed away mercilessly at his violin, heedless of the abrasive tones it produced. The middle child, Princess Constantia, slumped over her cello with a limp despair that made it clear she, like the audience, wished she could be anywhere else. The youngest, Prince Domenico, had been given the onerous task of playing the viola, an instrument forever cursed with the role of harmony rather than melody. The little prince performed earnestly and enthusiastically, and with some skill, but in doing so completely drowned out the melody produced by the other two siblings, making the entire composition unintelligible and more or less unlistenable.

Irina sat with a fixed smile on her face. Ambassador Boz was to her left, and Captain Aguta to her right, both with similar expressions.

After being subjected to these "performances" on a weekly basis for months now, they had learned to tune out the wretched affair while still appearing as enthralled as the empress. Irina did not know Her Majesty well, but thought she seemed an intelligent and astute woman. As such, she wondered if even she was faking her fondness for her children's weekly renditions of traditional Aureumian airs that should have been recognizable but were not.

At last the ordeal was over and the guests began to rise from their seats. Irina glanced around, mostly to appreciate the quiet suffering etched onto the faces of her fellow guests, and noticed that Zaniolo was not present.

"It seems our favorite general was able to get out of this week's recital," she murmured to Boz.

"I'm not surprised, considering recent events," said Boz.

"Such as?" asked Irina.

"Apparently the empire is in quite a state."

"Oh?"

"The Uaine are currently at large, though how one hides a ravenous horde of undead is anyone's guess. The Izmorozians, meanwhile, seem to finally be grasping the concept of national unity, making the empress's plans for an easy reacquisition much less tenable. And most recently of course there is the shocking tragedy that took place in Colmo."

"Shocking tragedy?" Irina felt a cold fist clench in her gut. "Nothing to do with my daughter, I hope."

"Difficult to say, my lady, since not a single soldier at the garrison survived." Boz's eyes glittered. "Apparently the event has inspired tremendous unrest throughout Raíz, as if suddenly bringing centuries of buried resentment to the surface."

"I see." Unfortunately, that strongly suggested to Irina that Sonya *was* somehow involved.

"But there may be some good news for you, at least," said Boz.

"For me specifically?"

"Yes. Apparently with all the uncertainty at home, the empress has wisely decided to recall her forces from Kante."

"She's giving up the campaign? Things *must* be dire."

"Indeed. But I imagine that means you'll be seeing your son again far sooner than expected."

Irina still had no idea how the ambassador gleaned so much information. She'd proposed to Zaniolo in her report that perhaps Boz had an invisible spy in her employ. She didn't know if that was even possible, but it seemed no less probable than the idea that Boz and Vittorio had conducted an elaborate pantomime purely for Irina's benefit. Zaniolo had not yet offered an opinion on either theory.

"That is heartening news regarding my son," she told Boz. "And if you come across any information concerning my daughter, I would be very grateful."

"I am but a humble gossip hound, my lady." Boz's eyes crinkled into a smile. "I expect if you spoke to Zaniolo directly, he would have far more information."

"It couldn't hurt," agreed Irina.

It wasn't merely Sonya she was concerned about. She was glad Sebastian was leaving Kante, but would the empress then send him to put down this Raízian uprising that might include Sonya? Irina didn't know if even the great city of Colmo could withstand another confrontation between her children. Surely Zaniolo would agree with her and urge the empress to keep Sebastian here at the palace.

Boz placed a gentle hand on Irina's arm. "Good luck to you, my lady. I hope you find what you seek."

"My thanks, Ambassador. Now if you will excuse me."

Irina made her way out into the aisle and saw that Cloos lurked by the exit, perhaps hoping to finally drag her to his "workshop" so that she could gush over his secret "project." As she passed, Irina made certain to be deep in conversation with an elderly count that she had briefly met a few weeks ago and whose name she could not recall. She could vaguely see Cloos attempting to get her attention out of the corner of her eye and she kept her full focus on the count so that it was believable she had not noticed his presence.

She knew she would eventually have to see Cloos's project, if such a thing truly existed, but right now she was more concerned with explaining to Zaniolo in no uncertain terms why it was for the good of *everyone* that her offspring not be forced into direct conflict again.

Once Irina had extricated herself from the count, who seemed to have gotten the mistaken impression from their brief conversation that she was interested in becoming his mistress, she headed straight for Zaniolo's office.

It was early evening, so the general might have gone back to his quarters by then. But if things were truly as tense as Boz suggested, there was a good chance that he was still trying to sort and disseminate the large volume of information coming to him from the south, north, and east.

As she hurried down the hall, she saw the unexpectedly familiar face of Sasha Rykov walking with his usual lumbering, disinterested air in the opposite direction. She had no idea why, but her son was deeply fond of the oaf. Sebastian had always been a sentimental boy, so perhaps he viewed the man as one might a beloved pet.

"Good to see you again, Private," she said as they passed.

"Sure," he said with his usual rudeness.

Irina thought about scolding him. While it was true he wasn't her son's servant any longer, such impertinence shouldn't be allowed to pass.

But no. She had more important business, and she didn't want to chance Zaniolo retiring for the day before she'd spoken with him. The doltish peasant probably wouldn't understand anyway. So she held her tongue and continued on her way.

Once she arrived at Zaniolo's office, she was glad to see his office door still open.

"General," said Irina as she entered. "I fear I must ask—"

She stopped in mid-stride and her heart lurched into her throat.

The last time Irina had seen a dead body was when her husband was killed. This time she had mercifully been spared witnessing the actual act. But there could be no doubt that Zaniolo, slumped in his chair, his eyes wide and vacant, a sword handle protruding from his throat, had been murdered.

59

Bad loves worse.

It was an old Izmorozian saying, which essentially meant that no matter how bad something got, inevitably something worse would happen, making the previous *bad* thing seem less awful by comparison. Sebastian could never decide if this concept was the purest expression of Izmorozian fatalism, or a depressing attempt at Izmorozian optimism.

He and the other officers worked until well after sunrise, assessing the damage, getting head counts of the soldiers, triaging those who were injured, and figuring out what, if any, supplies remained. When Sebastian nearly passed out again from fatigue, Barone told Marcello to get him over to the apothecary station for a restorative, then take a break.

The two now sat on a pile of bricks that had been a house the day before and sipped at the foul-tasting restoratives the apothecaries had whipped up. Normally they didn't taste quite so bad, but the food stores had been severely damaged and there hadn't been enough fruit or nectar left to hide the bitterness.

"Well, I'm not going to say I told you so," Marcello said after a long period of silence.

"Thank you," said Sebastian.

"But I damn well did tell you not to get so soft on those Kantesians."

"I suppose you did."

"To think they'd wreck their own newly restored town just to spite us. The bastards. They can't have gone far. We ought to run them all down and make them pay."

"Like they did to us."

"Huh?" asked Marcello.

"Well, here they were, just living their lives, and the empire comes in, destroying everything in sight and killing indiscriminately. Then we rebuild the town for our own purposes while denying prisoners of war much needed medicine. What did we expect? Gratitude?"

"It's war, Portinari. We did what we had to."

"No, we did what we *wanted* to."

"Well General Barone said—"

"Never mind what General Barone says. What do *you* say?"

"You just...don't understand. I'm the general's aide-de-camp. Whatever he says, goes for me, too. It *has* to."

Sebastian looked sorrowfully at his friend. It was the same sort of blind obedience he'd once felt toward Vittorio.

"I *do* understand," he told his friend. "I used to feel a similar loyalty to a different commanding officer. I thought him the wisest and most noble of men. A paragon of virtue. But then I learned that in the end, he was just a man, and not a very good one. I think Barone is probably a better man than the one I once followed, but perhaps that makes it even harder for you to break off and find your own way."

"What are you talking about, my own way?" demanded Marcello. "What other way is there? I would be happy to not have to withhold medicine from old ladies and children, so please, Sebastian, show me this *amazing* other way you've found where we all get to be nice to each other and nobody has to die anymore."

Sebastian looked at his friend and realized he had no response.

"Exactly," said Marcello after a moment.

They sat there in silence for a little while, occasionally grimacing as they sipped their bitter restoratives. They were near the western edge of the ravaged town, so they were the first to see the rider galloping across the meadow toward them. It was a lone man in imperial uniform. He was riding one horse while another galloped unencumbered by his side.

"An imperial messenger," said Marcello.

"How can you tell?" asked Sebastian.

"He's probably switching back and forth between horses so they don't tire out as easily. It must be something urgent. Let's go see."

The two stood up and hurried to intercept the messenger. He reined in his horse sharply and looked carefully at the two officers, then nodded.

"I must speak to General Barone immediately, and no one else."

"I'm his aide-de-camp," Marcello told him proudly. "I'll take you to him at once."

Sebastian tagged along as Marcello led the messenger to the makeshift shelter that Barone had set up to command the recovery. The general had found one of the few buildings that still had two joining walls intact. He had taken an only slightly singed section of canvas from a tent and stretched it across to make a roof. Now he sat in its shade poring over tally sheets spread out on a tabletop supported by charred bricks.

"General Barone, sir!" The messenger saluted sharply.

The general looked up at him, a bushy white eyebrow rising when he realized this soldier was newly arrived. "Yes?"

"I have an urgent command from the empress herself!"

Sebastian and Marcello exchanged a look. A command directly from the empress? This was serious.

"I see," Barone said gravely.

The messenger handed him a sealed envelope. He examined the seal for a moment, then carefully broke it. His expression did not change as he read the contents of the message but once he was finished, he closed his eyes and rubbed at the bridge of his nose.

He looked over at Marcello. "Bring me Totti, Branca, and Dandolo at once."

"But...not Captain Reyes?" asked Marcello, looking a little unsure.

"No, not Reyes," agreed Barone. "In fact, if at all possible, avoid contact with him or any of the Viajero troupe."

Marcello still looked confused, but he gave a sharp salute, said, "Yes, sir!" then hurried off.

Barone turned to Sebastian. "Captain, I pray it won't come to this, but if necessary, do you think you have enough strength for a serious confrontation?"

"Right now, sir?" asked Sebastian.

"Indeed."

"I'll...do whatever is necessary for the safety of our men."

"Well said." Barone nodded. "And keep drinking that potion, Portinari. I know it tastes like the devil, but if it comes down to it, we might need every last drop of energy you can muster."

They waited in tense silence until Marcello returned with Totti, Branca, and Dandolo in tow. They looked as weary and filthy as Sebastian felt. The idea of any of them getting into a confrontation right then seemed ill advised at best. And anyway, a confrontation with whom?

"Gentlemen, I'm afraid I have some troubling news," Barone said.

"*More* bad news?" asked Dandolo.

Bad loves worse. Sebastian could practically hear his mother invoking the old saying.

"I have just received an urgent summons from the empress," said Barone. "We are to pack up immediately and return with all possible haste to Magna Alto."

There was a moment of stunned silence.

"I'm sorry, General," said Totti, his face pale. "Did you just say that after everything we've been through, after all we've lost and suffered, we're *retreating*?"

"We're falling back for the time being," said Barone. "I'm afraid more pressing concerns call us back."

"What could be more pressing than the campaign in Kante?" demanded Branca.

"And why...," asked Dandolo, looking around, "isn't Reyes here? Shouldn't he be present for this announcement as well?"

Barone looked gravely at them. "None of us have any doubt of Reyes's loyalty, or the loyalty of his troupe. But there seems to be great unrest in Raíz right now, and there is...*concern* at the palace that our Raízian comrades may find themselves conflicted as to where their primary loyalties lie. So in the interest of pragmatism, we have been ordered to take Reyes and his troupe into custody during our return trip."

Silence once more fell on the group.

Finally Dandolo said, "This is preposterous! I trust Reyes with my life!"

"As do I," said Barone. "But I cannot risk the life of every single soldier in the battalion. Hopefully Reyes will recognize and accept this...*complicated* situation and allow himself and his men to be placed into temporary custody until we reach Magna Alto and get it all sorted out. But if not..." He glanced meaningfully at Sebastian. "We must be prepared to take action to ensure his compliance, one way or another."

60

It would have been too obvious to assemble the entire battalion, so Barone ordered Totti to gather his "best men." Once that small but formidable group had been brought together before the general, they formed up and marched to the section of Kleiner where Reyes and his Viajero troupe were camped.

The late-afternoon sun cast the turbulent, cloudy skies of Kante in a liquid gold. The wind had picked up, pulling at Sebastian's hair and uniform. It gave him some relief, cooling his cheeks, which were flushed from the troubling idea that he might have to inflict harm on men who were supposed to be his allies. No matter what, he promised himself, he would not lose control. No one would die that day by his hand.

Reyes was sitting among a group of his Viajero and they were passing around a bottle of something, no doubt enjoying a well-deserved rest after laboring all day to recover from the previous night's attack. Reyes said something to his men that Sebastian couldn't hear, but he saw many of them laugh and nod. Reyes had always seemed like a man who was much loved by those under his command.

Reyes took a sip from the bottle being passed around. As he handed it to the man beside him, he glanced over and saw the formation of soldiers marching toward him. His head cocked to the side, more curious than concerned, and he stood.

"General? Has something come up?" he asked casually, though he didn't come any closer.

Barone lifted his hand and the formation came to a halt, still twenty feet or so from the troupe of Raízians.

"I'm afraid so, Captain," he called across the open space between the two groups. "We just received orders to return to Magna Alto with all possible haste."

"An emergency at the capital?" Reyes's pose remained calm, but his sharp eyes scanned the group of men before him, perhaps intuiting their tension.

"A great deal of turmoil, in fact," said Barone. "Some of it stemming from violent unrest in Colmo."

Reyes was silent for a moment, then he said, "I see."

"You have a lot of family in Colmo, don't you, Ernesto?"

Sebastian found it strangely discomfiting that the general would choose to use the captain's first name in that moment, and Reyes seemed to feel similarly, because his posture straightened, and his eyes narrowed.

"I do."

"We have fought side by side many times."

Reyes nodded. "Indeed we have, Paolo."

"I hope I might appeal to our many years as allies when I ask you to willingly place yourself and your men under custody during the journey to the capital."

Reyes was again silent for a moment, his face unreadable. Then he asked, "And what crime is it we're accused of?"

"No crime, Ernesto. But the empress understands the difficult position you and your men are in and doesn't wish to take chances with the lives of any of her men. So until she can judge where your loyalties lie, she has asked me to safeguard against any potential sympathizers within your troupe."

Reyes's expression darkened. "After everything we have done for the empire, and for you, this is greatly disappointing, Paolo."

"I won't deny that the situation is troubling," said Barone, his tone becoming harder and less conciliatory. "But I have my orders, and now so do you. Stand down and allow yourself and your men to be restrained until we return to Magna Alto. As a soldier and officer of the imperial army, you are sworn to obey."

Reyes glanced at his men. Some of them looked alarmed. Some looked openly angry. Sebastian would have been furious as well. No matter the justification, it seemed like the empire was betraying them after their years of loyal service.

"I may be a soldier, but I am a person first," said Reyes. "A person with integrity who doesn't cast aside years of *friendship* to appease the will of privileged royalty who have never known a day of true hardship and sacrifice in their life."

"Do *not* disparage the empress," Barone said coldly. "No amount of friendship would allow me to forgive such a thing."

The two men glared at each other in silence. Both groups were tense, with hard expressions, stiff postures, and hands hovering much too close to their weapons. Sebastian supposed that the underlying tension between the Aureumians and the Raízians had always lurked beneath the surface. He'd caught brief glimpses of it now and then. The Aureumians thought the Viajero were arrogant and snobbish, and the Viajero thought the Aureumians were coarse and insensitive. And now that buried animosity had risen to the surface with potentially disastrous consequences.

At last Reyes spoke. "In the interest of avoiding violence, I will surrender myself into custody."

"And your men," said Barone.

"I will not order my men into unjust captivity," Reyes said flatly. "I *cannot*. Nor can I stand idly by if anyone tries to capture them by force. You have only me, or no one at all."

"I see." Barone turned to Sebastian. "Captain Portinari, subdue the Viajero and their captain."

Sebastian stared at the general. Why must it be him? What about all the men behind them bristling with swords and hostility? When Sebastian turned to Reyes, he saw the look of scathing judgment in his fellow captain's eyes.

"Do as your conscience dictates, Captain Portinari," said Reyes.

Sebastian felt the shame burn in his chest. First, the willful neglect of wounded prisoners of war, and now the betrayal of allies who had done nothing to provoke distrust. This was not what he had joined Barone's battalion for. It was not what he had come to Kante for.

"Captain," said Barone. "You are a soldier of the imperial army. You have your orders."

"Come on, Sebastian...," muttered Marcello. "You know how this is going to end one way or another, so don't be on the wrong side of it."

Sebastian felt his stomach churn as he took hold of his gem.

"So be it," said Reyes. He raised his hands. "First Movement! Begin!"

The Viajero began a complex combination of dance and song that Sebastian had seen before in treating severe pain for a large group of injured. In moments it would render Sebastian and all of Barone's men insensible for several minutes. Long enough for Reyes and his Viajero to escape, or if they were angry enough, kill them all.

But Sebastian had read imperial history. He knew that the reason the Viajero hadn't participated in the Winter War was because the cold interfered with their ability to cast magic. So he drew the heat out of the air around them. In moments their movements became stiff and their voices faltered. Even the graceful Reyes found himself shivering uncontrollably and barely able to stand on his feet.

"Colonel Totti, the Viajero have been rendered temporarily powerless," Barone said. "Move in quickly and restrain them."

Totti gave a sharp, eager salute. "Yes, sir!"

"*But*," said Barone. "Bloodshed is no longer necessary. I will view any acts of brutality as disobedience."

"Yes, sir." Totti seemed slightly less eager, but he motioned his men to move. They quickly bound and gagged Reyes and his men.

Barone turned to Sebastian. "Good work, Captain. You did what was necessary without causing unnecessary loss of life."

Sebastian felt so ill he could not bring himself to respond. Reyes's words echoed in his mind. *Do as your conscience dictates.* Mere hours after criticizing Marcello for following questionable orders, Sebastian had done the same.

Marcello gripped Sebastian's shoulder and gave him a sympathetic look. "We all have to follow orders we don't like sometimes."

His friend probably hadn't meant to twist the guilt deeper, but he did.

"Indeed," said Barone. "Even I must follow orders I am uncomfortable with, Portinari. Such selflessness is the fullest expression of being a soldier."

If that was true, thought Sebastian, perhaps he should not be a soldier. Perhaps his father and sister had been right all along.

It was a painful thought, one that made his innards writhe. But he was done avoiding painful lessons. He was done hiding from difficult truths.

61

It was rare for Jorge to visit the Viajero Quarter. Frankly, it had always made him a little uncomfortable. The Viajero all had such an ease about them. Such a casual warmth. Just as with the Izmorozians, he was keenly aware that there was a distance between the Viajero and himself that perhaps no effort on his part could ever hope to bridge. The difference was, these were supposed to be *his* people.

Yet even though the Viajero Quarter reminded him of just how unlike most of his countrymen he was, he was here anyway. Maria was worried about Sonya, and since he was her best friend, she had asked him to come down and talk to her.

Jorge didn't know precisely what the problem was. Maria had been vague on the details. But he could guess at least some of it. *Someone* had slain the entire imperial garrison. Who else could do that except Sonya? But what had happened after? Had she been killed and brought back to life again by her goddess during the attack? If so, then the change of appearance, and possibly of behavior as well, would no doubt have alarmed Maria. Of course he had *warned* his sister something like this might happen. Maybe it was the shame of that which had made her skimp on the details of her request. But whatever had happened, and whatever Sonya had become, Jorge had to hope that he could still help his friend.

His family had insisted he take protection with him to the quarter, so Ignacio followed at a respectful distance. Jorge had been

329

embarrassed at first. He felt it was bad enough being a member of one of the Great Families "slumming it" in the Viajero Quarter. He couldn't understand why his sister had never been similarly self-conscious about that.

But now that he had reached the quarter, he was grateful for Ignacio's protection. He had not felt this kind of unease since before the battle at Gogoleth. Everywhere he looked, he saw it in people's eyes. A terrible, desperate eagerness. The sort of self-righteous impulse that overrode reason and made people fling their lives away. They were still Viajero, of course. Still laughing and singing and dancing. But there was an edge to it all. An aggressiveness that was not typical of the usually easygoing artist community.

The farther he got into the quarter, the more overt it became. He began to see anti-imperial slogans painted on the walls. FREE RAÍZ! and DEATH TO THE GREEDY EMPIRE! He saw a massive portrait of the empress with a pig nose. It was all fairly coarse compared to typical Viajero work, but what it lacked in finesse, it made up for with a seething fury that seemed to lurk beneath each brushstroke. The music that drifted down from open windows was no less unnerving. Hard, scraping guitar, sharp staccato drums. It made walking through the streets of the quarter feel like passing through a thunderstorm.

Finally he saw a familiar face. Lucia was a relatively young Viajero, but her natural gift for singing, fierce artistic discipline, and her fiery passion had already made her a well-respected presence in the quarter. It was said even the renowned Raízian playwright Pedro Molina would doff his hat to her when they passed each other in the street, and there was rumor that he was currently writing a new play with her in mind for the lead role.

But now Lucia was working with a small group of dancers who were marking through the choreography of something that even without the energy and commitment of a performance made Jorge ill at ease. Something about it seemed terribly old. And ominous.

"No, Francisco!" she shouted at one dancer. "Do you want us all to be turned inside out, our guts flung into the faces of our enemies? Is that what you want?"

"N–no, Lucia!" Even though the man was much larger than her, he was clearly cowed by her presence.

"Then God damn you, pivot on that right heel like I told you!" She let out an explosive sigh and threw her hands into the air. "Or else kill me now!"

Jorge was afraid to interrupt her, lest her explosive temper turn on him, so he continued to watch them practice for a short while until she eventually noticed him.

"Ah, Jorge. Maria said you'd be stopping by."

She shifted from fierce commander to cavalier artist with sudden and jarring ease.

"Forgive me for interrupting, Lucia," he said.

"Think nothing of it." She flipped her hand at the dancers. "Everyone go practice. When I come back, I expect to see it done perfectly."

She strode over to him. "Okay, little brother, you want to see your lover?"

Jorge didn't know why she thought she could talk to him like that, but more importantly, he had to clear up the bigger misunderstanding.

"Er, Lucia, Sonya and I are not—"

"Oh I know," she said. "I can smell a virgin a mile away."

"Ah…" This was why he didn't like being around Viajero. Not only did they make him feel stiff and formal, they *shamed* him for it. "So how *is* Sonya?"

Lucia waved her hand, as though shooing a fly. "Like I told Maria, it's nothing to worry about. Just a spell of melancholy. It happens to all artists. Perfectly natural."

Jorge decided not to argue whether it was natural or not and instead said, "All the same, I'd like to see her."

"Of course, of course," Lucia said agreeably. "Melancholy may be normal, but it never hurts to have a good friend to help you through it. And who knows when those imperial pigs will try to come back. I respect another artist's process, of course, but the sooner you can get her back into a fighting mood, the better."

She led him down one of the narrow, winding streets this part of Colmo was so famous for. It was said that the great Viajero architect

Joaquin Fortuny had designed this neighborhood with the Viajero specifically in mind, claiming that its circuitous ways and irregular passages were conducive to the creative spirit. Jorge merely found it conducive to getting lost.

But Lucia knew its routes well, and led him through the maze to one building nestled in among all the rest with no distinguishing features except a newly painted mural of an arctic fox that looked down balefully at him from above the entrance.

"I take it someone did that for her?" he asked Lucia.

Lucia nodded. "We wanted her to feel welcome, you know? So we asked Felix to do it. He's one of the best at painting animal likenesses in all Raíz. You've probably seen his work all over the city."

Jorge could rarely differentiate one artist's work for another, but he nodded as though he could. Yet again, there was this unspoken pressure to appear creative and cultured in a way he was not, and probably never could be.

Lucia glanced meaningfully at Ignacio. "You'll want to leave the muscle behind."

"How dare you—" Ignacio began, looking deeply offended.

"No, she's right," Jorge said gently. "I'm sorry, Ignacio. Will you wait here for me?"

Ignacio took a moment to regain his temper, then nodded. "As you wish, Señor."

"Wonderful," Lucia said dryly. "Shall we enter then, *most honored* Señor?"

The shades inside were all drawn and there were no candles or lanterns lit so the place was quite dim.

"How does she even see to piss?" muttered Lucia.

"She can see in the dark," said Jorge.

"Impressive."

"Sonya?" he called. "It's Jorge."

"Hey."

He heard her voice faintly but he almost didn't recognize it. Her moods had shifted quite a lot since they'd been forced to flee Izmoroz, but this was much more stark a difference. She sounded listless. Hopeless, even. That didn't make sense, though. If it was true that she'd just killed a bunch of imperial soldiers, she should be rather cheerful.

He went farther into the room, his eyes straining in the dim light. Finally he found her lying on a cot in the corner near a shuttered window. The tiny slits of sunlight that filtered through showed her lying on her back staring up at the ceiling. He paused, not sure what to do.

Lucia was apparently not as intimidated by this scene. She flopped into a nearby chair. "I brought your rich boy, Sonya."

"Thanks," said Sonya, although she did not sound particularly thankful and still did not bother to look at them.

"Go on." Lucia waved impatiently to Jorge.

Although he didn't like being pushed around, he moved over to Sonya and after a moment sat down on the gritty stone floor beside her cot.

"Sonya," he whispered. "What happened?"

It took her a while to respond, but he could tell she was working toward something, so he remained silent and waited.

"I killed them all," she said softly.

He waited for more, but that seemed to be the end of it.

"Sonya, I hate to say this but you've…killed a lot of people. What made it different this time?"

"*I* made it different," she said.

"How do you mean?"

"A Ranger of Marzanna is supposed to believe that death is natural. There's nothing wrong with dying or killing, provided there's a purpose for it. I accepted that and it didn't use to bother me. But the justifications I clung to: freeing my people, serving the Lady…I lost them. So instead I started killing for money. For community. For acceptance. Honestly, just for something to do."

She finally turned to look at him. The small bands of sunlight shone across her watery golden eyes.

"And it was easy, Jorge. So easy. Maybe I could have just floated along like that for years, but it all felt…trivial. So when Lucia came to me with something that sounded important, I jumped at it. I went into that garrison thinking finally I'm getting back to doing what I'm supposed to do. Even if I wasn't in Izmoroz, I was still a Ranger of Marzanna."

She looked back to the ceiling. She closed her eyes and a tear streaked down her cheek.

"Sonya...," Jorge said. "I still don't understand what's wrong."

"I realized that I don't want to be a servant of death anymore, Jorge," she whispered. "But without that, I don't know what's left of me."

62

The journey from Kante back to Magna Alto was exhausting. Each morning they awoke, ate a cold breakfast, then began at the fastest pace the infantry could muster. They continued with only short breaks until sunset, then set up camp and fell into deep slumber. The following day they did the same thing, and every day after.

The grueling pace left the entire battalion weakened, but there wasn't much risk of attack in the middle of the vast Aureumian heartland. And since they were returning to the capital, they did not need to be fresh and ready for battle when they arrived.

As a captain, and one of the few soldiers with a mount, Sebastian was required to ride up and down the line during the march, making sure that none were slacking. He was under orders to immediately punish any who fell behind, and was grateful it was something he rarely had to do.

In addition to the march itself, there was also the matter of keeping guard over the Raízians, supposed allies that they must now treat as prisoners. The Aureumian soldiers seemed able to change their disposition toward their Raízian allies quite easily. Some even seemed eager to do so. Sebastian had a difficult time understanding that.

When he expressed his concerns one afternoon to Marcello, his friend said, "Oh, that's because you're not really Aureumian."

"How do you mean?" asked Sebastian.

"Well, you're only half Aureumian by blood, and you were raised in Izmoroz. So it makes sense that you don't think or act very Aureumian."

"I *meant*," said Sebastian, "what does being Aureumian have to do with a blatant disregard for one's allies?"

"That's just it, Portinari." Marcello looked a little frustrated. Or perhaps defensive. "You're looking at it wrong. People are scared, that's all. We *have* to keep these Viajero tied up and gagged. If even one of them were to slip free, it could be the death of us all."

"Surely that's an exaggeration," said Sebastian.

Marcello shook his head stubbornly. "You really don't get it, do you? I guess it can't be helped. After all, you're not Aureumian, and you're a wizard, too. You've never had to worry about other people having magic while you have none. Aureumians have always had to come down hard on magic users. Otherwise it would be the end of us."

"So you've always lived in unspoken fear of your allies?" asked Sebastian.

"Well, not *fear*, of course," Marcello said quickly. "We're not cowards, after all. But a certain amount of caution. A man would have to be foolish to think someone with special power wouldn't try to take advantage of it if they could."

"I . . . see."

Sebastian wondered if he was also among the people the Aureumians viewed with unspoken "caution."

The tensest period of each day was when it came time to feed the prisoners. The Viajero needed to have their gags temporarily removed so they could eat, which of course presented them with an opportunity to free themselves, and perhaps seek retribution for their betrayal. To discourage this, they were only fed one at a time, and each was heavily guarded while they ate. Because Captain Reyes had been so respected, he was now equally feared. In order to assure everyone that it was under control, Barone ordered that none other than the imperial wizard would guard Reyes as he ate.

"I don't need to tell you what sort of bloodshed might ensue if you shirk your duty, Captain," Barone had told him. "On *both* sides."

"No, sir. I suppose not," said Sebastian.

So he sat in the dirt with the man who had so impressed him with beauty and grace and watched as the Viajero desperately shoveled his meager daily allotment of cold porridge between his raw, cracked lips.

"I'm sorry, Captain," he whispered. "I'm so sorry."

Reyes paused for a moment, and gazed at him with weary eyes. "Your words sound sincere, Captain. But your actions belie them."

Then he returned to finishing his food before his time ran out.

Sebastian felt the hard crush of guilt in his chest as he retied the gag. Of course the man was right. How could he think an apology meant anything when he continued to participate in such terrible and unjust treatment? He tried to tell himself that he was there to keep things from getting worse, but he no longer believed his own self-justifications. Regardless of anything else, he was still complicit.

He had just left the prisoner area when he heard a shout from behind.

"One's slipped his gag! Look out!"

Sebastian turned back to see that one of the other Viajero had stood up, his mouth open as though ready to speak or sing. There was a desperation in his eyes. A madness, almost. Sebastian watched his chest rise as he filled his lungs with air.

But whether it had been to sing a dangerous magic or merely to beg for more food, Sebastian would never know. Before the man uttered a sound, three swords pierced him. One in the chest, one in the throat, and one in his mouth. The soldiers gripped their swords tightly, their faces hard as stone as they kept the blades in place while the Viajero choked, and gagged, and bled to death.

Sebastian remembered once wishing he could be more like his Aureumian countrymen. Now he was grateful that it still seemed an impossible goal to attain.

63

At last the majestic, soaring towers of Magna Alto came into view, but it did little to ease Sebastian's troubled mind. Once they passed through the main gate and into the city, they were met by a large escort who took charge of the Raízians.

"What will happen to Captain Reyes and his troupe, sir?" Sebastian asked the general as he watched them marched off toward the brig.

Barone sighed. "I don't know, Captain. Hopefully they will just be kept under watch in a comfortable environment until the empress is assured of their continued loyalty. But..." He shook his head. "These are complicated times."

Sebastian did not find that explanation satisfying, but there was little he could do or say. "Yes, sir."

Before dismissing the infantry, Barone addressed them from horseback.

"I know this was a difficult and discouraging mission. Rest assured that once peace and unity has been restored to the empire, we will return to Kante to continue the work we started. For now, get as much rest as you can. I expect we'll have new marching orders soon enough."

Once the infantry had been dismissed, Barone, Sebastian, Marcello, and the other captains took the spiraling road to the palace. Sebastian barely noticed as they passed through the Silver Ring, the splendorous neighborhood where some of the wealthiest people in the empire lived. Even entering the palace stirred little within him. He dully wondered if it was merely the exhaustion that tempered his previous wonder, or his growing disillusionment.

Once Barone dismissed the officers, Sebastian went straight to his mother's apartments. He found her sitting in a chair, calmly drinking tea and ignoring the cookies, just as he'd left her. She seemed not to have changed at all.

"You've returned at last, darling," she said. "I was..."

She trailed off as she got a good look at him. Her already pale face took on a deathly pallor and she came to her feet. "Sebastian! My God, what happened?"

"It's okay, Mother." He moved to her and took her hands, forcing himself to smile reassuringly.

She pulled one hand away and touched his hair. "So much gray, my darling...And your face..." She cupped his cheek with her cool hand and gently stroked the dark pouch beneath one of his eyes with her thumb.

"It looks worse than it is," he said.

"It *looks* like you've aged twenty years in only a few months," she said bluntly.

He winced. "Thank you, Mother. You always know just how to put things."

"Sit," she commanded.

He hardly needed convincing, and immediately sank into one of the chairs. He found he didn't have much appetite, but poured himself a cup of tea. His mother sat back down beside him and took up her own half-full cup.

"It's the magic, isn't it?" she asked.

He nodded as he cupped his mug of tea with both hands, finding some small comfort in its warmth.

"If that is the case," his mother declared, "clearly you must stop using magic."

He smiled bitterly. "Galina said the same thing."

"She always did have a great deal of sense." His mother sighed. "I wish things had worked out between you. I was genuinely fond of her, despite the fact that she was a conniving bitch."

339

His smile grew teasing. "Are you sure you don't mean *because* of that?"

"Perhaps," she conceded. "But betraying you was the one thing I couldn't forgive."

He stared down into his tea, watching the steam drift off the surface. He suddenly wondered what Galina would make of his current doubts. Would she be pleased? Would she see it as vindication for what she had done?

"There's something else bothering you," his mother said.

"You always know."

"Of course. Now, out with it. I detest lengthy interrogations."

"Do you think I made the right choice in joining the imperial army?"

She regarded him carefully for a moment before speaking.

"At the time you made the choice, yes. It was the only way to ensure our safety in such a precarious situation. And later, with all of Izmoroz as your enemy, what else could you do but flee to Aureum and the relative safety it offered?"

He looked up at her. "But now?"

She was again silent, as though weighing what she should say next.

"You've asked before what happened to your grandparents and your aunt, and I've always said I would tell you another time. Would you still like to know?"

"Of course."

She nodded, then poured herself some more tea. She took a sip and her eyes drifted away, as though seeing old memories rise.

"I met your father shortly after the war. The attraction was mutual and instant. Ever a man of action, it did not take him long to ask your grandparents for my hand, and our engagement took place soon after.

"There were many among the nobility who disagreed vehemently with our engagement. Still hurting from their defeat and subsequent loss of power, they considered it tantamount to betrayal by the Turgenev family. I suspect it particularly rankled them because I chose the imperial commander who defeated them over Lord Prozorova, arguably the most respected and sought after young noble in the country. It was a telling indication of the dramatic shift of power in postwar Izmoroz.

"But your grandparents were thrilled with the engagement. They understood that Izmoroz had been irrevocably changed, and by allying themselves through marriage to the most powerful imperial personage in the region, they were ensuring their own standing within the new order. Your aunt was not old enough to become engaged, yet she already had several extremely influential suitors, noble and imperial. The future looked very bright indeed for the Turgenevs."

She looked down at her tea. After a moment, she placed it carefully on the table, then folded her hands together on her lap. When she looked at Sebastian, he was stunned to see her eyes now brimming with unshed tears. He had never seen such open emotion from his mother in all his life. But her voice remained clear and firm as she spoke.

"Unfortunately, your grandparents underestimated the lengths to which people would go to appease their resentment. In those days, the Turgenevs had two homes. The townhome on North Veter Street that you have seen many times, and a large manor just outside the city. On the night of our wedding, your father and I retired to the townhouse, while your grandparents and your aunt, who was not yet fifteen, returned to the manor."

She paused for a moment and took a slow breath. Her eyes continued to brim with unshed tears but she seemed able to prevent them from falling somehow, perhaps by sheer force of will. After a moment, she continued, though now her voice wavered.

"The next morning..." She took another breath. "I learned that the manor had been set on fire, and all within had perished in the blaze."

She did not look at Sebastian as she spoke, but stared fiercely off into empty space. Her hands grasped each other so tightly they were white. But still she did not shed her tears.

After a moment, he asked, "The Izmorozian nobles did it?"

"Or they had the peasants do it. The details hardly matter."

"But...aren't you angry with them?"

She sighed, and all the tension seemed to drain out of her. She carefully dabbed at her eyes as she said, "With the Izmorozian nobility?

341

Not particularly. They were small-minded, frightened, resentful, and petty. Like most people in this world. They had been brutally conquered by your father, a man who truly earned his savage reputation as Giovanni the Wolf. Did they not have a right to be angry as well?"

"I suppose, but still . . . what did their terrible actions accomplish?"

"Nothing of course. But if you think war is meant to accomplish something, you haven't been paying attention." His mother now seemed back to her old self and spoke with lucid clarity, as though giving him a history lecture like she had when he was a child. "War exists because weak and arrogant fools desperately try to prove their strength, and other weak and arrogant fools retaliate in kind. It is a never-ending cycle of reprisals, retributions, and sometimes naked vengeance."

"Surely there must be some way to stop it," said Sebastian. "To end the cycle."

"Of course," she said. "One side must stop retaliating, even in the face of hideous cruelty. And I'm sure you already have some idea how difficult it would be for even the most generous of souls to watch their loved ones brutally slaughtered and not lash out in kind."

Sebastian thought of the wrathful peasants who had rebelled within Gogoleth. They had likely been retaliating against his actions in Les and elsewhere. He thought of Isobelle and her fellow Kantesians watching with satisfaction as their giant metal monster smashed through the enemy who had destroyed their town and killed so many of their people.

"Why do you tell me this?" he asked.

"Because, my darling boy, you aren't really asking me if you made the right choice to become a soldier when your father died. You are asking me if you should be one now. While I would never tell you what to do, I thought you were ready to have a clearer, more mature picture of what it means to be a soldier in wartime."

"But wouldn't it still be a risk to both of us if I abandoned my post now?"

"Things have changed at the palace in your absence, Sebastian, and our position here is less secure. Our primary ally, Zaniolo, has been murdered."

Sebastian stared at her. "How? By whom?"

"Stabbed to death in his own office, although the killer has not yet been found."

"And it happened right here within the palace?"

She nodded. "And that's not all. The Uaine forces have apparently vanished from Izmoroz. It's suspected they are somehow making their move on Magna Alto. Any day now, the outer wall could be besieged by a horde of undead and we'll be stuck in a siege."

"My God. No wonder the empress called us back."

"And hopefully you now understand why this place is no longer a safe haven for us."

He leaned in close and said quietly, "Should we flee, Mother? Right now?"

"And go where?" she asked.

He thought of Isobelle. "I...know of some potential allies in Kante."

"Do you have a way to contact them?"

He shook his head.

"Do you at least know where they are?"

Again he had to shake his head.

"We would have to be quite desperate to find ourselves wandering the Kantesian countryside looking for people who would only be *potential* allies."

"I...see your point, Mother."

"I have been forming some alliances of my own with the other expatriate guests here at the palace, so I am not without some support."

"That's comforting to know," said Sebastian.

"For the moment, I think we should continue as we are, but we must remain flexible. Barone and his battalion will be sent south to deal with the Raízian uprising, but with any luck, you'll remain here to help defend the palace in case the Uaine attack."

"Yes, it would be best if I was here to protect you," said Sebastian.

"For another reason as well," said his mother. "I'm sure it won't surprise you at this point to learn that your sister has gotten herself mixed up in the mess down in Colmo."

"Yasha is working with the Viajero insurgents?"

"Apparently so."

Sebastian's mother was right. He wasn't surprised. But he was worried.

"What if I *do* get sent to Raíz?"

His mother sighed. "It is a distinct possibility."

"Mother...I don't know if I can fight her again," he confessed. "I don't think I *want* to."

"Well, that's good to hear," his mother said, looking unexpectedly relieved. "Perhaps you're maturing more than just physically."

"But I thought—"

"Sebastian, I am a simple woman."

"Come now, Mother, you're one of the most complicated people I've ever met."

"Hardly. It's the world that is complicated, and it is my steadfast commitment to simplicity that makes me such a confusing anomaly. I have never cared for politics, ideals, nations, cultures, or any number of 'causes' that people sacrifice themselves and their loved ones for. Since the moment I lost my mother, father, and sister to that fire, I have cared only for the remaining members of my family. Everything I have done, and everything I continue to do, is intended to ensure their continued survival. I care not one whit for any oaths you may have made to the current ruler of this arbitrarily drawn land. You and your sister come first. Always."

He stared at her. As was often the case, he didn't quite understand what she was implying. But at least now he had the courage to admit that.

"What do you think I should do, Mother?"

"If you are sent to Raíz, I say empires, armies, and righteous goals be damned. Do whatever it takes to ensure that both you and your sister come out of this conflict alive."

64

General Barone had been right in surmising that it wouldn't be long before the battalion was once again deployed. In fact, Sebastian had only three days to rest before there was a quick knock on his door. He opened it to find Marcello.

"Hello, Portinari, how are you holding up?" he asked.

"Okay. And you?"

Marcello grinned. "I must have slept for two days straight, then ate for another day straight. I feel nearly myself now."

"Just in time to get deployed again, huh?" asked Sebastian.

Marcello's smile faded. "I'm afraid so. The general asked me to come get you. He and the empress want to have a word."

"I assume immediately." Sebastian took his uniform jacket from the closet and put it on.

"Nobody makes the empress wait," agreed Marcello.

Sebastian nodded, then walked with Marcello down the hall as he buttoned up his jacket. He wondered what the empress wished to speak to him about. It wasn't really necessary for her to give him his orders personally, after all.

"Ah! Welcome back, Sebastian."

Sebastian glanced over and saw Vittorio standing nearby, his head bowed respectfully. It was a jarring moment because he had almost forgotten the strange frail creature his former mentor had become.

"Oh, hello... Franko." It still felt uncomfortable to call him that. "How are you feeling?"

"Quite well, thank you. And I'm glad to see you're still in one piece."

"Thank you. Yes, there wasn't a great deal of battle."

"Still, you must be disappointed to be brought back before you could accomplish your goals."

"I suppose so..." Sebastian gazed at the sweetly smiling Vittorio and realized he simply had no idea how to talk to this person who now truly seemed a stranger to him. He didn't want to be rude or cruel, but he felt ill at ease in his presence.

"Well," Vittorio said brightly, "a little angel told me that good news awaits you."

"Is that so?" Sebastian wondered just how far gone the man had become.

"Indeed." Franko beamed. "I think the news will lift your spirits during this trying time."

"Er, thank you, Franko."

There was an awkward moment as the three of them stood in silence, Vittorio smiling pleasantly, Sebastian and Marcello giving each other confused glances.

"Well," Sebastian said finally. "I'm glad to see you are settled in now."

"Oh my, yes. Now you better be off. You don't want to keep Her Majesty waiting, do you?"

"R-right."

Sebastian and Marcello continued on their way down the hall, leaving the smiling ex-commander behind.

"Was that Franko the traitor?" Marcello asked under his breath.

"I take it you know him?"

"Only by reputation," said Marcello. "*He* is the former commander you were talking about?"

"Yes."

"Well no wonder you're leery of following orders. If half the things I've heard about him are true, he's an utter brute."

"I can't argue with that."

"Really I don't know why people still admire him."

Sebastian glanced at him sharply. "What do you mean? The man's a convicted traitor. How could *anyone* admire him?"

"It's from before my time, but apparently he was right up there with your dad as one of the most beloved officers in the empire. And the fact that he survived a fall from the tower, just like Emperor Alessandro, well... some people wonder if his talk about angels and divine intervention isn't so crazy after all."

"That's absurd."

Marcello shrugged. "I'm not arguing. It's just what some of the soldiers have been saying. Their fervency is almost cult-like, frankly."

Sebastian frowned. How could Vittorio still inspire such loyalty after all he had done? And apparently without even trying?

Marcello led him to the throne room, where two honor guard wordlessly opened the doors for them.

Once inside, Sebastian's eyes were immediately drawn to the massive stained glass above the throne that depicted the Ascendance of Alessandro Morante, first emperor of Aureum. Did people really believe Vittorio had ascended like him? Sebastian found it impossible to believe such a thing. Then again, as he considered the original story, which he had once found so inspiring, he couldn't help wondering if even the original story had been true. Would God really command the emperor to subjugate everyone on the continent in His name? It seemed more likely a made-up story to justify what the empire had done. Or if it truly was God's will, Sebastian had to ask himself what sort of God that was...

"Captain Portinari, so good of you to come."

The empress's satin voice pulled his gaze from the stained glass. She sat upon her throne, as regal as the first time he'd seen her. Barone, looking much restored, stood beside her.

Sebastian and Marcello knelt before her and she did not bid them rise so they stayed on one knee.

"I am honored by your summons, Your Majesty." He wondered even as he said the words if he truly meant them.

"I hear things took an unexpected turn in Kante, and that it was only your timely rescue that saved our officers."

"Oh, uh, I suppose so, Your Majesty."

The empress glanced at Barone for a moment, then a slight smile crept onto her dark red lips. "Or perhaps I should thank the young Kantesian nurse who lured you away from your bed that night?"

Sebastian felt himself blushing. "Y-Your Majesty, I—"

She held up one hand and he was silent.

"You have no need to apologize, Captain. It is a weakness common among young men, after all." Then she frowned. "Although I confess I find your appearance troubling, because you don't really look like the young man I sent off to Kante. Is there some truth to the notion that wizards age prematurely?"

Marcello turned his head sharply and gave his friend a concerned look. Sebastian smiled sadly at him, then looked back at the empress.

"I'm afraid so, Your Majesty."

"I see. That's ... unfortunate. But I suppose it's all the more reason to make the most of you while we still have you."

It seemed a heartless thing to say. Perhaps the empress didn't realize that it was their use of him that was speeding up the process. Or perhaps she simply didn't care.

"Yes, Your Majesty," he said because he knew that was what he was expected to say.

She paused for a moment, perhaps wondering at his sincerity.

Then she said, "I don't often apologize, Captain. And even more rarely in a formal setting such as this. So I hope you appreciate the enormity of this when I say that I am sorry I had to pull you so suddenly from your quest to find more constructive applications of your magic, and I am doubly sorry that, like your old commander Vittorio, I am sending you into a situation where you will once again need to use your magic for destructive purposes."

"I ... see, Your Majesty."

"I considered keeping you here at the palace in case the Uaine show up, but according to Zaniolo's reports, your magic is not particularly effective against the undead."

"I'm afraid that's correct, Your Majesty." Sebastian's heart sank. He knew exactly where this was going.

"So instead you will continue to serve in General Barone's battalion, which will deploy in two days for Colmo. There you will use any means the general deems necessary to restore order. Is that understood?"

"Yes, Your Majesty."

"Perhaps you already know that your sister is among the insurgents down in Colmo."

"Oh, uh, I have heard something to that effect," admitted Sebastian.

The empress glanced at Barone before continuing. "I know you are haunted by what happened during your last few confrontations with her. But surely you are also aware that you might be one of the few people who can stand against her. If you are left with no other choice but to once again unleash your full power to stop her, I will take responsibility."

The empress paused, watching as what she said settled on him. She was giving him permission in advance to destroy the entire city of Colmo if that's what it took to bring down his sister. She was telling him that she *expected* him to do the thing he had sworn never to do again, "generously" adding that she would take responsibility. As if that was any consolation. As if it made the deaths of countless innocents any more acceptable, or that those deaths would weigh upon his conscience any less.

He looked at Barone, but the general's expression was unreadable.

Morante asked quietly, "Is that understood, Captain?"

A cold calm fell over Sebastian as he considered his response. There was, he decided, a certain feeling of power in completely masking one's intent. Was this how his mother felt when she so carefully manipulated those around her? Might Galina have felt it when she nodded along in agreement with his own pathetic justifications for the slaughter of innocent peasants?

Doing the right thing did not automatically make one a good person. It just made the right thing get done. As such, Sebastian didn't need to think himself any better of a person in order to do the right thing now.

"Yes, Your Majesty. I will fulfill your orders by any and all means at my disposal."

Lying for the sake of his sister and all those innocents in Colmo felt sweet indeed.

"Wonderful." Then the empress smiled, suddenly looking more cheerful. "Oh, I do have one bit of news that should please you, Captain."

"Your Majesty?" He couldn't imagine what it might be, but it reminded him of Vittorio's strange words on their way to the throne room.

The empress nodded to the honor guards by the door. "Bring him in."

Sebastian turned, and felt himself breaking into the first genuine smile in weeks.

"Rykov! You're back!"

The hulking, silent, redheaded Izmorozian nodded casually, as though they'd only just parted.

"I thought you might be pleased, Captain," said the empress. "General Barone has expressed some concern regarding your health, and so Private Rykov will be accompanying you to assist in any way he is able."

"I am very grateful, Your Majesty," said Sebastian, and this time he meant it. So often during the deployment to Kante he had found himself missing his old aide-de-camp. He'd never truly appreciated how much the quiet, unassuming man had done for him. And his loyalty was without question. No doubt he would be a huge help in working things out with Sonya. Perhaps they would all get through this yet.

INTERLUDE

There was a place in the Eventide, if the Eventide could be said to have places, that appeared to be a giant magnificent tree of light, with leaves and roots at both ends, extending in all directions infinitely. Or perhaps the ends merely curved into each other. Infinity could be inscrutable like that.

"You've maneuvered that little pawn of yours quite well, my dear sibling," said Marzanna as they lounged among the dense, glowing branches. She picked a pulsing globule of potential from one of the thinner branches and ate it. It held a bitter sort of flavor, as overripe potential was wont to have, but she did not mind it.

"I always knew I might lose my hold on the Armonia at some point, so I set him there quite early as insurance. I certainly wasn't about to let Mother's pet spoil what might be my greatest victory of all time."

"Do you anticipate this to be a victory?" asked Marzanna.

"I haven't seen anything yet from *your* efforts that might contradict that belief."

Zivena scanned the branches carefully, looking for one of the sweeter potentials. Sadly, there were none left in that part of the tree.

"I confess there were a few moments where I thought you might have outmaneuvered me," she admitted. "And I still don't quite understand what your two servants and that doll are doing in the north. But at this point, I'd say my position is strong enough that I have little to worry from you. The Armonia on the other hand…"

Zivena gave in and plucked one of the overripe potentials, and reluctantly took a bite. She made a sour face and handed it to her sibling, who ate it gladly.

Once Marzanna had finished eating, she said, "You're afraid he could go blundering in at the last moment like the Armonias usually do and steal the spotlight."

"Precisely!" Zivena picked another overripe potential, but this time instead of taking a bite, she crushed it between her massive, throbbing hands, splattering its juice everywhere.

Marzanna licked the juice of bitter potential from her bone-white cheek with her long, black tongue. "I do love seeing you excited, dear sibling. But don't count me out just yet."

PART FIVE

SEIZURES OF DESTINY

"Change is a convulsive and unpredictable thing. Not even those who incite it can predict its outcome."

—Stephano Defilippo, former personal apothecary to Her Imperial Majesty, Empress Caterina Morante the First of Aureum

65

Perhaps Galina Odoyevtseva had changed more than she'd realized. She used to prefer feeling in control of a situation and, when she hadn't, would bend all her thoughts on achieving control, or at least influence, regarding whatever matter was at hand.

Yet ever since that night in Les when the people officially chose her to lead them, she did not feel as though she truly was in control anymore. It was strange, because the lives of countless Izmorozians were in her hands, ready and willing to do whatever she asked of them. But Galina did not feel that she was a wielder of that power, so much as a vessel for it. She was in a poetical mood, so perhaps she might now truly consider herself a hollow porcelain doll—one filled with the will of a downtrodden people ready to demand a better life for themselves. There was something almost intoxicating about the idea.

She stood at the bottom of the ancient black stone steps that led up to the Duma of Gogoleth, a building nearly as old as the College of Apothecary. Like many of the oldest buildings in the city, it was a large, brooding structure with several swirling domed roofs that jutted out at irregular intervals.

The Duma lay in the very center of Gogoleth, and for centuries had been the seat of power in Izmoroz where the Council of Lords waged their endless debates and theoretically governed their people. But during the two decades of imperial occupation, it had been left empty and allowed to fall into disrepair. So when the new Council of Lords was formed, the first law proposed, as well as the first law enacted, unanimously, was to renovate the building in which they worked.

That was, to Galina's knowledge, also the *only* law so far enacted by the new council.

Galina adjusted her mask, squared her shoulders, and took a deep breath. Then she slowly ascended the steps, flanked as always by Andre and Tatiana.

An arch held up by two pillars framed the entrance to the Duma, looking somewhat out of place, both because pillars were more an element of Aureumian architecture than Izmorozian, and because they were clearly quite newly added, made of wood, and painted a garish blue. Although many had been eager to shed the empire and return to "the old ways" of Izmoroz, Galina thought it interesting how some aspects of Aureumian culture had become so embedded over the last twenty years that people did not even see them as foreign influences anymore.

For a moment, Galina gazed at the thick, timeworn oak door, so different from the frame that contained it. There was an iron knocker with the face of a bear fixed to it, pitted with rust. Then she nodded and Andre opened the door for her.

The Duma's lobby was brightly lit with a great many oil lamps along the walls. Quite a waste, really, considering it was empty.

On the other side of the lobby, behind a set of newly made doors, she could hear a cacophony of booming male voices, all attempting to talk over each other. Really, if this was how they "debated," it was no wonder they never accomplished anything.

She walked across the thick red carpet of the lobby to the closed doors. Tatiana lifted one leg and pulled one door open with her clawed foot, while Andre opened the other with his great clawed hand.

Then Galina stepped into the Duma Council Chamber, the first woman to ever do so.

At first, none of the assembled nobles noticed the historic moment. They sat on tiered benches, which curved in a semicircle that descended to the floor. It reminded Galina of a theater, partly because the men were behaving rather theatrically, shouting down at the man who currently held the floor in a most strident manner, while the man shouted back at them all with equal fury. A black banner stretched across the back wall with an image of a snarling bear embroidered in silver thread. Beneath the image was the Old Izmorozian phrase *Svoboda i Bratstvo.*

"Freedom and brotherhood, indeed," murmured Galina as she watched the men posture and preen before each other like peacocks preparing to fight over a mate.

Eventually, the man who held the floor, the only one facing in her direction, took a breath from his condemnations and noticed the masked woman and her two ominous escorts at the back of the room. That man happened to be Galina's father, Lord Sergey Bolotov Prozorova of Roskosh Manor. He stared up at her with such obvious astonishment that even the most passionate of his political adversaries was eventually forced to pause in their tirades long enough to turn and see what he was gaping at.

There was a moment of blessed silence as they all seemed to collectively struggle with the presence of a woman in their midst. Galina decided not to squander that opportunity.

"Good afternoon, gentlemen," she said.

That alone was enough to break the spell. Everyone except her father began shouting once again, demanding to know what right she thought she had to be there. There also seemed to be some vague recognition as well, as though they may have heard rumors of some masked woman stirring up trouble among the peasants. Astonishing that even such a threat had not been enough to unify them. Perhaps they simply could not comprehend their own obsolescence.

She waited for a few moments, but when it seemed they might continue like this for some time, she turned to her Rangers.

"Quiet them down, won't you? But please don't kill anyone."

"Yes, Mistress!"

Perhaps she should have been a little more specific, especially given the eager gleam in their eyes. Belatedly, she realized that if the noise was bothering her, it must be downright painful to their sensitive ears.

Tatiana strode over to a shouting, red-faced man on the aisle of the tenth row. The Ranger gazed at him impassively a moment, then lifted one knee and impaled his foot with a single talon, piercing boot and flesh, possibly all the way through to the floor.

The bone-rattling shriek that arose from his lips was enough to drown out everything else. Within the suddenly silent room, all eyes watched the man grovel before Tatiana and beg her to release his foot.

Tatiana looked questioningly at Galina, who nodded. Then she slowly lifted her leg. The wet sound of her talon sliding free of his flesh was quite audible, and several noblemen began to look ill. Once he was free, the man collapsed onto the bench, whimpering and clutching at his bloody shoe.

"I do apologize for my Rangers," Galina said to the assembly with a tone utterly lacking in regret. "They aren't accustomed to verbal abuse and are surprisingly sensitive souls once you get to know them."

She had been pleased to note that her father had not joined in with the rest, but had instead remained silent as he stood alone on the floor, his face slowly draining of color.

Now he spoke haltingly to her. "M-my Galechka...is that you?"

"I'm pleased that you know me so well that you could see through my minimal disguise, Papa," she said. "But I'm afraid I am no longer *yours*, and have not been since you decided to indulge in this"—she gestured to the frightened noblemen around them—"*pageantry*, rather than getting on with properly governing your people."

"*That's* what this is about?" He seemed astonished, as though he considered his absolute failure in leadership to be only a minor concern. "Now look, Galina, I told you—"

"I recall full well what you told me, and I would caution you not to take such a stern tone with me. My Rangers do not care for impertinence, and while I would not want you to be harmed, I certainly can't be seen to play favorites at such a pivotal moment in our nation's history."

He drew himself up, looking angry. "Are you *threatening* me, Galina Odoyevtseva?"

She gave him a pitying look. How quickly he had gone from

beloved father to posturing fool in her eyes. Did all parents ultimately disappoint their children so?

"No, Father. I threatened you months ago when I said that if the council continued to drag its heels, there wouldn't be a future to protect. The world around you heaves with revolt, yet still you sit here and argue like children." She shook her head sadly. "And you wonder why it's come to this."

Lord Prozorova was clearly struggling to contain his temper. That tic in his right eyelid was starting to flutter, and his skin was shifting to a reddish purple. But he was an intelligent man and clearly understood that he and his daughter could no longer play the roles of parent and child.

"What, exactly, is it you wish to accomplish here, Galina?" he asked.

"Oh, I've already accomplished what I wanted, Papa. I'm merely here as a courtesy to inform the Council of Lords that your services as the governing body of Izmoroz are no longer required."

His eyes bulged. "No longer *required*?"

"Steady, Sergey . . . ," one of his fellows muttered nervously.

"In truth, you were little better than anarchy," said Galina. "So it behooved me to form a proper government in your stead."

"You? A seventeen-year-old girl govern the country?" Lord Prozorova looked incredulous, as though he simply couldn't wrap his mind around the idea. "By what authority?"

"If you will quiet yourself a moment and listen carefully, you will know." She turned to Andre. "Please open the doors to help those hard of hearing to better understand."

"Yes, Mistress."

Andre shuffled back up to the entrance and opened the doors wide.

The noblemen stood, glancing nervously at each other. Some looked more shocked, others more offended. One opened his mouth to speak, but a sharp look of interest from Tatiana discouraged him.

As the silence continued, a low rumble from outside the Duma became increasingly evident.

"What *is* that?" demanded her father.

"Come with me, gentlemen, and I will show you where true authority lies."

She turned her back on the noblemen and walked slowly through the doors and into the lobby, with Andre and Tatiana once more flanking her. She did not look back to see which noblemen were following, because it might have given them the impression that she cared.

She did, however, quietly murmur to her Rangers. "How many are coming?"

"Roughly half," said Andre.

"Good enough. And my father?"

"He is among them."

Galina was surprised by how much that pleased her. Despite his failings, she still loved him dearly and would have been sad if he'd chosen to side against her.

Her Rangers opened the venerable front doors, and the moment she came out onto the top step of the Duma, she was greeted by the thunderous cheers of her people. She smiled and waved down to the hundreds of peasants and townsfolk who had been asked to gather. Then she looked back at the dumbfounded noblemen who had followed her.

"This is the only authority that matters," she told them. "The will of the people and the power to enforce that will. What authority did *you* have? Tradition? Misplaced sentiment? Perhaps merely a lack of alternatives? Well, that time of short-sighted mediocrity is over. Izmoroz deserves better. And I shall give it to them. Or..." She turned and waved to the people, who cheered with increasing fervor. "You can take it up with them. It is their mandate, after all."

The noblemen looked at each other with tense, unsure expressions.

"I'm about to make a short speech to my people," she said. "You are welcome to join them."

"Join...*them*?" one of the other nobles asked, eyeing the unwashed crowds below.

"Nobility does not guarantee status or authority in the new Izmoroz," she said. "For the time being, I have decided not to completely strip you

360

of your titles and lands because I think you may be of some use. But should you prove an obstacle..." She shrugged. "Well, I do hope you won't force my hand on the matter. I know it would upset my mother terribly to no longer be Lady Prozorova."

The nobles stared at her aghast. It was a threat that frightened them at least as much as physical violence, as she knew it would. After all, being a noble was wrapped up in their very concept of self.

"Well? What's it to be?" she asked after a moment. "Join the rabble, or go skulking back into the Duma with the other frightened children to be... *disciplined* later."

Several winced at her word choice, and made a hasty move toward the crowds. Others followed them with some reluctance. Galina's father lingered before her a moment.

"Galina, I..." His expression seemed a battleground of emotions. "I don't know what to do."

She smiled and fondly touched his cheek. "I suppose you'll just have to trust that you raised me well enough, Papa."

A look of relief spread across his face, as though this acknowledgment of his contribution to her efforts gave him great comfort.

"I suppose I must."

"Now, Papa." She picked a piece of lint off his jacket as though they were back in his study. "If you wouldn't mind hurrying along, the longer the crowds stand about cheering like this, the more rowdy they become, and the more likely they will be to damage public property in their exuberance."

He gave her a sheepish smile. "Very well, daughter. Since apparently I bear some of the blame in your brazen coup, I have no choice but to support you completely."

"There, that wasn't so hard, was it?"

He shook his head in bewilderment and walked down to where the other noblemen stood looking distinctly uncomfortable next to the clamoring masses.

Galina turned her attention to those crowds that had supported her for so long and so passionately. The momentum from her speech in Les had been like a blizzard stretching across the land. If the nobles in

361

Gogoleth had heeded even some of the rumors about her, or been able to agree upon a proper course of action, they might have stopped this from happening. But as always, they had disregarded the will of the people. It was not a mistake she intended to ever make.

She held up her hand until the crowds grew silent.

"Thank you, everyone who has brought us to this moment. The history books will write of this day, the rebirth of Izmoroz. No longer the poor cousin in the north, we will be a force respected and admired throughout the continent."

This time she was a little more prepared for the spontaneous cheers that erupted. She let it go for a few moments, then just as it began to peter out, she continued.

"Whether it is the Uaine and their loathsome undead, or the imperial thugs who return to conquer us, we must all come together and be ready to not merely repel, but resoundingly defeat them. Only then can the true work of building our greatness begin. I have spoken to the Council of Lords, and the wise among them have seen reason and joined in our cause."

She gestured to the group standing with her father, and there were more cheers, this time with a distinct tone of relief. Even now, the peasants seemed to fear the nobles, and were glad to have at least some of them on their side.

"Most of you know me as Mistress Kukla," she continued. "It was necessary to conceal my identity for a time, but now that the last holdout of the old order has been swept aside, I stand here before you, unmasked."

She untied the ribbon that held on her porcelain mask, but hesitated before taking it off. It had become such a part of her image. Would the people be disappointed? Would she lose authority going from symbol to mere woman? Perhaps. But she also felt it important that they know her fully. It was, in a way, their last chance to turn back before she completely owned the power they were giving her. And she liked that she felt confident enough to give them that choice.

She took off the mask and smiled down at them.

"My name is Galina Odoyevtseva Prozorova, eldest child of Lord

Prozorova. I was once engaged to the imperial wizard, Sebastian Turgenev Portinari, son of Giovanni the Wolf. I thought that I could
convince him to use his power—power I didn't think I possessed—
to help our poor suffering land. But when I saw how the empire
was corrupting him, I rejected him and turned to his sister, Ranger
Sonya Turgenev Portinari, because she also had power that I thought
I lacked. Together, we began a rebellion that even now continues to
ripple across the continent. But in time it became clear that she too
was compromised by her family, as well as her fondness for the Uaine.
In the end, she fled the country, abandoning us all."

She paused for a moment, finding that she had begun to enjoy the
rapt attention of their gaze. The stillness of the crowd. The sense of
unity among them.

"Again and again, I sought those I considered more powerful than
myself to achieve my vision of a stronger and more just Izmoroz. Wizards, Rangers, nobles. Again and again they failed me. But you, the
so-called *common* people? You did not fail me. So from this day forth,
I, Galina Odoyevtseva Prozorova, dedicate my life to your service and
the service of Izmoroz. And I will not fail you."

Andre lifted his big furry head and in a roaring voice shouted,
"ALL HAIL HER MAJESTY, GALINA ODOYEVTSEVA PRO-
ZOROVA, FIRST QUEEN OF IZMOROZ!"

As the crowds exploded once more into cheers, Galina stood and
smiled. Now that the speech was over and her ambition realized, she
wanted nothing more than to retreat to the comforts of Roskosh
Manor and a good book.

But those were the impulses of a child, and she was a woman with
a great deal of work to do.

66

Jorge had returned to potion-making. Not because he had rekindled his passion for apothecary, but because the turmoil of the Viajero Quarter had spread throughout the city, and he suspected it would soon reach a fevered pitch that would result in the need for as many healing potions as could be obtained.

He had decided to take the travel kit out into the garden. He'd found a nice spot by the fountain near where his mother sometimes liked to paint. The soothing magic of the garden helped him focus, and somewhat mitigated the anxious shouts, music, and occasional splintering of wood or crash of glass that could be heard over the walls of Cassa Estío.

"Jorge, you need to talk to Maria." Hugo hurried from the house, looking so tense it seemed not even the calming Viajero magic could reach him. "*Immediately.*"

Jorge looked at him a moment, then turned back to grinding aliento leaves with his mortar and pestle.

"About what?"

"Don't play dumb with me," said Hugo. "She's somehow involved in all this...*anarchy*, and you know it!"

"And what would I say to her?" asked Jorge as he continued to work.

There was a pause. Jorge imagined his brother was probably staring at him in consternation, but he refused to look.

364

Finally, Hugo said, "Tell her to stop it, of course!"

"First of all, at this point I doubt she could. Second, why would I?"

"Because it's a threat to the Elhuyar family! Merchants are starting to close their shops for fear of riots. The market is practically empty. We have warehouses full of stock and nowhere to sell it!"

Jorge put down his mortar and pestle, and looked at his brother.

"I understand those things are important, Hugo. But so is this."

"What, people acting like wild savages?"

"No," Jorge said. "People finally standing up against the empire to claim their freedom."

"What would *you* know about such things?" demanded Hugo.

"Oh, didn't I tell you?" Jorge asked mildly. "I took part in the revolution in Izmoroz."

He went back to his work, and this time he could hear his brother making strangled noises. Despite everything that was going on, he couldn't help smiling a little at that.

"Jorge!" came his sister's voice. "Thank God, there you are!"

He once again put down his work and saw Maria hurrying up the path from the front gates. She looked even more tense than Hugo, her face unusually pale and her eyes squinted almost to slits. He didn't know if he'd ever seen her so anxious.

"What is it, Maria?" he asked with genuine concern.

"Sonya *still* hasn't left her bed."

Jorge sighed. "I told you. She's going through a lot right now and I can't make her do something she doesn't want to do."

"But we're running out of time!" Maria said. "Lucia says the imperial army is back from Kante and already marching south. They should be here in a week, maybe sooner."

Hugo looked like he might faint. "The empire is *attacking Colmo*?"

Jorge frowned. "I see."

"Do you really *see*, little brother?" demanded Maria. "The Viajero can't handle an entire army on their own. Your revolutionary friend was supposed to *help* them. But instead she's lying in bed moaning about her Lady or whatever."

"I *told* you that could happen," snapped Jorge. "I warned you she was unstable. That she wasn't ready for something like this. But you refused to listen to me!"

"I can't believe this!" groaned Hugo. "You are both missing the most important thing! Who cares about your little friend, or who said what when. The empire is coming and *we are all going to die!*"

"Such commotion in my garden."

All three siblings froze at the dry voice of their father. They turned to see Señor Arturo Elhuyar walking toward them, as calm and stern as ever, hands clasped behind his back. His wrinkled, jowly face remained expressionless, but his eyes burned with a cold, chilling light. The señor was displeased.

"Papa!" Hugo looked the most stricken.

"All this shouting," their father said, "is not becoming for the Elhuyar family."

"Apologies, Papa," said Maria, her eyes downcast.

"Now tell me, what is so important that all three of you felt justified in abandoning your dignity?"

"Papa," Hugo jumped in first. "These two have joined up with the rebels."

"So?"

Hugo stared at his father for a moment. "W–well, such unrest could have terrible consequences for our business. For our *family.*"

"It is a risk that some families would shy away from," said the señor. "Families that are cowardly and unimaginative. Is that our family?"

Hugo's face drained of color. "N–no, of course not, Papa."

"No," agreed the señor. "You were perhaps too young at the time to remember this, but the Elhuyars were not always the most powerful family in Raíz. We were at best a middling family, respected, true, but not revered as we are now. It was the conflict and uncertainty of the Winter War that brought us opportunity. When other families hedged their bets, it was I who forged new trade agreements with the empire that would ensure strong supply lines to Izmoroz. And because we upheld our agreements so honorably, they naturally sought us out when establishing trade and supply lines into Kante. Was all this a risk? Of course. But, my son, one does not become the most powerful family in Raíz by shying away from conflict, and one does not *remain* the most powerful by fleeing from it."

"Y-yes, Papa." Hugo looked completely deflated.

Jorge had not known that the Winter War had been the source of the Elhuyar wealth and power, and while he felt some awe at his father's bold dealings, he also felt some horror. Without his family, was it possible Izmoroz might never have been conquered? Were the Elhuyars war merchants?

The señor turned to Maria. "The Elhuyar family does not cling to the status quo, do we?"

"No, Papa," she said.

"We look ever forward." Then he turned to Jorge. "And we do not shy away from risk, do we?"

"No, Papa," he said.

"This is why we are respected in Raíz and throughout the empire. Not because of money. Because of our character." He turned back to Hugo. "Do you understand now, my son?"

"I do, Papa."

"Good. Because now is the time for the three of you to work together. To complement each other's strengths, and shore up each other's weaknesses for the good of the family. Hugo, your diligence is to be commended, but you lack insight and boldness."

"Yes, Papa."

"Maria, you have great vision for the future, but you become easily disordered and lack discipline."

"Yes, Papa."

"Jorge, you have great courage and intelligence, but you are too content to let others lead."

"Yes, Papa."

It was so strange that this man, who hardly ever seemed to be paying attention, could, in a moment, cut right to the heart of each of them like that. It was true that Jorge was the only one in the family to leave Raíz, and the only one to seek his own goals. It was also true that he preferred to follow Sonya rather than take the responsibility of leadership. Perhaps with his friend struggling, he owed it to both of them to step forward.

"We will not disappoint you, Papa," he told his father.

The señor nodded, looking satisfied. "I know."

Then he continued his slow walk through the garden.

Once their father was gone, Jorge looked at his siblings, a new-found and surprisingly thrilling determination burning in his chest. "I have an idea."

"Oh?" Maria asked.

"The last time Sonya and I went up against an imperial army, we recruited our own army to fight them."

"What army could we possibly find in less than a week?" asked Hugo.

Jorge looked surprised. "Why, the one that's been working for our family for decades, of course."

67

By Sebastian's estimation, he had only two friends in the world. He'd like to think he had three, but Isobelle had made it clear that while she hoped to be friends with him one day, present circumstances didn't allow it.

And so Sebastian traveled down the Advent Road to Colmo with his two friends, the Aureumian Marcello Oreste, aide-de-camp to General Barone, and the Izmorozian Sasha Rykov, newly appointed lieutenant of the imperial army thanks to the generosity of Her Majesty. Although Rykov was still a lower rank than Sebastian, he was no longer a direct subordinate. To Sebastian's mind, that meant they could now speak freely to each other and truly be friends. Not that Rykov had ever been particularly subservient. Or talkative. But still.

Rykov and Marcello were dissimilar in nationality, class, and temperament. Really, he couldn't have found two people less alike if he'd tried. And yet, he desperately wanted them to get along. The trouble was, since Sebastian had such limited experience in having friends, he didn't know how to accomplish it.

Things seemed to come to a head shortly before the army crossed the Raízian border, when Marcello brought up Sonya.

"So I'm finally going to meet this crazy sister of yours, huh?"

The three rode side by side at the front of the general's entourage, with Sebastian in the middle.

"I suppose so," said Sebastian.

"This time we'll kill her for sure," said Rykov.

"Actually, Rykov—" began Sebastian.

But Marcello jumped in, looking furious. "Good God, man, that's his *sister*!"

Rykov shrugged. "That was the order."

"Not specifically," said Marcello. "We just have to subdue her."

"Good luck with that," said Rykov.

"Really, Rykov—" protested Sebastian.

"I understand she's *special*, and it won't be an easy task." Marcello's face was flushed red with irritation. Apparently he disliked Rykov's blunt conversation style. "But you can't just go around talking about killing a man's sister."

"Sebastian agrees with me."

"He most certainly does not!"

"Both of you! Enough!" Sebastian turned to Rykov. "Sasha, the thing is . . . well, I know Sonya has done some terrible things, but so have I. I want to believe that *I'm* capable of redemption, but how can I do that unless I also believe she is capable of it as well? So I want to try talking things out with her. In earnest this time."

"Huh." Rykov's eyes widened with uncharacteristic surprise.

While his friend didn't press any further, Sebastian felt that perhaps he owed him some additional explanation. They hadn't seen each other in months and he suspected the difference in his views might be quite jarring.

"This is actually something I've been meaning to talk to you about, Sasha. You see, if Sonya has some sway over the Raízian rebels, then perhaps she and I might be able to act as intermediaries. We might even be able to find a way to address the concerns of the Raízian people without further bloodshed."

"Concerns?" asked Marcello.

"Certainly," said Sebastian. "People don't risk their lives in direct confrontation with their government unless they have serious grievances. If I can learn what those grievances are from Sonya and bring them to the general, it may be possible to address the root problems without violence."

Now it was Marcello's turn to look mystified. "Are you mad, Portinari? You think the general will give the Raízian rebels concessions after they slaughtered an entire regiment? They must be *punished*, not rewarded."

"But that sort of punitive, tit-for-tat mentality will only escalate things," protested Sebastian. "If left unchecked, the only solution will be a contest to see who can kill the most people."

"Fine by me," said Rykov.

"That's what war is, after all," said Marcello.

Sebastian looked first at one friend, then the other. It appeared he'd helped his friends find common ground, and unfortunately, it was in disagreeing with him.

He said nothing more on the matter as they continued the march south. He'd hoped that Rykov could help keep him from losing his temper when he sought out Sonya, but now he wasn't sure his friend was even willing to give her a chance. Marcello was supportive of Sebastian's protectiveness toward his sister, but apparently that generosity didn't extend beyond the bounds of family to the people of Raíz. And of course Sebastian's entire plan was predicated on being able to actually find Sonya before any fighting broke out, which would be no small feat.

In fact, the closer they got to Colmo, the more Sebastian wondered just how feasible his idea was. The road between Magna Alto and Colmo was supposed to be thick with trade at all times, and yet they saw no one on their march south. Not a single merchant wagon. The emptiness of the road and surrounding countryside lent an air of unease that seemed to permeate the entire battalion. As the temperature slowly climbed, and the lush rolling hills of Aureum gave way to the dry craggy rock of Raíz, the infantry grew increasingly restless. They spoke in muttered whispers at evening meals, glancing often at the Raízian night sky, which somehow seemed bigger than northern skies. Dark and vast, as though longing to swallow them all up.

The battalion's morale had not truly recovered after abandoning all their hard work in Kleiner, then enduring the forced march to Magna Alto. To be given this new and potentially graver deployment immediately after those trials was clearly taking its toll on the men.

Jon Skovron

Sebastian thought General Barone might give them some encouraging words, perhaps a short rousing speech, especially once they were only a day or two's march from Colmo. But the general remained silent, almost withdrawn. During the day he rode in silence surrounded by guards, and at night took his supper alone in his own tent. In Kante, Barone had elected to sleep in the larger officers' tent, and Sebastian found it a troubling sign that the general had chosen to isolate himself.

One night, after breaking up a petty fight between two soldiers, he decided to speak to the general about his morale concerns.

"General Barone? Might I have a word?" He stood at the entrance to the tent.

"Portinari? I suppose. Come in."

The tent was quite small compared to the officers', but impressively large for a single person. A single guttering candle revealed a sharply austere quality to the furnishings that did not seem indicative of the general's personality at all.

Barone lay in his cot reading, and did not get up, or even look up, when Sebastian entered.

"Thank you for agreeing to speak with me, sir." Sebastian saluted.

"At ease, Portinari," Barone said, still not looking up from his book. "What is it you wish to say?"

"I, uh . . ." In the past, Barone had seemed to hold some affection for his men, but none of that was on display now, and it took Sebastian a moment to adjust. "I'm concerned about the morale of the troops, sir."

"As well you should be, Captain," said Barone.

Sebastian waited for further words, but none came.

"So . . . you are aware of the issue."

Barone licked his thumb and slowly turned a page. "I'm old, Portinari, but not yet senile."

"M-my apologies, sir."

Again Sebastian waited, perhaps for the general to say that he had things well in hand. But no such assurances came.

"Well, sir . . . don't you think we should do something about it?"

Finally Barone looked up from his book. "And what, pray tell me, do you think I should do?"

372

"Begging your pardon, sir, but I know everyone would appreciate some inspiring words from you."

"And what sort of inspiration do you think I have?"

"Sir?"

"The empress broke her word to both of us, Portinari. She promised us a rescue and recovery mission. She promised an opportunity for our battered souls to heal in constructive activity, saving lives rather than ending them. But you see, that was a promise of convenience, and broken the moment it became inconvenient. Why? Because you and I are good at sowing destruction. Others see it as a gift, but we know it to be a curse. So what would you have me do? Give our men false hope? Feigned enthusiasm? We go now to kill or to die, and as you well know, there is nothing grand or inspiring about that."

Sebastian stared as the general went back to his book. He hadn't realized that they were so similar. Barone was just as weary of war as he was. Probably more so. When the general had spoken of redemption so passionately, it was because he understood what it was like to seek it. Sebastian didn't know what terrible things the general had done in the past, but now he could see how they weighed on him.

And despite both of their intentions, present events had only made things worse. They'd failed in Kleiner. Then they'd been forced to arrest Barone's long-time friend, Captain Reyes, and treat him like a prisoner. Sebastian wondered if he should share his plan with the general. Perhaps the idea of a bloodless solution with the Raízians would help Barone shed this dark despair. But he remembered what the general had said after arresting Reyes. *Even I must follow orders I am uncomfortable with, Portinari. Such selflessness is the truest expression of being a soldier.*

No, it was too big a risk to tell him now. Perhaps if Sebastian was able to find Sonya, convince her to work with him despite all the terrible things he'd done, and learn what it was the Raízians sought, then he could present his plan to the general.

So instead of sharing anything further, Sebastian saluted again.

"Thank you for taking the time to explain it to me, sir."

Barone nodded without looking up. "Dismissed, Captain."

373

68

It was rare to see all three Elhuyar siblings together outside of their home. In fact, Jorge couldn't remember the last time all three had gone somewhere together in public. It hadn't been on purpose, but once they'd become adults, they'd each had their own interests. Sometimes it took adversity to unite family.

Now Jorge, Hugo, and Maria stood before the entrance to the Anxeles Escuros guild. The guard stared at them in astonishment.

"We'd like to speak with Xefe Arzak," said Maria.

"R-r-right away, Señorita!"

He hurriedly opened the door for them. "Do you need me to show you the way?"

Maria patted his cheek as she walked past. "Thank you, but I know where to find him."

The three siblings walked through the dimly lit hallways that smelled of leather, sweat, and steel. Or so Jorge imagined. It certainly had a similar . . . *aroma* to an Uaine tent.

"Really, Maria, how many times have you been here that you know your way around so well?" Hugo was clearly nervous in this unfamiliar environment, and was expressing it, as he often did, by being critical of others.

"You should be grateful. The Great Families may be the brains of Raíz, and the Viajero the heart, but the guilds are the backbone, and nothing moves without that."

Hugo looked like he wanted to argue, but he surely knew that as uncomfortable as this encounter might be, the fate of Colmo and perhaps all Raíz hung in the balance.

A few guild members walked past, and to their credit, did not miss a beat when they stopped and saluted.

Finally they reached the door to the Xefe himself, Javier Arzak.

Arzak had been a fixture within the guilds for so long he was practically a legend. There were tales of him driving off Victashian pirate raids single-handedly and negotiating peace treaties between Great Families that had hated each other for generations. There was also a legend about a string of heartbroken lovers he'd left behind, but Jorge was pretty sure that many of the details in those stories were not even physically possible. Regardless, Jorge had grown up believing that there was no finer or fiercer man in the world than the Xefe. There were even those among the Great Families who said it was a tragedy that he had never settled down and had children, because he would have had a good chance at becoming one of them.

Perhaps because she had already met him, or perhaps because she was less impressed with childhood stories of heroism, Maria didn't hesitate to knock on the door.

There was a commotion inside, and what sounded like a stack of parchment falling, followed by muttered curses. But then the door swung open.

Javier Arzak was every bit as magnificent and imposing as Jorge imagined. His thick gray beard was braided immaculately, and his eyes shone with a vibrancy unmatched. His presence was at once powerful and thoughtful. Perhaps the years had tempered his strength and forcefulness with wisdom and kindness. That was how a hero should be. At least Jorge thought so.

"My, my," Arzak said upon seeing the three siblings. "To what do I owe this profound honor?"

"We have need of your services, Xefe," Hugo said with his usual rigidity.

"I see! Well, please come in so we may discuss it!"

Arzak gestured for them to enter. It took a while for them to find seats among the clutter, and Jorge was shocked by Maria's impudence when she sat at Arzak's own desk. But the Xefe seemed not to mind and instead limped over to a small bar.

"May I offer you some wine?" he asked.

"Of course," said Maria.

"Thank you," said Jorge.

Hugo gave Jorge a sharp look. "When did you start drinking?"

Arzak chuckled. "I suspect one does not live through an Izmorozian winter without something to warm the insides."

"That is true," said Jorge. "Although I really don't drink that often. But the Uaine drink when discussing matters of great importance, and I thought that applied in this instance as well."

Arzak's bushy gray brows rose. "Great import, is it?"

"We think so, Xefe," Hugo said.

"Indeed..." Arzak poured a glass for Maria, Jorge, and himself.

Hugo seemed to notice that he was the only one without a drink, and sighed. "I suppose if it's customary in such circumstances, I'll have to suffer through."

Arzak grinned as he poured another glass. "Very generous, Señor."

Once he had handed Hugo the glass, he gazed at them all in silence for a moment. "Well, how shall we proceed?"

Jorge cleared his throat. "You may be aware, Xefe, that an imperial battalion will arrive in Colmo in a few days' time."

"Is that so?" Arzak looked neither surprised nor concerned as he took a sip of his wine.

"Er, yes." Jorge took a sip of his own drink and was surprised to discover he didn't mind it. In fact, compared to the vodka and whiskey he'd had to imbibe in Izmoroz and Uaine, it was rather pleasant.

"So, Xefe," Maria pressed on. "We would like to hire as many guild members as you can spare to defend the city."

Arzak looked at her for a moment, then Jorge, and finally Hugo. His gaze remained on Hugo, the eldest, as he asked, "Am I to understand that the Elhuyar family supports Raízian independence?"

It seemed to cause him some pain, but Hugo's voice remained

steady as he said, "Yes. We believe that the Elhuyar family must lead Raíz toward an independent future."

"I see." Arzak took another sip of his drink, then looked apologetically at Maria. "Then I am sorry, Señorita, but you cannot hire the Anxeles Escuros for this task."

She stared at him. "Why not?"

"Because we are Raízians. This is our land and our people. To demand payment to fight for our own independence..." He shook his head. "It would shame us."

Understanding dawned on Jorge. "So...you *will* fight?"

Arzak's face suddenly lit up in a grin. "Of course! Do you know how long I have waited for this moment? For years I have hoped for one of the Great Families—just *one*—to align themselves with this cause. And now the greatest of the Great Families comes to me? How could I refuse?"

Relief swept over Jorge. "Xefe, I cannot tell you how happy we are to hear this."

"It is only the beginning, Señor," said Arzak. "Once other Great Families hear of your stance, many of them will feel obligated to fall in line. And then other guilds will join as well. Never before have the guilds and the Viajero come together in common purpose. We will be a force unlike anything seen in history. The three of you have started something grand this day. Perhaps even something that will change the whole world."

69

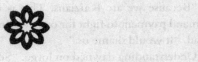

Irina decided that she had not been getting out of the palace often enough. She sat in the back of a carriage and gazed through the window as the awe-inspiring homes of the Silver Ring slid past her view. The Aureumians may not quite have a handle on noble decorum, but they certainly understood decadence. Polished marble, delicately shaped bronze, and so much gold gilding it seemed like a national compulsion. The sheer number of homes that indulged in such extravagances made words like *garish* or *gaudy* meaningless. When everyone was doing it, it was merely the style.

The gardens, too, were breathtaking and highly impractical. Not quite as impressive as the gardens in the palace, but still, one sprawling bouquet of color after another. They were filled with so many delicate and finicky annuals that it would have been impossible to maintain without a full-time gardening staff, which Irina suspected was partly the point. Any household that could afford to keep a full gardening staff had a great deal of wealth, and it was clear the residents of the Silver Ring enjoyed showing off that wealth.

The city of Magna Alto itself was more humble of course, but still quite fine. Irina found the atmosphere refreshingly different from Gogoleth. Although she'd always enjoyed the rowdy bustle of Nadezhda Square, she had mostly done so from the comfort of her balcony. By contrast, the merchants of Magna Alto seemed to be a cultivated sort, imploring her to stop her carriage and take a look at their wares with a veritable avalanche of compliments and enticements. And what wares they had! Even a quick glance through the window made it evident that she would find beautiful treasures here that could never be seen, much less obtained, in Izmoroz. And when she did not stop, but merely smiled and waved to the merchants, they took the rejection graciously and expressed hope that perhaps she would stop on her return trip.

Sadly, Irina was not traveling through the largest trade hub on the continent to shop. In truth, she had no money to spend anyway, but even if she had, she was on a much graver mission. Before he left, Sebastian had entreated her to check in on Captain Reyes, for whom he had enormous respect, to make certain he was not being abused. Irina had agreed to do so, partly because she was pleased to see him expressing such thoughtful, mature concern, and partly because she hoped to find yet another potential ally within the walls of Magna Alto, should things get worse. She didn't know exactly what she feared might happen, and that made her all the more uneasy. Best to be prepared for any eventuality.

On the far west side of the city lay the barracks, where the common soldiers were housed. Beside the barracks was the brig. It was a squat, unpleasant-looking brick building with only a few, narrow barred windows.

She asked the driver to stop in front of the brig. Once he'd done so, he came around to help her out of the carriage. He was an older Aureumian palace servant, and as she stepped down onto the cobblestones, he gave her a concerned look.

"Shall I accompany you, my lady?"

"Thank you, but I'll be fine, I'm sure."

If she did manage to discuss a potential alliance with Captain Reyes, she did not want a palace servant within earshot.

"If you say so..." The driver didn't look convinced. "I'll stay with the carriage, then?"

"Yes. Hopefully I won't be long."

She gathered up her skirts and approached the brig. There were no guards out front, so she opened the door and found herself in a small room with benches lining the walls. A large, locked gate was set into the far wall, presumably barring the way to the prison cells.

Off in the corner, a soldier sat behind a desk meticulously packing a pipe with tobacco. He looked up when she entered, and did not try to hide his surprise.

"Uh...ma'am?" He put his pipe on the desk and pushed himself to his feet, looking wary. "Is there something I can help you with?"

"My name is Lady Irina Turgenev Portinari," she told him calmly.

She wasn't sure if he was responding to her title or the Portinari name, but he suddenly looked stricken and his whole bearing took on a more conciliatory air.

"A-apologies, my lady."

She nodded. "My son, Captain Sebastian Turgenev Portinari, has just been deployed with General Barone's battalion to Raíz. He asked me to look in on his old comrade-in-arms, Captain Reyes, in his absence."

"Oh, I see..." The soldier looked flustered.

"Is there some problem?" she asked.

"Er, no, it's just...the cells ain't exactly a fit place for a lady, begging your pardon."

"Then perhaps you can bring him out here for a few moments?"

He looked even more uncomfortable.

"You do realize that only a month ago, Captain Reyes was a commanding officer in the empress's army? And now you're telling me you don't trust him enough to fetch him from his cell for a short while?"

"With all due respect, my lady, a Raízian never commanded anyone but other Raízians. I don't think the men would have stood for it."

"Is that so? It seems the vaunted Aureumian cosmopolitan attitude toward other cultures does not extend far beyond the palace, then."

"My lady?" Now he just looked confused.

She sighed. "Never mind. It appears that in order to carry out my son's wishes, I must brave the unladylike atmosphere beyond that gate. Will you accompany me?"

"Of course, my lady."

He unlocked the gate, took a torch off the wall, and looked back at her. "Please mind where you step, my lady. I wouldn't want you to muss those fine shoes."

"I appreciate your concern," she said.

She followed him into the dark, windowless corridor beyond. It was lined on either side with iron-barred doors. The lone guttering torch did little to reveal much in the cells, but the smell of unwashed bodies and excrement was so overwhelming, she was forced to cover her mouth and nose with her handkerchief.

She observed a puddle trailing into the aisle from one of the cells, and understood what the soldier had been getting at. Apparently some of the inmates had either overturned their waste buckets or simply not used them. In either case, she had to pick her way carefully so as not to sully her soft leather shoes with urine.

As they continued, Irina became aware of mutterings and restlessness within the cells. She still couldn't see anything beyond huddled shapes, however.

"YOU!"

A hand suddenly reached through the bars of one cell in an attempt to grab her.

"Back off, worm!"

The soldier accompanying her spun around and thrust his torch at the arm. The prisoner howled with pain and quickly withdrew. The muttering from other cells stopped immediately, and there was a sudden silence that was even more unnerving.

At last the soldier stopped before one of the cells. It didn't look any different from the others, despite containing a decorated officer of the imperial army.

The soldier raised the torch so that it illuminated the cell better. Irina could see a man slouched on the floor in the very back of the cell. He had long black hair that had once been in traditional Raízian braids, but was now half unraveled. It was no wonder, since his hands and feet were still bound, despite being in the cell. He was also gagged.

"Why does Captain Reyes have additional restraints?" she asked. "He's already locked in a cell, so the bindings seem not only cruel, but unnecessary."

"He ain't just a regular Raízian, my lady. This here is a Viajero. And one of the best. All it would take is one song or dance, and we could both lose our minds forever."

"How does he eat?"

"Once a day, he's ungagged while under guard by five men. He eats his meals with a sword at his throat, but he eats all right. We ain't cruel, my lady."

She gave him a withering look. "Is that what you think? Can you remove the gag now so that I may speak with him?"

"Apologies, my lady. Regulations say we need at least five men guarding him whenever the gag is removed."

She sighed, then turned to the prisoner. She could not see his eyes in the gloom, but as far as she could tell, he had taken no notice of her.

"Captain Reyes, I apologize for my discourtesy. It's hardly seemly for me to converse with a man who cannot respond in kind. And yet, I promised my son that I would look in on you."

She waited, but there was no acknowledgment.

"My son, Captain Portinari, has expressed both his admiration for you, and his concern for your well-being. He asked me to tell you that his actions, though regrettable, had been intended to de-escalate a situation that likely would have resulted in severe casualties on both sides. He hopes that you still think of him as a comrade and ally, and upon his return to Magna Alto, he will do all he can to make certain you and your men are not only reinstated, but recompensed for your unfair treatment."

She waited, but still there was no visible response.

"As for myself, Captain," she said in a gentler, less formal tone, "I find your treatment not only unfair, but inhumane. Rest assured I will take it up with the empress personally upon my return to the palace."

"Nnn." He shook his head.

"No?" she asked. "So you have given into despair and resigned yourself to martyrdom, then?"

No response.

Her voice took on a more crisp, businesslike tone. "Well, I'm afraid that plan doesn't quite suit me, Captain. As you may or may not be aware, the situation grows increasingly more fluid in Aureum. *Alarmingly* so, if you want my opinion. I count anyone who has earned the respect of my son among my allies, and I find in times like these, one does not squander allies or allow them to indulge in romanticized self-destruction. So I'm afraid that *despite* your wishes, I will speak to the empress about these deplorable conditions and do my utmost to see that they are improved."

Captain Reyes leaned forward, his head cocked slightly to one side in curiosity, as if truly taking an interest in her for the first time. Then he nodded, and leaned back once again.

"Wonderful. I'm glad that's settled."

She turned to the soldier, who was looking at her with a great deal of confusion, as if he only dimly understood the agreement that had just transpired. Or at least, she hoped that was the case.

"If you would kindly escort me immediately from this dreadful place, I would be very grateful," she told him.

"At once, my lady."

70

As Irina rode back through town in the carriage under darkening skies, she wondered whether an alliance with the imprisoned Captain Reyes would be of any help. It seemed unlikely, but it had cost her very little to propose. She wasn't sure that she could convince the empress to improve the truly intolerable conditions of the Raízians on her own, but perhaps she could interest Ambassador Boz in getting involved. It seemed like her sort of meddling.

Then the carriage jerked to a halt so abruptly that Irina had to put her hands out to stop from smashing her face into the front panel.

"What on earth is going on?" she demanded as she fixed her tousled white hair.

"Apologies, my lady," said the driver from his perch in the front. "Someone's stepped out into the road."

Irina leaned out the window and saw a lone figure trudging across the road. They were just entering the Silver Ring again, where pedestrians were uncommon, so the person's mere presence was unusual. They wore a thick hooded cloak that concealed them almost completely from view, and walked with a stiff, unsteady gait.

"You there!" the driver shouted to them. "Get out of the way or I'll run you over!"

The figure continued their slow, laborious walk without responding.

The driver looked back at her. "What should I do, my lady? I gave fair warning, so we're within our rights to trample right over him."

"I've seen enough awfulness for one day," said Irina. "They might be drunk or feeble-minded. Just go down and push them aside."

"Yes, my lady."

The driver climbed down from the carriage and hurried over to the shambling figure.

"Listen, friend. Her ladyship has a kind heart, so rather than crush you under the wheel, she asked me to move you over to the..."

As the driver took hold of the figure's shoulder, the cloak slid to the ground. Underneath was not a person at all. At least, not anymore.

A gray, desiccated corpse with patchy strands of dingy hair was dressed in a ragged brown tunic. It stopped and slowly turned its head to look at the driver with yellow, bloodshot eyes.

The driver stood as if frozen. His mouth worked open and closed, but only a whimper escaped.

With surprising speed, the undead drew a rusty short sword and stabbed him in the chest.

The Uaine are here, thought Irina as she reached through the small window of the carriage to grab the horse's reins. They were not merely laying siege to the city, but already within the walls. She had no idea how that was possible, but it was a mystery to be solved later. Her only option at present was to flee to the palace. Even if the city was overrun, the palace had its own defenses.

She snapped the reins. The horse gave a shrill whinny, then charged forward, crushing both the undead and the now dead driver under its hooves.

It was difficult for Irina to steer the semi-panicked horse by reaching through the window while it raced up the road. And worse, she saw more of the cloaked, shambling figures ahead. At first only one or two, but as she got closer to the palace, more and more. Were they already converging? If so, going to the palace might not be the best option. In fact, if the city was truly being overtaken already, her best bet might be to return to the brig and free the Viajero, perhaps the only people in the city powerful enough to defeat an army of the dead head-on.

But just as she began coaxing the horse to slow down so that they could turn around, a cold, gray hand grabbed her arm through the side window.

It was the undead from before, fixing her with its lidless eyes. Apparently when she'd run it over, it had latched on to the underside of the carriage and slowly climbed up to reach her.

She instinctively yanked her arm out of its grasp, but in doing so, also jerked the reins suddenly. The horse tried to turn sharply and staggered, neighing loudly in alarm. That brought the attention of more undead, who quickly converged on the horse.

As the carriage careened wildly through the Silver Ring, Irina opened the door and kicked furiously at the undead clinging to it. The thing was heedless of pain, and she was not strong enough to dislodge it by force. Even when she jammed the toe of her shoe in its eye, puncturing the orb so that fetid goop ran down its cheek, it did not stop, or even hesitate.

The horse shrieked in terror as a mass of undead grabbed it. It twisted wildly about, tipping over the carriage and bringing horse, carriage, undead, and Irina crashing to the ground.

Irina lay dazed amid the wreckage of the carriage. Her head and right arm throbbed painfully and it was difficult to see with the blood pouring into her eyes from the gash on her forehead. She struggled to rise, but then a gray hand shot out of the rubble and grabbed her by the throat. Her right arm was clearly broken and flailed uselessly, but her intact left hand scrabbled just as ineffectively to free her throat.

She watched with dimming vision as the undead, still throttling her, rose from the wreckage. Its other hand had been completely severed, and half its face crushed, but it did not seem to notice. Its sole focus in that moment was on ending Irina's life.

"Stop."

The voice was feminine, neither loud, nor particularly forceful, but the undead let go immediately.

"Move along," commanded the voice.

The undead stood, even though one leg was grotesquely twisted, and began limping away, joining others of its kind as they spread out through the Silver Ring.

Irina turned to see a young woman dressed in brown robes. Her hair was as white as Irina's and her skin even more so. She stared down at Irina, her brow knitted together and her mouth open, as though she wished to say something. But then she turned and followed after her undead charges.

Irina lay there for a moment, alternating between desperate gasps and violent coughs. Her broken arm throbbed and her head still felt muddy, most likely from a concussion. But she knew she couldn't stay out in the open. She needed to find shelter somewhere. The problem was, she didn't know where. Go back to the town? Return to the palace? She had no way of knowing which was less dangerous.

She forced herself to her feet, gritting her teeth against the pain and fighting off the urge to faint. She winced as she put her weight on her right ankle. Not broken, but at least injured. She looked around and saw that while the previous undead had moved on, there were more coming, both from the direction of the palace and the town. Had they already infested all of Magna Alto? Was the fight over before she even knew it had begun?

Perhaps if she'd been clearheaded enough at the time, she could have surrendered to that strange, brown-robed woman. But now the only thing around her were the glassy-eyed undead, and she doubted they would even understand her.

She spotted a nearby manor with an open door. Perhaps she could hide there? Unless the undead were inside, of course. But even so, it was better than standing stupidly in the middle of the road among the wreckage of her carriage.

The undead hadn't been paying much attention to her before, but once she began moving toward the manor, they took notice. There were five of them, and they weren't especially fast, but neither was she.

She hobbled along as best she could, but the undead seemed attracted to her increasingly desperate movements. She stopped, hoping they might lose interest, but now that she had their attention, they continued toward her.

"Lady Portinari!"

Irina looked up to see Captain Aguta and Hexenmeister Cloos

riding down the road from the palace. They charged fearlessly into the crowd of undead. Aguta slashed about with a sword, which he used to lop off arms and legs, leaving a helpless, writhing head and torso on the ground. Cloos held a long halberd, which he used to keep the undead at a safe distance so that Aguta could make his way over to Irina.

He grinned as he held out his hand to her.

"My lady, care to accompany me back to the palace?"

She forced a tight smile as she accepted his offer. "I've been waiting for you to sweep me off my feet."

He pulled her up behind him and wheeled his horse around.

"Cloos!" he called. "Time to go!"

The Kantesian nodded tersely, and they headed back up the hill with as much speed as they could wring from their horses.

"Is the palace safe?" she asked Aguta as she clung to his waist with her good arm.

"So far they've been completely ignoring it," said the Aukbontaren. "We seem to be safe there."

"For now," said Irina.

Aguta nodded grimly. "For now. But at this point, *now* is all we have."

71

"This way," Rowena called to a small group of sluagh gorta that were milling around a large, polished marble fountain. They tended to cluster if left to their own devices, and Mordha wanted them spread as widely around the city as possible as quickly as possible, like a net being cast across Magna Alto. If the Aureumians were prevented from gathering in large numbers, the townspeople might stay put, and with some luck, they could seize Magna Alto with only minimal bloodshed. At least, outside the palace, anyway.

That woman with white hair had looked so much like Sonya that Rowena had instinctually called out when she'd seen the sluagh gorta strangling her. A relative, perhaps? Regardless, Rowena probably should have just let her die. It wasn't as though Sonya would forgive her or the Uaine for what they had done simply because she's spared a distant family member for a few minutes. Judging by her injuries and general lack of fortitude, the woman was unlikely to make it to safety before being overtaken by another pack of sluagh gorta. Not that there was any true safety in Magna Alto anymore.

"Have you heard how they're faring at the barracks?" asked Blaine as he trotted over to her, his blood-slick sword laid flat on his shoulder.

She shook her head. "Run into some trouble?"

He glanced at his sword and shrugged. "Small imperial patrol. They hadn't even realized what was happening."

"That was the point," she said. "Surprise assault from within."

"Seeing their stupid, shocked faces as I cut them down gets dull quickly," he said. "I would have preferred a real fight."

"I'm sure you're not alone," said Rowena. "But we've still got a long way to go yet before we reach our goal, and time grows increasingly short. We have to be sparing with all our resources. Even headstrong young men with a death wish."

He scowled at her. "I don't have a death wish."

"Ever since you lost Sonya and Jorge, you have thrown yourself into every fight with a recklessness that suggests otherwise."

"What does it matter? You can always just bring me back as a sluagh gorta."

"I would rather keep you as you are for as long as possible."

"Why? You don't even like me."

"True," admitted Rowena. "But your brother did, and I promised him I'd look after you."

He grunted, clearly not pleased that she was once again bringing up his brother. But sometimes she had to be harsh to snap him out of his foolishness.

"Ah, there you are!" Lorecchio rode up to them on one of the tall Aureumian horses. "Glad to see you're both doing well."

"Do they need me at the barracks?" asked Blaine. "The soldiers putting up much of a fight?"

Lorecchio pursed his lips and looked around. "I suppose things are pretty well in hand here. If you're pining to go down there and split a few imperial heads before they're all gone, I won't stop you."

Blaine nodded, a dark eagerness in his eyes. "I'll see you both later, then."

Rowena and Lorecchio watched him hurry off.

"His father really should speak to him," said Lorecchio.

"He has," said Rowena. "It didn't end peaceably."

"Ah," said Lorecchio.

"What did you expect? He was excluded from our inner circle for months, and latched on to the only friendly faces he could find. Then we got rid of the friendly faces."

"We only excluded him because he's a terrible liar."

"And that's his fault?" asked Rowena. "We are not all as gifted with scheming and duplicity as you."

"I can't tell if that was an insult," said Lorecchio.

"I know," she said. "More's the pity."

He regarded her for a moment, then sighed and shook his head.

"I suppose I better get going."

"To the palace?"

Lorecchio nodded.

"Should be quite the spectacle."

He gave her a pained smile. "Our ally does seem to have a flair for the dramatic, doesn't he? I'll get word to you and the rest of the Bhuidseach once everything is settled."

Rowena watched him canter up the hill toward the palace. Then she turned back to the vast manors and sprawling gardens that surrounded her. She'd thought Gogoleth opulent when she'd first seen it, but it was a poor cousin compared to this place. Foreigners said the sluagh gorta were hideous abominations. But to her eye, this "Silver Ring" was far more grotesque. To have so much wealth concentrated in such a small place for such a small group of people. It was easily the most unnatural thing she had ever witnessed.

This was the power of the gods gone unchecked. She did not like these methods, but if this was what it took to finally tear them and their machinations down, she would gladly accept it.

72

There we are, my lady," said the apothecary as he finished wrapping Irina's splinted arm. "Apply the salve every morning and take care not to jostle it, and you should be fine in a couple weeks. Usually I say a week at the most, but given your age, I suspect closer to two."

Under normal circumstances, Irina would have had sharp words for anyone who used the phrase *given your age*, but she was numb from exhaustion, pain, and shock and could only nod.

Once the apothecary was gone, she looked at Aguta and Cloos, who had been hovering anxiously in the background during the unpleasantness of setting her broken bone. "Thank you both again for coming to my rescue."

"It was the hexenmeister who realized that you were missing," said Aguta.

"I had been looking for you because I'd hoped you might have some free time to see my project," Cloos said earnestly.

Irina chuckled bitterly. Even now the man would not let it go. Still, his fixation might have saved her life, so she could hardly complain.

"Let's see if I understand this correctly," she said wearily. "The main Aureumian force is engaged at Colmo. The Uaine somehow knew this, and knew a way to get into the city without being spotted."

"That does seem to be the situation," Aguta said grimly.

"By any chance, has anyone seen Ambassador Boz today?" she asked. They both stared at her.

"Why, my lady?" asked Cloos.

"I know she has been conspiring with *someone* these last few months. Perhaps it was the Uaine."

"You really think her capable of betraying the empress's trust like that?" asked Aguta.

"She is an ambassador," said Cloos. "Surely such an act on her part would provoke some sort of international incident."

"Only if there are any of us left alive here to start one," Irina said bleakly.

The two men exchanged worried looks. She felt pity for them both. Cloos may have chosen the wrong side after all, and poor Captain Aguta had most assuredly washed up on the wrong shore. Of course, she was no better off, but self-pity was not something in which she indulged.

"My lady. Gentlemen."

Irina looked up to see a soldier standing in the doorway.

"All nobility and guests of the empress are summoned to the throne room at once."

"Good," said Irina. "Hopefully the empress will share some insight on what's going on."

"Not for me to say, my lady." The soldier had an odd intensity. A brusqueness almost. She noticed he was also armed, which was unusual inside the palace for any soldiers besides the imperial honor guard. "Follow me."

"Even during such crisis, a *please* would not have gone amiss," she muttered as she, Aguta, and Cloos followed after the soldier.

As they walked down the hall, Cloos sidled up beside her. "My lady, once the empress has dismissed us, now would be an excellent time for you to, uh, view my project."

"Hexenmeister, please. If you hadn't noticed, the imperial capital is overrun with the undead. It hardly seems the time for such things."

"On the contrary, it's all the more urgent."

"And why is that?" she asked.

He glanced at the soldier nervously. "Apologies, my lady. I am perhaps being too forward. Another time, then."

393

"I should think so."

Her tone sounded indignant, but there was something about the way Cloos had looked at the soldier that expressed a similar unease to her own. Why *was* this soldier armed? And why had he gone to fetch them when it was usually a servant who came to fetch her for a royal summons?

Two more soldiers that she did not recognize stood outside the throne room. They opened the doors without a word and the soldier who had been guiding Irina and her companions motioned for them to go first. Once they had crossed the threshold, all three soldiers followed, firmly shutting the doors behind them. Irina heard the steely hiss of those soldiers drawing their swords just as her eyes took in the horrible sight before her.

The empress sat on the throne beneath the dazzling stained glass, just as she had the first time Irina had laid eyes on her. But her face was ashen and her hands clutched at her armrests. Her honor guard lay in a heap at her feet, their golden armor dulled with drying blood.

Other nobles and guests of the court were pressed against the walls on either side, among them the empress's three children. They were guarded by grim-faced soldiers similar to the ones who had brought Irina.

Two men stood before the empress. One was an Aureumian man about the same age as Giovanni, although he wore a roughly constructed mess of hardened leather and wool. The other man was impossibly large, hideously scarred, and dressed in the same barbaric fashion.

Despite her evident fear, the empress glared at the Aureumian.

"Lorecchio. I might have known you were behind this."

The man named Lorecchio smiled faintly. "Though I appreciate the compliment, I am merely a humble adviser. It is the mighty Tighearna Elgin Mordha, chief of Clan Greim and warlord of the Uaine, who commands this army."

"But it was you who managed to secret them past the outer defenses of Magna Alto, through the city, and into the palace with my honor guard unaware. It was you who mustered enough disloyal soldiers to aid you."

"Again I am flattered, but do you really think these stalwart soldiers would follow a disgraced deserter of the Winter War in open rebellion of their empress? No, someone with significantly more prestige and access to the palace was required. Although I do confess that when the person in question offered an alliance, I certainly advised the Tighearna to accept it."

"Who——" began the empress.

"It was me, of course."

Irina's stomach sank as she recognized the voice. Not Ambassador Boz, but the other—and to her mind far worse—suspect:

Franko Vittorio.

The former commander stepped out of the crowd of nobles and guests and walked in his clanking, shambling steps to the center of the room. Within his gaze now was a madness that did not seem like it could ever be appeased.

"Franko?" The empress was dumbfounded. "I thought——"

"That I loved you?" he asked pleasantly. "Or that I was helpless?"

He nodded, smiling his gentle smile as he looked around the room.

"Death has a way of changing a person," he said. "When God sent his angel to rescue me, just as he had your great-grandfather, I understood that my greatest crime was in loving you. It was that love which had imprisoned me. And it was only when that love turned to hate that I was able to be free."

"You think you have ascended like my great-grandfather?" demanded the empress. "You're even more mad than I thought."

Vittorio shrugged. "I no longer require your approval or acceptance. It matters not if you believe me. And it does not even matter if these soldiers loyal to the empire believe me. Because it is as clear to them as it is to me that whether or not I am worthy may be debatable, but you most certainly are not."

"How dare you! The empire has thrived under my rule!"

"Has it?" he asked. "How many lives and resources were lost in claiming Izmoroz? And to gain what? Heaps of snow, a coarse and ungrateful people, and a middling college with delusions of grandeur. Rather than attempt to annex those heathens into the empire, we

395

should have razed the entire place, then stripped the barren land of its ore, which was the only thing of true value it offered."

"You can't be serious."

"Not only am I serious, it is what I intend to do once you are out of the way."

"You have no claim to the throne!" The empress's regal defiance was beginning to crack. "You may have swayed a few discontents, but when the mighty armies of Aureum return, they will crush you like the vermin you are."

Vittorio nodded agreeably. "You do have a point. I lack validity to be emperor. But I have no intention of *being* emperor. It seems a cumbersome role, anyway. I'll need a suitable figurehead to represent me." He turned to his soldiers. "Bring me the children."

"No, Franko!" The empress was in a state verging on panic now, her countenance gone from pale to red as she shouted at him. "For God's sake, don't you dare harm them or I will make you suffer."

Irina understood why the empress was growing so desperate, but surely she realized her hysterics were only feeding Vittorio's sadism.

Now he smiled blandly. "You already did make me suffer for years, Caterina. Or had you forgotten?"

The three royal children, Prince Valentino, Princess Constantia, and Prince Domenico, were brought up. All three were crying, sniveling wrecks. It seemed clear to Irina that none of them had been raised in strict discipline. She would have been ashamed to see Sebastian or Sonya act in such a pathetic way during a crisis.

Vittorio gazed thoughtfully at them for a moment.

"The youngest, I think."

Almost before he'd finished speaking, both of his hands shot out toward Valentino and Constantia. He held a needle in each hand, which he stabbed into their necks. He quickly pulled his arms back in to steady himself with his crutches and watched with unabashed pleasure as the two began to shake violently. Their eyes rolled back, their tongues bulged out of their mouths, and they fell to the ground.

The empress shrieked as she watched their heels slap convulsively on the marble floor, and she continued to wail long after they had grown still. She slid out of her throne like she had lost all her bones, and crawled over to their lifeless bodies, weeping all the while.

Vittorio savored her misery for a few moments, then turned to the hulking Uaine named Mordha.

"Thank you for indulging me, Tighearna." He gestured grandly to the crying empress. "I believe it is customary for you to kill the leader of your vanquished foe."

He stepped aside and watched Mordha with evident anticipation.

The Uaine, however, did not seem to relish his victory. Irina was surprised to see a look of sorrow on his scarred face.

"You thought yourself chosen by the gods, little empress. And perhaps for a time you were. But now you see how fickle is their affection."

Then he reached down, grasped her sobbing head with one massive hand, and broke her neck with a sudden twist.

Vittorio chuckled with an almost childish delight, then walked over to Irina.

"You did warn them that it was too risky to keep me around," he said.

Her expression was grim. "I did."

"Perhaps you wonder what will happen to your beloved Sebastian now," he suggested.

Irina only looked at him. If he was hoping she would fall into hysterics like the empress, he still did not understand the steel that dwelled within Izmorozians.

"Well." Vittorio shrugged. "He's young. He'll adapt. He trusted me once, perhaps he'll learn to trust me again."

"And if he doesn't?" she asked coolly.

"Your son has always been something of a risk. His power has made him a formidable ally in the past, but there has always been the potential for him to become a dangerous enemy instead. That is why, very early on, I established some . . . *insurance*, should he ever get out of hand."

Irina fought to keep her expression neutral. Disdainful, even. But judging by the satisfaction in his gaze, she was not wholly successful.

"Would you like to know what that insurance is?" he pressed.

"You seem quite desperate to tell me," she replied through a clenched jaw.

"Do you recall that big, redheaded oaf who always followed him around?"

Her heart sank. Of course. Sasha Rykov. One of the few people her son actually considered a friend.

Franko observed her for a moment, smiling all the while. "Yes, you remember him. And I suspect that you already understand he is not truly Sebastian's man, but mine. I encouraged him to always be there to support your son. To help him. Unless of course he steps out of line. Then it's a knife in the ribs. So you had better hope that Sebastian's willing to follow me again."

Irina had never been a particularly religious woman, and after her family was killed she'd been openly dismissive of anyone who was religious, including her own daughter.

But now, as she glared up at the gloating Vittorio, she prayed for the first time since she was a child.

She prayed to the Lady Marzanna that Sonya would somehow find Sebastian and save him from Vittorio's backstabbing minion. And she prayed for a way to kill this monster standing before her who had brought such suffering to her family.

Dear goddess, I will give you whatever you want. My body, my soul. I will give you everything if these prayers be answered.

73

A *new pact has been struck.*

Awake, Lisitsa...

Sonya's eyes snapped open, her heart hammering in her chest.

She had lain in her bed for some time now. She wasn't sure how long. Every once in a while, Lucia, Maria, or Jorge would come and try to get her to eat something. But everything had seemed impossible. She'd told them to leave her alone. She wasn't worth the effort. Perhaps she wanted to die, but she wasn't sure the Lady would allow it, and she was more afraid of what she might become if she returned. So she lay there in a state somewhere between consciousness and dreams.

Perhaps it was that liminal state which allowed her to hear the Lady's words so clearly, like shivering razors that hissed beside her ear. Even now, she could still feel her presence lingering in her spine like a chill wind.

She stood up and scanned the dark room with her fox eyes. It was empty. But outside she could hear a low but steady roar, like thousands of voices. Through the windows she could see the flicker of fire. Something had happened, or was about to happen. Something the Lady didn't want her to miss?

No, it wasn't just that. The Lady had said something else to her. Even as Sonya pulled on her black guild vest, trousers, and boots, as she tied her greasy, unwashed black hair back into a ponytail, shouldered her bow, and belted on her knife, she tried to recall what had shocked her awake. It hovered just out of recollection.

Sonya stepped out of her apartment and into the cool evening breeze. But the air was thick with the sound of restless voices and the scent of anger and fear. What was going on?

She climbed the side of the building. With the hot climate of Raíz, windows were plentiful, so she reached the roof quickly and easily. There she was better able to understand.

Below her, the streets were crowded with people chanting, shouting, brandishing weapons and torches. A mob—no, a full-fledged riot. And in the distance, she saw why. A battalion of imperial soldiers had arrived, no doubt in retaliation for her attack on the barracks.

Once again she had made things worse for people.

Maybe she could surrender herself and no one else had to die. But how could she even get close enough speak to someone in order to claim responsibility? No doubt the soldiers would shoot a fox-eyed, pointy-eared, fanged archer on sight.

As she stared at the two groups that moved slowly but inevitably through the streets toward each other, she dimly recalled that Jorge, Maria, and Lucia had come to tell her that this would happen. They had sounded so urgent, but even then she had not been able to muster up the will to join them. And so they had left her. It was tempting to think of her inaction merely as cowardice. But she knew better. It had been despair.

So what had snapped her out of it? She was weak and hungry, dizzy from even the easy climb to the roof, but she forced herself to think through it. What had been the last thing the Lady had said?

Bratishka.

Little brother.

Sebastian was here.

Maybe she could convince him to accept her surrender in lieu of starting a war. Surely he would be glad to punish her for all the trouble she'd caused. All the death and suffering she seemed to leave in her wake. She didn't know if that was what the Lady would want her to do, and she no longer cared.

Sonya sprinted from roof to roof in the direction of the imperial army. Her stomach twisted with hunger, and she felt far too light-headed to be leaping from building to building. But the army and the riot would soon meet, and once they did, there would be no going back. She had to find Sebastian first. She had to convince him that punishing her alone was sufficient.

Once she drew close to the army, she dropped down to the street. The riots were now behind her, but their sullen roar was still easy to hear, even over the rhythmic footfalls of the marching soldiers. She darted through the alleyways that ran parallel to the main street. The soldiers looked grim and sullen. Exhausted, despite the fact that the fighting had not even commenced.

Sonya's golden eyes scanned for some sign of her brother. Her ears strained to hear his voice. Her nose...

There he was. She could smell him. That specific scent she'd known most of her life that could only be him. She moved swiftly toward the source of it, keeping to the shadows in the alleys, ducking into doorways whenever a soldier happened to glance in her direction, or a scout clumsily passed by.

Then at last she saw him, riding behind a group of infantry with two other officers. One was the large redheaded Izmorozian who had been with him in Gogoleth, the other was an Aureumian she didn't recognize.

But then she looked more closely at her little brother, and her heart lurched. He looked like he'd somehow aged decades during the months since she'd last seen him. His hair was shot through with gray, and dark pouches hung beneath his eyes.

"What happened to you, Bastuchka...?" she whispered, and stepped out of the shadows.

As if somehow able to hear her over the tread of his soldiers, or perhaps sense her presence, his head turned just as she stepped into view. His eyes went wide in recognition. He saw her. Now what would he do?

He tapped his chest, then nodded to her. He was coming to her? That was surprising. He said something to the officers beside him. The Aureumian looked confused, and the Izmorozian merely shrugged.

Then Sebastian pulled his horse out of the line. But instead of heading directly down her alley, he led it down the next alley, as though he didn't want to give her exact position away to his fellow soldiers. What was going on with him?

She moved back into the shadows, watching carefully as the two officers he'd spoken to continued to march along with the army. She heard her brother's horse and decided to meet him there where they'd be out of direct view. If that's what he wanted, she was happy to comply, even if she still didn't understand what his intention was.

He climbed off his horse and looked around, his eyes squinting in the dark. Even a normal human should have been able to see her in such darkness. Whatever had happened to age him prematurely had also taken a toll on his senses.

"Sebastian?" she said quietly.

He gave a start, then turned and looked at her with an unfamiliar intensity. Not the righteous anger she'd seen before but something raw and vulnerable.

"Yasha...," he whispered and took a step toward her.

Without meaning to, she reached out her hand toward his face, her voice aching. "What *happened* to you, little brother?"

He gave her a smile sadder than any she'd ever seen. "It's the magic. The more I use it, the faster I age."

"Then don't use it, dummy!" she snapped, forgetting in her frustration that she was here not to argue but broker peace.

But he didn't seem mad. In fact, he let out a soft, bitter chuckle.

"It's not funny, Bastuchka!" she said. "Why are you doing this to yourself?"

"Me? What about *you*?" Now he looked irritated. He gestured to her face. "Why are you giving away pieces of yourself, huh?"

"Because I don't know why!" she snapped.

"Well, me either!" he retorted.

They stood there and glared at each other.

Then, perhaps it was merely dizziness from hunger, but for a moment she could see herself from the outside. Here they were, after all their struggle and suffering, acting like children while the city around them was poised on the edge of chaos. It was absurd.

A hiccup of laughter escaped her lips before she could stop it.

Sebastian looked taken aback, then he too laughed. Before she knew it, the two of them were laughing without restraint, something they'd also done as children. Sometimes they'd get into such fits of laughter that by the time they subsided, neither could remember how it had begun.

Except they were not children anymore. Soon Sebastian's laughter took on a hysterical edge. Tears began to course down his cheeks and his increasingly convulsive laughter changed to sobs.

"Sebastian?"

She put her hands on his shoulders, but was not at all prepared for his sudden fierce hug.

"Yasha," he wept into her shoulder. "I'm so sorry, Yasha. It's all my fault. I've ruined everything."

She stiffened, taken aback by his sudden embrace, or perhaps by his sudden honesty. But after a moment she relaxed into the hug and stroked his gray-streaked hair soothingly. "Bastuchka, it's okay..."

"It's not. I've done terrible things."

"So have I," she said.

"I've done worse."

"Do you really want to turn this into another sibling rivalry?" she asked dryly.

Laughter mixed back in with his tears and he gave her a weary look.

"I've missed you, Yasha."

"I've missed you, too, little brother."

He released her and took a step back, his expression abruptly grave and determined.

"Will you help me?"

"With what?" she asked carefully.

"You know the leaders of this Raízian revolt, right?"

"Well..."

"Surely they have a list of grievances. Perhaps if you and I worked together, we could bring both sides to a negotiating table to address the problems and avoid this unnecessary bloodshed."

Her golden eyes widened in surprise. "Your superiors are open to that?"

403

"I'm . . . not sure," he admitted. "Maybe. I hope so. Perhaps if we've already worked out the Raízian side and present it to him in the right light, he would at least consider the idea."

"That does not sound very encouraging, little brother," she said.

"I know, I know, but what else can we do?"

She shrugged. "I was just going to throw myself on your mercy and beg you to punish me and leave everyone else alone."

He frowned. "Why would *that* work?"

"I mean, I'm not proud of it, but I was the one who killed all those soldiers."

"By yourself?"

"Not exactly," she admitted. "The Viajero had them all under some kind of trance spell."

"So who's the more dangerous in that scenario, the person who stabbed some helpless people, or the group who magically turned trained soldiers into helpless people?"

"Okay, I see your point."

"And besides, it wouldn't solve anything. If you and the Viajero were punished, it might appease the empress's wrath, but the underlying problems in Raíz that began the conflict would still exist."

"True." Her eyes narrowed. "You've *maybe* matured just a little since we last saw each other, Bastuchka."

He gave her a sour look. "You're still a wiseass, though."

"It's part of my charm," she said.

"Uh-huh," he said. "Is that why the Uaine kicked you out of Izmoroz?"

Her expression hardened. "That's a whole different matter and something we'll need to talk about later, once we've brought the Raízians and Aureumians to the negotiation table."

"Agreed."

"Now, I think I can find the leader of the Viajero, but it's going to be——"

She froze.

"Yasha?" Sebastian asked.

"Someone's coming."

She pulled him back into a doorway just as the Aureumian and Izmorozian officers from before led their horses around the corner into the alleyway.

"Marcello! Rykov!" Sebastian stepped out of the shadows and turned back to her. "It's okay, Sonya. These are my friends."

Sonya hesitated for a moment. She might trust Sebastian more now, but she wasn't sure about the other two. Yet he was looking back at her with hope in his bleary eyes.

She sighed and stepped into the moonlight.

"My God, she really does have fox eyes!" gasped the Aureumian who, judging by the sound of the names, was probably Marcello.

"You." Rykov immediately reached for his sword.

"Rykov, stop!" Sebastian's eyes were imploring, but his hand was now on the massive diamond that hung from his neck.

Rykov looked at Sonya, then back at Sebastian.

"What are you doing?" he asked bluntly.

"I told you, we have to try to prevent this conflict from escalating. If the army kills these rioters, it's going to provoke civil war."

He seemed to mull that over for a moment. "So you're joining with her?"

"My sister? Yes."

"It *is* a complicated issue, Rykov," said Marcello. "Surely you can see that."

"Shut up," Rykov told him. Then he turned back to Sebastian. "So you changed sides?"

"Don't you see, Rykov?" pleaded Sebastian as he moved closer to the hulking Izmorozian. "Aureum, Izmoroz, Raíz... There are no sides. Not really. It's just people. People who don't need to die. And we can save them. Together."

Sebastian reached out toward Rykov, as though beseeching this stoic man to reconsider his views. Sonya was actually impressed with her brother in that moment.

"Okay," said Rykov.

Sebastian's whole body relaxed, and he let go of his diamond. "Thank you, Sasha."

"Sure."

But Sonya heard the quiet hiss of a small blade leaving its sheath.

She shoved Sebastian aside just as Rykov thrust with his knife and the blade pierced her chest.

While blood poured into her lung, Sonya grabbed Rykov's knife hand and twisted it, breaking his wrist. Then, even as her legs gave out from under her, she yanked the knife from her own chest and stabbed his thigh, slicing downward as she fell so that it cut straight down the side of his leg all the way to mid-calf. He bellowed in pain as his trousers quickly soaked with blood, then fell to the cobblestones beside her.

But that was it for Sonya. She couldn't finish the job. Instead she lay on the ground, her chest gurgling and blood spilling from her mouth. Sebastian dropped to his knees beside her, tears streaming down his face as he shouted her name. He kept saying he was sorry over and over. She tried to tell him that there was nothing to forgive. She was happy she could do this for him. That she could finally save her little brother. But the only thing that came out of her mouth was more blood. So she merely touched his sagging cheek and smiled, then closed her eyes and drifted away.

74

Sonya awoke once more on the bank of the Eventide River. She knew by the still, scentless air before she'd even opened her eyes.

But the river looked different now: black, flat, and as impenetrable as the night sky. The Lady Marzanna stood on its surface, her pale bony frame clothed in dark robes that seemed a part of the river itself. Her black eyes sparkled in her gaunt white face.

"Welcome, *Lisitsa*." The goddess's voice broke on Sonya's face like the lashing of icy waves. "I wondered when I'd see you next."

"You knew it would be soon." Sonya surprised herself by the disrespectful tone in her voice.

She was also surprised that the Lady did not seem to mind.

"I didn't know for certain," replied the goddess, "but I suspected it would be."

"Is it true what *Rosomakha* said? That you don't really care about Izmoroz? About us?"

Lady Marzanna seemed to genuinely consider the question, as though it had never occurred to her before.

"As I told you once before, I am the goddess of all death, all winter, and all change. I am not merely the goddess of such things in one small corner of the world. I do not have the . . . *luxury* of choosing favorites."

"So the Rangers are merely tools to you."

Again she considered carefully before responding.

"Perhaps before this is all over, you will understand."

While Sonya appreciated the thought the Lady seemed to be putting into her answers, she still found them unsatisfying. So she took a deep breath, braced herself, and said:

"I don't want to be a Ranger of Marzanna anymore."

But to her amazement, the Lady only nodded and said, "Then you must make a choice."

"A...choice?"

"You fulfilled your vow to rid Izmoroz of the empire. As such, you are no longer beholden to me. I consider our pact fulfilled and will allow you to die."

"Oh." So Sonya had been right? The Lady didn't really care about her anymore?

"However," continued the goddess, "if you pass beyond the Eventide now, your brother, your mother, and your friends will fail in their attempts to bring a new peace to the continent. In all likelihood, they will suffer and die without purpose. Or worse."

"Why do you care what happens to them?" asked Sonya.

"I don't care about them," admitted the Lady. "But I do care about the change they might bring. So if you want to see your brother's dream fulfilled, I am willing to bring you back once more." She smiled wide, her long black teeth gleaming in the unreal light of the Eventide. "For a price of course."

"And that is?" Sonya asked.

"Your beautiful midnight hair."

Sonya had just been reunited with her brother. And clearly, despite whatever maturity he'd gained, he was still a poor judge of character when it came to placing trust in people. He'd talked about stepping outside the power struggle to help everyone, be they Aureumian, Izmorozian, or Raízian. Was this the change that the Lady spoke of?

"I'm worried about what I'd be like if I came back," she said. "I don't think I'd do my brother much good as a mindless beast. If I give you any more of my humanity, will I still be me?"

Lady Marzanna tilted her head to one side and gave Sonya a disturbingly innocent look. "What is *me*, I wonder?"

Sonya glared at the goddess. "You're not going to tell me."

"I don't even understand the question, so how could I?"

"Come on. You know what I mean...*Me*. The person that I am. Sonya Turgenev."

"Hmm." The Lady blinked slowly, as though carefully considering what she said. "And what is this *me* comprised of?"

Sonya groaned. She honestly couldn't tell if the Lady was mocking her or genuinely confused. "Forget it. Fine. I'll pay the price."

She'd barely finished the words when dark tendrils shot out of the river and wrapped her in a cocoon from the neck down. They lifted her off the ground and brought her close to the goddess.

Lady Marzanna smiled her dark, toothy smile. "I'm so pleased, *Lisitsa*."

She grasped Sonya's face with a bony hand, covering it almost completely. With a clawed finger of her other hand, she cut across the soft flesh of Sonya's forehead just at the hairline. Then she carefully sliced down her temple, over her ear, along the nape of her neck and back up the other side. It traced a burning line of pain around Sonya's scalp that made her writhe and whimper. She found herself biting the palm of the goddess's hand that held her. But rather than flesh, it felt like her sharp teeth scraped on a solid block of ice, causing her even more pain.

Once the goddess had finished tracing all the way around Sonya's hairline, she grasped her hair in one fist and slowly pulled. The delicate flesh that joined her scalp to her skull tore, making a wet sound like a shell being peeled from a boiled egg.

And along with the top of her head, something else was ripped free from Sonya.

Something deeply human.

It was this wrenching loss that finally made her scream, like a tortured beast, into the cold grip of winter. Of death. Of change.

75

During the battle to liberate Gogoleth, Jorge had felt little interest in seeing the violence firsthand. He knew that some men enjoyed such spectacle, but he was not one of them. Yet while he was just as reluctant to observe the conflict in Colmo, this was his city, and it was now his people under attack. He felt that as a son of the Elhuyar family, it was his obligation to bear witness to their struggle.

He and Maria stood on a balcony several blocks from the conflict. The two groups looked like toys in the streets below. To the left were the neat, orderly rows of marching imperial soldiers. To the right, the seething mass of townspeople. It appeared to be merely a disorderly rabble of discontent peasants. But of course theater was a Raízian national pastime, and if the imperial leadership did not suspect the true nature of the mob, then they did not understand their one-time allies nearly as well as Jorge thought.

"Lucia said this should be a safe enough distance," Maria assured him. "We might still feel the effects, but it won't be overpowering."

"Are you worried for her?" Jorge asked.

She gave him a weary smile. "Why do you think I brought this."

She held up a bottle of fine, centuries-old wine, clearly taken from the Elhuyar cellars.

"Does Papa know you took that?"

She shrugged as she began to twist the corkscrew. "He said wine of this vintage should only be opened for the most important occasions.

I believe that watching my beloved lead a battle for the liberation of Colmo qualifies."

Jorge hesitated for a moment. "Do they know? About you and Lucia, I mean?"

"We certainly haven't talked about it, if that's what you're asking." She popped the cork off the bottle.

"Does it bother you that they will never acknowledge her?"

"I don't need their acknowledgment." She took a swig from the bottle and winced. "Probably should have let that breathe a little."

Jorge looked with new appreciation at his sister. He might be more experienced in war and conflict, and more well traveled. But he was still such a coward when it came to the approval of his parents. He wondered if he ever saw Blaine again, could he live a similar life split between love and family? In his mind, those two things overlapped so much, it was difficult to see how he could possibly keep them separate. But perhaps...

Well, it was unlikely he would ever see Blaine again, so it was probably pointless to tie himself up in knots over it anyway.

"They're getting close." Maria's face was tense as she took another swallow, her eyes on the two tiny masses of people.

She offered the bottle to Jorge, but he shook his head.

"You sure? It'll help soften the impact."

"Hm, I suppose you're right."

She grinned as she handed him the bottle. "That's the spirit, *hermano*."

He took a swallow and agreed that they should have let it breathe a little, but even so, the quality of such an old wine was undeniable.

"What does *hermano* mean?" he asked.

"Brother."

"How do you know so much of the old language?"

"Viajero sing in the language of our people, so Lucia knows a lot of it," said Maria. "She's been teaching me."

"To what end?" He handed the bottle back to her.

She gave him an odd look. "Because it's *our* language. It's something all Raízians should know if we hope to completely divest ourselves of the Aureumians."

"You think, after generations of speaking the imperial tongue, we can just switch back like that?"

"It'll probably take a few more generations, but I don't see why not."

Jorge gazed at his sister a moment. "You know, Papa was right. You really are a visionary."

"You sound surprised. I guess you've never seen me as anything other than your bossy big sister."

"Because you are."

"Shut up and watch." She pointed down to the streets.

"I rest my case," he murmured, but did as he was told.

The two groups had at last come together in the marketplace. All the stalls had been dismantled and stored away days ago, so it was now merely a large open space. The soldiers came to a halt and prepared their vaunted shield and spear lines. The rioters stopped their advance in the face of the wall of bristling steel, but continued to shout. The archers in the back line of the imperial column drew back their bows, ready to rain arrows down on the people.

The tension hung there like that for several moments. The imperial army poised to unleash violent and bloody death, the rioters shouting and gesticulating. Perhaps the imperial officer in command was hesitant to strike the first blow in what appeared to be a crowd of unarmed townspeople. Whoever it was, that consideration, though admirable, was misplaced.

The deep, resonating sound of a gong rang out through the marketplace, followed by the steady thud of a bass drum. With that, the feigned chaos of the rioters dropped away. In breathtaking unity, the people stepped into the largest Viajero dance that had been seen in a hundred years. Their hard, almost lurching movements made it seem like they were all drunk, but each sway, each wobble, was perfectly controlled. Along with their movements, the shouts of the Viajero turned to song, deep and guttural.

"The Dance of the Five Despairs," murmured Maria. "Lucia told me about it, but of course I've never seen it before."

The imperial archers were able to let one volley fly before the performance hit them. Even more than five blocks away, Jorge felt it. The wave of passion struck him like a blow. It was blunt and coarse, like the style of the performance, and made his body feel so heavy, it was a struggle to lift his arms.

"First Movement," Maria said in a hoarse voice, her hands grasping the balcony railing for support. "Awareness of Burden."

It was clear the soldiers were feeling it far more intensely at close range. Some fell immediately to their knees, unable to rise. Others were able to widen their stance and stay on their feet, but holding up the heavy, iron-bound shields was too much.

That was when the mercenary snipers from Anxeles Escuros rose from the nearby rooftops and began to pick off the now-unprotected spear soldiers.

A command went out to the imperial soldiers and they began stuffing what looked like wax in their ears.

Blocking out the sound lessened the effect, but a Viajero performance was more than just music. In order to truly protect oneself from the Viajero, a person must also block out their vision. Yet being both deaf and blind in battle was a dangerous proposition.

To bolster the strength of the visual component of the dance, the air painters that had been in the back of the crowd stepped forward, wielding their massive brushes with grace and elegance. The singers and dancers shifted to something slower, almost lulling. Above that, the painters wove complex glittering patterns of periwinkle, lavender, and white in the air. The combined effect deepened the weightiness Jorge had been feeling into a slow lethargy.

"Second Movement," Maria murmured. "Embrace of Melancholy."

Protected from the sound at least, a number of the archers managed to shoot another volley. But their aim was off, and many of the arrows fell short or veered to the side. A few reached their targets, but it wasn't enough to impact the performance. Meanwhile, the shield and spear lines struggled to close the gap with the performers, all the while fending off arrows from the Anxeles Escuros sniper squads on the nearby rooftops.

Seeming to sense their advantage, the Viajero's performance quickened in tempo. The style became short and sharp, and the paint colors darkened into navy, eggplant, and slate. Jorge felt shudders of unease ripple through him that quickly turned to fear.

"Third Movement." Maria's voice was pinched, and her face was tense. "Succumb to Dread."

The imperial soldiers in the front lines wavered, then finally broke formation, peeling off to either side. There they were met on the flanks by Anxeles Escuros swordsmen, who cut them down easily.

"H-how are they not affected by the song?" Jorge asked, his voice tinged with panic.

"Acclimation," said Maria. "If you experience a performance enough times, it stops affecting you so strongly. They've been training since we first spoke to the Xefe."

"Like building up an immunity to poison."

She nodded tersely.

Although the imperial front lines had broken, the secondary lines filled in the gap, and the archers still managed to get off intermittent volleys. The Viajero were taking heavier losses as the soldiers drew closer.

But the Viajero were now lost in their performance and didn't seem to even notice the comrades falling around them. Or perhaps they used it as inspiration. Their sounds grew more frenetic, their movements more aggressive until it almost seemed like they were attacking the air before them. Above them, the painters cast seething red and mottled orange that swirled fitfully. Jorge could feel the fear within him shifting, darkening, heating up into anger.

"Fourth Movement," Maria said through clenched teeth. "Grip of Wrath."

Violence burst forth among the imperial soldiers, but it was not directed toward the Viajero. Instead they turned on each other, stabbing their comrades with spears, bashing them with shields, or shooting them at close range with arrows. Those who had lost weapons attacked others with fists, or even teeth.

"God damn it, this is monstrous!" Jorge fumed. He knew the performance was making him overreact, but it truly was horrifying to see magic that could turn people against each other so quickly, and the savagery that resulted. It was as though the entire front half of the army had succumbed to sudden, frenzied madness.

Of course, it was only the front half. The back half of the army, less dramatically affected by the Viajero, had been frantically reorganizing itself.

The catapults rolled into view at the very back of the column, and he understood. If he hadn't been so filled with anger, the sight of soldiers lighting a row of pitch-filled siege engines would have struck renewed dread in his heart.

"No!" Maria gripped the railing so hard her knuckles were white. "Those damn monsters will raze the whole city rather than lose!"

"If they can't have it, they'd rather no one have it at all," Jorge said grimly.

The flaming pitch sailed into the air in a strangely dignified arc before splashing down in the midst of the Viajero. The dancers came to a halt as people screamed in agony, trying to get the sticky, flaming substance off their bodies. Nearby buildings caught fire and the square filled with dense black smoke that choked the singers and obscured the bewitching colors of the painters. With a single stroke, the entire Viajero resistance had been routed.

The soldiers began to press their advantage. Both the snipers and swordsmen did their best to cover a retreat, but they were easily overwhelmed by greater numbers. Jorge clenched his fists and looked on helplessly at what could turn out to be a massacre of the greatest talent in Raíz, a loss from which his people might never recover.

A deep, booming horn was sounded and the soldiers stopped their advance. The horn came again and the soldiers actually began to retreat.

"What on earth just happened?" demanded Maria. "I—I mean, I'm grateful they didn't just kill everyone, by why would they stop now when they could have completely crushed us?"

"The only reason I can think of," said Jorge, "is something even worse than a Raízian uprising has just occurred."

76

If it weren't for his sister, Sebastian would be dead. He'd been glancing back at her, relieved he'd managed to convince Rykov to stand
down. He'd seen the momentary flash of shock in her golden eyes. Still
he'd been too slow, too damn clumsy to do anything. She'd shoved
him aside and by the time he'd grasped his diamond again, it was over.

He knelt on the ground cradling Sonya's lifeless head. It was so
heavy. And so still. Rykov sat nearby clutching at the massive gash
that ran down his leg with his one uninjured hand.

"Why, Rykov?" Sebastian shouted through his tears. "*Why would
you do it?*"

"It was an accident," Rykov said, although rather than his habitual
brusque indifference, his face was pinched with pain. "I was trying to
kill you."

"I know that!" snapped Sebastian. "But why would you try to kill
me? I thought...I thought we were friends."

Rykov's eyes narrowed. "Why would you think that?"

That brought Sebastian up short.

"Wh–what do you mean?"

"I followed you around because Commander Vittorio told me to.
He said if you ever got out of line, I should kill you. That was my job."

"F-from the very beginning?"

"Sure."

"That...can't be right..." Sebastian stared at this man who he'd

416

thought of as a friend for so long. Rykov had been his first, and for a long time, only friend. He remembered all the times in Izmoroz when Rykov had been there to help him and care for him. The words of encouragement and support. The bowls of broth and reminders to get to bed. He had presumed that had come, at least in part, from a place of affection and concern. But had those months of companionship during such dark times meant nothing to Rykov? Had their friendship only ever been in Sebastian's head?

Yes. He finally understood now. He really was the needy, naive fool everyone thought him to be.

With that thought, he felt a heavy darkness bloom in his chest. It unfurled and spread slowly like a blotch of ink in water, casting a pall over his heart.

"But, Rykov...," said Marcello.

Sebastian had almost forgotten he was there.

"Vittorio isn't even your commander anymore," pointed out Marcello. "Why are you still following the orders of a convicted traitor to the empire?"

"Because he's in charge of the empire now." Rykov looked confused. Like he'd expected them to already know that.

Marcello's eyes widened. "You're saying Vittorio staged a coup?"

"Sure. I guess that's what it's called."

Marcello laughed, though it sounded shrill. "Impossible."

But Sebastian knew. Rykov didn't have it in him to make something like that up. As the dark wrath continued to spread through his chest, he understood that Vittorio had been playing a very long game, and Sebastian was merely a pawn who had outlived his usefulness.

"I think he's telling the truth, Oreste."

"But..." Marcello looked first at the maimed and wounded Rykov, then at Sebastian kneeling in the alley with his dead sister's head cradled in his lap. "How could it be?"

"You were the one who said Vittorio still had supporters," pointed out Sebastian. "'Cult-like' is how you described them."

"No." Horrified realization stretched across his face. "I have to warn the general! Sebastian, I–I'm sorry—"

"It's fine." Why would Sebastian expect loyalty from anyone at this point? "Do what you must."

Marcello nodded sharply, vaulted into his saddle, and sprinted after the army that had already moved on without them.

Sebastian watched him ride off for a moment, then turned back to Rykov. By then the darkness had spread throughout his chest and into his limbs. It felt heavy, but there was something soothing about the weight of it. He gently placed his dead sister's head on the cobblestones, then slowly stood.

"I was wrong about you."

Perhaps there was something frightening in his gaze because Rykov flinched. "Look, I was just following orders."

"That's right." Sebastian's voice was heavy. Gravelly. Like the darkness had spilled into his lungs, filled up his throat. "You're a pawn. Like me."

"Sure. We're the same."

Sebastian fingered his diamond. "No, Sasha. We're not the same. Because I'm still a wizard, and you killed my fucking sister."

Panic seemed to push Rykov past his pain. He began to drag himself down the alley with his one good hand and one good leg. As though he could somehow escape his fate.

"It's not right or fair," continued Sebastian, watching Rykov's pointless effort. "But the world doesn't care about either of those things. It only cares about strength and cost."

As he gripped his diamond, Sebastian felt the darkness spread all the way through his body. It swirled within him like an oily whirlpool, endless and hungry.

"Therefore, Sasha," he continued, "you should never anger someone with great power. Because the cost will be beyond anything you might have imagined. When I'm done with you, there won't be anything left. Not a body, or even a soul."

He took the hungry void that swelled within him and focused it on his diamond.

And then he smiled. But it was not his smile. He had let something in. Something from outside himself. Maybe something from outside everything. But whatever it was, it understood his suffering, and turned it into raw energy. He poured that energy into the diamond. The gem vibrated so hard that his hand grew numb. But he did not let go.

"Beyond life, beyond death, she waits." Sebastian spoke in a grating, guttural voice, his words no longer entirely his own. "She is endless and ravenous. None on this plane can truly comprehend her, yet she is all around us. I wonder, Sasha, can you sense the great goddess Mokosh? Can you feel the insatiable Damp Mother Earth?"

Sebastian released all that gathered power at once upon this man who had betrayed his trust and killed his sister.

Rykov halted in his pathetic crawl for a moment. Then he reached out one shaking hand toward the main street. But the hand convulsed, and he gasped. Shivers went through him. Then he slowly curled on himself into a fetal position. The shivers grew convulsive, and his injured limbs flailed helplessly as his stomach caved in. His spine curved forward in violent jerks, as if being folded again and again, the sharp pops echoing through the alley. He opened his mouth to scream, but his rib cage collapsed, crushing his lungs, sending a gush of blood that splashed across the cobblestones. His eyes grew red, then darker, until they at last burst in his skull, sending puffs of pink mist into the air. But still he wasn't dead. Still he suffered and writhed. His torso compressed like an accordion of flesh. The bones of his legs and arms shattered into powder so that his limbs were mere sacks of skin and muscle that were then sucked into his center of gravity. At last there was nothing but a shapeless torso attached to an eyeless head. The neck collapsed, then the skull began to cave, cracking loudly until it softened enough to be drawn into the center as well. At last even the compressed torso shrank down, like something was consuming it from within, or perhaps like water down a drain.

Finally, not a single piece of Rykov remained.

Sebastian looked down at his hand and saw that his diamond had crumbled into powder.

The darkness drained away from him, leaving him cold and weary, and he wondered what kind of power could shatter even his diamond.

What had he tapped into? The goddess Mokosh? That couldn't be. There was no religion that worshipped such a terrifying entity. She was a fairy tale. A nightmare to scare children. So why had her name come unbidden to his lips?

In the distance he heard a sudden burst of strange music. Viajero music. It was followed by fierce, angry shouts.

The battle had begun. Apparently Marcello hadn't been able to warn the general about Vittorio's coup in time. Now they were all killing each other. And for what? Was there even an empress to obey any longer?

Sebastian had set out to do two things when he left Magna Alto. Save his sister and prevent unnecessary bloodshed.

He'd failed at both.

Then his sister suddenly sat up with a loud gasp, her golden eyes wide, her blood-drenched chest heaving.

"Y-Yasha?"

She turned and grinned at him as she tried to get her breath under control.

"Hey, little brother," she said between pants. "I hope you didn't think," she gasped, "that was the end of me."

He stared at her, his eyes filling with relieved tears.

"How did you..."

"Eh, I just made another bargain with the Goddess of Death." She shrugged like it wasn't a big deal. "Don't worry, though. Just a one-time thing. I don't serve anyone but myself now."

"I...see."

He reached out and tentatively touched the top of her head. Instead of long black hair, she now had short fluffy white fur, like that of a fox.

"Well?" she asked, and there was a hint of anxiousness in her expression.

"It's very soft," he assured her.

She looked relieved. "Great. But don't think you can go petting me anytime you want."

77

ust like that," murmured Irina as she walked numbly down the hall toward her apartments. "In a single stroke, Vittorio has changed the very course of civilization on this continent."

She knew she should be grateful that Vittorio wanted her alive, at least for now. She should also be grateful for the fact that though she was confined to the palace, she could move about inside without restriction. Yet the obvious implication of this—that she was utterly helpless and posed no threat to Vittorio's regime—rankled deeply. Mostly because it was so true.

"Lady Portinari!" called Cloos as he hurried down the hall toward her.

He was the last person she felt like dealing with in that moment, but allies, even tiresome ones, were few, so she turned to him and managed a strained smile.

"Hexenmeister, how are you holding up?"

"Oh, it's all so dreadful." He wrung his hands anxiously. "This was not what I expected when I fled my homeland to the safety of the empire."

She let out a mirthless chuckle. "I know the feeling."

"How are the others, do you think?" he asked.

"Captain Aguta is playing it very carefully, as he should," said Irina. "He is no threat to Vittorio, but also serves no purpose. He lives purely at the new emperor regent's pleasure."

"What about the ambassador? I don't think I even saw her in the throne room."

"No," agreed Irina. "It seems she wasn't the mastermind behind this coup, but I suspect that she at least got wind of it and decided to leave before she was forced to share our fate."

Cloos's eyes widened. "And she didn't warn us?"

"Presumably doing so would have compromised her own safety or given away some Victashian state secret or another. I suppose I do not begrudge her that choice. After all, at times like this, we must all take care of our own first and foremost."

"I see..."

He looked away, as though considering that for a moment.

Finally, he asked, "What about you? You always seem so clever. Surely you have some plan or other."

"While I am no threat to Vittorio, I do at least serve some purpose for the time being. He intends to convince my son to join him, and he would have a much harder time doing so with my blood on his hands. I could also be used as a means to keep my son in line if he joins."

"And how likely do you think it is that your son will join him?"

Irina sighed. "Given our most recent conversation, I would say it is extremely unlikely."

Cloos leaned in closer, a desperate expression on his face. "A-and then what would happen?"

"It's difficult to say. Vittorio might use me as a hostage. Or he might simply decide to kill me to punish Sebastian for refusing him. He's never been the most clear-thinking fellow."

Cloos looked even more anxious now. "This...this is unacceptable. It cannot happen!"

"I appreciate the sentiment, but I do wonder how you would prevent such a thing."

He glanced nervously away, then back to her again. "Lady Portinari, will you come see my project now?"

She wanted to strangle him. She wanted to shout: *This? Now of all times, you go back to this?*

But what good would it do, other than alienate one of her few remaining allies? So after a moment, she nodded.

"Very well, Hexenmeister. I know it means a great deal to you."

He suddenly looked relieved, as though all his cares had been vanquished. His clammy hands clutched at hers and he smiled beatifically at her.

"Thank you, my lady! Thank you! And I hope you will soon be as excited as me!"

"Er, yes . . ." She was already starting to regret her acquiescence, but clearly it was too late now.

"Please, follow me." He turned and hurried down the hall, frequently turning and beckoning to her.

She wished she'd had the sense to wait until Aguta was with them, or even some imperial guard, but the stress of the day was clearly taking a toll on her ability to think rationally. All she really wanted to do was go back to her apartments and sob into her pillow at the horrible deaths of the empress and her children. But instead she took a deep breath, squared her shoulders, and followed the Kantesian through the palace.

His apartments were set apart from the others, and once they entered, Irina understood why. It was not a traditional living space, but rather a massive workshop that happened to contain a bed in the corner. The room was filled with all manner of mechanical devices, scraps of metal, and tools with which to fashion and shape them. There was even a large furnace at one end that glowed a sullen orange.

Cloos passed by all of it without a glance as he made his way to one corner of the room. Irina followed him to what she initially thought was a partial suit of armor on display.

But no, it couldn't really be that, unless it was armor intended for a giant. The helmet alone, which covered not just the top of the head, but the face as well, was easily two feet high. And it was oddly shaped. The front seemed to have been molded to that of a human face. A distinctly feminine face. In fact, the likeness was quite familiar . . .

"Hexenmeister," she said sharply. "Is that meant to represent *me*?"

"You recognized it immediately! I'm so relieved!" He grinned like an excited schoolboy on his Name Day. "I have been studying your face for months now, trying to make sure I captured its likeness exactly."

She struggled to keep her voice calm and level and not express the mixture of alarm and disgust that weighed upon her chest.

"Pray tell me, Hexenmeister, what is the purpose of this...*composition*? Clearly it's too large to be a suit of armor. Is it some sort of sculpture, perhaps?"

"Oh, no, no, no!" he exclaimed in delight. "It is a Kantesian construction called a golem. Or at least, the beginning of one."

"I fear I am unfamiliar with much of Kantesian culture. Please elaborate."

"Of course, of course. You see...well, where should I begin..."

He was clearly excited to speak about his work, but perhaps was not particularly good at explaining it.

"Ah, I know! When we first met, I was struck by your astonishing beauty, and by the heartbreaking tragedy that age had already begun to ravage it."

She gazed coldly at him. "You are making a poor start of your explanation, Hexenmeister."

His exuberance turned quickly to panic. "I do not mean to offend, but only to tell you my process! I was never satisfied with the ugly golems that my countrymen make. Massive, clumsy, *monstrous* things. Certainly, they serve a purpose, but I prefer beauty! Elegance!" His expression turned dark. "And do you know what they called me?"

"I dare not guess," Irina said uneasily.

"Superficial! Frivolous! As if aesthetics have no value!"

He looked furious now and Irina finally understood that what she had on her hands was not some creeping sex fiend but an obsessive and highly temperamental craftsman.

"Such fools," she said encouragingly.

"Exactly!" He looked greatly pleased. "Beauty is its own reward. It requires no reason beyond itself!"

"Well said." Irina didn't agree, but it hardly seemed the time to argue.

"Be that as it may," said Cloos, "I am forever troubled by the *impermanence* of beauty. I had just begun work on this new project and was pondering how best to give it shape when I met you. I looked at you and decided that your beauty should exist for all humanity to cherish for eternity."

"So you decided to capture it in a metal sculpture?"

He shook his head. "Beauty is more than the shape of a chin or the line of a cheekbone. There must be some . . . *inner life* to it, or else it is but a poor substitute. I don't merely wish to make your likeness eternal. I wish to make *you* eternal."

He looked at her expectantly.

After a moment, she admitted, "I don't follow you."

He sighed in frustration. "As an enchanter, I am able to transfer someone's life force—their very soul—into an inanimate object. So I am in the process of building you a new, magnificent, and eternal body made of the finest metals."

"A new body . . . for me?" She turned back to the massive metal face with its empty eyes.

"I still need to construct the arms and legs of course," Cloos said quickly, his eyes looking almost feverish with excitement. "And obviously, I welcome any design input that you might have. It will be your body, after all, so it should be something that pleases you."

Irina tried to imagine how tall it would be with proportional arms and legs. Ten feet? Perhaps twelve? She would barely be able to fit through a door.

"So once it is finished, you would want to transfer my mind into this . . . metal monstrosity?"

"*Nein*, Frau Portinari. Metal *beauty*!"

She let that pass for the moment. "What would happen to my original body?"

"Unfortunately, the flesh construct is destroyed in the transfer process."

"So there would be no going back."

He looked uneasy. "That is correct."

"Would it hurt?"

He looked even more uneasy. "I believe there would be some discomfort during the transfer. But once finished, you would never be plagued by physical pain again."

That gave her pause. "Are you saying I would be *invulnerable*?"

"Nearly. The soul is actually condensed into a jewel in the center of the golem. As long as that jewel remains intact, any damage to the outer shell merely needs to be repaired by a skilled metalsmith."

Irina continued to gaze upon the metal form. It was... unnerving, but she could not deny that Cloos was indeed a skilled craftsman. It had its own strangely haunting beauty. More to the point, it might be her best chance of survival.

"Would I be strong?" she asked.

"Stronger than any man alive," Cloos said with quiet eagerness, as though sensing that he had found an angle that interested her. "Strong enough to defeat your enemies."

"I see." Irina thought of her prayer to the Lady Marzanna. She had offered up her body and soul in exchange for a way to kill Vittorio. Perhaps the goddess had taken her quite literally.

"You would be strong enough to escape this place, too," Cloos pressed. "None could hope to stop you. Then you could find your children and protect them from *any* who would dare seek to harm them. Why, you might be able to take on an entire imperial battalion all by yourself."

She was silent for a few more moments as she stared at her metal visage. Cold. Perfect. Unstoppable.

There were, she decided, worse ways to spend one's autumn years.

"How soon can it be completed?"

78

The maddening smell of blood, smoke, and burning flesh filled the air. Sonya sat behind Sebastian on his horse and tried to focus on filtering out everything except clues of Jorge's whereabouts. All her senses had taken a massive leap forward after this latest bargain with the Lady. She felt nearly as overwhelmed as she had the very first time, before Mikhail had taught her how to dampen them. Every footstep, every breath, was as loud as a shout to her. Even at a distance, screams from those who had been wounded in the battle—PREY—hardly allowed her to think. And she still had not fully recovered from getting stabbed, so there was a constant dull pain in her chest that spiked every time she shifted her torso.

"Yasha, are you okay?" Sebastian asked as he looked over his shoulder.

"I'm fine, *bratishka*," she said as the horse walked slowly down an alley in the darkness. "I mean, I did just die and come back to life, though, so I'm a little tired."

"R-right, of course."

Unfortunately, that wasn't all she felt. Clashing with her weariness was a murmuring feral excitement. It was as though *Lisitsa* was closer to the surface than ever before. Perhaps because the heavy smell of blood—HUNT—permeated the air. If so, she hoped the feeling would ease once they escaped the area. Or perhaps it wouldn't. She really didn't know. She still felt like herself, and yet . . . something had definitely changed within her. It was too soon to say what.

427

"Yasha, you're certain this Raízian friend of yours will help..." He hesitated. "*Us?*"

"Don't worry. Jorge's my best friend. He'd help me no matter what. And he has a big sister, too, so he probably sympathizes with you a lot."

Sebastian still seemed skeptical, but he nodded, and the two of them continued on through the smoky streets of Colmo.

The night sky was still a sullen orange from the fires that hadn't been put out yet. Occasionally someone hurried furtively past—PREY—but mostly the area was empty.

"We failed them," Sebastian said quietly. "I'd hoped we could stop this all from happening, but..."

"Well, it would have been a whole lot worse if you'd been fighting with the imperials," said Sonya. "There might not have even *been* a Colmo anymore."

He nodded, although it didn't seem to ease his guilt. Sonya still didn't know what had happened to her brother to change his perspective so drastically. There would be time to learn all that later, once they were gone from here.

At last she caught the familiar scent—MATE—of her best friend. It was muddied by the smoke and her tired, frenetic brain, so it took longer to locate him than it should have. But at last she saw him kneeling next to an old woman—PREY—who sat slumped against a building. He was carefully pouring one of his potions into her quavering mouth.

"Jorge!" She clambered off the horse and hurried over to him.

The old woman looked ready to bolt—PREY—at the sight of Sonya, but Jorge put his hand gently on her shoulder.

"It's okay, Rosa. This is my friend. You just rest while I talk to her."

Jorge handed the potion to the old woman, then stood up. He gazed at Sonya—MATE—for a moment in silence with a pained expression. Then he said:

"It happened again."

She nodded, running her fingers through the new white fur she had instead of hair. Sebastian was right. It was very fluffy and pleasing to the touch. Probably not an even trade for the strong animal urges that now kept intruding on her thoughts. But it was something, at least.

Jorge gave her a searching look. "Are you...okay?"

"I'm, uh, not sure yet," she admitted. "Still trying to figure it all out. But I can't do that here. I need—*we* need to get out of Colmo. Probably out of Raíz altogether."

"We?" Jorge looked over toward Sebastian, who was still astride his horse. Jorge squinted, probably finding it difficult to discern her brother's features by nothing but moonlight and distant flickering fires. But after a moment, his mouth opened wide.

"Sebastian?"

"Sebastian Turgenev." Sebastian dismounted and bowed slightly. "Pleased to meet you."

Despite her assurances to Sebastian, Sonya hadn't been completely sure how Jorge would react. So she was relieved when her friend broke into a warm smile. Even so, she hadn't expected him to grab Sebastian's face and kiss his cheeks.

"Thank you for making peace with her," he said to her brother.

"Uh..." Sebastian's face was beet red. He apparently hadn't been prepared, either.

"It's a Raízian thing," said Sonya.

"Ah," said Sebastian.

"Oh, yes, sorry..." Jorge looked sheepish. "It's been a long night, so my emotions are perhaps a little too close to the surface."

"Where's Maria? Is she okay?" Sonya asked.

Jorge nodded. "Lucia had a bad burn, so Maria is treating her with some ointment I gave her. I've just been trying to help out others like Rosa here."

—PREY—

"I'm fine now, Señor." Rosa waved him off. "You take care of your friends."

"Keep taking small sips of that," he said.

"I will, I will."

He looked back at Sonya and Sebastian. "So you're leaving?"

—FLIGHT—

She nodded.

"Where will you go?"

"There are some people in Kante who I hope will take us in," said Sebastian.

"Kante? I see."

"Do you want to"—MATE—"come with us?" Sonya asked.

He shook his head. "I can't leave my people. Not now. Not after what's happened. And what might come next."

"It looks like you pushed back the empire this time, but I'm sure they'll be back," said Sonya.

"That's just it, though," said Jorge. "We didn't push them back. They routed us. But instead of finishing us off completely, they suddenly retreated."

"Hm," said Sebastian. "I wonder if Marcello got word to General Barone about the coup after all."

"What coup?" asked Jorge.

"There was a plot by Franko Vittorio to seize power in Magna Alto, although I don't know if it succeeded."

Jorge stared at him for a moment. "Would that be...a good thing for us?"

"I doubt Vittorio gaining power is good for *anyone*." Sebastian groped for the diamond that no longer hung around his neck, and his brow creased. "Though I'm not sure what we can do about it now."

Sonya patted her brother's shoulder. "We'll figure something out." Then she turned back to Jorge. "And once we do, we'll be back. I promise."

"So," said Jorge, "I guess this is goodbye?"

"For now," she said.

They stood awkwardly for a moment.

"Ah, hell." She grabbed him with both arms and squeezed. He was so close she could hear his pulse and he smelled so nice that she couldn't help herself. She pressed her nose against his neck—MATE—and inhaled deeply.

He shivered. "Uh...Sonya?"

"Sorry, sorry…" She stepped back and gave a nervous laugh. "Still trying to adjust to things. Impulse control seems to have, uh, suffered some." It was a bit of an understatement, but she didn't want to alarm her friend.

"It's even worse now?" Jorge gave Sebastian a pleading look. "Please try to keep her from doing anything horribly insane."

Sebastian nodded. "It'll be just like when we were kids."

"That's comforting," said Jorge.

There was another awkward pause.

Then Sonya said, "So… can I have my horse back?"

He laughed quietly. "Of course."

They followed Jorge back to Cassa Estío. Jorge gently suggested it might not be a good idea for them to come inside right then, so they waited out front while he brought out Peppercorn.

Sonya grasped his chubby face. "My *Perchinka*. I hope you enjoyed your vacation, because it's time to get back to work."

Peppercorn nickered, carefully sniffed her new furry head, then nuzzled against her.

"I missed you, too," she said.

The sun was just starting to come up as Sonya and Sebastian left Colmo. The fires had all been put out, but smoke and the smell of death—PREY—still lingered.

The imperial army appeared to have left, heading north back up the Advent Road, probably hoping to wrest power from Vittorio before he cemented his position. Sonya didn't know what their chances were, but at least it was keeping them from putting all their resources into finding their renegade wizard and his outlaw sister.

So Sonya and Sebastian followed east along the coast toward the Blindaje Desert. Sebastian said he knew someone who might help them. Maybe. Hopefully.

A half-wild beast person and a broken wizard. Sonya should have been deeply uneasy about their prospects. And yet, whenever she turned to look at her brother, his bleary gaze squinting in the clean morning sun, she couldn't help feeling the first small stirring of real hope she'd felt since leaving Izmoroz. After all, she was nobody's servant now. She was completely free to do whatever she liked. And rather than be daunted by that prospect, she was thrilled by the vast possibility before them.

Before all this began, Sonya had wondered what she and her brother might accomplish together if they were united in purpose. Now it was time to find out.

79

*T*o Her Royal Majesty, Queen Galina the First
From Ambassador Ceren Boz of Victasha

*Congratulations, Your Majesty, on ascending the throne to become the
first monarch of Izmoroz, and doing so without bloodshed. A most astonishing feat, to say the least. I do hope you will share some of your strate-
gies with me when we have more leisure. Unfortunately, I suspect we will
not have that kind of respite for some time. Although I wish this missive
was merely to congratulate you and your people, I fear there are pressing
concerns that affect us all.*

*Until recently, I was stationed in the imperial capital of Magna Alto.
But I was forced to flee when I learned of the impending Uaine invasion.
I have since discovered that the invasion was part of a larger plot by
Franko Vittorio to overthrow the empress. He was successful, and soon
after murdered Her Imperial Majesty, as well as her two oldest children.
He then propped up the youngest, merely a boy of eight, as emperor, and
himself as regent. For all intents and purposes, Vittorio rules the empire
now. I am given to understand you know this man well, and therefore
have a deep appreciation of just how dire the situation is.*

*But there is yet some hope on the horizon. The Raizians have man-
aged to expel the empire from their land for the first time in centuries. I
believe your old comrade Sonya Turgenev was somewhat involved. It was*

a narrow victory, however, so I suspect if you were to offer an alliance with the Raízians, they would be most amenable.

If you do not have any contacts in Raíz, I would be happy to provide you with some introductions. Furthermore, I think it worthwhile to also consider an alliance with the Kantesians, who have been successfully keeping the empire at bay for several years now, although at great cost. Again, I am happy to furnish some contacts in Kante, should you need them.

Victasha has a vested interest in seeing stability returned to your continent as soon as possible, preferably without Vittorio or an army of undead in power. While the combined might of Aureum and Uaine is indeed formidable, I believe that a triumvirate alliance between Izmoroz, Raíz, and Kante might be able to match it. I am therefore eager to assist you in achieving that goal in any way that I am able.

Should you need to get word to me, please deliver your message to Sezai Bey, the man who has given you this letter, and he will communicate its contents to me with all possible haste.

Your humble servant,
Ambassador Boz

"Hmm," said Galina as she carefully folded the letter and placed it on the desk before her.

She looked over at the large, muscular brown-skinned man dressed in colorful silks who waited in patient silence by the door.

"Hmm," she said again.

This was indeed dire news. An empire run by Vittorio was already too awful to conceive, and adding the gruesome might of Mordha's undead army raised it to catastrophic proportions. An alliance seemed not merely wise but essential. And yet, she knew she must be cautious in dealing with Victasha, a country she knew little about.

"Sezai Bey?"

"Yes, Your Majesty," the Victashian said.

Galina was still getting accustomed to being called *Your Majesty,* but the way he said it sounded quite fine.

"I would like for you to remain an honored guest of the crown while I consider my response to the ambassador."

He nodded his head. "As it pleases you, Your Majesty."

"Masha, settle our guest in to one of the rooms and make certain his needs are seen to."

"Yes, Your Majesty." Masha turned to the Victashian. "Right this way, sir."

Masha led him from the room, leaving only Galina and her Rangers behind.

It was tempting to immediately take Ambassador Boz up on her offer to coordinate an alliance, but she thought it best to first attempt to use her existing connections before becoming reliant on an unknown foreign power.

"Tatiana *Sova*."

"Your Majesty." The Ranger stepped in close, as was her wont, and stared unblinkingly at Galina.

"You are the swiftest subject in all of Izmoroz."

"Thank you, Your Majesty."

"As such, I wish for you to take a message to a Raízian whom I believe to be in Colmo."

"Which one, Your Majesty?"

"I'm afraid I only know one. But his family is quite powerful, so I hope he will be able to assist us."

"And what is his name?"

"Jorge Elhuyar."

"Ah, I think I have met this lemming before. He is *Lisitsa*'s companion."

"That's the one," agreed Galina. "He may harbor some resentment if he suspects my involvement in ousting Sonya from Izmoroz, but I hope he is intelligent enough to see beyond such minor concerns."

"What shall I tell him, Your Majesty?"

"That we seek his aid in forming an alliance between Izmoroz and Raíz to fight the imperial menace."

"And what if *Lisitsa* is still with him?"

Galina shrugged. "Presumably she still enjoys killing imperials. Hopefully she will not hold a grudge against me."

"And if she does?"

"Do what must be done to clear a path to our alliance with Raíz."

"Even if it means sending the little fox to the Lady's embrace for all time?"

"Even that," agreed Galina.

Tatiana snapped her mouth opened and closed a few times, which Galina knew typically indicated eagerness.

"It has been long since I had the pleasure of fighting one of my own."

Galina gave her a hard look. "Only if necessary, Anya."

Tatiana pursed her thin lips for a moment, then gave a single sharp nod. "Yes, Your Majesty."

Galina wasn't sure she fully believed her, but time was of the essence and there wasn't much she could do to enforce the promise.

"Go now, and may the Lady speed your steps."

Tatiana left without another word.

"What did the letter say, Your Majesty?" asked Andre.

"Essentially," said Galina, "it states that the world is ripe with possibility for those with the courage, strength, and vision to seize it."

"Those such as us, Your Majesty."

"Indeed."

EPILOGUE

The goddesses sat on the edge of spring, gazing at the summer that lay before them.

"I suppose you think yourself very clever, manipulating the Armonia into reuniting with your precious *Lisitsa*," said Zivena.

"Moderately clever at best," Marzanna said deprecatingly. "For anyone who understands the underlying nature of mortals, it was fairly evident that all it needed was the occasional push. The bond between siblings can be quite useful."

"Well, you haven't won yet, my sibling!" said Zivena.

"Of course not. I only warned you not to count me out. Now I'd say we are more or less on an even playing field."

"Only if you can get those willful, atheistic Kantesians to cooperate."

"True," agreed Marzanna, although for some reason she did not seem particularly concerned.

They were silent for a few moments.

Then Zivena said, "It was surprising to hear that name again after so long."

"Mokosh, you mean?"

"Yes. Do you suppose Mother is even more cross with us than usual?"

"Why?" Marzanna asked teasingly. "Have you done something that warrants it?"

"Not I," asserted Zivena. Then her liquid eyes narrowed. "Have *you*?"

Marzanna's smile stretched into a broad grin that showed her rows of gleaming black teeth.

"Who can say?"

The story continues in ...

THE WIZARD OF EVENTIDE

Book Three of The Goddess War

Acknowledgments

This book, and indeed this whole trilogy, would not have been possible without Nerea Aragones. I have known Nerea for a very long time. She lived with me during my junior year of high school as an exchange student from Spain. Those first few months were quite an adjustment for both of us, but by the end of the year it really did feel as though we were siblings. I am grateful that we have remained friends in the decades since, that we know each other's children, and that we can still share important aspects of our lives. I am even grateful that she can still convince me to do things like eat a pizza topped with whole roasted crickets.

I also want to thank *both* my editors. Brit Hvide helped me with those awkward early drafts, courageously soldiering on despite the fact that she was pregnant during a pandemic. She hung in there nearly until her due date before finally handing over the reins to Angeline Rodriguez, who stepped smoothly into the middle of a trilogy as though she had always been there. It's rare to get insight from two different editors, and I believe this book benefited greatly from the range of perspective.

As always, I would be remiss if I didn't thank my agent, Jill Grinberg, and the rest of the team at JGLM. I cannot imagine getting along without them, and I never tire of expressing my gratitude for everything they do.

extras

orbitbooks.net

about the author

Jon Skovron is the author of the Empire of Storms trilogy and several novels for children and young adults. His short stories have appeared in publications such as *ChiZine* and *Baen's Universe*. He lives just outside Washington, DC, with his two sons and two cats. Visit him online at jonskovron.com.

Find out more about Jon Skovron and other Orbit authors by registering for the free monthly newsletter at orbitbooks.net.

if you enjoyed
THE QUEEN OF IZMOROZ

look out for

LEGACY OF ASH
Book One of the Legacy

by

Matthew Ward

A shadow has fallen over the Tressian Republic.

Ruling families plot against one another with sharp words and sharper knives, heedless of the threat posed by the invading armies of the Hadari Empire.

The Republic faces its darkest hour.
Yet as Tressia falls, heroes rise.

Wind howled along the marcher road. Icy rain swirled behind. Katya hung low over her horse's neck. Galloping strides jolted weary bones and set the fire in her side blazing anew. Sodden reins sawed at her palms. She blotted out the pain. Closed her ears to the harsh raven-song and ominous thunder. There was only the road, the dark silhouette of Eskavord's rampart, and the anger. Anger at the Council, for forcing her hand. At herself for thinking there'd ever been a chance.

Lightning split grey skies. Katya glanced behind. Josiri was a dark shape, his steed straining to keep pace with hers. That eased the burden. She'd lost so much when the phoenix banner had fallen. But she'd not lose her son.

Nor her daughter.

Eskavord's gate guard scattered without challenge. Had they recognised her, or simply fled the naked steel in her hand? Katya didn't care. The way was open.

In the shadow of jettied houses, sodden men and women loaded sparse possessions onto cart and dray. Children wailed in confusion. Dogs fought for scraps in the gutter. Of course word had reached Eskavord. Grim tidings ever outpaced the good.

You did this.

Katya stifled her conscience and spurred on through the tangled streets of Highgate.

Her horse forced a path through the crowds. The threat of her sword held the desperate at bay. Yesterday, she'd have felt safe within Eskavord's walls. Today she was a commodity to be traded for survival, if any had the wit to realise the prize within their grasp.

Thankfully, such wits were absent in Eskavord. That, or else no one recognised Katya as the dowager duchess Trelan. The Phoenix of prophecy.

No, not that. Katya was free of that delusion. It had cost too many lives, but she was free of it. She was not the Phoenix whose fires would cleanse the Southshires. She'd believed – Lumestra, *how* she'd believed – but belief alone did not change the world. Only deeds did that, and hers had fallen short.

The cottage came into view. Firestone lanterns shone upon its gable. Elda had kept the faith. Even at the end of the world, friends remained true.

Katya slid from the saddle and landed heavily on cobbles. Chainmail's broken links gouged her bloodied flesh.

"Mother?"

Josiri brought his steed to a halt in a spray of water. His hood was back, his blond hair plastered to his scalp.

She shook her head, hand warding away scrutiny. "It's nothing. Stay here. I'll not be long."

He nodded. Concern remained, but he knew better than to question. He'd grown into a dependable young man. Obedient. Loyal. Katya wished his father could have seen him thus. The two were so much alike. Josiri would make a fine duke, if he lived to see his seventeenth year.

She sheathed her sword and marched for the front door. Timbers shuddered under her gauntleted fist. "Elda? Elda! It's me."

A key turned. The door opened. Elda Savka stood on the threshold, her face sagging with relief. "My lady. When the rider came from Zanya, I feared the worst."

"The army is gone."

Elda paled. "Lumestra preserve us."

"The Council emptied the chapterhouses against us."

"I thought the masters of the orders had sworn to take no side."

"A knight's promise is not what it was, and the Council nothing if not persuasive." Katya closed her eyes, lost in the shuddering ground and brash clarions of recent memory. And the screams, most of all. "One charge, and we were lost."

"What of Josiri? Taymor?"

"Josiri is with me. My brother is taken. He may already be dead." Either way, he was beyond help. "Is Calenne here?"

"Yes, and ready to travel. I knew you'd come."

"I have no choice. The Council ..."

She fell silent as a girl appeared at the head of the staircase, her sapphire eyes alive with suspicion. Barely six years old, and she had the wit to know something was amiss. "Elda, what's happening?"

"Your mother is here, Calenne," said Elda. "You must go with her."

"Are you coming?"

The first sorrow touched Elda's brow. "No."

Calenne descended the stairs, expression still heavy with distrust. Katya stooped to embrace her daughter. She hoped Calenne's thin body stiffened at the cold and wet, and not revulsion for a woman she barely knew. From the first, Katya had thought it necessary to send Calenne away, to live shielded from the Council's sight. So many years lost. All for nothing.

Katya released Calenne from her embrace and turned wearily to Elda. "Thank you. For everything."

The other woman forced a wintery smile. "Take care of her."

Katya caught a glint of something darker beneath the smile. It lingered in Elda's eyes. A hardness. Another friendship soured by folly? Perhaps. It no longer mattered. "Until my last breath. Calenne?"

The girl flung her arms around Elda. She said nothing, but the tears on her cheeks told a tale all their own.

Elda pushed her gently away. "You must go, dear heart."

A clarion sounded, its brash notes cleaving through the clamour of the storm. An icy hand closed around Katya's heart. She'd run out of time.

Elda met her gaze. Urgency replaced sorrow. "Go! While you still can!"

Katya stooped and gathered Calenne. The girl's chest shook with thin sobs, but she offered no resistance. With a last glance at Elda, Katya set out into the rain once more. The clarion sounded again as she reached Josiri. His eyes were more watchful than ever, his sword ready in his hands.

"They're here," he said.

Katya heaved Calenne up to sit in front of her brother. She looked like a doll beside him, every day of the decade that separated them on full display.

"Look after your sister. If we're separated, ride hard for the border."

His brow furrowed. "To the Hadari? Mother . . ."

"The Hadari will treat you better than the Council." He still had so much to learn, and she no more time in which to teach him. "When enemies are your only recourse, choose the one with the least to gain. Promise me."

She received a reluctant nod in reply.

Satisfied, Katya clambered into her saddle and spurred west along the broad cobbles of Highgate. They'd expect her to take refuge in Branghall Manor, or at least strip it of anything valuable ahead of the inevitable looting. But the western gateway might still be clear.

The first cry rang out as they rejoined the road. "She's here!"

A blue-garbed wayfarer cantered through the crowd, rain scattering from leather pauldrons. Behind, another set a buccina to his lips. A brash rising triad hammered out through the rain and found answer in the streets beyond. The pursuit's vanguard had reached Eskavord. Lightly armoured riders to harry and delay while heavy knights closed the distance. Katya drew her sword and wheeled her horse about. "Make for the west gate!"

Josiri hesitated, then lashed his horse to motion. "Yah!"

Katya caught one last glimpse of Calenne's pale, dispassionate face. Then they were gone, and the horseman upon her.

The wayfarer was half her age, little more than a boy and eager for the glory that might earn a knight's crest. Townsfolk scattered from his path. He goaded his horse to the gallop, sword held high in anticipation of the killing blow to come. He'd not yet learned that the first blow seldom mattered as much as the last.

Katya's parry sent a shiver down her arm. The wayfarer's blade scraped clear, the momentum of his charge already carrying him past. Then he was behind, hauling on the reins. The sword came about, the killing stroke aimed at Katya's neck.

Her thrust took the younger man in the chest. Desperate strength drove the blade between his ribs. The hawk of the Tressian Council turned dark as the first blood stained the rider's woollen tabard. Then he slipped from his saddle, sword clanging against cobbles. With one last, defiant glare at the buccinator, Katya turned her steed about, and galloped through the narrow streets after her children.

She caught them at the bridge, where the waters of the Grelyt River fell away into the boiling millrace. They were not alone.

One wayfarer held the narrow bridge, blocking Josiri's path. A second closed from behind him, sword drawn. A third lay dead on the cobbles, horse already vanished into the rain.

Josiri turned his steed in a circle. He had one arm tight about his sister. The other hand held a bloody sword. The point trembled as it swept back and forth between his foes, daring them to approach.

Katya thrust back her heels. Her steed sprang forward.

Her sword bit into the nearest wayfarer's spine. Heels jerked as he fell back. His steed sprang away into the streets. The corpse, one booted foot tangled in its stirrups, dragged along behind.

Katya rode on past Josiri. Steel clashed, once, twice, and then the last wayfarer was gone. His body tipped over the low stone parapet and into the rushing waters below.

Josiri trotted close, his face studiously calm. Katya knew better. He'd not taken a life before today.

"You're hurt."

Pain stemmed Katya's denial. A glance revealed rainwater running red across her left hand. She also felt a wound high on her shoulder. The last wayfarer's parting gift, lost in the desperation of the moment.

The clarion came yet again. A dozen wayfarers spurred down the street. A plate-clad knight rode at their head, his destrier caparisoned in silver-flecked black. Not the heraldry of a knightly chapterhouse, but a family of the first rank. His sword – a heavy, fennlander's claymore – rested in its scabbard. A circular shield sat slung across his back.

The greys of the rain-sodden town lost their focus. Katya tightened her grip on the reins. She flexed the fingers of her left hand. They felt distant, as if belonging to someone else. Her shoulder ached, fit company for the dull roar in her side – a memento of the sword-thrust she'd taken on the ridge at Zanya. Weariness crowded in, the faces of the dead close behind.

The world lurched. Katya grasped at the bridle with her good hand. Focus returned at the cost of her sword, which fell onto the narrow roadway.

So that was how the matter lay?

So be it.

"Go," she breathed. "See to your sister's safety. I'll hold them."

Josiri spurred closer, the false calm giving way to horror. "Mother, no!"

Calenne looked on with impassive eyes.

"I can't ride." Katya dropped awkwardly from her saddle and stooped to reclaim her sword. The feel of the grips beneath her fingers awoke new determination. "Leave me."

"No. We're getting out of here. All of us." He reached out. "You can ride with me."

The tremor beneath his tone revealed the truth. His horse was already weary. What stamina remained would not long serve two riders, let alone three.

Katya glanced down the street. There'd soon be nothing left to argue over. She understood Josiri's reluctance, for it mirrored her own. To face a parting now, with so much unsaid ... ? But a lifetime would not be enough to express her pride, nor to warn against repeating her mistakes. He'd have to find his own way now.

"Do you love me so little that you'd make me beg?" She forced herself to meet his gaze. "Accept this last gift and remember me well. Go."

Josiri gave a sharp nod, his lips a pale sliver. His throat bobbed. Then he turned his horse.

Katya dared not watch as her children galloped away, fearful that Josiri would read the gesture as a change of heart.

"Lumestra's light shine for you, my son," she whispered.

A slap to her horse's haunch sent it whinnying into the oncoming wayfarers. They scattered, fighting for control over startled steeds.

Katya took up position at the bridge's narrow crest, her sword point-down at her feet in challenge. She'd no illusions about holding the wayfarers. It would cost them little effort to ride straight over her, had they the stomach for it. But the tightness of the approach offered a slim chance.

The knight raised a mailed fist. The pursuers halted a dozen yards from the bridge's mouth. Two more padded out from the surrounding alleys. Not horsemen, but the Council's simarka – bronze constructs forged in the likeness of lions and given life by a spark of magic. Prowling statues that hunted the Council's enemies. Katya swore under her breath. Her sword was useless against such creatures. A blacksmith's hammer would have served her better. She'd lost too many friends to those claws to believe otherwise.

"Lady Trelan." The knight's greeting boomed like thunder. "The Council demands your surrender."

"Viktor Akadra." Katya made no attempt to hide her bitterness. "Did your father not tell you? I do not recognise the Council's authority."

The knight dismounted, the hem of his jet-black surcoat trailing in the rain. He removed his helm. Swarthy, chiselled features stared out from beneath a thatch of black hair. A young face, though one already confident far beyond its years.

He'd every reason to be so. Even without the armour, without the entourage of weary wayfarers – without her wounds – Akadra would have been more than her match. He stood a full head taller than she – half a head taller than any man she'd known.

"There has been enough suffering today." His tone matched his expression perfectly. Calm. Confident. Unyielding. He gestured, and the simarka sat, one to either side. Motionless. Watchful. "Let's not add to the tally."

"Then turn around, Lord Akadra. Leave me be."

Lips parted in something not entirely a smile. "You will stand before the Council and submit to judgement."

Katya knew what that meant. The humiliation of a show trial, arraigned as warning to any who'd follow in her footsteps and dare seek freedom for the Southshires. Then they'd parade her through the streets, her last dignity stripped away long before the gallows took her final breath. She'd lost a husband to that form of justice. She'd not suffer it herself.

"I'll die first."

"Incorrect."

Again, that damnable confidence. But her duty was clear.

Katya let the anger rise, as she had on the road. Its fire drove back the weariness, the pain, the fear for her children. Those problems belonged to the future, not the moment at hand. She was a daughter of the Southshires, the dowager duchess Trelan. She would not yield. The wound in Katya's side blazed as she surged forward. The alchemy of rage transmuted agony to strength and lent killing weight to the two-handed blow.

Akadra's sword scraped free of its scabbard. Blades clashed with a banshee screech. Lips parted in a snarl of surprise, he gave ground through the hissing rain.

Katya kept pace, right hand clamped over the failing left to give it purpose and guide it true. She hammered at Akadra's guard, summoning forth the lessons of girlhood to the bleak present. The forms of the sword her father had drilled into her until they flowed with the grace of a thrush's song and the power of a mountain river. Those lessons had kept her alive on the ridge at Zanya. They would not fail her now.

The wayfarers made no move to interfere.

But Akadra was done retreating.

Boots planted on the cobbles like the roots of some venerable, weather-worn oak, he checked each strike with grace that betrayed tutelage no less exacting than Katya's own. The claymore blurred across grey skies and battered her longsword aside.

The fire in Katya's veins turned sluggish. Cold and failing flesh sapped her purpose. Too late, she recognised the game Akadra had played. She'd wearied herself on his defences, and all the while her body had betrayed her.

Summoning her last strength, Katya hurled herself forward. A cry born of pain and desperation ripped free of her lips.

Again the claymore blurred to parry. The longsword's tip scraped past the larger blade, ripping into Akadra's cheek. He twisted away with a roar of pain.

Hooves sounded on cobbles. The leading wayfarers spurred forward, swords drawn to avenge their master's humiliation. The simarka, given no leave to advance, simply watched unfolding events with feline curiosity.

Katya's hands tightened on her sword. She'd held longer than she'd believed possible. She hoped Josiri had used the time well.

"Leave her!"

Akadra checked the wayfarers' advance with a single bellow. The left side of his face masked in blood, he turned his attention on Katya once more. He clasped a closed fist to his chest. Darkness gathered about his fingers like living shadow.

Katya's world blurred, its colours swirling away into an unseen void.

Her knee cracked against the cobbles. A hand slipped from her sword, fingers splayed to arrest her fall. Wisps of blood curled through pooling rainwater. She knelt there, gasping for breath, one ineluctable truth screaming for attention.

The rumours about Akadra were true.

The shadow dispersed as Akadra strode closer. The wayfarers had seen none of it, Katya realised – or had at least missed the significance. Otherwise, Akadra would have been as doomed as she. The Council would tolerate much from its loyal sons, but not witchcraft.

Colour flooded back. Akadra's sword dipped to the cobbles. His bloodied face held no triumph. Somehow that was worse.

"It's over." For the first time, his expression softened. "This is not the way, Katya. It never was. Surrender. Your wounds will be tended. You'll be treated with honour."

"Honour?" The word was ash on Katya's tongue. "Your father knows nothing of honour."

"It is not my father who makes the offer." He knelt, one gauntleted hand extended. "Please. Give me your sword."

Katya stared down at the cobbles, at her life's blood swirling away into the gutter. Could she trust him? A lifetime of emissaries and missives from the north had bled her people dry to feed a pointless war. Viktor's family was part of that, and so he was part of it. If his promise *was* genuine, he'd no power to keep it. The Council would never let it stand. The shame of the gallows path beckoned.

"You want my sword?" she growled.

Katya rose from her knees, her last effort channelled into one final blow.

Akadra's hand, so lately extended in conciliation, wrenched the sluggish blade from her grasp. He let his own fall alongside. Tugged off balance, Katya fell to her hands and knees. Defenceless. Helpless.

No. Not helpless. Never that.

She forced herself upright. There was no pain. No weariness. Just calm. Was this how Kevor had felt at the end? Before the creak of the deadman's drop had set her husband swinging? Trembling fingers closed around a dagger's hilt.

"My son will finish what I started."

The dagger rasped free, Katya's right hand again closing over her left.

"No!" Akadra dived forward. His hands reached for hers, his sudden alarm lending weight to his promises.

Katya rammed the dagger home. Chain links parted. She felt no pain as the blade slipped between her ribs. There was only a sudden giddiness as the last of her burdens fell away into mist.

Josiri held Calenne close through the clamour. Screams. Buccina calls. Galloping hooves. Barked orders. Josiri longed for the thunder's return. Bravery came easier in moments when the angry sky drowned all else.

The church spire passed away to his left. Desperate townsfolk crowded its lychpath, seeking sanctuary behind stone walls. People filled the streets beyond. Some wore council blue, most the sea-grey of Eskavord's guard, and too many the garb of ordinary folk caught in between.

Ravens scattered before Josiri's straining horse. He glanced down at the girl in his charge. His sister she may have been, but Calenne was a stranger. She sat in silence, not a tear on her cheeks. He didn't know how she held herself together so. It was all he could do not to fall apart.

A pair of wayfarers emerged from an alleyway, their approach masked by the booming skies. Howling with courage he didn't feel, Josiri hacked at the nearest. The woman slumped across her horse's neck. Josiri rowelled his mare, leaving the outpaced survivor snarling at the rain.

More wayfarers waited at the next junction, their horses arrayed in a loose line beneath overhanging eaves. The town wall loomed through the rain. The west gate was so close. Two streets away, no more.

A glance behind revealed a wayfarer galloping in pursuit. A pair of simarka loped alongside. Verdigrised claws struck sparks from the cobbles.

To turn back was to be taken, a rat in a trap. The certainty of it left Josiri no room for doubt. Onward was the only course.

"Hold tight to me," he told Calenne, "and don't let go."

Thin arms redoubled their grip. Josiri drove back his heels.

Time slowed, marked out by the pounding of hooves and the beat of a fearful heart. Steel glinted. Horses whinnied as wayfarers hauled on their reins.

"For the Southshires!"

The battle cry fed Josiri's resolve. The widening of the nearest wayfarer's eyes gave him more. They were as afraid of him as he of them. Maybe more, for was his mother not the Phoenix of prophecy?

Time quickened. Josiri's sword blurred. A wayfarer spun away in a bloody spray. And then Josiri was through the line, his horse's greedy stride gobbling the last distance to the west gate. The mare barely slowed at the next corner. Her hooves skidded on the rain-slicked cobbles.

Calenne screamed – not with terror, but in wild joy – and then the danger was past, and the west gate was in sight.

The portcullis was down, its iron teeth sunk deep. A line of tabarded soldiery blocked the roadway and the branching alleyways to either side. Halberds lowered. Shields locked tight together, a flock of white hawk blazons on a wall of rich king's blue. Wayfarers filled the street behind.

Thunder roared, its fury echoing through the hole where Josiri's heart should have been. He'd failed. Perhaps he'd never had a chance.

"Everything will be all right." He hoped the words sounded more convincing to Calenne than they did to him. "Mother will come."

Calenne stared up at him with all the earnestness of youth. "Mother's already dead."

Spears pressed in. An officer's voice bellowed orders through the rain. Josiri gazed down into his sister's cold, unblinking eyes, and felt more alone than ever.